Love and Fallout

For Esther

Love and Fallout

by

Kathryn Simmonds

Seren is the book imprint of
Poetry Wales Press Ltd
57 Nolton Street, Bridgend, Wales, CF31 3AE
www.serenbooks.com
Facebook: facebook.com/SerenBooks
Twitter: @SerenBooks

Print ISBN 978-1-78172-146-9
Kindle ISBN 978-1-78172-148-3
Ebook ISBN 978-1-78172-147-6

Typesetting by Elaine Sharples
Printed and bound by CPI Group (UK) Ltd, Croydon, CR0 4YY

The publisher works with the financial assistance of
The Welsh Books Council

Things

There are worse things than having behaved foolishly in public.
There are worse things than these miniature betrayals,
committed or endured or suspected; there are worse things
than not being able to sleep for thinking about them.
It is 5a.m. All the worse things come stalking in
and stand icily about the bed looking worse and worse and

worse.

(Fleur Adcock)

Saturday Morning

We are waist-deep in water and marching. At the poolside our instructor bounces on her toes, her compact body tight-sprung like one of the machines in the gym. 'That's it ladies!' she calls, 'keep working!' Maggie marches behind me as the circle rotates. If she wasn't so keen on Aquafit it's unlikely I'd be here, not on a Saturday morning, but then friendship, like marriage, is sometimes a matter of compromise.

The class is halfway through. The dance music is pounding. I've nearly finished a To Do list in my head when I catch sight of a figure crossing the far edge of the pool – a girl of about twenty, her hair a mass of curls. She raises a hand to wave at someone, and as she smiles my list breaks apart and all at once the past comes crashing in. I jerk my chin back with a gasp as if to keep from taking in water.

'Careful, Tess!' Maggie is at my shoulder. I start moving again before there's a pile-up behind me, trying to keep track of the girl as she heads towards the diving boards to scale the silver ladder.

The lesson continues. It's only a girl, I tell myself. A girl swimming, that's all.

Our instructor is bouncing with new urgency, her voice more insistent, the same tone used at fairgrounds when the rides speed up. Twelve women jump on the spot, spinning invisible hoops on their forearms until their muscles burn. The girl dives into deep water and disappears.

In the changing room, citrus shampoos mingle with the chemical tang of chlorine as we go about the business of dressing and undressing. Pool noise swells and fades with every flap of the swing door.

'Honestly Tess, there it was, large as life. Larger. It practically needed its own introduction.' Maggie is drying her hair with a beach towel. 'He didn't have a moustache in the photo. You need to be prepared for something like that. It was…' she reaches for the word, '…transfixing. Over dinner, I had to stop myself from feeding it.'

I laugh and button my shirt.

'And it wasn't just the facial hair. I mean that doesn't have to be a deal-breaker, but there were other things he didn't mention. Like his age.' Beside us a woman has a foot on the bench and is buckling her roman sandal with infinite care. Never too concerned about discretion, Maggie doesn't seem to notice her lean nearer.

'His profile said forty-nine, but if he was a day under sixty, I'm an Olympic athlete. Why do they think lying is all right?'

The internet dating has been going on for a while, but the only men she's meeting seem to be deficient in some respect: the one who never paid for anything; the one who turned out to be married; the one who had a previously undisclosed enthusiasm for re-enacting historic battles.

'We could try Salsa dancing,' I say, thinking that might yield a few possibilities. 'Do people still do that?'

Maggie says they do, but wouldn't I rather go with Pete? For a moment I try to picture us in a community hall gyrating our hips. It's been suggested in the room of the two-seater sofa that we should spend more time together – could a Latin beat improve the rhythm of our marriage? Possibly. But Pete's never been much of a dancer – six foot three, beardy, size twelve feet, he's more at home on a rugby pitch. Anyway, that isn't a conversation for the communal changing room and, still musing on the idea of a shared hobby, I wring out my costume as Maggie tells me about a fantastic dress she's spotted.

'Just your colour,' she says, sliding a comb through her bob.

'Do I have a colour?'

'You know you do … Colour me Lovely?'

A birthday gift three years ago – how could I forget the Colour me Lovely lady? I stood in her living room for an hour while she held material swatches against my face and told me I should be wearing more prune, ivory and sage green. She also said I could do topaz, lemon and pink (as long as it was tawny rather than baby). I thanked her, put my cycling helmet back on and pedalled home.

Maggie slows the comb. 'That was fun, wasn't it?'

My agreement seems to make her happy, and she sings to herself as she fastens an earring. On paper we may seem unlikely friends, but shared childhoods can easily thicken water to blood, and forty years on from our first meeting in a Stevenage back garden where we made perfume from fistfuls of her mum's roses, Maggie's more like my sister. A louder, more extravagant sister.

'Doing anything this afternoon?' I ask.

'Not especially.'

Her response is uncharacteristically brief and I raise an eyebrow. 'Another date?'

She smiles, 'Something like that,' and whisks her make-up bag to a bank of mirrors. Whatever it is will keep until next Saturday, or a mid-week phone call.

The key to my bike lock isn't in the pocket of my jeans, or the pouch of my shoulder bag, and I'm on my knees feeling under the bench, when I hear someone say *Excuse me*. I look up. Her curls are wet now, but it's the girl from the diving boards. At close range, the resemblance turns my heart: the same almond-shaped eyes, arched brows, wide mouth. I move aside. She grabs a towel from the hook and enters a cubicle to dress.

When Maggie reappears I'm sitting on the bench with the bag gaping open on my lap. My legs feel useless, as if from the effort of treading water.

'Are you all right?'

'Fine.'

She regards me with a frown, and I nod to reassure her, to reassure myself.

'Just… I can't find my bike key.'

'Tessa, you and keys.' Together we finish the search.

It's usually me with an eye on my watch, but today it's Maggie who's eager to be off into the Cambridge sunshine. But I don't ask any more questions – wherever she is or isn't going is her business. She brushes my cheek in a quick goodbye.

When she's gone I remain on the bench, not wanting to admit what I'm waiting for, or rather who. In a few minutes the girl has finished dressing. I stand, ready to leave. My pulse throbs high in my neck as I approach and ask for the time.

She glances down at her sports watch then into my face.

'Twenty-past twelve.'

'Thanks.'

It is remarkable, her eyes are green, and at the corner of her lip is a beauty spot. I hesitate, wanting to speak, wanting to say *You look like someone, someone I knew years ago.* Could she be a relative? A distant cousin? But nothing comes. Instead I'm simply staring at her while women file past us barefoot towards the pool. The changing room is too hot and I have to get out.

'Sorry,' I say, accidentally brushing her shoulder in a move to the door. *Sorry. Sorry.*

Part One

With our lovely feathers

1

Saturday Afternoon

Pete lowers his paper and quietens one of his trumpet-playing jazz legends. We exchange a smile and I make sure to give him a kiss, albeit a slightly self-conscious one, because Valeria has reminded us that mutual acknowledgement is important and these small acts of appreciation will help re-establish intimacy. If we're going to keep paying her sixty quid an hour for her advice, I for one am going to take it.

'How was the class?'

'Fine.' My mind brushes against the girl from the pool, then withdraws. 'Have you trimmed your beard?'

He passes a hand around his jaw. 'No harm in looking presentable.'

'None at all.' Something else is different. The Hoover's been out because our worn carpet is without fluff ball or paperclip. 'Spring cleaning?' The pile of newspapers usually stacked beside the bookshelves has disappeared; the broken dining-room chair propped against the wall for a fortnight has gone, and there's no hint of the usual low-level clutter. 'Looks great.' Pete's obviously trying too.

Assembling a cheese sandwich, I notice the fridge is whiter

and all the kitchen surfaces have been recently wiped down. It smells lemony.

'Where's Dom?' I ask, eating the sandwich standing up.

'Working on his tan.'

That's a joke. If he's not plugged into Goth Friendly, his social networking site, the details of which he keeps a deliberate mystery, he'll be locked in a garage with his band mates rehearsing for greatness.

'There's a Hitchcock on soon,' Pete says. But I tell him I should get the seed potatoes in, then crack on with the leaflets.

'What leaflets?' His eyes leave the sports section.

'For Heston Fields.'

'Why are you doing them?'

'Someone's got to.'

He asks how much else I'm taking on, and I tell him we're just working out a few ideas then stop because there's a definite wrinkle in his brow, the wrinkle that leads to a frown and then on to the open highways of disagreement.

'You're running another campaign?'

We've had the Heston Fields discussion. Or row, as it turned out, and as far as Pete's concerned, if the council wants to sell a chunk of neglected land so a developer can build luxury flats there's no point losing any sleep. He calls it scrubland, or backlands, but the truth is, it's public land. All right, it's a bit tussocky, but kids play football there and people cross it to reach the parade that qualifies as Heston's high street. We used to play cricket there with the kids. But I know there's no point reminding him of this because Heston Fields has become what Valeria would call a trigger point. Unwilling to provoke an incident, I stuff my mouth with a final sandwich crust.

When Pete appears at the garden door to say the film's starting, I'm on my knees making divots in the soil. He seems unusually agitated.

'What's got into you?' I ask, shading my eyes. That's meant to sound teasing but it comes out as stroppy. Valeria's right, communication isn't easy: words have so many ways of defying your intentions.

'Nothing.' He pauses to assess me. 'What have you got on?'

My shorts are in the wash, so I'm wearing an old pair of his, khaki and belted at the waist. 'They're only for the gardening.' My tone goes wrong again. He retreats. Should I call after him? But what will that achieve? We'll end up having an involved conversation about shorts which could easily escalate, just as other ordinary conversations have done, until we're not discussing shorts at all, we're arguing about why he doesn't want to help me save the local library and I don't want to watch him referee rugby.

The April breeze is warm and fresh and the hum of a lawnmower floats over from a neighbouring garden while I kneel, cutting seed potatoes into sections, spacing them in a row. All long relationships suffer strain, it's only natural, every couple has their own argument playing out in different forms, the subjects they return to again and again, pressed like bruises that never fade. I sit back on my haunches. We never thought we'd end up seeing a therapist. In fact we probably wouldn't have if Pete's sister hadn't discreetly suggested it to him after a lunch visit. Of course we didn't row in front of her, but we gave ourselves away all the same. Lack of eye contact? Flinching when the other spoke? Plates clattered too loudly in the kitchen? Who knows. But because neither of us wanted to quash the idea, because we agreed the sessions were only a precautionary measure, we found ourselves in Valeria's tranquilly decorated living room with its South Asian tapestries and life-affirming pot plants.

I make another divot and turn my thoughts elsewhere, wondering what Pippa's up to at university on a sunny Saturday afternoon. Would it bother her if I called later? Perhaps a text? But it's impossible to say anything in a text – all those paraphrased thoughts, at every sign off the hopeful: 'be nice to spk sn, love mum xx.'

After a few minutes the doorbell chimes. It chimes again so I call to Pete. He must have his headphones on. I slip out of my clogs and hurry through the living room expecting to find Pru on the doorstep with a question about the meeting agenda. But when I open the door, Pru isn't standing there. Instead, smiling at me is a thin woman in her early forties who has the gloss and wing-mirror cheekbones of a former fashion model. Behind her is a camera crew. *A camera crew.* And there, waving, is Maggie. For a few stupefied seconds I can't work it out: in some bizarre coincidence she's stopped by at exactly the same moment as a TV crew.

'Are you Tessa Perry?' asks the thin woman.

Partly shielded by the door and ready to close it at any moment, I confirm my identity.

'Excellent,' she says, 'because we're here to…' Then she raises her arms along with her voice and everyone cries in unison, 'Make You Over!'

The penny teeters, bright and coppery at the edge of my comprehension then drops into a slot and rolls away. Maggie has *brought* these people here. Before I know what's happening, they're piling inside.

The living room, which was empty just minutes ago, is now crammed with bodies. One of the crew switches off a bright light and Jude, the woman with the cheekbones, declares, 'We're going to work a little miracle, darling. In a couple of days even your own husband won't recognise you.' Pete enters on cue carrying a tray of coffee mugs and proffers a plate of biscuits towards Jude. 'Gingernut?'

She looks at them as if they might be about to get up and tell her a joke. 'Not for me,' she says, flashing a stellar smile. That smile seems familiar now from the blur of television magazines racked up in Sainsbury's.

'Did you know about this?' I ask Pete. The spring cleaning suddenly makes sense.

'Not until the last minute.'

Maggie kisses my cheek, 'Isn't it brilliant?' She's wearing a turquoise dress I've never seen before. Her hair is shining. And another conversation is explained, the Colour me Lovely lady. Nothing comes out of my mouth, though there are thoughts, half formulated, careering at speed on unfinished tracks. But there's no time for discussion because the director, a wiry young man who's introduced himself as Zeb, gathers us together and we watch as the scene that's just played out is replayed on a tiny monitor.

There's me, startled in Pete's shorts, and there's Jude at the door saying, 'It's all thanks to your best friend,' and then Maggie stepping forwards for a hug, the camera framing us in close up, a faint streak of mud striping my cheek.

'Perfect!' Zeb claps his hands.

The waves of weirdness subside until I'm touching reality again, and when it comes my voice has an untethered quality, 'Wait!' The room falls quiet and the man who's been twiddling a valve on his headset stops twiddling. I look around at them trying to reason, like someone speaking to hostage takers. 'There's been a mistake. I don't want a make-over.' I turn to Maggie and repeat it, as if she might translate. 'I'm not going on *television*.'

Zeb steps in.

'Tessa, Tessa, don't worry, lots of our guests are nervous but we've got a great package lined up. We had a look at Maggie's letter and we're going to start with the Greenham Common angle, then bring in your charity work. Everything will reflect you, organic products, fair-trade fashion...'

'Greenham Common angle?' My stomach drops at speed, like a bucket freefalling down a well shaft.

He consults his clipboard, 'You were *there*, weren't you?'

'Well yes, briefly, but...' The sentence fades away. Greenham Common tumbles about in my head like dirty laundry as Zeb continues his spiel. While he speaks I'm bumping through images from the past, images I've not thought about for years, or rather not since this morning, when that green-eyed girl appeared at the pool.

He's asking if I've any photos I could dig out. 'We like to give the viewers some back story, a feel for who you are.' But I don't want the unidentified masses to feel me. And I certainly don't want a discussion about Greenham Common. 'You'd be very now,' he says, 'with your environmental charity, and your…'

'Issues,' says Jude, with an eye on my shorts.

The clematis bush has caught Zeb's attention; he thinks we could do some nice shots beside it for the reveal. I have to make this stop.

'I'm sorry, but this programme isn't for me.'

Zeb says the programme is for everyone, it will be wonderful, it will change my life and amazing things will happen. I tell him I'm quite happy with my untelevised life. Our exchange goes on until Pete steps in and diplomatically suggests the TV people leave. Zeb now has a harassed expression. He looks from Pete to me as if he might find a solution.

'Tell you what, we'll give you guys some space,' he says. 'Talk things over. Give me a ring later, or in the morning if you like.' I accept his card but say I won't be changing my mind.

When they've finally trooped back into their people-carrier there's only Maggie left in our living room.

'Tess,' she begins, and stops, as if unsure of what should follow. Her lipstick has bled away but a stencil of pink liner remains.

Pete collects a couple of coffee mugs and retreats to the kitchen. Then Maggie starts with a pitch just like the telly people, how exciting it's going to be, how they're going to spend a small fortune doing me up. I tell her I'm not a semi-detached. We'd usually laugh off cross words before it got to this, but in fact, I can't remember how it got to this at all – wasn't I planting potatoes?

'I thought it would be fun,' she says. 'I wanted to give you a treat, a helping hand.'

'If you wanted to help me you could distribute a few campaign leaflets, not arrange a lynching.'

'Tessa, you're overreacting. Most women would be thrilled.'

'About what? Getting shown up on national TV by their best friend?'

Maggie manages a pub, she always dresses the part and sometimes a little extra, but that's all right, that's who she is and I wouldn't try to change her, so why is she trying to change me?

'What about Colour me Lovely? You enjoyed that,' she says. I look at her for a second, she's giving me no choice. 'No, I didn't, I only went because you'd brought the bloody thing as a present. What else was I going to do?'

A ripple of hurt breaks over her face. I turn my gaze towards the newly tidied bookcase and wish none of this was happening. 'And anyway there's a big difference between that and going on telly. What was in your letter?' This is what I'm anxious to know. 'What's Greenham Common got to do with anything?'

She shrugs, as if I might as well know the truth. 'That's where it all started.'

'All what started?'

'Your saving the world thing.'

'My what?'

'You know what I mean.' Her tone is matter of fact.

My heart thuds. Do I know what she means?

She sighs. 'Look, this was supposed to be a nice surprise, a way to treat you, give you time for yourself, get you out of the bag lady gear for a...' She stops short.

'*Bag lady?*' The words are neon-lit, they're a massive Blackpool extravaganza and we're standing beneath them. The letters are ton-heavy, teetering on a wire, sparking, ready to come crashing down between us.

'God, I didn't mean...' she reaches at the space between us.

'What did you mean?'

We stare at each other. When Pete appears from the kitchen, Maggie is in the hall still apologising, but this has been enough for one afternoon and I walk away while Pete sees her out.

Afterwards me and Pete sit on the sofa. He puts out a hand uncertainly then settles his fingers on the small of my back and makes circles while I try to understand. *Bag lady?* Okay, there are lots of jeans and jumpers in my wardrobe, but I can dress up if I want to. My hair is an average brown with the first traces of silver running through. Sometimes I wrap it with a scarf or clip it up with combs. I don't wear make-up because I don't like the feel of it, or the palaver.

'She wouldn't have wanted to upset you; you know what she's like.'

'I can't stand the idea of those programmes.'

He nods. 'She wanted to give you a boost, a bit of, what do they call it, me time.'

'*Me time?* Seriously?' He shrugs, the circles stop and he removes his hand.

I can't help thinking this is the second time she's gone behind my back, even though we never discuss the first, having tacitly agreed years ago never to mention it. I say *bag lady* aloud, hoping Pete might rush to my defence but he doesn't, he tells me not to worry about Maggie, she was simply being clumsy.

My hands are resting on my lap, nails ridged with dirt from the planting, wedding ring grazed after years of wear, crosshatched with the knocks and scrapes of daily life. We bought the ring in Broadstairs when we were camping. Sunburnt under our shirts from three hot days, the sky threatening rain, fingers interlaced as we climbed a steep slope away from the beach. What must we have looked like asking to unlock cabinets and inspect the jewellery? But I think we enjoyed looking out of place, all that love everywhere we went, dancing invisibly around us like the flecks of salt in seaside air.

The question I've been resisting finds its way out.

'Do you think I need a make-over?'

'No,' Pete says. And then adds troublingly, 'You're just you, aren't you.'

An hour later The Heston Fields Action Group are gathered around my kitchen table. News of the Make me Over visit has caused a minor frenzy.

'When's it going to be on?' asks Pru, who is well into her seventies but has more vim than most thirty year olds.

'But Pru, I'm not actually going to *do* it.'

'You're not? Oh,' she says, disappointed. 'I do love Jude – what's she like in real life?'

We chat about Jude for a while until I manage to steer the conversation back to Heston Fields. This is only our second meeting and there are fewer people involved than in our drive to save the Post Office.

I begin checking my notepad, 'So David, if you could investigate the planning laws, as agreed?'

David Parish nods with a 'Will do'. He's a retired architect. Excellent with detail. I run through, ensuring everyone's happy with their roles, assign someone to write to the local paper and someone to circulate a petition. I'll design leaflets, create the web page and ring local friends.

'Eventually we could build towards a placard walk. But for now we need to think about ideas for fundraisers.'

'A placard walk?' repeats Alice Ainsley. This is the first time she's done anything in the way of campaigning. 'Do you... do you think that's necessary?'

'We need to be visible, Alice. This is common land, public green space. It'll take work but we can turn things around.'

She nods as if willing herself to believe it and we begin to brainstorm publicity ideas. Pru, who's been unusually quiet for the past few minutes, sits up. 'You know Tessa, I've had a thought, something to get the message out.' Everyone looks towards her. She pauses, 'Television!'

I laugh. 'Full marks for positive thinking but that's slightly beyond budget.'

She smiles and lays down her pen. 'But doesn't one of us have the opportunity to become a television star?'

'Oh marvellous,' says David Parish, 'top drawer.'

Oh God, she's right. If I go on the programme and mention the campaign it'll be the best publicity we're ever likely to get. Then again, what about the Greenham Common angle? An uneasy feeling trickles into me. Television? No. I can't.

'Things are so busy at work,' I say, which is true. It's only a two-person office and we're approaching a funding review, Frieda can't get everything done by herself.

Four pairs of eyes fix on me. Pru's gaze is unwavering. 'I'm sure filming is swift.'

But I couldn't have them package me up as a Greenham Woman, not after everything that happened. While the others talk, memories start to move around in my head like uninvited guests at a party, they initiate unwelcome conversations and hold forth with embarrassing anecdotes and pass around snapshots which I attempt to snatch away: a journalist in a burberry hat, a bicycle with a bent wheel, a flaring camp fire on a winter afternoon.

Pru knows the format of the show, she says they could easily include a couple of minutes on Heston Fields. We could make it a condition. Whatever my personal feelings, I can see it's a brilliant idea. Imperilled, like a woman balanced on a high diving platform, I agree.

Coffee cups are chinked in celebration. David Parish, who's taking notes in his beautiful copperplate handwriting, asks if he should amend the minutes with a new action point and his fountain pen hovers over the page: Tessa to appear on television.

It takes a while to find the right shoebox, and in the process I sift through a succession of others crammed with the odds and ends accumulated over years – cards from long-forgotten restaurants, books of souvenir matches, wedding invitations with felty corners, a handful of snaps from the early days with Pete. In one strip of pictures we're squashed together in a passport booth, me on his lap, him pressing his mouth to my cheek in an exaggerated comedy kiss. Strange to stumble upon that intimacy again after so long, almost an intrusion, like passing lit windows and glancing at figures caught in an embrace.

Among the memorabilia are photographs which have never been sorted into albums and I find a picture of Mum in her early thirties, hair backcombed into a beehive, showing off her slim legs in a mini dress printed with overblown pink and orange roses. There's a photo I thought we'd lost, Pippa as a newborn, soft and curled into herself, staring solemn-eyed at the camera. In another she's sitting on my lap after her fourth birthday party, giggling while I hug her to me. I stare at the photo for a long time. Then I remember what I'm supposed to be looking for.

The Greenham stuff must be under the bed. I feel around behind a tartan rug and an old pair of trainers until the Freeman, Hardy & Willis box slides free. It's a few seconds before I lift the lid. Inside is a badly knitted scarf – an early attempt before I gave up knitting for good – and beside that a few handwritten leaflets, two snapshots and an exercise book, the cover smeared with ancient splatters of mud. I pick it up as if it might bear radioactive traces and, with a deep breath, flip it open.

28 October 1982
Hope this wasn't a mistake. Too late now. Met a girl called Rori (sp?) who helped me put up my tent. They've all gone to a meeting somewhere. Not sure what I'm supposed to be doing. It's freezing. Fingerless gloves a mistake.

As I unravel the scarf, a little velvet box drops into my lap. Inside is a pair of silver earrings in the shape of peace symbols. They feel as strange as tiger's teeth after all this time.

The photos are smaller than I remember. The first is a shot of a blockade. I'm squeezed up with a dozen other women, singing. This is the one I'll show to the TV people. But the other is not for public view. I pick it up by the edges, and there we are, me and Rori with our arms slung around one another, the heads of passing women blurring in the background and at the far corner of the frame a child grasping a stick with a paper dove attached, just in shot. On the back of the photo, in handwriting that hardly resembles mine any more is written *Embrace the Base, 1982.* We're both laughing at some private, lost joke, faces turned towards each other, eyes meeting in an instant of joy. And the day returns with all the sharpness of cold weather. Rori's smile, her springy curls spilling from her hat, the two of us clamped together as if we could stay like that forever.

I sit on the edge of the bed gazing down into the image and her lovely face rises up from where it's been buried so long.

2

Life and Death

Mum sat on the settee peeling a saucepan of potatoes with the smallest, sharpest knife in the drawer, something she could do while barely taking her eyes off the six o'clock news. It was September, still warm, and outside a few kids were kicking a ball about before their mums called them in for tea. When a clip from Greenham came on, Dad mumbled to himself and turned his attention back to his *Daily Express* while I took a deep breath and said, 'I was thinking, I might join them for a bit.'

Mum gave a quick little gasp as if she'd cut herself. 'What?' Her hands stopped in mid flow, a strip of peel drooping over her wet thumb.

'The camp. I've decided to go and visit.'

Dad let out a snort. 'We better get you some dungarees then.'

'Don't be daft, you can't go and live on the roadside with that lot,' said Mum.

'They don't live on the roadside.'

'They do.'

'No they don't. They live in tents.'

'Pitched by the roadside.' She looked at me closely, the way she did when she thought I was coming down with something.

'What about your job, they're not ten-a-penny these days.' And, after a pause, because she was still harbouring hopes we'd get back together, 'what about Tony?'

'I've told you, me and Tony are finished, and anyway, I'm not hanging about just because of some bloke.'

'She'll fit right in,' said Dad.

'It's not funny, Brian.' Dad put down the paper then and pointed the new remote control to silence Moira Stewart, who was reading a story about the Iran-Iraq war and regarding us with her serious woman-in-a-man's-world expression. I knew instinctively that in another life, Moira would be doing her bit to safeguard humanity.

'What's put this into your head?' said Dad.

'Nothing's put this into my head. *I've* put this into my head. One nuclear warhead can do the damage of twenty-nine Hiroshimas.'

I reminded them about the dangers of cruise missiles, even though I'd gone through it with them all before; bits I'd got from the CND meeting at Knebworth village hall, bits I'd picked up from Tony, snippets I'd filleted from *The Guardian*. They exchanged a look that said *Do you think she's serious*? I thought Dad was going to tell Mum it was just as well I didn't go to university, the way I'd overheard him saying once when they were washing up. That was soon after I'd given them a lecture about the cruelty of factory farming and told them I was thinking of going vegetarian. 'But you don't like vegetables,' Mum said. I didn't have an answer for that one.

'It's that bloody leaflet isn't it?' said Dad.

'No.'

'The one with the bloke making a bunker under the stairs?' asked Mum, still clasping her half-peeled potato. 'Oh Tess, you don't want to worry about that. Just because some little lad in the civil service is handing out leaflets, it doesn't mean me and your dad will be panic-buying pineapple chunks.'

'It's not a joke.'

'I know it's not, you sleeping on the cold ground with that lot.' She contemplated the murky saucepan.

'That leaflet was written by the Ministry of Defence,' I reminded her.

Protect and Survive advised, in illustrated steps, how best to cope before and after a nuclear strike. A shelter was vital. *You and your family may need to live in this room for days after an attack, almost without leaving it at all.* That alone sounded pretty awful, like Christmas Day and Boxing Day but without any decent food or telly, only the promise of a radioactive dust cloud if you tried to step outside. The leaflet said a pair of stout boots should be kept on standby for trips beyond the front door and that these trips should, if possible, only be conducted by people over thirty.

The problem was, we didn't have a cellar or a bunker, our house was a new build and there was hardly enough room to keep the things we needed, let alone stock-pile things we didn't. The people on Bishops Road would be all right because their houses had big cupboards under the staircases, I knew that from babysitting, but we couldn't very well rush to Bishops Road and start knocking on doors with only four minutes warning. And anyway, who'd let us in? If you didn't have the facilities, the leaflet suggested making a lean-to: there were drawings of a man carrying sandbags and looking busy with a hammer as if he were enjoying some Sunday DIY. He'd nailed three doors together but it didn't say where he'd got them from. I couldn't imagine Dad taking our doors off their hinges.

Mum seemed to have forgotten about the potatoes. 'How long are you planning to go for?' I told her I wasn't sure yet, my visit was open. 'How will you wash?' She glanced at Dad whose eyes had slid back to the mute TV. 'What about your monthlies?' She mouthed. I made a shushing face. 'Perhaps you should find another job, love. That place isn't stretching you much, is it, and you could be earning a better wage too. You don't have to stay in Stevenage now you've got your licence, you could go anywhere. Letchworth. Baldock. Or you could get something in London if you really wanted, couldn't she Brian, go up on the train?'

Dad sighed. He was looking at me as if I were a map of somewhere foreign.

But I wasn't bothered about getting on the train every day. I'd always known Hirshman & Luck was a temporary measure until I'd decided on the next step, and while I was going out with Tony, I didn't care what the next step was. I loved clocking off and leaving it all behind, not having to think, let alone worry about anything until the next morning. Even when I was there I could use half my mind for the work and the other half for sifting through thoughts of our time together. But then Tony dumped me in the middle of a routine phone call about weekend plans. There'd been the slightest break in the conversation, and I knew it was coming, sure as an F16 out of a clear blue sky.

'I was thinking, what if we put things on ice for a while?' he said.

On ice? What did that mean? I wasn't a polar bear. I didn't want to be put on ice while he strode into the white wilderness and found himself a dozen Eskimo girls, giggling in their beaver skin dresses.

He stumbled something about really liking me but thinking it was best for both of us. There was a pause before he added that he thought we could be friends, but when it came down to it, he needed someone he could really talk to. I knew what he meant, he meant about current affairs and politics. He'd just finished his degree at the Polytechnic and was going to move to London. He said he was going to be busy, he had plans.

'I have plans too. It's not as if I want to hang around in Stevenage all my life.' That's what I said. Not bad. Not true either because actually, yes, I would have hung around in Stevenage, I would have hung around anywhere if Tony was there to hang around with. Instead we agreed it was a big world and he told me again how much he liked me and I just about maintained my dignity until we reached the end of the conversation and I was free to cry in the privacy of my bedroom with The Human League turned up loud to disguise the wailing.

After Tony dumped me, I carried on at work, soothed by the repetitive rhythm of the days: the post at nine-thirty, tea-break, minute-taking, the little tapes of dictation clattering onto my desk at intervals, each containing the slow drone of Mr Hirshman's voice telling me where to put my full stops and when to start a new paragraph; the reassuring presence of Peggy, the senior secretary, the deliberate way she'd stop at exactly one o'clock every day and stretch up her arms to the ceiling saying, 'Rest for the wicked, Tessa,' then rise from her desk to retrieve her foil-wrapped sandwiches – chicken roll with piccalilli or tinned salmon and cress. Routine offers a modicum of comfort when your heart has been broken.

Mum and Dad knew I was suffering. Mum made me my favourite dinners for a week and I'd catch Dad giving a concerned sideways glance while we watched *Nationwide*, though he never said anything because he didn't know what to say. He got all the information off Mum. They'd both liked Tony – Mum said he had lovely eyes and reminded her of a young Gene Pitney. But it didn't matter what they thought about him anymore, it didn't matter if they knew he'd sold *The Socialist Worker* in the student union bar, because I'd never be bringing him home again. Tony was in the past. There were no more phone calls late at night just when I was giving up hope. There were no more trips to his friends' parties. Those parties belonged to a different chapter of my life, and if he wanted to start something with that girl Lisa the social sciences student – I'd heard them having a long, flirtatious argument about the monarchy – then that was up to him.

Without Tony I could see my life for what it was, and what I saw was small and disappointing. Stevenage was ugly: its endless mini roundabouts, its purpose-built breezeblock towers, the fountain where teenagers sat on summer evenings knocking back cider as the sun glinted orange off the Co-op, young mums smoking cigarettes with one hand and rocking a pram with the other. If I stayed it would be the death of me. And as the days went by, the true meaninglessness of my afternoons of copy typing began to scare rather than soothe me, and my walk home through the town centre became a journey through my own colourless future.

What I needed to do was make my life count for something. If I could expect any life at all. Day by day I thought more about what was happening in the world, and with Tony pushed to the side, I had time to dwell on the real issues, the life and death of it. I kept the *Protect and Survive* leaflet beside my bed and woke up worrying, or fell asleep and dreamed of the line-drawn man sheltering his family ineffectually in the homemade bunker. Four minutes, that's all we'd have. And the weapons were real. They were coming. The Americans were going to park them here as a defence against the Russians and Mrs Thatcher thought it was a great idea.

On TV the Greenham women sang their songs, sisters under the skin, and it was suddenly obvious: here was a way to make a difference, a way to sacrifice my pathetic life for something noble, something meaningful and something I believed in. What's more, now that I was no longer the object of someone else's love, I could devote myself entirely. And the camp was a place Tony would never be part of, however many copies of *The Socialist Worker* he sold.

Every night at the tea table Mum tried a new angle on me, but like Margaret Thatcher, I wasn't for turning. Dad ate his shepherd's pie, disconsolate after another long day at the yard. Three years ago, after he damaged his back, they'd put him onto deliveries and supplies, and now when he came home he had a tired look around the edges and never talked about work. Not like when he was doing an extension or knocking through a living room. I hadn't heard him say any of his builder's words for ages – newel, or screed, or mitre. The money wasn't so good either. Mum had taken a part-time cleaning job, and then two. I wondered if they'd miss my board money.

Late one night I heard them talking downstairs; our house was too small for secrets.

'Let her get it out of her system,' Dad said. 'She won't last long without central heating and a warm bed.'

'D'you think?' Mum had that note in her voice, the one when she allowed herself to defer to Dad even though she didn't quite believe what he was saying. It was the same note that came out when she'd painted the kitchen walls a nasty yellow, and Dad told her it would dry two shades lighter.

'She gets these ideas doesn't she. Remember that time she was going to make her own clothes?' he said.

'Oh yes, I'd forgotten about that.'

'And when she started learning the guitar, how long did that last?'

'Or when she was going to be an au pair in Switzerland,' said Mum, who was now taking comfort in her own memories of my failed attempts to define myself as someone interesting. But I'd heard enough and went to lie on my bed, turning over my greatest flops as I stared at the ceiling. This wasn't the same, I said to the zigzag crack that ran like a fault-line from the light fitting to the curtain rail. This was important. This would be the beginning of something. Goodbye to Mr Hirshman, goodbye to Peggy and the biscuit tins and the spider plants. Goodbye to evenings at The Old Volunteer, the pool table with its worn purple baize and the fruit machine that never paid out. Apart from Mum and Dad, the only person I was sorry to leave was Maggie.

*

From our table beside the door we had unrestricted views of the entire pub, which meant Maggie could chart the position of any decent men like battleships on a grid. She'd come straight from aerobics, and the satin v-neck of leotard showed under her denim jacket.

'You've got to give it a go one night, you'd love it. And there was a complete stud on the running machine,' she said, exhaling a plume of smoke from her B&H. The thought of a good-looking bloke seeing me in my tracksuit bottoms was no incentive. We chatted for a while. She described her new manager at the pub who had trouble changing the optics, and I told her about Mr Hirshman's decision to create a stationery log-book to prevent the disappearance of propeller pencils, but actually I was working up to my announcement. After I'd made it there was a pause.

She blinked. 'Is this my mum's fault?'

'What? No, it's got nothing to do with your Mum.' Though it did, a bit. Me and Paula always had good chats when I called for Maggie. She'd lent me a few copies of *Spare Rib*, one of which contained a three-page feature about Greenham, *For years men have left home for war but now women were leaving home for peace*. I'd carried it around all week, re-reading it under my desk. Maggie, twizzling her cigarette, fixed her eyes on me.

'Because she only went for the afternoon, and anyway, she's going through the menopause. She's got a book.'

'I've handed in my notice.'

'Te-*ssa*.' She said my name the way she'd say it if I'd just given ten pounds to a tramp, then took a deep disbelieving drag on her B&H. 'Why?' The smoke filtered into a smog between us.

'Because this is more important.'

She flicked her ash. 'But those weapons aren't even here yet.'

'That's the point – to stop them coming.'

She assessed me. 'Listen, I know you like politics, and to be honest,' she held up a hand, palm flat, 'fair play. You're clever.' Maggie always insisted on my intelligence because I'd taken A levels, but she was the one could park on a sixpence and add up half a dozen drinks in her head. 'Just answer me honestly…'

I waited.

'Is it because of Tony?' She didn't wait for an answer. 'You need to get away, right? Because I know what it's like, not wanting to bump into someone.' Maggie had experienced at least five break-ups by my reckoning. 'But there are alternatives. You could get a job at Butlins. Theresa Matthews got a summer job helping with the kids' club, she said it was brilliant.'

'Maggie, I'm not going to Butlins, I'm going to Greenham Common.'

She exhaled and pressed the orange cigarette butt into the ashtray. 'Honestly Tessa, I don't get you sometimes.'

'You're supposed to be my friend. You're supposed to support me.'

'I am your friend, and a friend would tell you not to go and live outdoors with a load of lezzers.'

I'd known Maggie too long to be angry. We listened to Graham stacking the glass-washing machine. The jukebox was broken again.

'I always thought he had a wonky eye,' said Maggie.

'Who?'

'Tony Mercer.'

It had never occurred to me.

'You'll come back won't you, you won't go for long?'

I didn't know how long I'd be going. Long enough to make a difference. Long enough to make a change. 'Come and visit.'

'Me?'

'Why not?'

'Yeah, okay.' But I couldn't tell if she meant it.

We moved off the subject then and she described plans for her twenty-first. She was hiring a function room in the old town, but wasn't sure whether to invite Kerry Granger because she had an idea Kerry was after Dale Abbot and she thought me and Dale would be perfect together. I could see it was her way of keeping me connected to Stevenage, but the possibility of romance with Dale Abbot wasn't enough, and as she talked, I was more confident than ever that I was doing the right thing.

*

The night before I left, Mum insisted I wash my hair thoroughly because God knew when I'd have the chance to get it near a bottle of Timotei again. She said I could ring them anytime and Dad would come and pick me up. I said that was nice, but I was nineteen, old enough to drink and vote and get married, and I'd be fine. She said I was to be sensible and not get myself into any trouble with the police because some of those women were bound to be rough and there would be anarchists about. She said she knew I could lead my own life, but she and Dad had been around a bit longer – those women weren't all there to ban the bomb, some of them were there for other reasons. Never mind what other reasons, she said, I could use my imagination.

I'd laid everything out on the bed the way I did before holiday, except this time there were no white plastic sunglasses or Bermuda shorts. Along with my new donkey jacket, jeans, jumpers and toiletries, I'd included: a bottle of tomato ketchup, an alarm clock, travel scrabble, a mouth organ (I'd learn), my diary, a copy of *The Female Eunuch* (this time I'd get past chapter two), *The Second Sex* (ditto) and Mum's copy of *The Wives of Sunset Strip*, which I'd pinched from her bookshelf and hidden at the bottom of my pack for emergencies. Actually Mum had never read the book, it had been an ill-judged Christmas present from one of the ladies she cleaned for. From the news footage I'd seen, it was clear that fingerless gloves were essential because they accommodated fiddly tasks such as lighting matches. I'd nestled a packet of Golden Virginia in my bag too: offering tobacco around might be a good way of making friends. Like in prison.

3

Eco Chic

They've promised Greenham will only be mentioned to add what the director calls a little background colour. They still want to use a photograph.

'May I see?' asks Jude, leaning forwards from her position on the sofa. She's dressed in wide-legged trousers teamed with a polka-dot blouse, and everything she says has a dramatic edge, as if a camera were permanently trained on her. 'Hell's teeth darling, where in the world did you get that stuff?' She holds the blockade photo nearer. 'Did you knit that? The poncho thingy?' I have decided to take this whole experience with a big bucket of salt. Thankfully the filming at Heston Fields is already in the can.

'No, but someone probably did. People used to drop off donated clothes.'

'Lulu! Come and see this.' Jude beckons a girl from the crew. 'The other side of the eighties,' she explains, 'but you won't be seeing any of that in Hoxton Square. Those dungarees! Shades of Dexy's Midnight Runners, I fear.'

Lulu doesn't look old enough to know who Dexy's Midnight Runners are but she nods in appreciation and says Cool. With her long chestnut hair she reminds me of Pippa.

'What was it like there?' she asks.

Jude raises an eyebrow, also curious, but I can only muster a cliché.

'It changed my life.'

She places a slim hand on my knee, 'And now it's being changed all over again, darling.' I laugh, then realise she isn't joking.

The conversation which follows is orchestrated to seem informal. Jude tells me to relax, pretend it's only the two of us. She asks me to tell her about my lifestyle, so I talk about Easy Green and explain our ethos, how we advise people on low incomes about sustainable living – heat insulation, mostly – which helps reduce their utility bills. Just when I'm working towards another mention of the Heston Fields campaign, she cuts in, 'Fabulous. Now, this is the key question. Ready?' She allows a pause before it comes. 'What do you want from your wardrobe?'

'Oh, um, right…' This is not a question I've considered much, but something is called for. 'Well the main thing is probably comfort.'

She re-crosses her legs and the gesture is like a sigh. 'Ah yes, our old friend *comfort*,' she says using the kind of intonation that might be reserved for the word enema. 'And where do you buy your clothes?'

'Umm,' I'm sorting through to remember my last purchase, a striped top from the new high-end charity shop in town. 'I get a lot of things second-hand.'

She nods as if some puzzle is becoming clear. I mention a few things about landfill and sweatshops, before Zeb the director steps in, 'We'll have to stay off this Tessa, if you don't mind. Don't want a political broadcast.'

'But I thought…' I thought this was part of the package, the eco-chic theme.

He shoots Jude a meaningful look and scratches the soft wires of his beard. 'Go again.'

'Right, shopping as protest,' says Jude seriously, pushing a chunky bracelet further up her arm and nodding towards my shirt. 'So you could say that particular pea-green garment is a sort of protest. Or is that just what people do when you put it on?'

Someone in the crew hoots. A board clacks, 'That's it!'

Jude pats my knee. 'It's for the camera, darling,' she says. 'Strictly tongue-in-cheek.'

I remind myself about the bucket of salt.

Lulu is sent to organise coffee, and since I'm not needed for the moment I escape with her to the kitchen for ten minutes of normality. While we gather mugs, my phone bleeps.

Sorry haven't rung. Things been crazy. Everything ok? Pip x

What sort of crazy? Probably not this sort. I've decided not to tell her about the TV show yet, and for once I don't encourage her to ring.

Hi kiddo – everything fine. Speak soon. Lots of love, mum xxx

The message vanishes and the screensaver reappears; the kids last year on Camber Sands: Pippa, suntanned under a wide-brimmed fedora, Dom beside her smiling with a closed mouth because he was still wearing his braces.

Lulu stirs the mugs and frowns. 'I can't remember if I put sugar in Zeb's.'

'Zeb. That's an interesting name, what's it short for?'

'Simon,' she says, lifting the tray and making for the living room.

It's another blossomy afternoon and sunlight falls in slats along the garden fence. Jude is already outside with a cigarette, which she raises in greeting.

'Hideous for the skin,' she says. I tell her I smoked roll-ups

37

back in the day and she says it's impossible to make a woodbine look stylish unless you're eighteen and working the retro-grunge look.

'You came around to the idea then?' she says. 'Zeb feared you were going to bolt. We had a Hare Krishna once and she refused outright.'

I shrug, reminding myself to play along. 'It's an experience.'

'Exactly,' she says. 'One you won't regret. And it's for your daughter too.'

'Is it?' I conjure Pippa with sudden alarm. 'Did she sign the letter?'

'No no,' Jude waves her cigarette hand. 'What I mean is, we learn what's acceptable from our mothers, don't we? What you're telling her is that this,' she takes me in with another sweep of her cigarette, 'is okay.'

I have a flash of Pippa in one of her outfits, mobile in hand, jumbo handbag on shoulder.

'Believe me, I have no influence whatsoever on my daughter. Sometimes I wish I did.'

Me and Dom get along fine, apart from the usual tussles over wet towels on floors and homework, but with Pip it's more complicated. I can't dispel the idea I'm not the mother she wants.

Jude regards me with interest. 'Even so, darling. It's going to make you feel like a new woman when we sort you out.'

Sorting me out includes hair and make-up, for which Bobby, an attractive black American man with heavy-framed glasses, has been drafted in. He tells me I have gorgeous eyes. People have remarked on my eyes before; they're hazel, like Mum's, with a double row of eyelashes. Once or twice I was told off at school for wearing mascara, even though I didn't have a make-up bag, it was Maggie who was always getting marched to the cloakrooms to wash her face. Maggie. My muscles tense at the memory of her in the turquoise dress. Pete's right, she wouldn't have meant to upset me, but haven't we been friends for long enough? Why would she think I'd actually enjoy a make-over? Especially that sequence we filmed yesterday called 'The right shape for your shape' which involved me standing in my underwear while Jude assessed my body from various angles. *Just don't put me in a hexagon* I said. But joking didn't make things any less harrowing. Would Maggie want to go through that? She's my oldest friend, we grew up next door to each other, and yes, we're different, but when you've known each other since you were riding bikes together or running away from boys, the differences count for less. Or so I thought.

Bobby sifts his fingers through my hair and says hmm a lot. He produces a booklet of nylon hair swatches, each tinted a different shade, and tests them against my face before settling on Firecracker. I struggle to imagine a whole head of Firecracker, but when I ask questions he becomes mysterious and says *Trust me*, so I sit back and let the mixing, separating and painting begin.

'All these products are organic so they're super gentle,' he assures me, and I remember 1982, the one and only time I tried to colour my hair – in the wintry outdoors with a bottle of bleach.

The hair takes ages. When it's done Bobby moves on to make-up. He tells me what good skin I have. He says he often finds this with curvaceous ladies; maybe it's all that blood pumping around their bodies giving them a healthy flush. What do I think? He says he once worked with Meryl Streep and she had the most beautiful skin of any actress he ever came across who didn't have an actual weight problem. Like porcelain.

When I've been dressed they stand around and examine me approvingly. I'm wearing a long green skirt made from crepey material – part of a fair trade couture range – which sways in fronds when I move. The rest is questionable. Particularly the pink bodice. I glance down and there are my breasts, lifted from the darkness and displayed like shy newborns quivering before an audience. I insisted to Jude that I'd never wear something like this, but she's of the flat-chested model physique and kept saying, 'You've got a lovely pair, Tessa, show them off.' After negotiations she eventually fetched a cream jacket with seed pearls and feathers stitched around the collar. I've been instructed not to button it.

My feet are shod in a pair of stiletto heels – nude because this will apparently lengthen my legs – and Jude has made me get into something called Miracle Tights, which are supposed to give an instant streamlining effect. The operation of putting them on was like struggling into a pair of washing-up gloves three sizes too small.

'Are you sure it all goes?' I ask, assessing what I can see of the ensemble.

'*Goes*,' Jude laughs. 'Co-ordinating handbags are for the MIFs darling.'

'The what?'

'The Milk In Firsts. Trust me, you look gorgeous.' Bobby agrees and says he should probably leave the room before he starts having heterosexual thoughts.

It is time for the unveiling. There's a hush. Jude steers me like the mother ship towards the mirror, gold-frilled, like the ones in picture books about Snow White. I'm half-suspecting someone will swing a bottle of champagne against me. The blindfold is supposed to heighten tension. Jude counts to three before untying it with a flourish.

And there is a woman I only partially recognise. I stare back at her, the woman with the cleavage, the woman with the bright orangey-red hair cut in slices around her face. She has swallowed me whole. I am blinking out of her generously mascara-ed eyelashes.

'Oh!' The woman wobbles back on her dagger heels. 'This is strange.'

'Strange?' Repeats Jude from off camera.

Zeb yells *cut* and asks if I want to take a minute. Jude strides over, 'What's wrong, darling?'

I look down at myself, put a hand to my hair. 'I don't feel like me.'

She throws her head back, 'That's the whole point! You're not supposed to feel like you. You aren't you.'

'Who am I then?'

At that moment Bobby arrives like a coach to a boxing ring. He sweeps a powder brush over my nose while Jude talks.

'Come on darling, we need to wrap this up. I don't think I can bear another night in a Travel Lodge.' She looks to Bobby, 'Jesus, remember when we used to have an actual budget for this show.'

We go through the scene again and this time I give them what they want, which is a gasp of pleasure followed by a twirl. Afterwards, Pete and Dom are ushered in. Dom is wearing his biggest, blackest Goth boots and an expression of bemusement. I hope he didn't tell his teachers why he's got the afternoon off. Pete is clasping a bunch of roses which have obviously been supplied.

'What d'you think of Mum's new look?' comes Jude's voice. Dom doesn't answer. Zeb checks his watch. 'It's all in the edit,' he says. Jude asks Pete what he thinks of me. There are two high spots of colour on his cheeks as if he's been drinking.

'She looks amazing,' he says. 'I can't believe she's my wife.' His eyes have gone like half-set jelly.

At last it's over. The crew reel up cables and pack them into boxes. Jude gives me a final hug, 'Remember you're a beautiful woman,' she says firmly. I thank her. I don't know why I'm thanking her, but she seems so sincere and I want her to leave so badly. And then she does.

Dom flops on the sofa. When I ask what he thought of it all he shrugs, says why did I let them make me a ginge, and asks what's for tea.

'You'll have to see to yourself tonight,' says Pete. 'I'm taking your mum out.'

He is looking at me as if we've just met.

'Great,' I say, 'I could do with a nice meal after that.'

He tells me I look a million dollars again and then, still with the slightly unhinged half-set jelly expression, he suddenly whoops me around in a circle like a cowboy with a cowgirl. We are laughing and I'm engulfed by a surge of sheer relief.

'Right, give me ten minutes, I'll just get changed.' My face feels cakey and the shoes are pinching.

'Changed?' He's stopped laughing. 'You are changed.'

'I can't go out like this.'

'They've spent all day dolling you up.'

I explain about the shoes. He says he wants to show me off. I tell him this isn't Crufts and then Dom chips in from where he's sprawled, 'You'd look a lot less freaky without all that stuff on your face.' Pete shouts at him. I pull Pete into the kitchen.

'Are you ashamed of me?' I ask in a low voice so Dom can't hear. I'm leaning on the counter for support, but benefitting from the extra height of the heels.

Pete shakes his head. 'No, no, I'm proud of you, that's the point.'

'Let me wash my face then.'

He wraps a hand around the back of his neck, as if I'm one of his more challenging Year Elevens. 'You are so bloody stubborn. Why can't you go out like you are, just for one night?' The jacket is scratchy and I drape it on the kitchen chair. 'Most women would love all that pampering.'

'Pampering? I've been pummelled about like a side of beef. Look, I'll be ten minutes, I can hardly walk in these shoes.'

He shakes his head.

'What?'

'You,' he says. 'Why can't I take you out when you're dressed up like a woman for once?'

I rock very slightly on the heels. He bangs the kitchen door shut.

4

An Alien Mug

What with my pack and the tent, getting off the bus took some negotiation. I'd asked the driver to let me know the stop and he'd made a harrumphing noise.

'One of them are you?' he said. 'Should have got the 302.'

He dropped me at the bottom of a hill on a main road flanked by wire fencing. At a quarter past three there was still enough light to navigate, although I wasn't sure which direction I was supposed to take. Dad was right, I should have set off earlier. Half hoping for a sign that said *Campsite This Way*, I started up the hill.

It was only after I'd been walking for a while that I realised the fence, which looked a good ten feet tall, must be the one containing the American air base. But there wasn't much to see behind it, only grass, a stretch of concrete and in the distance a collection of low buildings in khaki shades, a few trucks parked beside them. The left boot of my new Doc Martens was beginning to bite at the heel but I pressed on until eventually the hill gave way to an unremarkable view of yet more fencing set against an expanse of pewter-coloured sky. Where were the women? What if the driver had sent me in the wrong direction on purpose? I pictured him in the depot, laughing with his mates over mugs of tea. A lorry rocked past at speed and I stepped onto the verge.

Why weren't there any signs? Eventually I made out a dot in the distance which transformed slowly into the shape of a person: a woman sitting on a garden chair, set back on a hillock of grass facing the road. I picked up speed. She must be one of them. She'd be able to help. I assumed a friendly expression, ready to wave and call out if she hailed me.

'Hello,' I said, quite bent under the weight of the rucksack.

The woman was oldish, wearing an Aran jumper with legwarmers pulled up to the knee and an enormous wax jacket. The placard staked into the ground beside her read PEACE in large hand-painted letters, and a dove was flying from one corner carrying a sprig of something green in its beak.

'I've just got here,' I said, because nothing else came to mind.

She offered a half smile and said *Welcome*, barely audibly, before getting on with some more staring.

Not having a chair myself, and unsure of protocol, I set my pack down in a spirit of camaraderie and perched. We sat like that, contemplating the road for a few moments, our silence interrupted every now and then by a passing car, while I thought of something to say. The woman, who hadn't introduced herself, cradled an enamel mug, which she raised, uttering the single word 'tea?' A Thermos balanced beside her feet.

'Oh. No thanks.' I'd never liked tea, and a quick glance inside her mug revealed strange leaves floating around in it. Nevertheless it was nice of her to offer. She had watery blue eyes, a plump face, and an aura of wisdom.

After a bit more staring I began to talk into the silence. I told her where I lived, what I'd been doing before, why I felt compelled to come, how wonderful it would be if every woman saw it as her duty, how it was only by individuals making their voices heard that we had any hope of changing the world. I went on like this for some time. When I'd got to the end of my speech, she closed her eyes.

Well that was just rude.

The wind crackled her jacket. Ordinarily, I would have made some comment about the weather, but this woman, with her mucky fingernails and her mucky tea, appeared to be impervious to everything, including the elements. She simply sat there with her eyes closed, a serene expression on her face. Maybe she was stoned? One of Tony's friends used to get stoned all the time, in fact that's about all he ever did. Once we went to a party and by the end of the night his legs had completely stopped working; we had to sit there for ages with Echo and the Bunnymen going around and around on the turntable before we could get him to the front door.

After a minute or so I stood up, feeling stupid. 'Better be off,' I said, as if I had some important shopping to do.

The woman opened her eyes and gave another slow smile like someone remembering a pleasant dream.

'Which gate are you going to?' This time I noticed her Welsh accent.

'Gate?'

'There's more than one.'

'Oh.'

She leaned forward and pointed, 'You're nearest Amber. Turn down that road when you get to the trees.'

Amber? I wasn't sure what she was talking about, but thanked her anyway and set off in the direction she'd indicated. This was Berkshire, but it was all alien territory to me and I didn't have a map.

The sky separated into darks and lights and the cars began to pass more regularly as the first commuters made their way home. I looked at my watch. At Hirshman & Luck, me and Peggy would be franking letters for the last post. I tried to think about the various boring tasks I'd liberated myself from, rather than the burning sensation of my blistering heel or my rising anxiety as I turned right at a clump of trees, still following the line of wire fencing. Mum had insisted on filling a spongebag with medical supplies and I hoped she'd included plasters.

The temperature had dropped and my hands, only partially insulated in the fingerless gloves, were bunched deep in my pockets. There was no sign of the gate, only a pin-prick of orange. A fire? Perhaps someone could point me in the right direction. I left the road and crossed a stretch of muddy grass, weaving towards the light through slender trees, their trunks patterned with white bark. Phrases from a song in composition drifted towards me... *you try to tie our mouths up but we sing*. A pluck as the singer changed chords, correcting herself... *you tie our mouths up but we cry*. Her accent wasn't English.

I followed the singing towards a handful of figures gathered around a smoking fire. The young guitarist sat on a log beside another woman who was reading a newspaper with great attention, the hood of her parka pulled up. The guitarist smiled.

'I'm looking for Amber gate, do you know where it is?' I asked. Little oddments of ribbon and bead were plaited into her hair.

'That is here,' she said. Her that was a *dat*. She could have been Danish perhaps. Or Norwegian.

'Oh thanks. So where's the gate?' I asked searching the dusk.

She frowned, 'But it is here.'

'Yes,' I said, realising it must be difficult conversing in another language, 'but could you tell me where the entrance is please?'

'Entrance?'

'To the camp.'

The woman with the newspaper lowered it a fraction and blinked at me through wire-framed spectacles. 'This *is* the camp,' she said in a pronounced northern accent. She might have been only two or three years older than me, but she spoke with the authority of someone twice my age. I glanced around, wondering if she was joking. A woman with a peroxide Mohican sat slouched in a car seat on the other side of the fire whittling a stick. Was this it? Where were all the women? Why weren't they making banners, or preparing a massive communal meal or practising a speech or something? It made no sense. Just then another figure appeared from the trees wheeling a carriage pram.

'Hello!' she called, pushing the pram right up to the fireside and pausing when she saw me. 'New recruit?' Springs of curly hair escaped her knitted hat. The others perked up noticeably as soon as she entered, as if the leading lady had walked onto a muddy filmset.

'She was looking for de entrance,' said the guitarist.

'Sorry, it's been a long journey,' I said.

The curly-haired girl smiled, bending to the pram and lifting from it an armful of wood. Even in the limited light her beauty was obvious, her face with its high cheekbones like a 1930s' film star. She squatted down and attended to the fire.

'Take a seat, we were just about to have tea,' she said in the sort of thoroughbred English accent guaranteed to thrill Americans. There were no empty seats, only a piece of sacking folded into a rough square. Mum's voice reminded me that sitting on the cold ground gave you piles.

'Shift up, Angela,' said the Mohican woman from her car seat.

'Thanks,' I said, glad to have some respite from the chafing boot, yet uncomfortable about squeezing so close to Angela and her newspaper, which she'd now folded into a neat oblong. 'Oh, that's a relief.' A rush of stars tingled pleasingly through my legs. I wanted nothing more than to take off the troublesome boot and start massaging my foot, but even if this was the outdoors, I was still very much in company.

'Are you weary?' asked the curly-haired girl, prodding the fire.

'I am a bit.'

'We get women from all over,' she said. 'Shetland. Belfast. I met someone from Malmo at Main Gate last week, imagine.'

'There's a couple of Yanks about too,' said the Mohican woman, her voice loud and Londony. 'Where you from?'

'Stevenage.'

'Stevenage?' The girl with the guitar made a quizzical face.

'Hertfordshire,' said Angela, still fixed on her paper.

'I'm Rori, by the way,' said the curly-haired girl, stepping back from the fire and admiring it. I wondered if I'd heard properly, but she'd already turned towards the others. 'Who else have we got?'

The handful of women introduced themselves. Barbel was the one strumming the guitar; Sam was the one with the Mohican. I'd already worked out that the one reading the newspaper was Angela.

'And who are you?' said Rori.

'Oh, sorry, I'm Tessa.'

'Well, Sorry I'm Tessa, your tea isn't far away, I'll put the kettle on.'

Putting the kettle on involved pouring water from a plastic canister into a bent teapot, which was then hung over the fire. Now it had flamed into life, the shapes around me began to take on definition. At our feet wooden pallets were arranged to make a short walkway because the ground had been churned to mud. It was black as pitch away from the fire, but I could see a length of plastic sheeting hung over a line suspended between trees, and a trestle table poked out alongside something which looked very much like a Welsh dresser.

'Been to Greenham before?' asked Sam from her car seat.

'No, first time.' I was still taking in what I could, aware suddenly of what I'd done. 'It's brilliant.'

It was like being in the aftermath of a bomb. A pre-taster of the apocalypse.

'You know it's customary to bring the tribe a gift,' said Sam, raising her voice over the discussion about who'd last seen Didcot Alan, who apparently delivered timber off-cuts. 'We like a gift, don't we girls?' Laughter. 'Got any booze?'

'No, sorry.'

'Chocolate?'

'Um, no.' Then I remembered the packet of Bourbons Mum had given me for the train. I scrabbled in my rucksack, happy to perform a service, feeling around for the biscuits which had slid down and were pressed against the soles of my trainers. They were broken when I eventually eased them out, but nobody seemed to mind.

While we waited for the kettle to boil I tried to be perky and interesting, though it was difficult knowing what to say. Angela was still engrossed in world events beside me.

Rori snapped a biscuit in half, 'Are you part of a women's group?'

'Not exactly. Um, I've been in CND.' Knebworth village hall had to count for something. 'Sort of.'

The Bourbons went round a second time.

'Before I forget, has anyone heard about Helen's trial?' said Rori, taking two more from the packet.

Angela looked up, 'I don't think we should go into it now.'

'Oh sorry. Loose lips sink ships and all that.'

'What do the loose lips do?' asked Barbel, strumming gently to herself.

Angela explained, 'It was a government slogan during the war.'

'The Falkland war, with the little island?'

'No, World War II,' said Angela, pushing her spectacles up the bridge of her nose. Out of everyone she'd offered least in the way of conversation.

Barbel repeated the slogan, perhaps storing it away in a file marked Strange British Expressions, while Rori stoked the fire with a black-tipped branch, which looked to be reserved for the purpose. Specks of white flew into the black air. 'We had some trouble a little while ago,' she said. 'A journalist infiltrated one of the camps looking for a story, you know, Left Wing Loonies Leave Kids, Potty Peace Women in League with Kremlin, that kind of thing.'

'They did one on Rori,' said Sam. '*Lady Muck*, wasn't it?' She whittled another chunk from her stick and snorted.

'Rori's father is in the royal family,' Barbel told me in a confidential tone.

'No he's not!'

'But I thought he takes dinner with the Queen?'

'He's a Viscount,' Rori muttered. At Barbel's request she explained with some awkwardness what that meant. In my mind

49

I was transporting her from the mud to a stately home where she was dressed in a long silk evening gown rather than a red mini-kilt over leggings teamed with a fisherman's jumper.

'Hey Tessa,' called Sam, 'see what company you're in?'

'No class wars tonight if you please,' said Rori.

Sam laughed. 'All right, Aurora.'

Aurora, the name rang in my head, gleaming from a bell tower.

'You're not a journalist?' said Barbel.

'Me? No!'

'Good. You don't look like one also,' she said to herself and strummed another chord. *You try to shut my mouth, but I will sing*, she declared tunefully and without any hint of embarrassment. We watched the kettle for a long time until it eventually began wobbling to and fro with its boiling cargo. The women passed their mugs towards Rori. Despite disliking the taste of tea, I decided this wasn't the time to fuss, Sam was right, this was a new tribe and I must respect their customs.

'Do you have a mug?' Rori asked. 'It's just we're rather short.'

Damn, I knew I'd forget something.

'She can use Jean's,' said Sam, 'I'm going for a piss, I'll get it on the way back.'

'There's no milk is there?' called Rori.

'What do you think?' came the cheerful reply. Someone laughed.

Drinking milkless, sugarless tea from an alien mug fetched by a woman who had just been urinating in the open wasn't my idea of a joke.

'So, you've come to live with us for a while?' asked Barbel. She could have been Swedish. 'Or only a day or two. The visitors come, the visitors go. It gets cold. You know, it's not their fault. They have jobs of course, and kids.'

'Me too,' I said. 'A job, I mean. But I gave it up to come here.'

'What was your job?' she strummed.

'A secretary.'

'Oh it's nice,' she said in her sing-song voice. 'Where is this?'

A woman's refuge, I wanted to say. A welfare centre for the victims of war crime.

'An estate agent.'

Angela glanced at me and returned her eyes to the newspaper.

In silence we watched a flame take purchase on a knobbly branch. My fingers and toes were warming even as my back chilled. It was like being a slice of baked Alaska.

I asked Rori if she'd been at the camp for long.

'About five months, on and off. More on at the moment.' She perched beside Barbel at the end of the log. Two silver hoops pierced the cartilage of her ear, and through both lobes she wore silver earrings shaped like peace symbols, their surface flecked by firelight. 'Angela's been here longest.'

Angela turned another page. Barbel stopped strumming and paused to calculate.

'What is the date today? Twenty-seventh of October?'

'Twenty-eighth,' Angela corrected.

'Then I have been here for two months. Before I was living on the Moshav,' she said in her up and down voice, 'and then the peace camp in Soesterberg. It was beautiful. And then I come here. Not so beautiful, but necessary. I come to make friends with all these crazy women, don't I?' She nudged Angela, who gave a pale smile, eyes still fixed on the print. 'But I better not speak too much because of my loose lips, that's right?'

'I'm really not a journalist,' I said. The smoke was beginning to make my eyes smart and I edged backwards.

'What's new in the world, Angel?' said Rori, crossing a long leg. I wondered who she was talking to, but saw it was Angela, who answered by reading out part of an article about Helmut Kohl, the new chancellor of West Germany. It was pretty dry stuff. After that she read a piece about a group called the Mujahideen who were fighting a civil war in Afghanistan.

'There you are, girl,' said Sam, who'd returned with the mug. Now I could see her in the light she looked quite a lot like the women from the enraged tabloid articles I'd seen. Was she a lesbian? I'd never met a real lesbian. She wore two jumpers on top of each other which came down to the middle of her thighs, and her Mohican, which stood about two inches tall, ran in a stripe down the centre of her head.

'Admiring the barnet?'

'Oh, no I was just…' I must have been gawping.

She winked and slumped back into her car seat.

'It's nice to have people to talk to,' I said. 'I met a woman on the way here but she wasn't exactly chatty,' I ventured, in a chums together way. 'She was sitting by herself on the side of the road.'

'That's Di. She's witnessing,' said Angela from inside her paper.

Witnessing? 'Oh. Right.' My face prickled. 'She seemed very nice anyway.'

'Everything set for this evening?' said Rori, filling my mug. The tea tasted faintly metallic, but it was hot at least. Bitter and hot. I sat quiet, afraid to get anything else wrong. 'We've a meeting later at Main Gate. I'd ask you to come along but we ought to be cautious just until we tell the others we have a visitor. After that nasty experience with the journalist it's made some of the women nervous. You understand?'

'Of course,' I said, not sure I did. Even if I was a journalist what were they going to do about it, how were they going to prove it? This was the sort of unjust treatment that a person wasn't supposed to expect when she was demonstrating against other injustices.

'I think I will cook,' announced Barbel. Her voice was interesting to listen to, every time she spoke she sounded as if she were surprising herself.

'Where's Jean?'

'Gone to visit Ruby gate.'

The women didn't look enthusiastic about the prospect of one of Barbel's dinners, and two hours later, after sharing a kidney bean and cauliflower stew, I understood why.

By eight-thirty I was huddled in my sleeping bag for warmth, my belly bloated. After the others had gone to the meeting, I'd done my best to locate myself, walking around the area with my torch, but I couldn't get the fire going properly and had given up in the end, retreating to my tent. I'd also given up trying to read Simone de Beauvoir and was thinking instead about Mum and Dad at home watching *Name that Tune*. They never missed it; Dad could say 'Boom Bang-a-Bang' before the contestants had their fingers anywhere near the buzzer. I usually made a big fuss when it was on, complaining at the sound of all that easy-listening piping its way into our living room, but the truth was I would much rather have been looking at Tom O'Connor than lying by myself in a tent on the frozen ground.

I'd tried my best not to think about Tony, but without distraction I began picturing him with his arm around Lisa the Social Sciences student, teasing her about her faulty grasp of Marxist theory in some romantically lit bohemian bar. There weren't any bohemian bars in Stevenage but he'd be in London by now, Camberwell, that's where he was headed. Well, who cared. I was making a new life too. I dug around for my exercise book, intending to make a note of Helmut Kohl in case his name came up in conversation, but in order to get to a fresh page I had to leaf through the old ones. Resisting a glance at the earlier entries was like resisting the sight of a motorway pile-up:

> Since you said your goodbyes
> the tears mist my eyes
> I'm a broken flower without feelings
> to be thrown onto vegetable peelings.

It didn't even scan. I flicked over and began writing up my journey, stopping to consider the women I'd met. Barbel with the guitar was nice, and Rori was brilliant, I'd liked her immediately, but that Angela was unnerving. The way she'd folded the newspaper into a rectangle and tucked her elbows in as I sat beside her, as if we were passengers on a bus. While I'd been putting up the tent Rori had mentioned that Angela had lost patience with all the fair-weather visitors coming and going. Perhaps that was it. I realised it had been a mistake to arrive on my own. I should have asked Maggie – it wasn't her sort of thing but she might have done it for an adventure, stayed a couple of days at least. Too late now. Mum and Dad and Maggie and Tom O'Connor were miles away; the tent, the lumpy ground, the wind plucking creepily at the canvas, these were all to be endured. I lay back and shut my eyes. I had my clothes on plus an extra jumper, but it was still freezing. An owl hooted unnaturally loudly. Now and again there was a thin rumble of traffic from the main road. Eventually I fell asleep.

Voices woke me. Bright lights somewhere outside. I propped up on my elbows, aware of the blood pumping at my temples. Laughter. Two male voices, or three? I unzipped the door flap. Branches obscured the view, but the glare was coming from car headlights, the driver leaning out of the window and shouting, his mate standing nearby.

'Smelly cow, why don't you piss off home!'

'This is my home!' It was Barbel's voice.

'Gyppo!'

'She's a Kraut.'

'Dutch, you idiot. Go away!'

'What you gonna do, have me arrested? She's gonna have us arrested, Dave.' Two more women came to join Barbel. From the shadows, I recognised Rori.

'Alright darling, gis a blow job.'

'She don't like fellers, do you?'

Another woman stepped protectively in front of her.

'That your girlfriend?'

All at once there was a noise, the sort of warbling Red Indians made in old films. A handful of other women came out of their tents until they half surrounded the car making their shrill cry.

You couldn't hear what the men were saying, you could only see the women and hear their tongues flicking, the same single pitch in unison.

Car doors slammed, then came the guttural rev of an engine.

I closed my eyes again and lay on my heart as if smothering it might stop it from beating so quickly.

5

Fallout

I'm trying to draw up a leaflet for the Heston Fields campaign: what I'm trying not to do is think about the argument, specifically the phrase *Like a woman for once*. After Pete stormed out I didn't feel like cooking so Dom ordered pizza. Now he dances the remote across channels, settling on a news story from Spain, where an encampment of young people are massed in a public square, banners and candles flickering against a purple-blue sky. They are chanting. Forty-two per cent of young people are unemployed, says the reporter. This annoys Dom and he begins to recount an article he's read about global economics. I listen, fiddling again with a format button before eventually asking his advice. He leans towards the laptop, taps rapidly a few times and realigns the page in an instant.

'How did you do that?'

'I'm a digital native,' he says, raising a slice of pizza until strings of hot mozzarella break from the box. 'You're at a disadvantage because you're basically operating in a second language.' I think about that, and the Spanish protest, how he'll be able to access the details in seconds, unlike years ago when we had phone trees and chain letters rather than webcams and instant streaming.

Madrid and the purple sky disappear but Dom is still thoughtful. 'So what were you doing in your camp?'

'Protesting against cruise.' He nods but the word is alien. 'You know, nukes. Weapons of mass destruction.'

'Right.' He chews on a lump of pizza the size of a golf ball. 'Dad said it was only for women.'

'Men could visit.'

'Did you have portaloos or what?'

I stop typing and raise an eyebrow. 'Is that your best question?'

'When Ed went to Glastonbury he said they were rank, he said it was like open sewage and he nearly puked, he had to hold his t-shirt over his face.'

'Thanks for that charming dinner conversation.' Ed going to Glastonbury is something we've been hearing a lot about recently and it's more than likely Dom will start petitioning soon.

'So?'

'If you really want to know we had a trench.'

'A trench?' This delights him. 'Nasty.'

'We were living outside, remember.'

'Commando style.'

I laugh this time. He considers. 'If you'd have met Dad by then do you think you would have gone?'

'I hadn't met Dad then, had I?'

'Yeah, but say you had.'

'Maybe.' A tiny window opens up, a window where Pete and I hadn't met. Would I be with someone else, or alone? And if there were children, what would they be like? I glance at Dom, my beautiful boy with his crazy teenage hair and his black clothes, and wonder who he might be: how much of him is himself, and how much is us.

He removes an olive from his pizza slice and sends it my way. I open my mouth obligingly. 'Did they have kids there?'

'Some of the women took their children.'

57

'Would you have taken us?'

'I don't know. It was just me then. Not Dad. Not Pippa. Not you.'

He loses interest in a world which doesn't contain him. The adverts are on and his eyes follow a bare-shouldered model as she exits the shower.

'Dad said they didn't do that much in the end. He said it was the Russians and the Americans who had a summit, that's why they got rid of the missiles.'

'Really?' I flick my eyes from the laptop, irritated by the idea of Pete holding forth, keen to make teacherly corrections, keen to ensure his son doesn't go running away with the wrong ideas. 'Why are you asking me about this if you've already talked to Dad?'

'Get your side.'

'Well Dad obviously thinks he's the one with the answers.'

There's a reflective silence before Dom announces that if those Spanish protests come to England he's going to join in. Definitely. He uses the word disenfranchised, which he's recently become fond of.

'I think it's good you went to your camp, Mum.'

'Thanks, love.' I pull him in for a quick cuddle, which he allows, because no one is here to witness it.

He picks off another olive. 'Did you ever get arrested?'

The ads are finished. I try a deflective move. 'You can watch a DVD if you've done your homework. Whatever you like, while Dad's out.' Since he's become a Goth, Dom's very into narratives which feature tortured heroes in floor-length black coats. Pete is losing patience, especially since he caught Dom in the bathroom experimenting with an eyeliner. That's another thing we've argued about: me wanting to let Dom be himself, or whatever new version of himself he's perfecting, Pete wanting him to be the boy he used to be, the one who was in football squad and spent every weekend outdoors.

Dom repeats his question about being arrested.

'I really need to finish this tonight, love.'

He sighs deeply, but gets up to fetch one of his films and I'm off the hook.

When Dom's in his bedroom I run a bath, easing gently into the heat. *Like a woman for once.* I swish at a cluster of bubbles as if to dispel the words, then lean back, wondering how it came to this. What happened to the booth, me on his lap, him puckering up for the comedy kiss? That photo would have been taken soon after we met, by accident, a real accident that had us sitting side by side in a hospital corridor.

I'd not long finished university in Leeds, and my friend Sabine had got tickets for a band. The gig was packed but we'd struggled to the front. Luckily there'd been a tall lad standing beside us and I used him as a marker when I went to the bar because Sabine was tiny, even in her high-heeled boots. The support band came on, and everyone was dropping their empties, so by the time the headliners appeared we were jumping on a sea of cracking plastic. All at once Sabine rocked over and crumpled in a heap. She was yelping, and I was trying to move with her through the wall of bodies when the tall lad appeared, picked Sabine up in a cradle hold and carried her out.

He found us somewhere to sit, and a girl in a leather jacket arrived and said she was a student nurse. She handed me her bottle of lager, put Sabine's child-sized foot in her lap and felt around while Sabine gasped and swore at her in French. The student nurse thought something might be broken, she said we'd have to get her to A&E. Before I could work out how to find a taxi, the tall lad offered us a lift. He had a kind face and long, floppy hair and he said his name was Pete. I thanked him but refused, I said he'd miss the band. He said it would only take twenty minutes, and anyway, he'd seen them before. Neither of those things turned out to be true.

We sat in A & E for three hours. Pete stretched out his long legs, one foot crossed over the other, and for some reason I noticed the left trainer had an eyelet missing, so the lace went straight through the hole. I don't know why I found that touching. We talked, nearly forgetting poor Sabine beside us, drowsing through her painkillers. He told me about teacher training college and said he'd always wanted to teach history. I told him about the politics degree I'd just finished, and my job at the women's shelter where I spent my mornings answering phones and the rest of the day in the kitchen. We looked at the people coming in and made up lives for them. I didn't tell him about the post-graduate student I'd been wanting to break up with, how I'd been secretly bored to death sitting in his bedsit having long discussions about the penal laws. Me and Pete made each other laugh. When he dropped me home in his dented Cortina he said, 'We should do this again.' I said I'd ask around, see if anyone else had something to break. And then we'd leaned forwards to kiss lightly on the lips, as if we'd been doing it all our lives.

Tess'n'Pete, Pete'n'Tess, tipping up at parties and festivals, a battered tent rolled in the back of his car, another event always over the hill. Eighteen months and we were married.

My trance is broken by a clank from downstairs. The bath water's gone lukewarm so I climb out, rub coconut moisturiser into my skin, put on a clean pair of pyjamas and get into bed. The curtains aren't completely closed, and a crease of light from the street lamp partially outlines the shapes in the room; Pete's guitar which he doesn't play much anymore, our shoes knocking around together in a heap by the chest of drawers.

Another clank. Then cursing. He's stumbled over something else, probably the cat's bowl or perhaps the mop and bucket the film crew kept moving while they were working out their shots. When I hear him on the stairs I roll onto my side and pretend to be asleep. He creaks down the landing, the bathroom taps run and the loo flushes, then he's in the room, the sound of unzipping, another thump. This time he giggles to himself and despite everything, I smile in the darkness. He must have tripped over his trouser leg.

'Tess.'

He smells beery. The alcohol has loosened whatever lock it is that keeps us distant in bed these days because he slides a hand over and lays it on my thigh. Once, after an argument, he would have laid his head on my breast. He would have looked up and made the puppy face, a trick he established back in our early days, back then it was endearing, a silly shorthand for sorry. All couples must have these signs and signals; there must be a couple in the Borneo Rainforest who know how to get around each other by tickling a particular part of the other's ear. But we have lost our recourse to that old matrimonial glue.

'Sorry,' he says.

'I don't want to talk about it now.'

He falls quiet. We lie still, thinking our own thoughts, not asking each other what they are. *Like a woman for once.* I rearrange myself so his hand is no longer on my thigh.

'I'm trying to apologise,' he says, directing his voice at the ceiling. 'I don't know what your problem is. You've been fussed over for two days and had a load of free clobber. They made you look gorgeous.'

The word *made* fills the darkness.

'Tessa?'

'But I didn't want any of it. How would you like it if I got a gang of people to mess you about?'

'I wouldn't mind, if they did a good job.'

'Yes you would. And what's the point of it anyway?'

'It was for you.'

'None of it was for me; it was for other people, if anything it was for you.'

'Oh don't get all *Woman's Hour* on me for God's sake.'

'I'm not getting all anything.'

'Yes you are, you're doing your Greenham Common bit.'

I flick the bedside light on and sit up. 'What do you mean, Greenham Common bit?' I blink against the lamp. 'You pretend to have your liberal middle-class values but you clearly thought

Greenham was full of woolly-minded women. You said as much to Dom.'

'Ohhh.' He lays a wrist against his forehead as if he's suffering a fever. 'No, I respect it, I do, but they got rid of the weapons after the INF treaty, that's fact.'

'Which made it what, a footnote to history? A twenty-year protest?'

'I'm not saying it wasn't well-intentioned…'

He's got his historian's hat on. It's infuriating when he tries to parcel up history as if he's qualified to make an absolute judgement, and I say the peace camp went worldwide, but he's not really listening. 'Oh look, you weren't there.'

He turns his head sideways on the pillow. 'Tell me about it then.'

'I'm trying to…'

'No, tell me what it was like for *you*. You never talk about it.'

Half a dozen images come at once: Rori's silver peace-symbol earrings catching the firelight; our boots plugging and unplugging the mud; the green-streaked inside of the roll-top bath; Di sitting with a placard beside the road; Rori turning away into a winter night as I call after her. I say something inconsequential about being young, only staying for a few weeks. He gives up.

'Well I'll never know what it was like, will I? Not that I could have been there.'

'The men got too aggressive, they wanted to take over.'

He looks at me, 'So you're telling me that none of those women acted like banshees. I remember the footage too.' He blinks at the ceiling. 'Why are we talking about this? God, if I knew it was going to end in a row I never would have…' He stops.

'What?'

'Nothing.' He shifts in the bed.

'You said I. *I* never would have…'

'Let's not have an argument.'

Suddenly it makes sense. 'You and Maggie were in this together, weren't you?'

He sits up properly, concerned. 'Look Tessa, she phoned me, ok? She phoned a few weeks ago, told me she thought it would be fun, and it was going to be a treat, and did I think it was a good idea. And I said yes. So she wrote the letter.'

'My own husband.'

'I don't see the problem.'

'No? Then why did you blame it all on Maggie?'

'I did it for you, Tessa.' He thuds the duvet for emphasis.

'No. You did it for yourself.'

I throw off my side of the duvet, cross the landing to Pippa's room and get into her bed. Behind my eyelids purple lava is bubbling. I try some diaphragmatic breathing, pushing my belly out on the in breath, but it doesn't help and in a couple of minutes I open my eyes again. How are we supposed to sort out our relationship if he's busy trying to turn me into someone else? Communication, in the corny language of therapy, that's the word Valeria always repeats. We are supposed to talk honestly. But what's honest about this?

All around are signs of my disappeared daughter: a framed swimming certificate, her rows of spine-cracked A-level text books bleached by the sun, an empty bottle of perfume on the dresser. I pick up a discarded magazine and leaf through. Pages and pages of fashion; an actress under thirty who already looks airbrushed to within an inch of her life. More fashion. A double-page spread featuring the best and worst products for busting cellulite, complete with close-up photos of dimply thighs and bottoms: *pinch a handful of skin and squeeze, do you see an 'orange peel' effect?*

I close the magazine, reminded of the afternoon I caught Pippa, hardly into puberty, with a measuring tape wrapped around the widest part of her thigh. The diets started when she was fifteen and I tried to talk her out of them, but they kept coming, one after the other, grim as prison wardens, each with a new set of restrictions, each making her pallid and irritable and tired. During her A-levels I left a copy of *Fat is a Feminist Issue* in her bedroom and found it again with a warning note: 'Please don't interfere.'

I turn onto my side, thinking about Pippa and playing back the argument with Pete. How long has he wanted me transformed? Was it simply a reaction to Maggie's idea? Another voice takes over in my head, a practical no-nonsense voice, reminiscent of Jean's from camp. *Come on old thing, stop feeling sorry for yourself.* This voice usually straightens me out when things go awry, but tonight I don't have the energy to listen. My mind lurches from Pete to Pippa, then floods with faces from the past until I fall at last into an uneasy dream.

6

Woman in a Bath

I woke up with pains in my legs and buttocks. The hood of my sleeping bag felt damp and my eyes stung from lack of sleep. After the men had vanished I'd stayed awake, enacting their return in my imagination, convinced of footsteps with every creaking branch.

The walls of the tent had sagged overnight and fluttered in the chill breeze as I lay still, trying to take charge of my thoughts, both of them: what am I doing here? And, what do I do now? In the end I roused myself with a verse of 'I want to be Free,' by Toyah. *Don't want to be nobody's fool*, I sang as I climbed out of my sleeping bag fully clothed, *Don't want someone living my life for me*, I sang, easing off my socks and putting thicker ones on, inspecting the O of my new blister in the process, *I want to be free* I sang, digging out the trainers from my rucksack. *I'm going to turn this world inside out, I'm going to…* I unzipped the tent and surveyed my new home. In the light of the October morning, things looked even worse than they had last night: it was as if someone had taken a skip and spread its contents thinly over an expanse of mud.

Between the tents and the igloo-shaped shelters dotted around the clearing, I could see a one-wheeled bike balanced upside down on its saddle, a washing-up bowl blown loose from its mooring, and a broken straw bale moulting in yellow shreds across the grass. A banner reading WOMEN AGAINST was strung droopily between trees. Obscured by branches, the missing word could have been anything – convention, war, washing-up.

I'd been camping with my parents once in Tenby, but our experience of the great outdoors had been tempered by the sight of other families happily adapting the norms of domesticity; mums pegging out washing, dads cooking sausages on Calor gas fires. Here there was no shower block, and there were no children playing Swingball either, although a half-deflated beach ball sat wrinkled in the mud not far away, like a strange fallen fruit. The overnight rain had calmed but the wind was still loaded with mizzle.

I'd filled an empty squash bottle with water for the train journey and now used some of it to brush my teeth, spitting a pool of foam into the mulchy leaves beside the tent. I knew there was a food storage arrangement beside the Welsh dresser, but since I'd brought a few supplies with me, it seemed easier to scoff down a bruised banana and a packet of salt and vinegar crisps. As to the problem of emptying my bladder, well, there weren't going to be any flushing toilets around, that was for certain, so using my Toyah force-field I navigated a path through the bracken and found a tree private enough behind which to squat, awkwardly, leaning backwards on my hands. I'd not quite finished when I glimpsed a woman wheeling a barrow in my direction. After a scramble to pull up my jeans, I recognised her as the woman I'd sat next to the night before, the one with the serious spectacles. Angela. I raised my hand in a weird half salute, still clutching my belt. She gave the slightest nod and carried on wheeling. I watched her small upright figure disappear towards the road, conscious of a damp spot on my inner thigh.

A low cloud scudded overhead, its belly swollen with rain. What did they do when it rained? In fact, what did they do, full stop? How did demonstrating against nuclear weapons work on a day-to-day-actually-filling-in-the-hours basis? Should I go and sit at the fire where two women were toasting bread on sticks and drinking tea? That would be a start. And yet it was all quite intimidating. Behind my tent the silver birch thickened into woods. Perhaps I should explore my new environment, get a feel for the terrain.

The trees smelled rich and damp as I walked. A chain of rusting chime bells hung from a low branch, tinkling when I rippled my index finger through them, and in the canopy a bird clapped its wings. As I moved further in, the loamy darkness became welcoming and quiet. Quiet-ish. I stopped still, listening to a faint, what was it – yes, a gnawing sound. There it was again. Could it be a squirrel? I crept towards the noise, eager for my chance to engage with nature, to appreciate the fact that I was out of that office, out of Stevenage and free. I edged closer, careful not to disturb whatever tiny animal might be at work, and as I peered from behind a tree the source revealed itself: there, with her back to me, someone was sitting in an empty bath, reading a book and crunching steadily on a carrot. A branch cracked under my foot and the figure turned.

'Hello there.' It was Rori, hatless, her curls bobbing free. 'Survived your first night?'

'More or less.' It felt odd to disturb someone in the bath, even if they were fully clothed.

'I imagine the welcome committee woke you?'

'What happened?'

'Drunks from Newbury who've nothing better to do. They wanted to piss in Barbel's tent.'

'Piss in it?'

'They're usually content to hurl abuse or rubbish, but occasionally they'll become more adventurous, try to impress each other by overturning our tents or stealing our belongings.'

'Sounds horrible.'

Rori shrugged and took another bite of her carrot. The bath had an old-fashioned roll top, with two exposed pipes where it had once been plumbed into a wall. Bricks propped it up at the back, but in the front its original claw feet survived.

'What are you reading?'

She flipped the cover as if to remind herself, '*An Introduction to Feminist Thought.* Something Angela lent me.'

'Any good?'

'Oh, it's all right. I've reached a chapter which discusses de Beauvoir's idea of immanence, you know the closed realm of the woman which keeps her passive and static, as opposed to the male state of transcendence. But Simone wouldn't think that if she were here, would she?' Rori leaned back and considered the twiggy sky. 'Then I started pondering that old existentialist idea that freedom is a burden and causes anxiety.' I nodded as if I knew this idea well and was regularly thinking about it. 'But we're compelled to be here, I mean at this camp, so the burden has lifted. Which is itself liberating.' She turned her head to me and raised a finely arched brow in a gesture which meant *What do you think?*

I nodded in a way I hoped looked ruminative.

'But the anguish always manifests somehow I expect,' she added, taking another chomp on the carrot. She was right. The idea of being urinated on while you slept was enough to anguish anyone.

'D'you have any books with you?' She'd obviously read de Beauvoir so I mentioned Germaine Greer.

'Oh,' she seemed disappointed, 'nothing else?'

'Well… not exactly…'

She leaned forwards, 'You're blushing!'

'I, um, borrowed it.' Shamed on my first day.

'What is it?'

'*The Wives of Sunset Strip*,' I said from my hot face.

'Ha! Thank God, something fun.' Rori sighed, laying the book down. 'Anyway, that's a classic feminist text.'

'Is it?'

'Of course, it's all about righting the status quo for subservient women in a male-dominated materialist culture.'

'Really?'

'Absolutely. And there's a good dollop of sex in it too,' she said, repositioning her leg. 'Who doesn't want to read about sex?' Her boot now rested on a tap freckled with rust. 'You and I are going to get on famously,' she declared. I felt my heart lift.

'So, do you actually have baths in there?' I asked, shifting my weight onto my other leg because there was nowhere to sit apart from the edge of the bath.

'Used to in the summer, with some effort. We dragged it behind the trees for the sake of privacy, then we'd shallow fill it and there you are, bathing en plein air.' She trailed a hand over the side. I imagined a cloth-capped ladies' maid pouring jugs of water over her back. 'Now I use it to read. Always read best in the bath. See,' she said indicating the corner of a tartan blanket, 'takes the chill off.'

Car seats, Welsh dressers, baths.

She gave the carrot a last bite and considered me. 'You look a little lost.'

I shrugged and did my best stiff upper lip smile.

'Come on,' she said, tossing away the green stump and climbing out. 'I'll give you the tour.'

The drizzle had cleared leaving a white sky. I followed as we left the trees and headed back into the camp, which Rori said was about half an acre in size.

'We're lucky to have space – at some of the other gates the women are sandwiched between the fence and the road. I love the gorse, don't you?' she said, not waiting for an answer. 'I slept in a caravan at Main gate when I first visited, but then the owner wanted to move, so I came here. But a bender's perfectly cosy. Amazing how one adapts.'

My trainers made sucking noises as we crossed through the

worst mud. I'd have to return to my Doc Martens before long, blister or no blister.

By far the best-looking of the feeble tents and shelters was a cloth tepee.

'That's Jean's wigwam. She's been here almost from the start, her husband was here too before it went women only.'

It was the sort of structure befitting a chief elder. 'Is she in charge?'

Rori laughed. 'No one's in charge. It doesn't work like that. But,' she considered, 'I suppose Jeany is rather the matriarch. She used to be a headmistress at an eminent girls' school.'

I reminded myself to smile if we passed anyone, the way I had on my first day at work, but apart from the two women at the fire drinking tea, there was no one around. Not until we encountered the humped figure of a woman stooping over a black bin liner.

'Morning Di. This is Tessa.'

The woman retrieved a crisp packet from the ground and deposited it in her sack like a peaceable Womble. It was the woman I'd met at the roadside, the one with the placard. Now aware that conversation wasn't her thing, I returned her smile without trying to engage her in chit-chat.

'Di's a Diamond,' declared Rori as we continued the tour. 'But she doesn't say an awful lot.'

While we walked, she explained that the fence around the base stretched for nine miles and women were camped at the different access gates.

'How many women are here?'

'At Amber? About eight campers at the moment, but we get a few visitors.'

Eight? Was that all? Rori registered my confusion. 'There are more at Main gate and the other women distribute themselves according to their leanings. Numbers are up in the summer. Are you a lesbian?'

'What?'

My reaction obviously amused her. 'Don't look so shocked,' she said, pushing a curl out of her eye. 'Women gravitate to whichever gate they're most comfortable, whether they're musicians, or Christians or they want to live with women of the same sexuality. Every gate has a different personality.'

'What's this one?'

'We're non-partisan,' she said firmly. 'All welcome.'

I felt lucky to have stumbled here first. We'd reached the edge of the clearing and were at the road. The fence ran as far as we could see, with a soldier standing at a gate in the wire.

'Is he an American?'

'British. You don't see much of the Yanks. Wait,' she pointed, as if spotting a rare bird, 'there's one. I've seen him before actually.' A tracksuited figure stopped at the gate. He looked tall even from our distance, and must have been at least six foot six. 'Day off, I suppose,' said Rori as he threw his arms into two wide circles, warming down after his run, before disappearing inside the base. She checked her watch, 'Time for Elevenses.'

I followed her back to the central muddle of the camp, to what she called the kitchen – two trestle tables sheltered by bamboo rods coved with a tarpaulin, which also protected the Welsh dresser, and a tall fridge, lacy with rust. The tables were stacked with tins.

'Bread's in here,' she said, lifting the lid from a large bale which housed a plastic bag and within that, another containing sliced loaves. 'In here for spreads,' she added, opening an oversized biscuit barrel. Tacked to the tarpaulin and decorated with browning ferns, a sign read, 'Please don't take more than you need,' and a smiling cartoon face indicated a non-dictatorial spirit. The jam was home-made, not the sort you found in the supermarket, but gooseberry, damson, greengage. 'We're lucky with donations,' said Rori. Another collection of plastic bins was marked with makeshift labels: pulses, muesli, veg, tins (various), herbs. Another container full of silver cans said simply 'Lucky Dip'.

'Labels came off,' explained Rori. 'Tea and coffee over there. Water's in that jug. The mains supply is down the road. There's only one standpipe,' she said, scraping a curl of cold margarine for her bread. 'We have to keep those containers full. No rota, just go if you see they're running low. Sometimes Jean takes the van, but it's close enough to walk.'

'Right.' I could carry water at least.

Not sure what I was looking for, I opened the fridge idly and took an immediate step back. Its insides were stuffed with paper bundles, tied with the same pink ribbon we used at Hirshman & Luck, or banded together and stacked in rocky piles which threatened to spill free at the slightest provocation. A manual typewriter sat on the bottom shelf.

'That's the office,' said Rori, 'for campaign letters and leaflets. We've a separate box with letters from the council, fines, that kind of thing. Jean looks after it.'

I nodded and shut the door carefully.

'How do they get here, the letters?' There were no front doors.

'Mail is passed on from Main gate.'

'What are you girls up to?' An older woman in a pair of army boots dropped a clutch of shopping bags onto the duckboard floor.

'Your ears must be burning,' said Rori.

'Not taking my name in vain are you?' The woman had a silver bob, and underneath her jumper the collars of her candy-striped blouse were sticking up Lady Diana-style.

'Quite the opposite. Tessa, this is Jean,' said Rori, licking jam from her knife.

'How d'you do?' She spoke with the voice of a newsreader. I remembered what Rori had said and imagined Jean in her previous life, on a stage before an assembly of girls, handing out lacrosse awards and leading the school in Jerusalem.

'I was just showing Tessa the office.'

'Administration, it's a necessary evil I'm afraid,' said Jean as she unpacked. 'I tell you, it was bedlam in Newbury. The number of people trying to get their trolleys around Sainsbury's. Madness. That's the last time I'm doing a shop on a Saturday morning.'

'Didn't anyone help?'

'Sam came along for the ride,' said Jean. 'Oh, by the way,' she turned to Rori, 'we've been given a heap of stamps and envelopes, so we'll make a push on those leaflets. Send them in bundles for the networks to distribute.'

'Good stuff,' said Rori, taking a bite of bread. I'd spread my own slice with gooseberry jam, wiping the knife on my jeans first.

Sam appeared through the tarpaulin with more shopping, her Mohican wilted by the weather.

'All right, girls,' she said, dumping the bags.

'How's tricks?' said Rori, poking about to see what she'd got.

'Same shit, different day,' replied Sam. 'I was telling Jean, it's time she did another blackberry crumble.'

Rori explained that Jean had devised a way of making an earth oven by digging a hole under the fire pit.

'Don't suppose you managed to find any lemon curd?'

Jean apologised, saying she'd completely forgotten, and Rori said not to worry, it was a filthy habit anyway and she'd been trying to kick it. We discussed preserves for a couple of minutes before Jean raised the subject of a blockade meeting.

'We need everyone for this one,' she said removing a small jar from her pocket. 'Fish paste. Don't tell the others,' she whispered, 'nothing's sacred in this place. Want a little taste?'

'Oh yes,' said Rori, looking genuinely excited.

'How about you, Tessa?' she asked, offering the tip of a knife for me to dip into the paste.

'Yes please.' I'd just swallowed a mouthful of gooseberry jam, but it seemed rude to refuse, even though I wasn't a fan, Dad spread fish paste in his sandwiches for work. Jean held the jar back for a moment.

'Fish paste is for women who earn it. Will you be coming to the meeting?'

'Definitely.'

'That's the spirit.'

I dipped the knife into the jar. Crab. Not too bad, actually.

7

Miniature Scotch Eggs

It's the evening of the broadcast and Pippa has arrived from Kent. Reclined in our ancient corduroy beanbag, wine glass on the floor beside her, she's telling me about someone she knows at university whose mother is friends with Jude.

'Apparently she used to have a terrible drink problem,' says Pippa, twining a ribbon of hair around her index finger.

'Did she?'

'And she believes in open relationships.'

'Is that so?'

She assesses me as if I might know something I'm not willing to divulge. 'What's she like? What's she *really* like?' So I tell her again about Jude, making the details as colourful as possible, recounting a few choice moments from our conversations with my best version of her voice, 'Do the model pose, darling. One hip out, that's it Scrumptious.'

'She called you Scrumptious?' Pippa whoops with laughter. I've forgotten how much I love that sound, the delighted gurgle which hasn't much changed since childhood. It's a treat to see her, even if it is because of this make-over show.

'I thought we could go on a walk tomorrow, see the bluebells in Fosset wood.'

'That sounds nice,' she says. 'What's her skin like up close?'

'Skin? I don't know, it's skin. Not as many wrinkles as some women her age I expect.' It'll be easier to catch up properly when it's just the two of us, when all the TV palaver is finished.

'Do you think she has Botox?'

'You know Botox is a poison, it comes from botulinum…'

'Yeah, I know, I know,' says Pippa in a *never mind that* voice. 'Did she have lines when she frowned?'

I try to think. 'Well, now you mention it, she did have a certain waxy quality.'

'Knew it,' she says, as if she's discovered vital evidence.

Pete enters with a tray of miniature scotch eggs, a plastic tray of salmon vol-au-vents from M&S and an assortment of crisps. 'Excited?' I glance at him without comment. 'You should be, a whole programme devoted to you.' He settles beside me and drapes an arm around my shoulders, which ordinarily would be nice, but tonight feels deliberate, a public gesture to prove everything's all right. Things have been less than all right since the filming, but he's obviously hoping to be vindicated as the world sees me turning into Rita Hayworth before their very eyes and my life is subsequently transformed with offers of personal appearances and invitations to open local branches of Asda.

Dom is in the armchair paging through the TV guide. He's wearing a new pair of chunky Goth boots with crepe soles and silver toe caps which he brought home proudly from Camden Market, much to Pete's horror and Pippa's hilarity. He leans over and palms some snacks.

'Not having any?' asks Pete, waving a bowl of Wotsits at Pippa, who shakes her head. 'You're getting too skinny.'

'Do you think I'm skinny?' she says, bright-eyed.

She's definitely thinner – I noticed it the minute she walked in the door but I've learned not to mention her weight.

The credits to the previous programme roll and Pete slides

up the volume '…This week Make me Over visits a woman from Cambridgeshire who's sartorially stranded at Greenham Common.' Pippa squeals. Dom lays down the TV guide. I take a huge gulp of my Sauvignon Blanc and the saxophone-heavy theme tune kicks in as Jude narrates: 'Forty-eight-year-old Tessa Perry left her fashion sense in a field at Greenham Common and, according to her best friend Maggie, she hasn't worn a dress since The Iron Lady was in power…'

'That's not true!' I exclaim as Maggie's face appears smiling on screen.

'Shhh!' says Pippa.

'But while the country rid itself of cruise missiles, Tessa never quite managed to rid herself of those Cold War fashion trends.' Cue an old photo of me in knitwear. '…so it's our job to stand up for a woman's right to look sexy. We're saying *No* to the drab (image of me in a checked shirt getting off my bike), '*No* to the shapeless' (me, unglamorous while putting out the rubbish), 'And *Yes* to a little Jude magic. Tessa Perry, it's time to MAKE YOU OVER!'

'There you are!' declares Pete.

And there indeed I am, smiling widely as the voiceover mentions our campaign. It's not a flattering shot, my hair is blowing around my face and my arms are outstretched as I stand before the five acres of grassland which is Heston Fields.

'Oh, Mum,' says Pippa, half sympathy, half dismay, 'why are you wearing *those*?' She means my orange trousers: linen, handy multi-pockets, drawstring waist.

'It's not about my trousers.'

But I can see from the shot that it very definitely *is* about my trousers.

The footage in the field is spliced together with a few images of me at work, one in which I'm giving a presentation to a local business about the economic benefits of sustainable practice, while apparently wearing an unsuitable jacket. In succession, these clips give a quick sketch of what Jude refers to as my lifestyle. Then it's on to the make-over. There's a view of me and Bobby the make-up artist at the kitchen table. He takes my hand as if he's going to hold it, but instead the camera examines my stubby nails. 'No more builders' fingers for you,' he says. I look tense. He recommends using formaldehyde-free nail polish, which is more environmentally friendly. Next he's mixing a face-pack made from honey, yoghurt and avocado: another close up and there I am in all my glory, a swamp creature, nodding with feigned interest as he tells me the avocado is rich in natural proteins and vitamin B6. Pippa and Dom roar. I can barely bring myself to look.

The programme is rushing by in a frenzy of skin pimpling vignettes, the camera swinging from one cringe-inducing sequence to the next. We've reached the scene in the bedroom where Jude has bullied me into stripping down to my underwear.

'And where exactly did these,' she hesitates before saying it, '*pants*, come from?' The knickers are not my best pair, but I hadn't thought they were anything to be ashamed of. They are averagely cut, plain and white.

The pink-faced woman on screen says, 'They're comfortable.'

'Ah, yes,' Jude flits a hand in the air, 'the C word again. Let me tell you something, Tessa, a bed is for comfort. An armchair is for comfort. But when it comes to underwear,' she twangs the back of my knickers, apparently lost for words. '*Lingerie*. It's French. It's about *sex*, darling. These...' another twang, '...are *not* sexy.'

Pippa groans. 'The shame,' she says, at the sight of her mother scrambling to cover herself. My face is now burning. Sheila next door will be watching this. My mum and her friends will be watching. The mothers from Dom's school will be watching.

It gets worse.

What I obviously wasn't party to were the 'behind the scenes' chats. There's a point when the camera flashes to Pete's face and sees him depressed by the contents of my wardrobe. There are chummy little shots of Jude and Bobby having a good laugh or throwing their hands up in despair. There's a snapshot interview of Maggie, prior to filming I imagine, saying I need to devote some time to myself because I'm always spending so much of it working on what she calls my causes. In the back garden, while I'm presumably inside being forced to try on yet another outfit, Pete leans against the garden wall and says with an air of wistfulness, 'It's not that I don't support what Tessa does but sometimes...' he makes a despairing face. A pain goes through my heart. Jude nods understandingly. I stiffen, but the next blow catches me off guard. 'You can see what I mean,' he says, and Jude sympathises.

Pete's arm is like lead on my shoulder. No one is eating the miniature scotch eggs.

'They've manipulated that,' says Pete. I draw away from him.

We move to the transformation scene. There is the obligatory before and after shot, 'from *that*' (oh dear) to *this* (wow), me going through my three looks: daytime, evening and what they refer to as 'full-on green glam', wobbling towards the camera in the dagger heels.

Of course, it is an illusion, I am still *that*, but now a more humiliated *that*.

We stare at the television all the way to the last painful credits, a shot of me and Pete gazing into each other's eyes, me wondering what is happening, he, presumably, thinking I want you to look like this always, fire of my loins, envy of other women, fantasy of other men.

The last word goes to Jude. 'Join us next week when we'll be meeting a pastry chef from Sunderland and transforming her from Eccles cake to French Fancy.' Then the saxophone theme tune again and it's all over.

Pete, whose arm is now resting on the top of the sofa rather than around my shoulders, uses his free hand to applaud against his thigh, while I reach for the control and flick the television off. We sit in the aftermath.

'What did you think, Pip?' asks Pete, with false brightness.

'Yeah, fun,' she says.

'How about Mum, didn't she look fantastic?'

Dom realises something is called for. 'Yeah. Well done.' He shifts his boots uncomfortably.

'To my glamorous wife,' says Pete, raising his glass. How can he pretend everything's all right after what he's said on national TV? The glass is still in mid-air. 'You looked fantastic.'

'But it wasn't me, was it? And it isn't me now. I'm still the before, not the after.' I get up to leave the room.

'Nice one Dad,' mutters Dom.

Pippa rustles in the beanbag. 'Come on Mum, Dad was only trying to help.'

Pete smiles at her, grateful.

'Pip, can't you see what a sham that programme was?'

'It was fun.' She readjusts herself, looking up at me. 'Things are different now,' she says. 'You don't have to dress like a man to be a feminist.'

'I don't dress like a man,' I say edging back into the room.

'Not you. But, you know, feminism is basically all over isn't it. Who wants to go around with armpit hair, banging on about equal rights.'

Armpit hair?

'And anyway, you can still be into all that and do it with lipstick on.'

'No one's saying you have to look a certain way to be anything.'

But she doesn't seem to be listening, she's going off on a tract of her own. 'Feminism is about allowing personal choice, isn't it? Individual expression. The point is, there's nothing wrong with wanting to look attractive…'

'Of course there isn't.'

'And just because you like to look good it doesn't follow that you're some sort of…' she casts around for the word but doesn't seem to find it, 'bimbo or something.'

'Who said anything about bimbos?' I lean on the door jamb. 'I've never been particularly bothered about fashion and make-up, have I? It's no criticism of women who are.'

'Yes. But all I'm saying is, women these days should be able to do what they want, because it's their choice.' Her brows have knit intensely together.

'Where's all this come from?'

Then Dom, who's been flipping back through the TV guide since the programme ended, chips in. 'It's because she's going in for Miss Student Body…'

Pippa shushes him.

'What?' I say to both of them.

Dom ignores Pippa and drops the magazine. 'I heard her telling Dad but she didn't want to say anything to you because she thought you'd freak.'

Now I glance at Pete who opens his mouth as if to say something and then changes his mind.

'What's Miss Student Body?'

Pippa's colour is up.

'It's a beauty contest,' says Dom.

She wriggles upright in the beanbag. 'Look, it's no big deal okay? We're post-feminism now. Post-post probably.'

'I don't believe this,' I say, unable to look at Pete.

'It's a bit of a laugh,' she says.

'At your expense.'

'No. Not at my expense.'

'She volunteered for it,' says Dom.

'It's nothing to do with you,' she snaps.

'Pippa,' says Pete reprovingly from the sofa. But I'm blocking him out. Presumably this is something else he wasn't going to share with me. I try very hard to keep calm. After some level-toned questioning, Pippa explains that Miss Student Body is a beauty competition for female students in the Eastern and Southern regions and she was invited to enter by a guy who approached her in a nightclub. As far as I can tell, the thing is organised by an outside events company and has nothing to do with the university.

'Pippa, this stuff is so out of date. I thought your generation had got beyond beauty contests.'

She runs a hand through her hair, the way her father does when he's wound up. 'No one's being exploited. We're doing it out of personal choice.'

Dom crosses one boot over the other. 'Sounds sad.'

'The prize is two thousand pounds,' she says, ignoring him. 'And they make a one thousand pound donation to a charity.'

'Oh well, that's all right then,' I say, 'if they dress it up like that.'

'See, I told you she'd be like this,' Pippa says to her dad.

'You could nominate Easy Green,' says Pete, which I imagine is his way of lightening the atmosphere.

'So you think this is all right? Having your daughter parading around in her knickers.'

'I won't be wearing knickers,' says Pippa, aghast. Dom laughs loudly. She tells him to shut up. I remind her that no one in this house tells another person to shut up. She says oh yes, that's right, sorry she was forgetting and asks me again why it was they were never allowed to play Monopoly. I close down that particular discussion before we go completely off topic.

'Pip, there are people fighting for university places. Students are out on the streets trying to protect their right to an education. Why do you want to waste your time with this nonsense? Just think about it, that's all I ask...'

'There's nothing to think about. It's no big deal.'

'If it's what she wants,' says Pete, 'I don't see the harm. We all do silly things when we're young.'

'It's not silly. Oh.' She rises from the beanbag, but with difficulty because beanbags aren't designed for decisive action. 'For some reason I thought someone might be, God, I don't know, pleased for me or something.'

'I can't say I'm hugely excited about my daughter parading around in her pants, no.'

'Well everyone's just seen yours,' she says, straightening up.

'That was different.'

'How?'

'I wasn't doing it for me…'

'Well I'm not either. I'm doing it for charity.' I give her a sceptical look and her brown eyes become fierce. 'You know how expensive fees are, you were the one who wanted me to go on the marches, remember?'

'This isn't the answer is it!' I knew she wasn't joining the women's society but I didn't expect this. 'If you're going to use that argument you might as well take up pole dancing, that probably pays a few quid.' She picks up her glass and heads towards the door. I try to calm my voice. 'Pip, you may think this is all a bit of fun, but there'll be people making money out of it. Making money out of *you*. You're a beautiful girl, of course you are, but you don't have to prance up and down to prove it. You don't have to feed the machine.'

'*What machine?* There is no machine!' she says flinging an arm up so the silver bangles on her wrist jangle and her wine sloshes. 'I'm sorry you haven't got a daughter who wants to sit in a field all day eating mungbeans and going on about global warming… I'm sorry I'm not kicking about in charity shop clothes getting neurotic about other people's heating bills or whatever it is you do…'

'Pippa!'

'…but that's not me, okay. And it never will be. I'm not like you.'

She makes her exit.

Dom shakes his head. 'She's mad.'

I have the urge to run upstairs, to suggest that walk in Fosset wood so we can talk things over and make our peace. But even as I'm thinking this I also want to shake her by the shoulders because for the life of me I can't understand her. A beauty pageant? And what was that about mungbeans? It's her first year at university, she's young, she wants to fit in, but even so, a

83

beauty pageant? Is her need to be accepted really that strong? I remember nineteen – the muddle of it – and I remember what it was like wanting to belong, only the gang I wanted to belong to had a very different agenda.

8

Singing Lessons

By three o'clock, at least twenty-five of us were gathered around the fire waiting for the meeting to start. Our numbers had been temporarily bolstered by members from Ruby gate, our nearest neighbours, who were camped half a mile away. Rori and I sat side by side on milk crates while Barbel, wearing a poncho made from a blanket, walked around the ragged circle handing out *Common Good*, the newsletter. Everyone accepted it keenly, even the couple with their arms slung around each other who seemed too deep in conversation to notice. I shared my copy with Rori and together we turned through the photocopied patchwork of handwritten articles, cartoons and announcements, pausing at the centre pages where a letter from a woman in prison had been reprinted. *Dear Womyn, missing you all like mad*, it began. 'She's incredibly up-beat,' remarked Rori, 'considering.' It was impossible to imagine being that woman writing letters from a prison cell.

My first day had passed enjoyably in Rori's company. After helping Jean unpack the shopping, we'd peeled potatoes together – well, me and Jean had done most of the peeling while Rori told stories about the month she'd spent hitchhiking in

Andalucia. Since cooking in the dark was hopeless, the women usually prepared the vegetables by daylight and left them in pots of water ready for the evening meal.

My eye fell on another patch from the newsletter – *Defending yourself in court?* it asked. *Confused by the rules? Come and join in skills-sharing workshop with other ♀ at Main Gate.* It was interesting to see what they did with that gender symbol. I was in the middle of an article about Gore-Tex, a wonder fabric which could both repel rain and let moisture escape, wondering if I could fit my fat sleeping bag inside a Gore-Tex sack, as suggested, when Jean raised her voice above the general chatter.

'Shall we begin?' The women hushed and Jean regarded the gathering over her half-moon specs. 'Wonderful to see so many here.'

It might have been the opening of a WI meeting, but despite the fact that many of the women were indeed drinking tea, there were no twin-sets or pearls on display. Instead the general look was one of utilitarianism – waterproofs, hiking socks, thick-soled boots, army surplus ensembles and the occasional flash of rainbow wool.

'Would any new women like to introduce themselves?' said Jean, casting around. Rori gave me a playful nudge and Angela, sitting cross-legged on a roll of carpet, glanced over. I got up in a half-stand to give my name. A few heads nodded in my direction.

'First of all,' said Jean, 'housekeeping. We do need to keep on top of the chores I'm afraid because it seems we're facing pressure from LAWE.' Jeers all around.

'Newbury residents' group,' explained Rori. 'Locals Against Women's Encampment'

'Or League of Absolute Wankers,' Sam added, pulling on her bootlaces.

Jean continued. 'I realise we're all grown-ups, but we do need to be diligent about litter collection and attending to the shit pit.' It was odd to hear the phrase on her lips. I thought fretfully of the peeing incident and Angela wheeling past with her barrow.

'In addition, let's be mindful about gifts. I know we've had this discussion before, but this collective must be about sharing rather than collecting.' I looked again to Rori.

'One of the women was stockpiling stuff we'd been given,' she said. 'Thermal socks, new sleeping bags. There was a scene.'

Jean ran through a few other points concerning camp life before getting on to what she called 'the meat of the meeting': the upcoming blockade. Conversations began about which groups could be approached for support, and someone suggested the Reading University Women's Society, when Sam, still tugging her bootlaces, spoke up.

'Blockading only gets us so far. The gravel trucks make it inside. They're late, but they get in. We need to up the ante. Everyone's used to seeing women sitting in the road, singing. Nothing's changed,' she said. 'We need to make a statement.'

'How?' came another voice.

'I've got an idea,' said a woman in a red hat. She looked around the group meaningfully. 'We should dress up as pigs.'

'Satire?' asked a young woman behind me. 'Like in *Animal Farm*?'

'No, PIGS. Police.'

A whoop of laughter. 'Brilliant!'

More voices broke in. 'Where are we supposed to get the uniforms?'

'We can't wear uniforms, we'll be as bad as they are.'

'But it's subversion.'

Everyone was talking together. Rori balanced a cigarette paper on her palm and with pinched fingers began sowing a seam of loose tobacco along its centre, taking care to protect the paper from the wind.

'What are the trucks for?' I asked.

'Building work on the silos. We blockade to stop them getting through.' Manipulating the tobacco into a neat roll, she skimmed her tongue over the paper's gummed edge, sealed the tube and then, tearing a small square from her Rizla packet, rolled and inserted a filter. Finally, she dipped a twig into the fire, lit her cigarette and inhaled. It was an operation of fluid beauty. She offered me the tin.

'It's all right thanks,' I said, reaching for my new pouch of Golden Virginia. 'Got my own.'

As the debate about costumes intensified, I made my first shaky attempt at a cigarette while Sam's strong voice rose up.

'Listen, this camp has been established for over a year, right? We've got to push forward. Surprise is our best weapon.'

'We shouldn't use language from the male lexicon,' someone declared. A discussion started up about gender-neutral language, but Sam wasn't distracted for long. 'We've got to remember why we're here.'

'What about the diggers? This is common land, or at least it was,' came another voice.

'Are they sending in diggers?' I asked Rori. I still didn't know what a silo was.

'No, she means the Diggers, you know, like the Levellers.'

'Oh, right.'

I glanced back at Angela. She had such a pale, serious face. Under the hood of her parka, she reminded me of a daguerreotype I'd seen in a history O-level book, a little girl wearing a bonnet and looking out with an old woman's stare.

I'd overfilled my cigarette paper and couldn't get control of it, and had just decided to extract a fat lump of tobacco when a gust of wind got up and blew everything away, leaving me with an empty hand. I made a disbelieving face. Rori giggled. Angela's eye landed on me briefly.

The red-hatted woman was speaking again. 'But we could make authority look at itself. Think about it: pictures in the papers, photos of police dragging away other police.'

Sam cut in. 'Stunts are well and good but I came here to do something.' There was silence, only the fire and a bird disturbing the trees. And then she said, 'It's time we cut the fence.'

It was as if she'd suggested setting someone alight. A chorus started up immediately, but Sam wasn't swayed and only raised her voice louder, 'Look at the ANC. They could only use non-violence for so long.'

'We're not the ANC, their human rights are being violated.'

'So are ours. The first human right is to live, isn't it?'

'Cutting the fence is an act of violence,' said a middle-aged woman in a snood arranged so that only her face was visible, like a nun's from her wimple.

'They're planning to put ninety-six nuclear missiles in there in a year's time and we're worried about cutting holes in some wire meshing. This is mad.' Sam shook her head, confounded.

'We're non-violent witnesses,' said the snood lady.

Everyone was talking over each other. The only one looking settled was Di, who sat knitting, the firelight playing on her round face.

Sam raised her voice. 'This is a resistance camp, we're involved in a struggle.'

'Shouldn't Jean do something?' I said to Rori as the voices grew louder still.

'She's not the chairwoman, there's no hierarchy.'

'Cutting the fence is a criminal act,' repeated the lady in the snood.

'I'm not going back to Holloway,' said a small woman, her black eyes darting fretfully around. 'I can't go there again.'

'You don't have to, Petra,' said her neighbour, a big woman in an even bigger cardigan.

'You don't know what it's like,' Petra looked tearful. The woman wrapped an arm around her. I'd lit a new cigarette but it kept going out before I'd had a chance to inhale. Anyway I was taking in more smoke from the fire because somehow I'd managed to sit in the wrong place again. 'It's horrible,' said Petra before disappearing back into the woman's armpit, like a mouse into a woolly hole.

Angela raised her hand. 'Shall we return to Monday's action?' she said, in her call a spade a spade accent.

A sort of calm descended and for a moment there was only the crackling of the fire. Angela produced a pencil and notebook.

'We'll need to be in place by 7am. According to information they're expecting a mass delivery of building supplies, so our presence will be holding back its safe passage.' All eyes were on her. 'As ever, we can't predict police response, and whoever volunteers for blockading may also be risking arrest.'

'They make you wee on the floor if you can't hold it in,' came Petra's voice from the big woman's armpit. Angela ignored her.

'Can we have a show of hands from volunteers?'

My cigarette had gone out for a third time but I didn't bother trying to relight it: I wasn't attending to anything apart from the word 'arrest' clanking with a cold echo in my head.

Sam's hand was in the air. Beside me, Rori raised her arm. Angela began the count. She came to me and paused. This was my chance: this was when I had to stop thinking about Tony and our fantasy semi-detached, dog-walking life together and start acting for the future. Plus I wanted to prove to Rori I had backbone; that, above all else, was suddenly vital. I forced away the thought of prison and raised my hand. Angela counted me in.

Darkness had crept up behind our backs and the tea-making ritual was repeated. Some of the women from Ruby gate stayed for a cup while others trailed homewards towards their own bent teapots and muddy firesides.

'At least this one didn't end in a row,' said Rori, yawning and raising her arms to the sky. As Sam stoked the fire, a wild flame leapt up and we whooped.

'Hey, it's Saturday night,' said the girl behind me as if she'd just remembered, which she probably had. I'd almost forgotten myself.

'They'll be having their disco at the base,' said Sam.

'They have a disco in there?' I asked, unable to imagine it.

'Oh yeah. You see the taxis going in, girls from Newbury all tarted up,' said Sam, poking the fire. 'Fraternisers.'

'They're young, they don't know any better,' said Jean.

'They should. Pathetic isn't it, we're out here trying to save their stupid arses, and they're in there rolling over for the military.' Sam pulled her jumper over her knees for warmth. 'Never mind. We can have our own party. Let's have a song, girls.' She began in her loud voice and a few other women followed. The words had been fashioned to the tune of da-do-ron-ron:

> *Sitting in the White House with his Stetson on*
> *They call him Ron with the Neutron Bomb*

Barbel crossed the mud to fetch her guitar. Impromptu group singing would normally have made me want to leave a room, but there was no room to leave, and anyway, I was here to become a new person. We sang several verses and it wasn't too bad because the song was upbeat, not the slow sort where someone wanted to do a solo with their eyes shut. After a slug from the circulating whisky, Rori broke off from singing and whispered, 'You know, I haven't had any action for nearly three months, which is positively sobering.'

I took my turn on the bottle. It was like taking a sip from the fire, but it made me forget my freezing earlobes at least.

'You said you did a protest at the main gate last week.' I passed the whisky on, my throat stripped bare.

She threw her head back in delight. 'I mean the *other* sort of action,' she said under her breath.

'Oh, I see.' Whatever face I was pulling made her smile and clutch my arm.

'You're not shocked are you?'

'Course not.'

The women had reached the chorus of the song again, *The neutron bomb, Ron, the neutron bomb.*

'Did you have a boyfriend back in… where was it?'

'Stevenage.'

Tony, Tony, Tony. My heart lurched despite myself. I thought of how he'd squeeze me to his side as we walked. I thought of the night in The Volunteer when he'd told me he loved me. How I'd made him say it again the next day to be sure.

'We broke up.'

'Because you were coming here? That happens.' She played with one of the silver peace earrings. 'They're afraid their girlfriends are going to turn into raving feminists.'

'It was before I decided to come.'

'I see. Is that why you came, broken heart – join the Foreign Legion?'

'No, not exactly.'

'Sorry, that was crass. Forgive me?'

She had a way of concentrating her attention on you, making you feel as if you were the most important person in the world. I shrugged, befuddled. 'I thought I should, you know… I wanted to do something meaningful,' I said. 'There was nothing for me at home anyway. It was very…' I couldn't think of the word.

'Limiting?'

'Yes, that's it.'

'I know what you mean.'

How? People like her didn't come from new towns made of concrete, they entertained, they had debates about foreign policy, they knew the plots to operas.

The nearly full moon was encircled by a fuzzy white halo. The women had moved on to a satirical song about being funded by the KGB and burning toast.

Rori nodded. 'We *are* doing something meaningful.' I smiled at her. 'So what was he like, this boyfriend of yours?' I told her a little about Tony and then we talked about relationships, though it was only Rori who spoke in the plural.

'It's so nice to have a girls' chat,' she said confidentially. 'I miss that.'

I warmed at her remark and yet puzzled over it. Wasn't the entire camp full of girls? 'But you and Angela are good friends?' I said, digging for clues; I'd seen the two of them talking before the meeting began but couldn't tell how deep their friendship went.

'Oh, I love her to bits but she's not exactly one for gossip and frolic,' said Rori. That much I'd guessed. 'So, you're over Tony?'

'Yes, I was a bit cut up... but it's fine now.'

I thought back to the wretched state of not belonging to the world, Mum and Dad moving around me as if they were behind glass. Rori fixed her attention on the fire.

'Things were bad for me for a while in my second year at university. Too much Sylvia Plath I expect,' said Rori. 'I didn't know how bad until a friend phoned my parents and they took me away.'

'Where to?'

'Nice country house for the posh nut jobs.'

Her way of speaking was so unselfconscious and direct. I didn't know what to say.

'Oh, don't worry, I wasn't in long, got myself out as quickly as I could. Worked out what they were looking for. Insight is key. Poor insight shows you have a lack of understanding about your condition – and you must acknowledge you have a condition, not merely a human condition like everyone else, but whatever condition it is they decide upon.' She said there was something called group therapy where the residents sat in circles and discussed their families. 'It's a bore, isn't it, listening to other people's mental distress. There've been a few evenings here where it all gets unpacked, childhood trauma and abusive uncles and God knows what.' She stopped abruptly and reached a hand to my arm, 'Don't listen to me. It can be dreary here sometimes but so can anywhere, and mostly it's wonderful. What everyone is doing is wonderful. And it's so liberating –

you'll see – like being a child again, an outlaw, living in the woods, playing, fending for yourself.'

She made it sound like *Swallows & Amazons* and I tried to recast the primitive settlement in her light. I wanted to know more, but Angela had risen from her carpet roll to join us. We shifted around to make room and conversation turned to the blockade. I told her I was looking forward to it, which wasn't quite true, and she nodded, offering me a slight smile.

'What's on your pin?' I asked, indicating the green and white button attached to her parka.

She glanced down. '*Pax Christi*. I represented them at university.'

'Angela was working on a Masters in Political Science,' said Rori, looping her scarf once more around her swan neck.

As she talked it was clear that Angela knew her ideological onions. Her sentences flowed together without ums or pauses, as if she'd written them down first. Listening to her reminded me of the time I'd seen Tony use the microfiche in his college library, that swoosh through swathes of information before the close-up seizure.

The bottle was coming our way. Rori took another swig, but Angela, who was talking about the glorification of the military, passed and the bottle was handed to me.

'What's disturbing,' she said, 'is the unquestioning acceptance of militarism and its promotion as a civilised and civilising force. War is bloody.' I took my sip, re-experiencing the sour-dry heat. 'The image of Margaret Thatcher riding on a tank draped with a union jack lends it a false credibility. After a while we become desensitised.'

Rori agreed. 'Living here, exposed to the elements, it sharpens you up,' she told me.

Militarism, said Angela, helped to give credence to a mode of thinking which took it for granted that whole nations should exist in fear of one another. She talked on in the firelight. *Fetishising. Atavistic. Proliferation.* 'Ultimately, arms-selling is

94

about power and profit,' she said. The determination in her pale face was impressive. What would it be like to be as clever as Angela, to live in a building of so many rooms filled with fascinating things and with plenty of space for storage? I lived in a two-up two-down but was hoping to extend.

Barbel played her guitar, fingers skipping along the fretboard. I didn't know any of the words, but when the song changed and slowed, I swayed left and right, picking up the general idea.

With our lovely feathers we shall fly

A dozen voices swelled around the fireside. Di gave me one of her smiles, then closed her eyes and continued knitting. I opened my mouth and, still cringing a bit despite myself, began to sing.

9

Green Woman Blues

Summer has arrived early and our clackety fan rotates in one corner of the office. We have to leave it on a low setting or the noise hampers phone conversations and paper is sent drifting and swishing to the floor. While Frieda takes a call, I sort through a box file of old invoices, having already re-taped its spine to keep it functional for another year. No one could accuse us of squandering money on overheads and we have the office to prove it: my desk, Frieda's jammed up beside it, a loo plumbed into an ex-store cupboard, a photocopier from ebay, and an ancient, elephant-grey filing cabinet on top of which piles of manila are balanced. One Sunday afternoon I'll have to confront them but for now I let them grow imperceptibly like mushrooms. Our kettle and mugs sit on a side table which gets pushed into the alcove beside the front door when we have meetings.

'Did you get back to Mr Naslund?' I ask, when Frieda is finished on the phone. We used to have a volunteer called Graham, a retired heating engineer who came in once a week to help with calls, but he met a widow in his creative writing class and they bought a bungalow together in Herne Bay. Now we deal with all enquiries ourselves and the red voicemail light is constantly flashing.

Frieda swivels her chair to reach the message book. As she does so, she catches some folders and also my eye. It could be my imagination, but she appears to be resisting a smile.

'Mr Naslund, Mr Naslund...' she repeats, leafing through.

'It's the hair, isn't it?'

She looks up with bewildered innocence. 'What?'

'You're good Frieda, but you're not that good.' She trained as an actress and still goes to the occasional audition between working here part-time.

'I need to get used to it, that's all,' she says, giving in to the smile.

'Me too.' I put a hand to my still-vibrantly-red hair. 'Hope it don't scare the kids.' My afternoon workshop is with a primary school in Huntingdon.

Three days have passed since the broadcast and I'm glad of the distraction of work because life on the home front has deteriorated further. Following the Miss Student Body revelation, Pippa went upstairs and packed her bag for the return to university. Before Pete drove her to the station she called me into the kitchen and said she thought it was better if we didn't speak for a while. No walk in the bluebell woods. No difficult but necessary conversation, hard truths spoken in the knowledge that we are mother and daughter and nothing should come between us. Only a perfunctory goodbye and an exit. My text messages have gone unanswered.

While I finish with the invoices, Frieda rings Mr Naslund's landlord about installing a water meter, something he's been reluctant to undertake. She manages to get him on side swiftly with her blend of charm and enthusiasm.

'Think that deserves a cup of tea,' she says, and I put in a request for PG Tips. In the two years we've been working together I've tried every fruit and flower combination imaginable but can't be won over to goji berry or hibiscus flower. Frieda is relentless in her pursuit of the new, whether it's tea or music or people, and as she fills the kettle she tells me about her latest man, a thirty-year-old sound designer. She likes the fact he's younger because he doesn't want to be tied down. *Tied down.* I wonder if that's what me and Pete are.

While I gather oversize polystyrene cut-outs for the workshop, we discuss any last bits that need doing before the council meeting next week. This one is crucial; our funding renewal hangs in the balance.

'Actually, there's something I've been meaning to speak to you about,' she says, setting down the mugs.

'Fire away.' I'm easing Mervyn the raindrop out from behind the filing cabinet where he's wedged himself. A grotty splodge discolours his nose so I pull paper towels from the dispenser and try to clean him down, stopping when I catch sight of Frieda's changed expression, intent and a little apprehensive.

'What is it?'

And as I sit with Mervyn on my lap, she tells me about a touring production of *Me and My Girl.*

'It was such a long shot, I didn't even bother mentioning the audition.'

We're on opposite sides of her desk, but I'm near enough to Frieda that I can see the tension in her eyes. 'Rehearsals start in a month. I'm sorry, I wanted to give you more time.'

'Don't be silly,' I put Mervyn aside and walk around the desk to hug her. In my head a tangle of new worries begin to flash their silvery bodies.

*

Pete and I are sitting opposite one another. For homework we were asked to spend at least an hour with each other, somewhere out of the house, somewhere we wouldn't be distracted by everyday problems. Go for a walk. Hold hands. Look at each other, said Valeria. Get yourselves in the dating zone. But after the week we've had, we're barely in the speaking zone, never mind the dating zone.

There's a white-bricked pub five minutes from Valeria's house and we've formed the unofficial habit of calling in for a quick drink before the counselling session because, although we don't admit it, the drink steadies us for the hour ahead. This evening, aware we haven't done our homework, we've allowed an extra half hour in the beer garden. I've been telling Pete about Frieda, which isn't strictly within the rules, since we're not supposed to discuss work, but it hasn't been an average day. He listens while a lad collects glasses around us.

'What if it's a sign?'

'A sign of what?'

He takes a sip from his bitter and leans back, fingertips resting on the table. 'You've achieved a lot, far more than most small charities. What if it's time to wind things up?'

I'm unsure whether he means this or if he's merely taking a position, adopting a counter-argument to test my commitment. This is a habit from the classroom.

'You know what Valeria said about finding more time for each other,' he says.

'She didn't tell me to give up work.'

'I'm not saying that.'

The conversation goes around in a circle for a few minutes and ends with silence. He turns over a discarded cigarette box with his middle finger: if he hadn't packed in smoking five years ago, this would be the point at which he'd have lit up and inhaled deeply.

His phone trills one short note and he smiles at a text message before tapping a reply. 'Pip' he says.

'Is she all right?' What I mean is, What does she say?

'She's fine.'

He doesn't offer anything else. He doesn't read the message out. The unwelcome thought occurs that he might be glad to have it for himself, he might be warmed by a little moment of triumph, the knowledge that he is the good father and I the bungling mother. But the thought is ugly and I push it away.

The late sun turns the pub roof bronze and he puts on his sunglasses. I follow the direction of his gaze to a young couple seated beside a pram. They're leaning into each other, his hand resting on her knee, her arm around his waist, catching some time together while the baby sleeps.

'Do you ever wish we'd had another?' he says.

I know he misses Pip. The week after she left for university I found him sitting on the edge of her bed, turning over the lumpy bear Mum knitted when she was born. I nearly reach out to take his hand, to rub my thumb over the wedding ring. But the moment passes. Before I can speak he supplies his own answer in a flat voice. 'You wouldn't have had time for more children.'

'Pete? We made those decisions years ago.'

'No, we didn't,' he says, still looking at the couple.

There are speckles of grey coming through his beard. I can't remember what he looks like without it now – he grew it on a whim when we were camping in Brittany, a holiday beard he decided not to shave off. The beard suited him, finished him. I remember putting my arms around him and calling him bear, and he was The Bear for the first few weeks of our return. He'd roar at the kids and chase them around the house.

'I don't understand you,' I say, which is the truth.

He shrugs. The young couple angle their chairs into the remaining sunlight. It's nearly seven.

'We ought to go,' I say, getting up.

During the walk to Valeria's house, I reel back in my mind: when Dom was two or three we could have had another baby, but it would have been a stretch; Pete was working full-time and I was in a fundraising job. There must have been conversations but I can't remember them now. Did we let them fade into the background of our day-to-day until they faded out completely? Was he still having that conversation in his head all along?

Perhaps we didn't make a decision then, not in definite terms. But surely that's the way of life, decisions that are not conscious, because often it's the accidents that link A to B rather than the plotted lines. A girl collapsing at a crowded gig. A lad with a car. A hospital waiting room. And then there are the chain reactions; I picture those hands circling the military base on a December afternoon, rippling and flying high into the freezing air, one current pulsing through a multitude. If I close my eyes, I can still feel that current pulsing down the years.

10

Women!

I yawned, sending a breath cloud into the freezing air. At half-past six on the morning of the Action we were gathered a quarter of a mile away from Amber gate. Our intention was to keep the blockade a surprise.

Jean, dressed in a Barbour and battered green cords, moved sociably around the visiting protestors in the smudgy light, sipping from the cup of her Thermos. The university students had turned up as promised, carrying a 'Reading Says No to Cruise' banner, and a few of them were chatting with a group of older women, some of whom wore lipstick and carried handbags. They had a banner too, 'Grannies Against the Bomb', beautifully stitched in appliqué on a linen background. Another small troupe, many of whom wore tie-dye, had brought an enormous papier mache puppet robed in a multi-coloured gown, her yellow wool hair streaming. They swirled the puppet on a stick so it looked as if she were dancing above the crowd. Even more compelling than the puppet women were the ones gathered near the side of the road, all of whom were dressed – trousers, coats, jumpers, scarves – in orange. They sang as they waited. Something Eastern. From where I stood, stamping against the cold, I could also see Rori swinging a loud hailer and talking with Angela. They were probably exchanging opinions about international policies and arms treaties and civil defence budgets. I couldn't yet follow all their conversations but the list in my exercise book was growing.

Things discovered/ yet to find out
Diggers – mid 15th Century. Rebels. Dug common land.
Silo – garage for nuclear missile.
Atavistic – (ask Jean)
Speak – a talk.
Sellafield – nuclear reprocessing plant. Was called Windscale.
Eco-feminists – women in woods??
Jus ad bellum – Justice before war.

My stomach gurgled. If I'd been spending a large proportion of time grappling with the concept of non-violent direct action, I'd been spending an equally large proportion grappling with my digestive system. Mum never bothered with pulses, and in their assorted beady shapes I'd always considered them more suitable for nursery school collages than hot dinners. Vegetables didn't interest me much either. But now these ingredients featured in every meal and thanks to a diet of unidentifiable stews and bubbling gruels, my guts were protesting. Greenham Gripe, Sam called it. I'd learned how much a person could value something once it was taken away. We all felt it about the right to live in a nuclear-free Britain, but privately I also felt it about bacon sandwiches.

At least if my stomach was restless I knew where to go – a dug-out ditch behind the trees, covered and re-dug at regular intervals. Despite the lack of official organisation, I'd come to understand how the camp worked. I'd taken my turn to collect firewood, and walked to the stand pipe carrying a canister of water which I'd dutifully filled and lugged back, proud as a hunter dragging a wild boar slain in the forest. It was only later that I realised the wheelbarrow was there to make life easier. Angela had pointed it out. After a somewhat chilly start, she'd warmed up a bit, but I got the feeling she didn't suffer fools, and I also sensed she wanted to protect her friendship with Rori. I looked over to where they stood talking. She seemed more animated than usual, but I could tell it was serious conversation rather than fun.

Me and Rori, we were the laughers, the chatterers, the intimates. In the short time since I'd arrived we'd fallen into a dizzy friendship, staying up late at the fireside, adopting voices to make each other laugh, exchanging confidences. I mused over what I knew about her. Born Aurora Constance Fleming in 1960, the year Brezhnev became president and Sylvia Pankhurst died, she'd grown up in Chelsea and attended a private boarding school from which she'd been expelled – something to do with smoking pot. Her older brother worked in the city. Her younger brother was at Winchester. As a child she'd wanted to be a naturalist and spent hours clambering about in rock pools whenever the family visited their holiday home on the north Cornwall coast. Her mother, Jocasta, loved parties and couldn't abide people with petty opinions and no politics.

Jean arrived at my elbow with her Thermos. 'Of course, one always hopes for more, but this will do very well, don't you think?'

I agreed. There must have been eighty or ninety of us altogether. Jean raised her arm in signal, and presently Rori stood before us, projecting her clear vowels, hardly needing the loud hailer. She thanked everyone for getting up so early, especially the students – they cheered themselves – and reminded everyone to register, to maintain a peaceful spirit and to support each other. She said the blockade was a celebration because we were life-loving women, and this action was a sign of our power. 'And I hope you're in good voice because we'll be handing out song sheets. Some of you may not have been involved with direct action before so I'll let Angela explain more.'

She smiled that wide cat smile and struck the air Lech Walesa-style so the pom-pom wobbled on her pink hat. 'Remember, arms are for linking!' I would have been ready to face an army with her, we all would. We cheered.

Then Angela stepped forwards and sobered us up.

'Our aim today is to disrupt entrance to the base by personnel and vehicle. Anyone who doesn't wish to sit down can add support by standing at the verge or acting as a legal observer, noting down anything we may need to refer to later.'

Like what? Did she mean in court? The griping sensation returned whenever I thought about prison cells.

'Women formed into small affinity groups make a large decentralised action easier to co-ordinate and service,' she continued, reminding me of the legal contracts we used to type up at work. 'The object is to create bonds of support so we take mutual responsibility for one other.'

Under Angela's direction, we began to form groups. Barbel grabbed my hand, and I turned, searching for Rori, but too late, another four women had joined us. Rosy-cheeked and warmly dressed, they looked ready for a long post-Sunday lunch walk. We exchanged greetings and promised to look after each other

Angela reminded us that Amber gate enjoyed reasonable relations with the police and asked that no one taunt them or the military. After she'd finished, the gathering was noticeably more subdued. Even the puppet had stopped dancing. But Rori revved things up again with the song I'd heard already, the one about the spirit being old and strong like a mountain. Barbel grinned at me. 'And so we're ready,' she said, pinning back a strand of plaited hair. This was it, my first action. With the mist lifting, we took up the song and began to walk.

As we neared Amber gate and our songs died away they were replaced by the faint but unmistakable sound of chanting – *We say no! We say no!* – which grew louder as we rounded the curve of the road. There outside the open gate a small horde of women were on the ground, blockading, arms linked, leaning against each other in a tangle. When they saw us a voice went up over the chanting. 'Women!' came the cry, followed by that strange Red Indian whooping.

'What's happening?' I asked.

'Sapphire-gaters,' said Barbel, tightening her lips.

'What are they doing here? This is our action.'

She shrugged. 'The news travels.'

A loaded gravel truck faced the blockade, poised to enter the compound. There were already two policemen on the scene and the younger began gabbling into the radio at his shoulder when he saw us coming. The truck driver pressed his horn. Then pressed it again. The older policeman went over to the cab window to speak to the driver and the chanting came with greater force. *We say no! We say no!* My guts quivered. The Sapphire-gaters were younger than our lot, a scrum of boisterous fresh-faced girls, some with punk hair, others with shaven heads, raucous and quite patently unafraid. One had a spider's web drawn across her face in purple eye-liner. Or it could have been felt tip.

'Oh dear,' said Barbel. 'At Sapphire gate they are quite, hmm, what's your word.'

'Rowdy?' I suggested over the new chanting which had risen in volume, despite the voices of Ruby and Amber singers, who were attempting a peace song.

'No. I can't think.'

The young policeman kept talking on his radio, while his colleague came forwards, caped against the cold, hands held up in black gloves.

'Stay back please, ladies.'

Angela and Rori were near the front with Jean. We all moved forwards.

'I'm asking you to stay back, I don't want to charge you with obstructing the public highway.'

'Blood on your hands!' called one of the Sapphire-gaters for no particular reason.

'Provocative,' said Barbel with relief.

'My colleague is calling for back-up,' a policeman informed Jean.

Barbel took my arm and we jostled nearer the front.

'Women!' shouted the Sapphire-gaters.

A few members of our group ran forwards to occupy the section of clear road between the heap of bodies already blockading and the wheels of the truck. The driver edged forwards to close the space, but the policeman gave a warning gesture, forcing him to reverse. That was it. The women darted in, taking position in the blockade while the policemen tried to keep them back and the truck driver leaned on his horn. 'Clear out the way you silly bitch!' he shouted, as another woman skipped in front of him. The students dashed ahead and sat down.

'Come on,' said Barbel pulling me towards the rows of women. I couldn't see Rori's pink hat.

'Pack in tight!' called a woman at my ear.

'Stay back!' ordered the policeman.

'Here you are,' said a voice from the ground, offering a hand to help me down. I squashed in, half falling on her, but she only laughed.

'I'm Debbie.' She sat cross-legged wearing a sheepskin coat and a blue hat. On the hat she'd sewn a CND badge, the stitching loose at one corner.

'Are you from Sapphire gate?'

'No, I'm local, but my mate is, Cat.'

She leaned forward to reveal Cat, who stared ahead, her scalp shaven but for one long rat's tail striping her neck.

'How long have you been here?' I asked Debbie over the noise.

'I don't know, an hour.'

Other women were collapsing around us.

'Take care of the goddess!' someone called. No one quite knew what to do with the papier mache doll, but she obviously couldn't sit in the blockade or she'd get her head crushed in, so instead she was passed to the grannies against the bomb, and remained tethered, robes streaming in the wind, while her owners sat down in the mesh of bodies.

'They don't know what to do,' said Debbie of the policemen. 'Look at them!' It was true; the young one with the radio was spinning around like a farmhand failing to herd cattle. Debbie began joining in loudly with the singing. I caught sight of a pink hat which might have been Rori's.

After two more songs a man cycled up to the front, dismounted and scratched his head. He was middle-aged, wearing bicycle clips. He tried wheeling around the arms and legs. 'Excuse me,' he said, pushing through. 'Excuse me. I've got to get to work. Excuse me.' But he and his bike were stuck.

'No chance,' said a woman at the back. 'Take the day off.' Laughter. The man with the bike tried to wheel nearer.

'Can't you get me in?' he shouted to the soldiers at the gate. But the soldiers pretended they hadn't heard.

'How many children are you going to kill today?' asked a woman.

'I work in the canteen,' said the man. He got back on his bike and cycled away.

11

Bolognese

Keeping in mind Valeria's advice about communication, I've sent my apologies to the Heston Fields committee and am preparing a meal this evening, a proper sit-down-and-talk meal. Cooking opens up a pocket of calm. Everything happens mechanically, my body obeying the bolognese-making habits of a lifetime, onions chopped and fizzing in oil, perfuming the kitchen as they slide around a cast iron pot. I pour a glass of Rioja, set the table for two and bring in a few sweet peas from the garden, arranging them in a yellow jug on the kitchen table. Dom's at band practice and the house is quiet but for the radio and the background laughter of a panel game.

The phone rings and I let it go to answer machine. It's Mum. She speaks in a rush, sending her love, but as usual she tries to cram too much information on the tape and it cuts off. Her voice – chatty, warm, reliable – causes me stop and stare through the kitchen window.

Six-thirty comes and Pete isn't home. I finish my glass of wine. Seven arrives and seven-thirty. I pour another and send him a text. Eight o'clock passes. I boil a small amount of spaghetti for myself and drain it, then regard it without appetite, leave it in the colander and settle on the old sofa beside the garden door. It's a worn chintz, something that once belonged to Pete's parents. I'm intending to make a list of grant application letters, but the list turns into a doodle and I get lost in a network of loops and boxes while evening springs up over the garden.

He comes in at nine-thirty. 'Sitting in the dark?' he says, turning on the standard lamp and draping his jacket over a chair. At the sink he fills a glass with cold water and drinks it down.

'You might have said you were going to be late.'

'Sorry. I went for a pint with Bill. Switched my phone off.'

'Right.'

'Thought you were at one of your meetings anyway.'

'Cancelled it.'

He says he's eaten so I go about spooning the Bolognese into a bowl for the fridge. He takes a fork and tastes it.

'Delicious.'

'It's only Bolognese.'

He sighs, sits down at the kitchen table and pours himself a glass of wine while I busy about making more noise than is necessary. After a tense pause he speaks. 'Look, we've got the Ofsted inspectors in next week and I can't handle this right now, Tessa. I've told you I'm sorry about all that make-over stuff. I don't know what else to say.'

'Sorry won't make everything slot nicely back into place.' I'm making room in the fridge for the cling-film-covered bowl. This wasn't how we were supposed to start off, and I definitely wasn't going to dig at him, but now the words are out.

He shakes his head as if at some private joke. 'Everything wasn't nicely in place.'

By this time we should be on the sofa side by side. This was supposed to be our turning point. I'd imagined laying my head on his chest, him stroking my hair.

'What d'you mean?' I say, closing the fridge. He's rotating his wine glass in small circles from the base. He gives me his weary face, shakes his head again and sighs.

'I'm not one of your kids, Pete, I don't want the Mr Perry treatment.'

'You *know* what the problem is: you're never here. You're always in a meeting, or at a committee, or off at some climate camp or other.'

'Twice, I went to the climate camp twice. And I've asked you to come to things.'

'I don't want to spend my evenings around more tables or my weekend in a tent.'

'You used to love camping.'

'We were younger then.'

'You want me to sit watching telly with you all night.'

'No.'

'What then?'

He looks at me squarely. 'I want a wife.'

His words go into me. 'What am I, a mirage?' I lean back on the counter.

'You're married to your campaigns. If it's not saving the post office it's the library and if it's not that it's rescuing a patch of scrubby field no one's bothered about.'

'*You're* not bothered about.'

'Don't you get enough of it at work all day?'

He stands up and goes to look out at the garden. One of the doors is open, it's a warm night but the perfume from the honeysuckle bush isn't soothing us. He massages the muscles at his neck.

'So I'm a disappointment,' I say to his back.

'No, no of course not. Don't be defensive.'

He's right, that is defensive, but I feel defensive. I pick up the colander of cold spaghetti and slide it into the bin. It has congealed, solid and contoured like a section of brain. 'You want a woman who has facials and hair appointments and spends Saturday in the shops.'

'It's not about how you look.'

'No? It is from where I'm standing.'

'It's the way you go about things. You don't have to save the world all by yourself. It's not always down to you.' That expression again, saving the world, the same one Maggie used. He softens his voice. 'I know you care and I respect that. But it's…' He stalls for the words, 'You're constantly distracted by the next great cause, as if your life depended on it.' He turns to face me. 'What's it for? You might as well still be living on that common for all I see of you, and when I do you're preoccupied, always on a mission. It's like an obsession, this need to be do-gooding all the time.'

'Do-gooding?'

He rakes a hand through his hair. 'What else is it?'

'I like to have a purpose that's all.' I'm still holding the colander. 'You want me to be someone else.'

'No.'

'Yes you do, why else did you agree to that programme?'

'A bit of make-up and some new clobber, is that such a drama? It was supposed to be a treat. Honestly. We've been through this…' It doesn't matter how many times we've been through it, it still hurts. He shakes his head as if he's decided something. 'But I tell you what, I don't want to live like this any more, I'm sick of you carrying on like a one woman United Nations. I'm sick of ethical bananas and carbon footprints and hemp bloody shower gel. I don't want a goat for Christmas. I don't want to walk around my own house in the winter wearing three jumpers. I want to fill the bath up, I want to…'

'You want, you want. Why don't you just have done and trade me in for someone else then?'

He recoils as if he's been struck, and the flutter that passes across his face exposes him. Because this is the man I've been married to for twenty-four years, I understand what the flutter signifies: it's guilt.

'Have you..?'

'No.'

In the still kitchen his breathing comes heavily. I'm at the sink holding the colander. He picks up the wine glass again and drinks. Oh my God. Surely not, that's mad isn't it? This is Pete, my husband, solid, bearded, practical Pete, Mr Perry, Head of History. The silence shivers between us, there's a sudden sick feeling in my stomach.

'Is there…?' I can't say the words *someone else* because they're too surreal. He blinks at me.

'Will you say something!' My voice is so loud it startles us both.

'It's over,' he says.

'What's over?' The colander is a dead weight.

He takes a deep breath and whatever it is he's going to say, I don't want to hear, but it's too late because he's saying it anyway. Or trying to.

'I did something stupid. It's over now, not that it was… it didn't mean anything… I stopped it, it could have gone on, but I didn't let it.'

It's an effort to match him to the words. The mouth moving is Pete's because it's the same one that reminds me we need to buy milk, but the words coming out are foreign. I have the odd sensation of being in a badly dubbed film. What my husband should be saying is, Let's forget about all this make-over rubbish and start again, but what he's actually saying is… what is he saying?

'You had an affair?' He's staring at me like someone hungry pleading for a morsel of food. I repeat the question.

'Not that no… it was more of an accidental… fling.'

'A *fling*?' He makes himself sound like a debutante in a Noel Coward play.

'But it's over.'

'…as in the flinging off your clothes variety?' The ground feels like water. 'So what you mean is that you've been sleeping with someone?' He says nothing. 'Who?'

It's a long moment before he gives up the information. The house is still but for the low purr of the fridge. 'A supply teacher.'

113

'Fresh out of teacher-training college?'

He looks up. 'It was nothing. I didn't want anything to happen.'

'Am I supposed to be grateful? I don't believe this.'

'Look, it didn't mean anything. I promise.'

'When did it start?'

'It's over. It only lasted a few weeks. It was a mistake.'

'When did it start? How?' I am shouting, trying to shout. My voice doesn't feel like my own. Nothing feels like my own.

He sighs. He is not answering. 'Tess, I'm so sorry.'

I start laughing. He's startled, spot-lit by the lamp, his hair sticking up like an exclamation mark from where he's raked through it.

'What a perfect day.'

'Tessa.'

I look away from the face I know better than my own, towards the sweet peas in their yellow jug. 'Get up, go to work, find out council isn't renewing funding for charity that's taken four years to establish. Come home, discover husband having an affair.'

'What? They can't do that,' he says. 'After all the work you've…'

His sentence dissolves. The letter came today. Two brief paragraphs telling us our grant has been pulled. We won't last more than another four or five months without it. He's the one I needed to talk to: he's the one I needed to come home to, because even if things aren't perfect he's my husband. But I don't know him. The familiar kitchen suddenly feels alien too, as if it belongs to someone else. I'm leaning against the sink, still holding the colander. The room and everything in it is a bleary mess.

12

The Arm of the Law

After half an hour of singing and swaying, nothing much had happened except the truck driver had got angrier, the women had got louder and my feet had got colder. Traffic had built up behind the truck but it was difficult to see exactly what was going on because there were at least four rows of women in front of me. My leg was going to sleep, but changing position was tricky in such limited space.

'Sorry,' I said, twisting into Debbie, 'pins and needles.'

'Jiggle when you need to, don't bother about me,' she said. I liked her, and talking was good, it made me feel calmer.

The Sapphire-gaters at the back started a loud jeering. 'Here they come,' said Debbie.

'What is it?'

Debbie and Cat, the girl with the rat's tail, were jeering too.

'What is it?' I repeated, raising my voice.

'Wagons.'

Through the gap between heads, I saw police officers tumbling from a van in a cascade of navy blue and lining up in pairs, ready to remove the first women from the road. My heart struggled for a way out of my chest.

One of the legal observers rushed towards the police. 'You're being *used*,' she cried, 'you're being *used*.'

'And you're obstructing the public highway,' said a policeman.

The officers set to work, lifting the protestors and dragging them away.

'Shame!' cried a woman at the front. The cry went up from the women on the verges. 'Shame! Shame!'

Grannies against the bomb started singing, 'We shall overcome.'

I rocked around, trying for a better view.

'Where are they taking them?' I asked Debbie.

'Dumping them out of the way, I should think. That's what they usually do, drag and dump.'

The truck driver looked on with his red face. Some of the women who'd been dumped were running back to the blockade. The police gave chase. It was like a crazed game of girls against boys.

I didn't hate the police. I'd never had any reason to. I'd never got on the wrong side of the law, never been caught shoplifting or drinking litre bottles of cider in the park.

'I've never done this before,' I said to Debbie.

She put her arm around me in a hug made awkward by the cramped position of our bodies, 'Don't worry.'

But I was worried. Very worried. 'What do I do?'

'What do you mean?'

Why was she being stupid? There wasn't time. They were fetching and heaving rapidly, soon their big gloved hands would be on me.

'When they come, when they come. The police.'

Debbie smiled like an indulgent big sister. 'Calm down,' she said, over the noise. Easy for her to say, she obviously enjoyed this sort of thing if she turned up for other people's actions. 'Don't struggle, they've been trained. Make your body go limp. If you struggle, it'll hurt more.' I'd heard that some police put their knees into you, or dug into your pressure points or pulled your hair.

Even with the women running back to sit in the blockade, the margin between me and the front line was thinning. Two policemen bent over the woman in front. 'Be careful!' scolded her neighbour, 'don't hurt her.'

'Come on then, we don't want to drag you,' said a policeman to the woman, whose hair was a soft spray of white. She obviously wasn't going to show weakness by standing with the grannies.

'I'm staying here.'

'Come on, love.'

'I am not your love. I've lived through two wars.'

The policeman sighed. 'Let's clear the rest,' he said to his colleague.

'They're preparing to store bombs in there,' said the white-haired woman.

'And you're obstructing a police officer in the course of his duty,' said the policeman as he got a grip on the woman beside her.

'Wake up!' she called, but the policeman said nothing and only worked around her.

Soon there was no one left between me and the front line, I *was* the front line. Two policemen were coming towards us. Debbie linked her arm through mine. 'Nooo!' she yelled. They stood behind her and hooked their arms under her sides, straightening up to take her weight, and as they pulled she resisted, yanking hard on my arm and crying 'No cruise!' She was making a proper song and dance. 'No, no, no.' I tried to get her arm out of mine, but she was locked in. They pulled again and she tugged me harder, so hard I thought my arm would rip from its socket. 'AOOwe!'

'You're hurting her,' said Debbie.

'No,' said the policeman, '*you're* hurting her.'

He had a point.

The policeman counted, 'one, two,' and quickly as possible I wriggled my arm free of Debbie's, so that on 'three' she was being carried off, giving the Red Indian whoop. I watched her boots kicking the ground as she was pulled backwards. She was flopping around like a fish. Now it was proper chaos again, the whooping was coming from everywhere, not only that, there was an awful miserable wailing starting up behind as if all the women had collectively found their dogs dead in the road.

'What is it?' I said to whoever sat behind.

'They're keening.'

'Cleaning?'

The woman didn't answer, something had caught her eye. 'Alma!' she said above the howling. 'They've got Alma!' she shouted. Now they were all upset. Alma was obviously popular. The wailing got worse.

'Calm down,' I heard myself saying. 'You'll make them angry.'

But they ignored me. Oh God, Oh God. The blood fizzed in my ears making me want to run, to get up in my big achy boots and run as if I were in a school sprint, but I knew I couldn't. There was an empty space beside me where Debbie had been. I had clear sight of another body going into the van.

Two officers bent down to me, a youngish one with sandy hair fringing his helmet, and an older one who leaned so close to my face I could see his nose in detail, red and bumpy like a planet. I tried to think of the Suffragettes – Emily Davison must have been scared too when the King's horses came thundering towards her.

'Come on.' He looked too old for this, in fact he could have been married to one of the grannies against the bomb. He gave a quick glance over my shoulder to see how much was left, like a farmer assessing a half-ploughed field.

'Nearly there, Don,' he said to the younger officer. 'Let's be having you,' he said to me. I wondered if he could see my fear. I wasn't singing or whooping or wailing. Before I could do anything about arranging myself for the move, he and Don had hooked their arms under my armpits and we were off. I remembered to make my body go limp. I was also trying to remember that I was furious about the war machine, but a large part of my mind was concerned about the amount of effort it must be taking them to drag me along – I could feel the mass of myself, arms and belly and thighs, heels scuffing the road as we travelled.

Abruptly I dropped onto wet grass. The old policeman leaned over me, his black helmet causing a partial eclipse. 'Don't try going back over there or I'll have you in the van, all right girlie?' I nodded into his milky blue eyes, and off he went to drag someone else from the pile while I lay, exhilarated, noise crashing around me, staring at the sky as if this were the first time I'd seen it, really seen it, the pale belt of cloud scudding quickly by, my body firing with adrenalin as if I'd escaped a deathly fairground ride.

'Hello.'

I looked up to find a concerned woman of about Mum's age beside me. She was one of the women I'd seen earlier, part of the group dressed entirely in orange. Her hair clouded her head in a fine halo of blonde like a dandelion clock. 'They didn't hurt you, did they?'

'Actually, my shoulder's a bit sore.'

'Oh.'

'But I think I'm all right.'

She nodded, assuming an expression of great empathy, and wrote something on a notepad. 'I'm Deeksha,' she said kneeling down. She looked more like a Carol. 'I'm here to observe.' We regarded the scene before us, the women still singing, police officers dragging others away, women running or splayed out on the road like starfish. Another police van had arrived and there was a struggle going on between two officers and three protestors who were trying to prevent their friend going into the van. I straightened, the woman going in the van was Cat, the Sapphire-gater who'd been sitting in my line. Nearby, two policemen were dragging Angela's light body rapidly across the ground. This must be her second removal from the blockade. I ought to be like her, I ought to go back and sit down.

'Do you want some of this?' asked Deeksha, producing a bottle of orange juice from her cloth bag. For a moment I wondered if she only consumed orange foods.

'It's freshly squeezed.'

'Thanks,' I said, taking a sip. 'Lovely.' And it was. Sweet and sharp.

A pair of policeman neared us and I moved aside in time for a woman to be dumped next to me: she sprang up like a jack-in-the-box, took a deep breath and ran back in the direction of the blockade. We sat there watching the scene from the verge, like spectators at a bizarre sports day. I knew I should go back. I should be brave. This is what I was here for. Where was Rori? I hoped she'd seen me getting moved by the police.

'Anything you want me to record?' asked Deeksha.

'Um, I don't think so.'

Around her neck she wore a string of beads with a circular medal in the centre containing a picture of a man who resembled an Indian Jesus.

'That's Bhagwan, my spiritual master. Want to see?' Before I could answer she'd taken the medal off and handed it to me. The beads were inlaid with silver, and the medal itself edged with gold. 'It's called a mala, everyone in my community wears one to remind us of his perfection.' The man in the tiny photograph had a beard like Jesus, but close up he looked creepy, his eyes were staring out like he knew what you were thinking. I handed the mala back.

'One of his commandments is to live wakefully. That teaching has brought me here.' She looked out at the chaos, appearing to contemplate something special. 'How did you get here?' she asked. It was obviously a spiritual question, could be she was trying to get me to live with her in an orange house. I considered my reply.

'Did you come on the coach?'

'Oh I see. No, I live here, I'm a camper at Amber gate.' Her expression transformed into one of admiration, softened with sympathy. I couldn't really call myself a camper, but it sounded better than visitor or stayer, the two other terms I'd heard.

'You women are so brave.'

I maintained a modest silence. From the corner of my eye I noticed Angela being dragged along again. For such a slight person she had a lot of energy. 'So brave. It must be difficult.' She touched my arm. 'You're doing this for all of us and we're so grateful.'

I nodded as if I could bear it well, unwilling to tell her I'd been living at the camp for precisely three days.

'We couldn't do it without your support,' I told her.

'Tessa!' I sat up straight to see Barbel waving from the other side of the road. The affinity group! I'd completely forgotten about the rest of them.

13

A Blast from the Past

It's half-past seven and the office blinds are drawn. Unable to sleep, I decided to come to work where at least I could be doing something. Or that was the plan. The Grants Directory lies abandoned while I tease at the knots in my head.

It's been a week since the night of the colander, a long and miserable week during which Pete and I have fallen back on the old routines of cohabitation. We cook, we watch news of distant crises unfolding in war zones, we nag Dom about his homework, we stack the dishwasher, but we are living without reference to one another. Or at least I am living without reference to him. We undress in the same room and arrange ourselves side by side, conscious of each other's breathing. He shifts and sinks into sleep, and I lie on my back, waiting for another day, waiting for the sun to come up and etch a lion's mane in the old furled roses of the wallpaper.

It's at night that I see them most clearly – him bearing down on her, pressing against her, tracing a line with his finger along the length of her thigh – and it's compelling, this intrusion into my husband's secret life. I see them curled in the half-light. I give them whispered dialogue. And then the wallpaper roses begin to bloom again and it's time to shower and eat and pretend for Dom's sake that everything is all right.

Her contact details are scribbled on an ear of notepaper and tucked into my diary. They weren't difficult to come by, I simply found the name of her agency, phoned and said I was from Pete's school and wanted to send one of their teachers an invitation to the summer barbecue. Twice I've picked up the phone and dialed her number, twice I've put the receiver down after her hello, blood thudding in my ears. It wasn't just the fear of not knowing how to articulate everything I'd rehearsed, it was the fear of her very real and immediate existence, the knowledge that I wasn't addressing a mute space but a person who had the ability to speak and feel and answer back. I didn't want to make her real because if I did she could say anything, that she was six months pregnant, that she was going to start a family with my soon to be ex-husband. Pippa's gone, Dom will be off to college in no time, so what's to stop him finding a nice younger woman and setting up home with her, filling the new breakfast room with cherubic two-year-olds? It happens all the time. And it might be too late for me to have more children, but it's not too late for him.

These are new sensations, new thoughts and they're strangely compelling. Pete only had one serious girlfriend before we met, Helena, an American student who eventually moved back to Illinois and in so doing broke his heart. One or two girls came and went after her, no one he spoke much about. But now, years later, after we've nearly forgotten our appeal to each other, let alone anyone else, this new woman, this shadow woman has lifted the bed clothes and settled between us, a live ghost. In the pauses between daily events – locking up my bike and unlocking the office, box-filing a report – there'll be a glimpse of her, a thought of her, and images from my own back catalogue sweep in. Pete racing Dom and Pippa across Holcolmbe Sands... Pete, flaked out after rugby, his head on my lap... Pete climbing an apple tree when we were first married... Pete tracing a pattern on her thigh... Pete presenting me with an apple... Pete pressing his mouth to her neck... Pete pretending to descend invisible stairs to make me laugh... Pete fitting his body around mine, kissing my neck... Pete fitting his body around hers, kissing her neck. And so it goes on.

We're due another counselling session but neither of us has arranged it because neither of us wants to sit on Valeria's pink sofa discussing this new parcel of sorrow, neither of us wants to unwrap it and examine it and work out what to do. And my head is already too full.

Since sliding that shoebox into the light, scenes from the past have been creeping up on me. I might be standing at the kitchen sink and suddenly I'm transported back to the common with its bowls of greasy water for the tin plates, and the red wire rack where they drained in the freezing air. My Greenham dreams have got mixed up with recent events: the night before last Pippa appeared in a bikini at one of the campfire meetings and I tried to cover her up with Angela's parka. By the illogical logic of dreams we were both nineteen but I knew she was my daughter. Then everything morphed into the set of a television show where the supply teacher played Jude introducing me to a studio audience, and I glimpsed Rori among the crowd of faces, saw her holding a placard and shouting something I couldn't make out. I woke with a lurch, prickling in a horrible after-shiver, the taste of the dream still in my mouth.

I make a crack in the blinds. Already the pavement is brightening. I fill the kettle and flip through a copy of *Third Sector*, glancing at the job pages: Head of Media, Account Manager, Direct Marketing Executive, they're roles that might be advertised in any large corporation and they're a long way from Easy Green. I could move back to working for another charity, but it's taken so long to build this one and I can't give it up now. The kettle reaches boiling point and leaks a small puddle of water. As I drop one of Frieda's camomile teabags into a mug, something returns to me – one of Valeria's strategies for confronting fears is to write them down. I jingle my laptop to life and think for a few seconds before typing:

What should I do about work?

The answer comes quickly because I've already half-formulated a decision:

Appeal to the council.

Another pause and then words I wasn't planning on:

Is this the end of my marriage?

The cursor blinks and I press delete, fighting a return to that image of Pete and the supply teacher, their breath fast and shallow. Instead I try to work on the problem of keeping the charity in business. But my thoughts won't be contained and they spill in other directions until I find myself typing something else:

If I was a good mother, Pippa would be able to talk to me.

The cursor pulses before a response appears:

She's still young. You didn't tell your mum everything when you were nineteen.

I consider that for a minute and type:

But I didn't resent her.

This exercise doesn't seem like such a good idea after all, but I've started now so in the shadowy office I think back over the past few weeks, my dissolving marriage, failing charity, misunderstood daughter, and type the one true thought, the thought that keeps drumming backwards and forwards like a wave.

I think I'm being punished.

And there it is for the first time, trapped like an insect under a glass. The cursor blinks at the end of the d, leading me on, but there's nothing else to say and nowhere else to go. I close the document, take another sip of tea with its faint taste of fields then click the cobalt blue e of the web. That little blue icon opens the door to swathes of human experience, it offers a chance to analyse what the great philosophers and psychologists have said about fidelity, or to summon tabloid articles in which footballers' wives battle to save their relationships after public blizzards of humiliation. Could I look her up again? Could I track her down on a social network? Is she mentioned on an education website? I have started this quest before but each tap into the search engine became an act of hollowing out, until by the end of twenty minutes, on the edge of my chair and nauseous at what I might find, I turned the computer off and went to bed in darkness, fully clothed.

The screen stares back, white as an eye. I don't know what I'm looking for. Not her. I resist that temptation and instead type Miss Student Body, then wait while a million search parties are dispatched invisibly to bring back news. And when it comes my spirits are not lifted. Photographs from last year's final are posted on the competition homepage: an array of pretty young women in evening dresses whose long shining hair gives them a similar appearance. The one in the centre is smiling hardest because she's been crowned with a silver tiara. I try to place Pippa among them. Is it really a bit of fun? They're so young.

I close the page and open my email, typing the password Frank, which is Pete's middle name. A dozen new messages are stacked in yellow envelopes: a circular from Amnesty and several other mailing lists, minutes from the last Heston Fields meeting, an online phone bill which I daren't open because I don't know how much Easy Green spent on calls last quarter. There's also something from Maggie. We've not spoken since the filming, but she's left two apologetic messages, and I meant to ring her but couldn't face it after Pete's bombshell. We've been friends for too many years to let this stupid programme come between us but even so I decide to defer my reply. One message jumps out. It's from Lulu, the Production Assistant. I click:

Hi Tessa
This came to the office. Isn't it great being famous?!! I hope you loved the ep. as much as we did, you looked fantastic!!!

She signs off with a kiss and a smiley face made out of a colon and half a bracket. I scroll down and read. And then re-read.

I'm sending this in the hope you can put me in touch with Tessa Perry, who featured on *Make Me Over*. We were at Greenham Common together. Many thanks, Angela Mullen.

Angela? Angela Mullen? I lean back in the chair and mentally add three exclamation marks of my own. Even as I try to picture her typing this – age her, offer her a setting (was this sent from an office? A kitchen table?), I cannot re-imagine the person I knew: pale-faced Angela, zipped into a parka, bending over her keyboard with a frown.

Part Two

Down at Greenham

14

Never Trust a Journalist

It was a wet Sunday afternoon in mid-November and the wind rampaged around the common like a mad woman. Our tarpaulin, set up in a gazebo-style arrangement to protect the main fire, had repeatedly collapsed, and finally ripped, leaving us nowhere to shelter, so in the end we'd retreated. I was in Rori's bender, listening to the weather as it warred with Barbel's experimental recorder-playing from next door. Barbel could play the guitar like a professional, but she'd never been forced to learn the recorder at primary school like the rest of us and now she'd decided to teach herself from a book.

'At least she's happy,' I said, as she started another round of 'London's Burning'.

'Yes, she has a gift for happiness,' said Rori, shifting to get more comfortable. We were propped on our elbows, a candle glowing inside a jam jar, bronze light pooling between us. 'She's one of life's free spirits.'

It was true, I'd never seen Barbel downhearted – even when the rain had seeped into our dry food supplies, ruining the flour and biscuits and turning the bread to wet sponge, she'd refused to complain.

'Do you think she'll stay long?' I asked.

'Difficult to tell. They're planning a peace camp in New York State, she wants to go and help.'

'The weather's got to be better at least.' The sheeting cracked hard in the wind and Rori sat up to re-tie a loose piece of plastic flapping near her head.

'Such a sloppy housewife,' she said, 'haven't dusted for weeks.'

'Well, I didn't like to mention it, but I noticed your antimacassars need a wash.'

She arched an eyebrow. 'What's an antimacassar?'

'You put them on the back of your three-piece suite.'

'Three-piece suite! You're hilarious,' she said, and flopped down again.

I didn't know what was so funny about a three-piece suite, but it was good to see her laughing. I'd noticed the melancholy she occasionally slipped into. Two days before, we'd been sitting by the fire, eyes fixed on the flames, and she'd told me about a time she'd walked into the sea. 'But it's harder to drown yourself than you'd think,' she said. Appalled by this, I'd put my arm around her and she'd smiled, not stoical but sad, and laid her head on my shoulder.

Rori's bender was more comfortable than my tent and more spacious too. She slept on foam spread over duckboard. The knobbles on the branches, which had been bent over to create the shelter's structure, acted as handy clothes hooks, while straw insulation kept in the heat. When the weather improved she'd promised to help me build a bender of my own.

The rain picked up speed and she sighed.

'Some days I'm convinced I've had enough, and other days this seems the only place to be.'

I knew what she meant. After a run of clear, cold nights I'd begun to enjoy being outside in a way I'd never have imagined when centrally heated in Stevenage. I liked the practical business of making do, the way women wrapped hot stones from the fire in cloth and put them in their sleeping bags. I liked listening to their stories as we cooked. I liked the sky, an ever-changing wallpaper. But in the rain it was a different matter.

'You know, being here is a little like playing tennis,' Rori said. I pictured hordes of women jumping over a net in their filthy whites. 'So much is about the inner game, the struggle with one's self.' She was inserting long fingers into her curls. Even if she hadn't washed or brushed them, the curls stayed springy.

'Still, this is far more enlightening than anything I've done before,' she said firmly.

'Even university?'

'Much.' The idea astonished me. 'I went to university and met exactly the same sorts I'd been at school with. All good fun of course, but hardly a challenge.'

I thought about that, and of the things I'd learned since being at the camp: that the suffragette colours were green, white and violet; nettles contain vitamin C and taste like a worse version of spinach; scattering catnip keeps away rats, and keening is symbolic of mourning. I'd also learned there are special ponds in London where women go swimming together, that a war was going on in Nicaragua, and that wooden pallets catch brilliantly on an open fire.

'What does your mum think of you being here?' I asked, chipping a cold drip of wax with my thumbnail.

'Jocasta? Oh she loves it. *Loves* it. She stayed for a night during the summer – those glorious warm evenings we had – though when it came to actually sleeping without a mattress, she was quite disabled by it all. Not that she'd ever admit it of course.'

'At least she sees why you're here.'

'Doesn't yours?'

I thought of Mum triple cleaning the worktops. 'She's not that interested in politics.'

A recent fragment of dream returned to me: Mum standing with her potato peeler removing Dad's post-explosion skin in long bubbly strips while he watched *Match of the Day* on a smoking television set. Since arriving at the camp my dreams had taken new and frightening turns.

Rori said her parents took opposing sides about disarmament. She was fond of her father, Corbert, but teased him for being right wing.

'They're poles apart on almost everything. Should have divorced years ago.'

'Why did they get married?'

'In their youth they were both exceptionally beautiful. It all comes down to sex in the end. But she married far too young, barely twenty. Actually, my being here has been very good for Jocasta. When there was that nonsense about me in the paper, the Lady Muck stuff, she was absolutely brimming, showed the page to all her friends. Greenham has boosted her no end. She can be quite...' she thought for the word, rolling a soft drip of candle wax into a bead '...unstable I suppose you'd call it. She's put her heart into fundraising.'

I'd got the impression from a couple of other things Rori had said, that unstable was a euphemism.

Outside the rain stormed on, but at least the wind had stopped hurling itself so violently against the bender.

'Do you think they have Sunday lunch inside the base?' said Rori, for whom thoughts of food were never far away. To pass time, we began planning a fantasy meal, working our way from starter to desert.

'You know what I'd die for? A poached pear with chocolate sauce,' she declared. 'Jocasta does them with a slug of cognac. Sprinkles them with crushed pistachios.' I'd been thinking about butterscotch Angel Delight. 'My elder brother, Ivo, did I tell you about him?'

'The one in the city?'

'He's incredibly impressed by these tiny meals on enormous white plates. Nouvelle cuisine. Absurd. Last year he took us to a smart restaurant for his birthday, and my main course was nothing but a spec of cod with a dribble of nothingy sauce.

Gone in two bites. And God knows what he paid for it. I blame that appalling fiancée – he hardly ever comes home since they met, and if he does it's only to show off to my father.'

That didn't make sense. 'Doesn't your dad have a title?'

'Oh yes, he has a title, but he doesn't have any actual *money*. Our house is practically bare floorboards upstairs. All the Nouveauxs have got the cash, haven't you noticed? Poor Dad, he'd love me to zip into a nice Laura Ashley and bag myself an aristo with a decent estate.'

We were on the cheese course, Rori scooping out the creamy insides of a Stilton, me cutting a generous wedge of Cheddar, when a head appeared. It wasn't like the heads of any of the women we knew; it was a head wearing a fawn Burberry rain hat.

'May I come in?'

The woman didn't wait for an answer, she was already crawling inside. 'Sorry to disturb,' she said, dragging after her a golfing umbrella and a leather bag like a beast on a leash. 'I'm April.'

'Here for a visit?' said Rori, as the woman rearranged the plastic sheeting to keep the weather out.

'In a way. I'm doing a piece about the camp.' She glanced around while simultaneously trying to settle herself on her knees.

'You're a journalist?' I asked.

'That's right. Freelance. Smaller papers mostly. Community news. Isn't it cosy in here,' she said, as if assessing the interior of Mrs Tiggywinkle's parlour. She wore a tweedy skirt with a pair of Wellington boots and the rain hadn't dampened the scent of her flowery perfume. I sensed Rori stiffen beside me and remembered her suspicion of journalists. But hadn't this one declared herself? April smiled.

'Would it be all right if I asked you a few questions?' she said, opting finally for an awkward half-squat half-kneel. 'I've been talking to some of the women at the Main gate, but I wanted to get an idea of what's happening at the smaller ones too.'

I glanced at Rori and whispered 'OK?' She shrugged as if she didn't mind either way. I'd never met a real journalist, and soon we were chatting away easily while I gave her the lowdown on our lives and tried to raise her consciousness. I was just in the middle of telling her about our water-carrying arrangements when Jean poked her head into the bender.

'Are you a journalist?' she asked. 'Because we don't permit the press into our living quarters.'

'I'm terribly sorry,' said April, looking to us.

There was no room for Jean to squeeze inside, so she remained suspended at the entrance, a disembodied head.

'Well then…' April made as if to go, but I interjected. 'It's pelting, Jean.'

Jean considered. 'I suppose we could use my tepee. But this isn't the way it's normally done.' There was a hint of schoolmistress in her voice I'd never heard before.

'That's very kind,' said April. 'Happy to come?' I was but Rori looked doubtful. 'I've brought coffee and chocolate digestives,' she added lightly.

There wasn't much Rori wouldn't do for a chocolate biscuit. Besides, April's presence was at least a spark of interest in an otherwise eventless wet Sunday so we crossed the puddled mud towards Jean's tepee.

The only figure visible in the thrashing rain was Di, un-pegging the WOMEN AGAINST CRUISE banner to keep it from being shredded by the wind. I called to her over the elements and she followed us.

You could get six women in Jean's tepee, which had a bristly doormat at the entrance to wipe the worst clods of wet mud from your boots. April collapsed her golf umbrella. Jean fetched mugs and spare cushions. Despite the faded mud splatters, the one she gave me was still pretty, fashioned from dark orange cloth, embroidered with an Indian elephant and dusted with pink sequins. Once upon a time it must have occupied a chair in Jean's home, a place I imagined to be walled with books.

April produced the flask of coffee. 'It has sugar, is that all right?'

'Brilliant,' I said. Sugar. I'd not had sugar in anything since I arrived. We didn't bother with it because it got damp quickly and crystallised into blocks.

April removed her hat, releasing a swirl of mostly dry strawberry blonde hair and smiled at us inclusively. Di smiled back, kneeling on her short legs, the rescued banner bundled beside her. I'd got used to Di's unspeaking presence; she always operated in silence, sometimes knitting silence, sometimes sitting with a placard silence, sometimes bending with a bin liner silence. That first time I'd met her by the side of the road was the longest conversation we'd had.

'Shall I be mother?' asked April, as the mugs made their way towards her.

'We don't have a matriarch,' I said. I felt we'd got quite friendly after our exchange earlier. 'We're not attempting to emulate patriarchal power structures.'

I thought that was quite good, but no one apart from April laughed. *Concentrate*, I told myself. *Don't muck about.* My mug said Great Ashfield Flower Festival 1975. There was milk in the coffee too. Milk *and* sugar. April produced the promised chocolate digestives.

The rain made a muted percussive sound against the thick canvas of the tepee and April's eyes moved again towards Rori, who she'd been glancing at with interest. 'I don't think I caught your name?'

'Bernadette,' said Rori. That was weird. April's pen hovered before she committed the name to the pad. 'Bernadette,' she repeated. 'Like the saint?'

'Exactly.'

'Can I ask how your family feel about you being here, Bernadette?'

'I'm not sure that's relevant,' said Jean.

'No, I'm not sure it is,' said Rori/Bernadette.

April nodded, not in the least offended. 'And how long have you been living at the camp, Tessa?'

I thought for a second. The days merged. Today was Sunday, but it could just as well be Wednesday. 'Two weeks.'

'Not long then.'

'It feels like longer… a lot longer…'

April smiled and wrote something down.

'I didn't mean, I mean, you know, it feels like home.' That wasn't quite true either, but it was better.

'So you like it here?'

I thought of everything at once. Weeing in a ditch. Conversations about politics. Learning songs. The vegetables. Laughing. Being friends with Rori.

'It's very educating.'

April seemed wary of Jean, and slightly unsure of Rori/Bernadette, so I found myself doing most of the talking, which was fine, she was very interested. Now and again she glanced over at Di, as if she might have something to contribute, but Di continued to sit quietly and listen. After we'd chatted for a while, April said, 'I suppose for the women to be here, children and husbands might have to take a backseat. What do you feel about that?'

'Many of us are here precisely because of our children,' said Jean. 'There are children living with their mothers at the other gates, as you know. And men are equally able to give childcare.'

'Some people think the women are supported by the Communists, what do you say to that? '

'By some people, you mean the right-wing press,' said Rori with challenge in her voice.

Jean laughed. The chocolate digestives had cheered her up a bit. She said the British didn't need help to protest and she talked about the Aldermaston marches she'd been on in the 1950s.

April nodded, as if she were thinking about it.

Rori said the country was in a deep recession and we were wasting millions trying to keep up with the arms race.

'But some people might say...'

'What might *you* say?' Rori asked, fixing the journalist with her green eyes.

April smiled. 'I'm simply playing devil's advocate. How would you answer the criticism that the Greenham women are well intentioned but misguided?'

Jean sighed. 'Misguided is spending vast sums of money on weaponry which can never conceivably be used.'

She and Rori talked more about the reasons for the original march from Wales. They were both clear and articulate, but they'd had practice with public speaking, and that's what it came down to in the end, you couldn't get better if you didn't practise. I took a deep breath. This was an opportunity.

'The thing is, April,' I said, 'the thing is... every cruise missile can do the damage of...'

A voice came from outside the tepee. 'Jean? Have you seen Rori?' It was unmistakably Angela. 'Oh,' she said, surveying the scene.

'You're very welcome to join us,' said April, turning around.

Angela took in the belted mackintosh and freshly washed hair, and though her face said *You've got a nerve*, she merely nodded and came inside.

Jean passed Angela a cushion of mustard corduroy and Angela sat down cross-legged beside Rori. When she pulled back the hood of her parka her fringe lay plastered in slicks against her forehead.

'So,' said April, glancing down at her pad. 'You were telling me about nuclear capability, Tessa?'

Angela's eyes settled on my face.

'Yes. You see, the thing is a cruise missile can do the damage of twenty-nine Hiroshimas, which is massive.'

'It is. Gosh. Twenty-nine.' April went to write it down.

'I think it's more like nine,' said Angela quietly, wiping her glasses dry.

'Is it? Oh. That's still a lot. Nine. Perhaps it depends which paper you read,' I laughed inappropriately.

April liked that, she made another note. I wanted to get her pen and cross it out again, but I couldn't. Everyone in the circle, particularly Angela, with her freshly cleaned glasses, was staring at me.

'Anyway, we're getting them because that's the policy they agreed to, the MAD one, Mutually Agreed Disaster.'

Hang on, that didn't sound right. April looked up with the slightest of frowns. 'Mutually Assured Destruction, do you mean?'

'Yes, sorry.' I knew that, I knew that, I'd got a bit muddled that's all. Angela was still scrutinising me. I had to prove myself. I opened my mouth to speak again. 'So on the subject of the um, NATO thingy… the thing is… other countries are supposed to get involved. So the Germans are having the SS-20s…'

'I thought the SS-20 was Russian,' said April.

'Oh yes, of course.' In my head a woman was ransacking the filing cabinets for information, but the files had got mixed up.

'I mean the Polaris in Germany.'

Angela broke in to make a correction.

'They have Pershing. NATO is countering Russian SS-20 with Cruise and Pershing based in Europe. The balance of terror.'

My face was going thermo nuclear. I remembered something Rori had said about Simone de Beauvoir and the existentialists.

'You see, women can help rebalance the power. Women are eminent and men are transcendent but here women are able to reach transcendence too.' I paused. 'Greenham is a subliminal place. I mean liminal…' That was one of the new words I'd noted in my exercise book. 'It's a liminal place, and…'

Could it be that Di's usually calm face had taken on a troubled aspect? Angela blinked through her glasses. April's pen wasn't moving anymore. Outside the rain slowed to a stop.

'What I mean is.' But I didn't know what I meant. The woman upstairs had run out of drawers to try and was lying exhausted on a chair, sweating.

April smiled kindly. 'You've been very generous with your time. I should probably make a move while the rain's eased off.' She replaced the flask in her bag.

Di coughed. April gave a little start, as if she'd forgotten Di were there, which is what happened to the rest of us much of the time. Then she turned her reaction into a question, 'Would you like to make any comment?'

Di nodded, 'The weapons are an abomination,' she said, in her soft Welsh accent. 'I'm here for my grandchildren.' There was something to be said for brevity.

Once April had ventured into the mud, Jean turned to her sewing box from which she produced a square of embroidery. 'Never trust a journalist,' she declared, squinting to thread a needle.

April had seemed nice. 'But some of them want to know the facts, don't they?' The mention of facts made me cringe.

'What that woman was interested in was the usual: how we cook, where we defecate, how we keep clean, who's looking after our children, are we lesbians. I hate to sound cynical, Tessa, but I've been here long enough to learn that. Even the sympathetic ones need a story.'

'But if we're nice to them they could tell other people.'

'*Nice?* We're not here to ingratiate ourselves,' said Angela, directing her irritation at me.

'I know but, if they knew we were just normal women.' I didn't like the edge to her voice, the way she could jump on things.

'As opposed to what? What's *normal*?'

She got up then and went outside with Rori to discuss a speech they were giving at a women's group in Oxford, leaving me with Jean and my own feelings of inadequacy. Di continued to sit with us companionably, a Buddha in a woolly hat.

If Angela hadn't arrived I wouldn't have felt so nervous and made such a fool of myself. I dug my fingernails into my palm, recalling the awful rambling.

Jean lifted the calico. 'How's it looking?' she asked, spreading out the fabric to reveal a bluebird and an emerald green butterfly. 'I'm stealing part of the design from William Morris.'

'It's beautiful.' I took off a glove and traced my forefinger over a silky primrose.

'It's for the group at home, they'll frame it and sell it to raise funds. Can you sew, Tessa?'

'Me? No.'

'Ever wanted to learn?'

'Isn't it a stereotype…?'

Jean turned the fabric to begin a new section and glanced at me over her half-moon specs. 'Have you been speaking to Sam?' Sam got annoyed about what she called mother-earth syndrome because it made women passive and she said women weren't all about feelings and caring and birth bliss. 'Sewing's a skill,' said Jean, 'if anything it binds women together, gives us solidarity.'

Jean was failing to thread her needle in the poor light, so I threaded it for her, glad to be doing something useful. Being useful felt important, and I welcomed any chance to contribute to the camp. I could peel vegetables and collect water, even if the public speaking needed work.

'What do you want to do with your life then, Tessa?'

Nobody had ever asked me that before. 'The careers teacher at school said I should think about town planning. But I ended up at secretarial college.'

'Did you want to be a town planner?'

'No, but I was good at Geography. Anyway, I failed my A levels.' Too many nights thinking about Tony and not enough revision, 'So Mum and Dad said I'd be better off learning a skill.'

Jean nipped at the calico with her needle, building dot-sized stitches into a pink bud. 'And what did you think?'

April had left us her chocolate digestives, I nibbled on one and shrugged.

The secretarial college was grey and concrete and filled with rooms which were filled with typewriters. We approached them every morning, removed their covers, rolled in our carbons and awaited instructions from Mrs Manningtree who'd worked at ICI for twenty-five years and could reach 95 words per minute without corrections. *Now is the time for all good men to come to the aid of the party* she sang, as we stumbled about on our keyboards like people in a dark room groping for the lights. Upstairs in a high-ceilinged classroom with flaky green walls, Mrs Plume taught us Pitman shorthand. She also instructed us about filing systems, appointment scheduling, telephone manner and good business dress: if you are tall, don't wear a box-style jacket; always attend an interview in a skirt, even if you prefer to wear trousers. A court shoe with a medium heel is best.

'You've got brains in your head,' said Jean. I felt doubtful. She gave another glance over the specs. 'At my school we taught our girls to think, not type. No girl of mine ever learned to type unless she was going to write books for a living.'

Well I wasn't going to write books. I thought of Peggy at Hirschman & Luck – was Jean saying her working life was invalid?

'There's nothing wrong with being a secretary,' I said.

'Of course there isn't. As long as it's what you really want to do. Too many bright girls are farmed out for office fodder.'

Jean finished another stitch and bit the thread.

'Do you want to have a go?' she asked as I rethreaded the needle with green silk.

'Me? I'll spoil it.'

'No you won't. We'll practise on scrap.'

She demonstrated how to mount the linen on a hoop so it was pulled taut, and then showed me a chain stitch.

'You can retake A levels,' she said, supervising over my shoulder.

We sat like that for two hours or more, Di with her eyes closed, meditating perhaps, me and Jean sewing, the rain clouds racing overhead and darkening the tepee. And as we talked I forgot that my sleeping bag would probably be damp when I got back to my tent, that I'd have no dry clothes to change into and that even when I tried my best to prevent it, everything I owned would become slaked with watery mud.

15

A Collapsible Bike

Two days later when the weather had finally cleared to reveal fresh blue skies, Rori suggested we cycle to Newbury to use the showers at the public swimming pool. I didn't have a bike, but she said I could probably borrow Angela's.

We found Angela sitting outside her bender on an aged sofa cushion, writing purposefully into a spiral-bound notebook. She shaded her eyes from the winter sun when she saw us. The hood of her parka was down, exposing her fine blonde hair, which fell thinly, like water, as if it had been poured on from a jug. If she wasn't reading a huge theoretical tome she was writing letters and if she wasn't writing letters she was co-ordinating actions, and if she wasn't doing that she was campaigning for Pax Christi or arranging speaks.

'What are you up to, Angel?' said Rori, who nicknamed everyone: Jean was Geni because she worked culinary magic, Sam was Tricks, Barbel was simply B or sometimes Barbie, which made me wonder if feminist mothers might not appreciate a Greenham dolly for their little girls, a rag-tag Barbie complete with change of jumper and detachable placard. Secretly I hoped Rori might one day find a nickname for me.

Angela laid down her biro, 'It's a letter to the council, I'm working out how to get another standpipe. This is a peopled community, so the fire services should have a water point here in case of emergencies. That's the case I'm putting.'

'Good idea, I could use a break from wheeling that barrow,' I said, wondering too late if that sounded like a moan, but wanting Angela to know I was doing my bit. Since the journalist's visit I'd felt awkward around her.

Rori explained our visit to Newbury and asked about the bike.

'Only if it's all right,' I added.

'Certainly,' she said getting up. 'But I'll need it back by four. I'm doing a speak at the Friends Meeting House in Newbury. Jean was going to give me a lift but the van's out of operation.' The van had been parked up waiting for a mechanic from Ruby gate who hadn't yet materialised. It was one of the few problems Jean couldn't fix herself.

A moment later, Angela appeared with a canvas bag from which she removed a complicated metal contraption. It was only as she unfolded a wheel that I realised she was transforming the contraption into a bike.

'Have you taken cycling proficiency training?'

Was that a joke? But Angela wasn't the type for messing about.

'I used to have a bike when I was a kid.' It was my cousin's hand-me-down, rusty blue and two sizes too big. It never got much use.

With another move Angela secured the saddle and there it stood, a thing with alarmingly small wheels and a long stem on which the wide handlebars were fixed. 'This is the lock,' she motioned to a plastic-covered cord. 'And this is the key. You'll need to keep it safe.'

'Right.' I tucked the key into the back pocket of my jeans.

'It only has three gears but you shouldn't need more.'

My large frame didn't compare well to that of the bike.

'You really are an Angel,' said Rori, hugging her spontaneously. Angela looked pleased and alarmed in equal

146

measures. You'd have thought she'd got used to all the hugging by now, it was a part of daily life – consoling hugs, joyous hugs, flirtatious hugs – but then Angela wasn't the sort to attract rushes of affection; contained, reserved and observing, zipped securely into her parka, attending to the world through her round glasses.

'Can we bring you anything from town?' asked Rori as Angela settled back to her notebook.

'I could do with another of these,' she said, raising her biro.

'I'll get it,' I said, refusing her offer of 10p. 'It's the least I can do.'

She thanked me and we exchanged a brief smile.

Only when we'd walked our bikes to the roadside and were safely out of sight did I offer my bottom experimentally to the saddle, which was higher than the handlebars, forcing me into a leaning stance. I spun the pedals, trying to settle my foot and the bike made a creak, obviously more used to Angela's light, boyish body.

'You *can* ride a bike, can't you?' asked Rori, steering her racer in graceful loops.

'Course,' I said, kicking the pedal into another accidental spin. 'It's been a while that's all.' I'd never seen a bike like this before, let alone ridden one.

'God, isn't blue sky glorious?' said Rori lifting her chin to the November sun. I agreed, afraid to look at the sky as I pushed off, afraid to look anywhere that wasn't the road ahead, swerving left to right as the bike gathered momentum.

'That's it, let it flow,' Rori called, keeping me in sight like a duck with her duckling.

The bike clicked and wheezed. Rori chattered about how fantastic it was going to be to have a hot shower, and I did my best to let it flow.

'It's good to see Angela looking brighter,' said Rori, appearing beside me. 'She's been through a hard time, there was a bereavement in the family before she arrived at camp.'

'Oh yes?' I said, an ear on Rori and two eyes on the road.

'She didn't give the details, doesn't talk much about herself. But she's deep.'

There was definitely a closed-off aspect to Angela, she had a way of retreating into herself even when surrounded by other people. Into herself or into a book. A biography of Saint Theresa of Avila, that was something she'd been reading at the fire, and I'd noticed the rosary beads she squirreled into her pockets if she was unexpectedly disturbed. Why wasn't she at one of the gates with the religious women if she was as devout as all that? Even though I was genuinely curious about Angela's dependency on heaven to re-configure global politics, it would have been unimaginable to actually ask her what she believed. She flowered like a winter crocus in Rori's presence, and she got along with Jean and with some of the others like Barbel, who loved everyone without restraint, but she and I had no natural connection. And now, after the journalist episode, I felt she might only be tolerating me for Rori's sake.

'We're nearly at Sapphire gate,' called Rori after we'd been cycling for a few minutes, 'that's where Sam used to live.'

'Why did she move?'

There'd been a wobble when a car overtook us at a narrow passing place, but otherwise I was beginning to enjoy the sensation of freedom.

'Some problem with her ex. And she said the mess was getting on her nerves, no one cleaned up.'

A clutter of tents and DIY shelters hoved into view, all jostling for space in the layby, and I caught the blur of a few placards: 'Hoot if You Hate Cruise' and 'Angry Wimmin'. I knew Sapphire had a lot of Rads and Revs, but wasn't sure what the difference was, only that neither group seemed keen on men. Rori waved hello as we passed, and I remembered Cat, the woman from the blockade, and wondered if she'd managed to escape the police cells.

'Tuck in behind,' called Rori as we approached the main road. The cold air stung my lungs, and the traffic thundered perilously close, but I followed, moving when she moved, stopping behind her at the lights, eyes streaming wind tears.

She twisted around. 'Ready?'

'Ready!'

'Let's go!'

With its market square and well-proportioned buildings, Newbury was more like Hitchin than Stevenage. It said cared for, comfortable, conservative. We walked into it like visitors from a ravaged country, bedazzled by shop windows.

After days of indeterminable vegetarian stews and canned food, we headed first to the bakery. 'Heaven,' said Rori, biting into her second jam doughnut. She was wearing the short red kilt over leggings, her black coat pinned with badges, the pom-pom on her hat nodding as we walked along discussing the outside world. Like mine, her DMs were crusted with dried mud. In the window of Our Price I caught a harrowing glimpse of myself reflected in the top 40.

Inside the bakery, the hot pies had gone some way to disguising the particular tang of wood smoke, a smell like old kippers, which clung to our clothes and hair, but in the newsagents we were unprotected. At least the shop was empty. Rori seemed impervious to the disapproving looks the newsagent kept throwing us as we stood scanning the papers for Greenham stories.

'Nothing,' she said, leafing through *The Sun*. I leaned towards a picture of Princess Diana with baby William. Mum loved the royals. On the day of the wedding we'd sat round the TV with the curtains shut to keep the glare off the screen, and she'd made a spread with a Victoria sponge and bucks fizz. Later, she'd bought every souvenir supplement going.

'God save the Queen and all who pay for her,' remarked Rori. 'That's this country's problem, the everlasting fawning.'

Before they'd agreed on Tessa, Mum had considered Elizabeth. I said nothing and picked up a copy of the *Telegraph* and turned a page.

'This isn't a public library,' called the newsagent from behind his hefty moustache.

'We'll be making a purchase,' said Rori, her tone light and pleasant. She picked up *The Mirror* and I reached for something called *The Berkshire Chronicle*. Leafing through the stories of small-scale fires and golden-wedding anniversaries, I stopped at the centre pages, opened my mouth to speak and aborted the operation immediately.

'Anything in that one?'

'Nothing,' I said, returning it to the pile.

'Oh, here we are, they're bound to have something in the *Newbury People*', said Rori, 'they're fixated.' I tried to put *The Berkshire Chronicle* out of my mind. 'Apparently they've had to expand the letters page because of us. This is from Mr Bernard Blume,' she assumed the voice of an affronted man. 'Dear Sir, Why do we have to put up with the continual presence of these so-called peace women in Newbury when they're hell bent on causing nothing but aggravation to local people. My mother was recently disturbed when two women, who had clearly been drinking, were attempting to. Oh.' She stopped short and frowned.

'What is it?'

There was a pause while she read on. 'It seems they were having a pee in her garden after the pub. Whoops. Ah, here's something from Mrs Cosgrove, she's always in here, let's see now,' she said. 'Yes, I think that's the full complement... waste of public resources... abuse of courts... eyesore... honest ratepayers. Bingo. What shall we award her?' I suggested a personally cooked meal from the lucky dip box, Rori suggested a full body massage from Sam, and we took turns suggesting until the newsagent bristled under his moustache.

'If you don't buy something you'll have to leave.' We were hunched over, giggling. Rori straightened up and walked to the counter.

'Good afternoon. Two Mars Bars please,' she said in her immaculate accent. He frowned, attempting to marry her ragamuffin outfit with her Minor-Royal's speaking voice. Meanwhile I selected a biro for Angela, testing it first to make certain the ink flowed.

Outside, the sun was still making bright shapes on the red brickwork of the town buildings.

'Thought there might have been something by that journalist woman, April thingumy,' said Rori, retrieving a surprise third doughnut from her pocket.

'I don't suppose everything makes it in,' I said, and changed the subject.

★

The smell of chlorine and wet towels took me back to school swimming lessons at Stevenage pool. A lady with damp hair passed through the turnstiles, fresh with the scent of citrus shampoo, her face flushed with exercise, and as I waited to pay, I thought of the dirt collecting in the cavities of my body, graining my belly button, rinding my toenails; the dried rain and woodsmoke seeping through my hat and into my hair. At camp we washed in buckets and bathed at a local supporter's house, a Quaker woman who let us troop through her home in our socks, but I was looking forward to a proper hot shower.

'One adult please,' said Rori into the plastic porthole.

The girl at the desk lifted her face from her magazine and blinked as if she'd just bumped into someone she wanted to avoid. 'Are you swimming?'

The badge on the girl's aertex shirt said Michaela; the badge on Rori's lapel said Cruise is Death.

'My friend and I are paying for a swim, yes.'

'But are you *swimming*?' repeated Michaela. Neither of us had costumes – like all the other women from camp, we were coming to shower, not swim. 'I can only let you in if you're using the pool.' She passed her eyes between us to make sure I was getting the message too, then tapped the window. 'It's on the sign.'

**Customers are required to swim
or entrance will be refused.**

Rori remained pleasant but her tone was firm. 'Could I see your manager please?'

If I'd been with Maggie I might have given her a nudge and suggested we get going, but I didn't want Rori to think I was the sort who buckled.

Michaela tucked her magazine out of sight and disappeared through a swing door, calling for someone called Keith, who arrived a minute later wearing a similar aertex shirt. His arms were surprisingly flaccid for someone who worked in a health facility, and his face, previously arranged in a 'How can I help you' expression, spasmed minutely at the sight of us.

'Is there a problem?' he asked.

'I hope not. We'd like to pay for a swim,' said Rori.

'The showers are for customers using the pool,' said Keith, indicating the sign.

'We are customers,' said Rori. 'That's discrimination.'

'No, that's the rule, Madam.' The word madam was given undue stress. 'If you come back to swim and you're wearing clean footwear, we'll let you through,' said Keith. 'Perhaps you could tell your friends. Thanks, Michaela.' The swing door flapped behind him.

'This is ridiculous,' I said, but no one was listening and Michaela had returned to her magazine. The thought of cycling back to the camp unwashed was too depressing.

'Okay,' said Rori, 'Time for plan B.'

16

A Pink J-Cloth

We stopped beside a set of railings. The previously patchy blue sky had been swallowed by white cloud and the wind whipped a stray thread of hair across my cheek.

'Where are we going?' I asked, hoping Rori hadn't decided on an outdoor pool.

'We're here,' she said.

'Where?'

'Here.' She pointed to the building. 'Hot and cold running water,' she declared opening the door of the Ladies public toilets.

Like all public lavatories, it was the sort of place you wanted to get in and out of as quickly as possible. Small frosted windows reduced the daylight, and the scent of disinfectant didn't quite mask a base-note of urine. A petite lady wearing an overall sat beside the door. She was reading.

'Good afternoon,' said Rori.

'Oh, you made me jump,' said the woman, dropping the book to her lap. The cover showed a woman in a red Spanish dress falling deeply into the arms of a Latin man.

Rori apologised. 'My friend and I were wondering if you might help us.'

The woman took in our generally unkempt appearance, her face settling into an expression of bemusement. 'You living on the common?'

Without obvious embarrassment, Rori confirmed that we were and then explained our predicament. 'We were hoping to use the shower at the swimming pool you see.'

'Looks to me like you need one.'

'We do rather.'

She fanned the air.

'It's the woodsmoke,' I explained.

'That what it is,' she replied cheerfully. 'Well, you better have a wash in here then.'

'That's very sweet of you,' said Rori, as if the woman had presented us with flowers.

'Got something to wash with?' We hadn't, we'd been expecting the jet force of a swimming pool shower to rinse us clean. The woman unlocked a cupboard and pulled out a cellophane packet. 'Couple of these should do the job,' she said, passing us each a new pink J-cloth. 'What are your names?'

'I'm Tessa and this is Rori.' She raised an eyebrow. 'Short for Aurora,' I explained.

'Sounds like a lady in one of my books,' she said appreciatively. 'I'm Vi. Short for Violet.'

After checking we had towels, she returned to her chair.

In the age-speckled square of mirror, the new me stared wonderingly back at herself, her usually white skin sporting a new smutty tan from the campfire, her hair mostly stuffed under a hat with a few greasy tendrils escaping about the ears.

'What a state,' I said.

'Nonsense, you look fabulous,' said Rori, 'grime's very this season.' I unzipped my sponge bag, but Rori's eyes were still on me, 'You've actually got a perfectly lovely face.'

Never sure what to do with compliments, I usually felt obliged to refuse them immediately, as if someone were trying to give me money. But Rori didn't listen.

'Take it from me, you're a peach,' she said, as if that was the last word on the matter. 'Where's your shampoo?'

I handed her the Timotei and she plucked off her hat, shaking out her curls. She'd already dispensed with her shirt and cardigan. I ran the hot tap until the water stung my fingers.

'Don't mind me,' said Vi, who'd been temporarily left out of the conversation. 'You get on with your wash and I'll read. Not that it's much cop this one.'

'Why's that?' I asked, pulling my jumper over my head and praying no one would come in. We had to be quick anyway because I wanted to return Angela's bike on time.

'Well, Fernando disappeared to his father's Spanish mansion just when Priscilla was expecting to marry him, so now she's in a right tizz because she's left her ritzy job as an air stewardess to be with him; anyway, Miguel, that's Fernando's brother, is sniffing around her, so it's obvious Fernando is going to leave the family crisis after his step-sister's funeral and come and take her back to Seville. That dispenser being tricky again?'

Rori was struggling to squeeze a dollop of pink liquid soap into her palm. Vi got up, removed the unit from the wall and shook it. I'd tried to plug the sink with a paper hand towel so I could mix the hot and cold water, which turned a cloudy grey within seconds of contact with my fingers.

'What do you girls do up there all day then?' asked Vi, reattaching the dispenser.

'We talk around the fire,' I said. 'We plan actions.'

'Actions?' Vi repeated, rubbing a spot on the sink.

'Come and find out,' said Rori, soaping the J-cloth around her neck and shoulders. 'You'd be very welcome.'

Vi laughed. 'Me? You wouldn't catch me sleeping out all weathers under a plastic sheet. Central heating and fluffy slippers, that's me. Still, good for you girls, that's what I say. Two fingers up to Maggie Thatcher. Bet she wouldn't want bombs on her doorstep.'

'What's that little splodge?' asked Rori leaning towards my waist.

I'd followed Rori's lead and stripped down to my bra, but unlike her I was holding my shirt to my chest to protect my modesty.

'That? It's my birthmark.'

'Is it! A birthmark.' She touched the tear of brown pigment. 'It looks like a skittle,' she declared. 'A little skittle. How sweet. I always wanted a birthmark.'

'Did you?'

'Yes, it marks you out, makes you special. Don't you think so, Vi?'

Vi glanced vaguely towards the birthmark, then up to my chest, only partially covered by the shirt.

'God didn't short change you, did he love?' she said, whooping with laughter.

My face warmed. Rori giggled, 'It's not fair is it,' she said. 'I think she's had my share.' Rori had neat patties for breasts, the sort that fitted nicely into t-shirts. Mine had a life of their own, sliding sideways when I lay down, flouncing about when I ran. I never wore a bikini or low-cut tops, and even when I wore T-shirts, builders gawped and yelled out, so that I'd instinctively cross the road for my own safety, like a water buffalo evading lions.

Rori had her head upside down in the sink and was trying to lather the Timotei.

'You'll never get anywhere like that,' said Vi. After another rattle in the cupboard she returned with a plastic jug. 'Here,' she filled it up and poured water over Rori's hair. 'Aren't you a curly top?' she said, working the shampoo into a foamy cornet.

'It's my grandmother, she has the curls in our family,' said Rori from upside down.

'*Grandmother*,' repeated Vi, with a wink to me in the mirror. 'Bet she's not best pleased with you sleeping rough?'

'I'm not sure she knows. She's gone ga-ga to tell you the truth.'

'Oh, me and my mouth,' said Vi, sounding anything but upset.

'That's all right. But I don't think she'd mind. Her mother was a suffragette.'

'Was she?' Vi stopped lathering. 'Chained herself to railings and all that?'

'I believe so.'

'Not just the curls run in the family then,' said Vi, refilling the jug.

Thankfully no one had come in so we were making progress.

'You next?' said Vi, lifting the jug in offering.

'I'll do Tessa's,' said Rori, towelling her hair, 'we don't want to disturb you.'

Rori massaged in gentle circles, sweeping shampoo from my neck with the flat of her hand.

With clean hair, I got out of my jeans and wrapped a towel around my waist. It was like getting changed at the beach.

'Honest to goodness,' said Vi. 'What would your mums say if they could see you?'

'Mine would have a heart attack,' I said, which was somewhere near the truth.

When the door went, Rori was buttoning her shirt and I had my leg stretched up to try and get my foot in the basin. The woman who entered was upright, well dressed, with a triangular rain scarf protecting her hair. She quickly took in the scene about her before entering a cubicle. We continued to dress as the tinkle of her urine flow became an energetic stream, finished off with a little pft before the flush. But though we made room at the taps, she didn't acknowledge us, even when I smiled at her in the mirror. On the way out she stopped at Vi's chair. 'I don't think the council would be pleased to hear that vagrants are abusing the facilities,' she said in a cream of Berkshire accent.

'They're not vagrants,' said Vi indignantly.

The woman gave us a backwards glance before leaving. Vi tutted. 'Snooty madam.'

We tucked in more layers.

'Vi, would you like one of these?' Rori said, removing a flyer from her rucksack.

'What's all this?' said Vi, scanning the leaflet.

'It's going to be huge,' I said. Like the other women at Amber gate, I'd been writing letters to form a chain: the letters were supposed to go out to ten women you knew, and those women were supposed to pass on ten more letters to women they knew. I didn't like to say that I couldn't think of enough women to send mine to. Maggie's mum would have liked one, but then again, if I could persuade Maggie to come to the demonstration she wouldn't want her mum there too. In the end I sat around writing the letters so it looked like I was involved, but they secretly ended up in the fire.

'We're planning to link up around the whole base,' I said, drying in between my toes before putting on clean socks. 'There might even be women coming from Europe.'

'Sunday,' said Vi. 'I'll be doing the dinner on Sunday. But good luck to you.'

She tucked the leaflet in her pocket. Rori tried to offer her a pound note for her kindness but Vi told her to keep it. 'Put it towards your camp,' she said. 'Or buy yourself a flannel.' We heard her laughter ringing behind us as we re-entered the street.

17

Brandy

It had rained while we'd been getting washed and the pavement was drying out in petals of damp. I was anxious to return Angela's bike but Rori waved her hand. 'Plenty of time for that. Let's have a drink.'

To get to the pub we needed to cross the market square, which meant passing two women who stood behind a table draped with a banner: LAWE Abiding Citizens.

'Keep Newbury clean. Peace women off our common,' repeated one of them into a hand-held microphone, the sort favoured by election candidates.

'It's her,' said Rori, pointing me towards the tweedy outfit and triangular rain scarf.

'Greenham women a drain on ratepayers.'

Our experience with Keith the swimming pool manager had emboldened me, so I followed Rori towards the trestle table, determined to be the first to speak this time. Anyway this woman was the same as anyone else, I'd heard her peeing in a public toilet. She lowered the microphone and stared us down spaghetti Western style, her face stern and powdered.

'This is victimisation,' I said. The woman fixed her eyes on me. 'What you're doing is inciting hatred,' I continued.

'No. This is an exercise of democratic speech,' she replied. 'You'll find we have public support on our side.' Her companion nodded but remained mute.

An old man with a Tesco's bag shuffled over to see what the fuss was about. He had the look of someone who lived on tinned soup.

'Sir, if you'd care to sign our petition, we're doing our best to protect the town,' said the woman. Before she could say anything else, Rori cut in.

'Did you know the airbase is built on common land?' she asked him.

'I remember a time before the War when you could walk all over, yes,' he said.

'Well, we want the land to be returned rightfully to the people who own it,' said Rori, checking her coat for a leaflet.

'Each missile costs twenty-five million pounds,' I put in. That was a fact I'd double-checked.

'Is that so?' said the man. There were two gullies down his cheeks as if his face had been folded and unfolded again. When I told him my Hiroshima statistic he shook his head. 'Terrible.'

'Meanwhile three million are unemployed,' said Rori.

'And think about how little money pensioners have to live on,' I added.

'This is it,' he said, warming to our theme, 'this is it.'

Impatient now, the woman from LAWE drew herself up like crown prosecution.

'Earlier today I witnessed these women stripped half-naked, washing themselves in the public lavatories,' she said, pausing for emphasis. 'Imagine it.' The old man averted his eyes, too abashed to imagine it. 'Public facilities. Think how one feels when confronted with such behaviour.'

'No, well, that's not on,' he muttered. She held the clipboard before him.

Rori slapped an anti-nuclear leaflet on the table and we walked away.

Most of the pubs didn't welcome Peace Women, but the landlord of The Feathers was an exception, and he'd even been known to drop by the camp in his Land Rover with a donation box. My usual drink was Bacardi and Coke, but Rori ordered brandy and soda in bulb-like glasses and we sat on barstools, sipping in the mellow light.

After reliving our experiences with Keith, Vi and the woman from LAWE, we'd been discussing plans for Embrace the Base, and then playing a game called I Have Never, which Rori knew from university. We didn't have money for more than one drink so we were playing with pints of water. There were quite a few things Rori had done that I hadn't. Hitchhiking. Jumping the fence at Glastonbury. Losing her virginity to a clarinet teacher. Nevertheless, the sorts of things I'd done – working for the summer in an ice-cream van, administering a home perm – seemed to delight and amuse her. When I said, 'I have never had a strip-wash in a public toilet,' we took a gulp of water. It was lovely stowing away under the low pub lights but time was creeping on and I reminded Rori about Angela's bike. She waved her hand. 'Oh forget about that, I'm having fun.'

On the other side of the bar two men waited to be served. Both had American accents, marking them out as off-duty military, and after some puzzling I recognised one as the tall serviceman I'd seen jogging near Amber gate. He seemed even taller in the low-ceilinged pub. His short blond hair was cut clean off his neck and nearly shaven at the sides. The sleeves of his cream V-neck jumper were pushed up, and underneath there was no shirt, only his chest with a few golden wires poking out. He looked like he should be called Brad, or Todd, or Chip.

I pointed him out to Rori, 'We saw him the other week near our gate, he'd been running.'

She glanced over. He and his friend had seated themselves on high stools like ours. His skin was paler than it should have been, but no doubt it responded to sunshine: he was the sort of man who should rightfully be finished with a golden sheen.

'They're all the same to me,' she said.

But he wasn't the same as anyone. I stared. Where did you get jeans to fit when you were that tall? Perhaps he wore American jeans bought from a special shop on the base. He turned his head, directing his brown eyes towards us and I smiled in a reflex, the only natural response to beauty like his, for he was unarguably handsome. His eyes slid past me to Rori, where they lingered, but he didn't smile at either of us.

'They're not supposed to even acknowledge us,' she said. 'They're fed all kinds of misinformation, that we're in league with the Russians and God knows what else. They think we wear razorblades sewn into our clothes.'

A couple of local girls, whose dirty looks I'd been trying to ignore, approached the bar, a real blonde and a dyed blonde, their hair combed and sprayed into flicked styles. The real blonde leaned on the bar as if she hardly knew the servicemen were there – the way Maggie might have done when she was pretending not to notice a man but wanted to make sure he noticed her – then she threw her head back and laughed at something her friend said. Whatever the friend had said probably wasn't hilarious, but that wasn't the point, the point was to make the men look up. I recognised that tactic too. The tall American swivelled on his stool and touched the real blonde on the elbow, wanting in on the joke. It was easy, that touch, an easy American gesture made by the sort of man who could catch keys one-handed or flip a cigarette from its packet straight into his mouth. It wouldn't be long before he and his friend would be buying the girls a drink.

The dyed blonde said something to the group and they turned their eyes our way and laughed. Rori finished her brandy, nonplussed. 'Shall we make tracks?'

I'd wanted to go straight back to camp, but Rori said there were a couple of things she needed to buy, so we agreed to meet at the bikes.

Sam had warned me to be careful of the phone boxes in Newbury, she'd heard they were monitored by the MoD, but I had no other way of reaching home and anyway it was doubtful whether my calls to Stevenage would be of much interest to them. Inside the box I caught my second urine whiff of the day, but at least the coin slots weren't jammed. I rang Maggie first and her mum answered.

'Are you okay there? Looking after yourself?'

'Everything's fine thanks, Paula.'

The radio buzzed in the background. Maggie's mum was in a constant battle to keep hold of Radio 4, but it always slid between Radio 1 and 2 when her back was turned. I had a quick mental glimpse of their house, messier than ours with Paula in the middle of it, glasses on her head, wishing she were somewhere else.

'You're doing great stuff,' said Paula, before Maggie took the receiver, swallowing a yawn.

'Sorry. We had a lock-in last night and I'm on split shifts.'

'Shall I call back?'

'Don't be daft. When are you coming home? It's not the same without you.'

I explained I wasn't but reminded her about Sunday's protest. She didn't sound too eager and mentioned something about the rota at work.

'Anyway, you've got all your new friends, haven't you.'

'Yes, but I miss you.'

It took a little persuasion, but eventually she promised to come.

Afterwards I phoned home, listening to the burr burr, steadying the ten pence piece, my thumbnail satisfyingly clean where it had recently been ridged with dirt. A vague figure appeared on the other side of the door, shuffling from side to side then stomping his feet, more to make a point than for warmth I suspected. I turned my back on him. What was wrong with people, why couldn't they allow other people to live without trying to martial them all the time?

Dad picked up. 'Tessa!' Then a shout off into the kitchen. 'Anne, it's Tess!' A quick scurry while Mum picked up the extension you could never hear on properly. One of Dad's mates had connected it without telling BT.

'Why aren't you at work?' I pictured him on the sofa wearing his house trousers.

'Taking a couple of days off.'

'Days off?' Dad never took time off from the yard. 'Why?'

'Give us your number and we'll call you back.'

'I can't Dad, there's a queue,' I said, glancing at my watch. I had to get back to the bikes.

'Well, they can wait can't they.' Also, I didn't want Mum to ask too many awkward questions.

'I don't think so. Anyway, it's only a quick call to see how you are.'

'Never mind us, what about you? We always have the news on just in case we catch a glimpse of you sitting in a tank.'

Mum cut in. 'Don't be silly, Brian. Aren't you cold at night, love? What are you eating? Me and Dad want to send you some money but we don't know where to send it to.' She sounded het up.

'I'm fine, honestly.'

'What do you do all day?' said Dad.

'We protest.'

'What, all day?' asked Mum.

'Being here is protesting.'

'Don't get yourself in any trouble,' said Mum, 'stick with the ones who sing the songs, don't go having any set-tos with the police will you? Why don't you come down, love. Get a good meal inside you and have your old bed back for a couple of nights.'

I pictured my old bed, my old room with the same posters and the view of the garages.

'How's the tent?' said Dad.

'I'm living in a bender now.'

'You what? Living with a bender?'

'IN a, oh stop being stupid.' I ignored him chortling at his own joke. 'It's a structure made from branches. You bend the branches over and cover them with plastic.'

'Oh God.' Mum's voice had taken a turn for the worse, I knew she'd be following her darkest imaginings, her only child developing trench foot and setting herself up for a lifetime on benefits.

'It's better than a tent, they're very warm.'

'Like a bivouac,' said Dad.

'A what?'

He started explaining that they'd learned to build them in the scouts before Mum interrupted, 'Why don't we come to visit?'

I made a half turn and caught a shadow of the man looming outside.

'They won't let me in, will they?' said Dad.

'But I could come?' said Mum.

'No don't. Please don't.' The pips started to go. 'Listen, I've run out of coins.'

'What did she say Brian? This phone's hopeless.'

'I've got to go, Mum,' I shouted.

'But we haven't told you our news yet…'

I didn't have time to listen to stories about next-door's extension, I had to get back to the bike.

'I'll ring you next week,' I shouted into the receiver as the line went dead.

Before I opened the door, I tucked an 'Embrace the Base' leaflet inside the phone book: protesting wasn't dissimilar to what it must be like being an evangelical Christian, the sort Mum hid from if she saw them coming first. The man waiting outside had a neat goatee beard and a teacherly face. Clean but

165

still clearly identifiable as a member of the camp, I held my nerve and looked him straight in the eye, anticipating more hostility. He took the weight of the door from me and held it open. 'God bless you,' he said. An unexpected warmth flowered in my chest, like the heat of brandy.

By the time we were back on the bikes, cycling freely into the dusk, I'd forgotten about the woman from LAWE and the girls in the pub, I'd even forgotten that Rori had kept me waiting for forty minutes while she finished her shopping. My thighs burned with the exertion of pedalling. It was good to be moving through the chill afternoon, clean and blessed by God, following Rori's red bike light towards the camp. She turned around.

'Come on Skittle, let's see what you're made of,' she called, changing gear and streaking away.

Skittle! She'd named me. Thrilling inside I leaned over the handlebars, powering forwards to keep up, pedalling the puny bike with the full force of my happiness.

I didn't hear the car until it was too late. At the sound of the horn I panicked, swerved violently to get clear, careering from the saddle into the side of the road, the bike scraping and twisting beneath me as I tumbled onto the unforgiving ground.

18

Earache

A belt of auburn light merged into an indigo sky. The previous afternoon when we'd taken a long stroll through the birchwood and admired the sunset, Rori had quoted a poem about the evening being spread out against the sky like a patient etherised on a table. But as I walked beside the bent-wheeled bike, my bloodied knee periodically flashing through my torn jeans, I wasn't thinking about patients being etherised on tables, I was thinking *What an idiot*.

'Mea culpa, Skittle. I shouldn't have made you race,' said Rori draping an arm around my shoulders.

'What am I going to tell Angela?' There was no chance I'd be able to fold the bike back into shape.

'It was an accident. She'll understand.'

I made no comment. With the thought of explaining all this to Angela my joyous mood had deflated along with the bike tyre. Better to get it over with quickly. As soon as I got back I'd find her, tell her and offer to get the bike repaired. Hopefully before Sunday when she'd ride it to mass.

Darkness had fallen by the time we reached camp, and a few figures were seated around the fire. Sam lifted a fork from her

Pot Noodle in greeting, 'All right girls?' It was okay for us to call each other girls, we were taking ownership of the word, but we shouldn't put up with it from outside. Sam said the police called us girls to reduce our status. 'Angela's been looking for you.' My heart lurched.

A woman I'd never seen before was reclined on the log, her head resting in Jean's lap. She wore black, the hood of her cape formed a cowl and her long dark hair fanned out around her. Jean was massaging the woman's jaw.

Rori leaned into her field of vision and gave a wave. 'Hello Vicky.'

The woman flitted her eyes weakly. 'Is that you Rori?' When she looked up I could see she must have been at least thirty, but she spoke with the voice of a little girl.

'I was having a bad time at Ruby gate, and then I got this terrible ear ache but I knew Jean would be able to help.'

'What have you done to yourself?' Jean asked, nodding at my knee with its flag of torn denim. Her fingers were still working in small circles around Vicky's jaw.

'It's only a knock,' I said. The cut stung like knives, and a warm pain had spread from my elbow to my shoulder.

'I can feel the heat in your hands,' said Vicky, lifting her head to regard Jean, who had her half-moon specs on a chain around her neck. 'You have a gift.'

Sam rolled her eyes and took another forkful of noodles.

'It often needs other people to point it out. That's how I knew about mine.' She relaxed her neck again and lay back.

'You might need some Dettol on it,' Jean said, ignoring the talk about gifts.

'Yeah. Nasty,' said Sam. 'Bike doesn't look too healthy either. Is that Angela's?'

'Was,' said Rori. Sam made a *Rather you than me*, face.

'Where is she?' I asked.

'Don't know, she was running around a bit hectic last time I saw her,' said Sam, scraping the bottom of her pot for the last re-hydrated pea.

'Have we got any more of those?' said Rori, meaning the Pot Noodle. She didn't seem worried by Angela or the bike.

'Thought they didn't eat this sort of thing in Poshfordshire,' said Sam. Rori didn't react. 'Just mucking about. They're in the kitchen box – came in a donation, they left a bag of clothes too. It's in the spare bender so you can help yourself. You might pick up another pair of keks, Tessa.'

Rori went off to get herself a Pot Noodle, but I felt queasy enough and declined.

'Ahhh,' said Vicky from whom the spotlight had evidently been absent too long. 'I know you can heal.'

'I'm simply massaging the lymph glands. They're connected behind the ear. Basic physiognomy. If I had some warm olive oil that would help too.' Jean knew everything and was capable of everything – map reading, embroidery, identifying wild mushrooms, lashing beams together – she had remedies for all kinds of problems and assumed the position, whether she liked it or not, of matriarch.

'No,' said Vicky firmly. 'It's because you have a gift.'

Jean asked what we'd been up to in downtown Newbury, so I explained about the swimming pool, the public toilet and the woman from LAWE.

'Honestly, it feels so much better now,' said Vicky, returning our attention to her ear. 'It was almost as if I had an evil spirit in my head.'

'Entertain a lot of evil spirits?' asked Sam.

'No.'

'So how do you know what they feel like?'

I'd never seen Sam being this confrontational with another woman. She pulled Rori's leg all the time about being posh, but it was clear Vicky really got on her nerves.

'What sort of clothes did they deliver?' Rori asked, appearing from the darkness with her Pot Noodle.

'Usual mish-mash. Need something special Aurora? Nice ball gown?' said Sam, with a wink.

'What flavour's that?' I asked Rori, conscious that Sam's class war games annoyed her.

She rolled the plastic pot around enquiringly, as if she hadn't thought to check. 'Chicken chow mein.' She studied the label a moment longer. 'Did you know they're made in Wales?'

'Meat is murder,' Vicky declared, her head still in Jean's lap. 'That was the other thing at Ruby gate, they said they were vegan but there was a woman who kept buying herself frankfurters. She'd eat them straight from the tin for all the world to see. Disgusting.'

There was a pause, during which my thoughts returned to Angela's bike, and then Vicky spoke again. 'I'd like to be a fruitarian.'

'What does that mean?' Rori asked.

'Nuts,' said Sam.

'Fruit,' said Vicky, ignoring the insult. 'I only want to eat what falls naturally.'

'Sounds dangerous,' Jean remarked.

'It's very pure, Jean. It's a way to avoid killing in all its forms.'

Rori prodded the fire with the poker-come-branch. Sam watched her shake the Pot Noodle and unpeel the lid. 'How much did she put away in Newbury?' she asked me.

'Do you want me to say?' I asked Rori, who crunched a curl of dry noodle between her fingers and laughed.

'A girl has to eat.'

For such a slim person, her appetite was astonishing.

'Right you are,' said Jean. 'I think we're just about done.' But Vicky didn't stir, her eyes were shut and she lay in Jean's lap, meek as a lab rabbit.

After her Pot Noodle, Rori went off to sort through the clothing donations. I said I wouldn't mind a look too, but she insisted I rest my leg.

'If I find any jeans, I'll grab them. What are you, a 16?'

'14,' I corrected quickly.

Jean went to fetch the Dettol from her teepee. Sam said what I needed was a nip of the good stuff and went to get her hipflask. I sat in the glow of the fire and made conversation with Vicky, who told me she lived in Maidenhead but didn't like its energy. She used to come to the camp with her friend Astrid, but since Astrid had been transferred to work in Bicester she'd completely changed, her aura had gone from bright green to a dirty shade of mauve.

'I'm glad I'm able to transfer easily,' she said, making herself sound like a gaseous vapour. 'The things I needed to learn would have been inhibited by Astrid. She was limited.'

'What did you need to learn?'

Vicky spoke deliberately. 'My craft.'

'Like what, weaving? Do you make the spiders' webs in the fence?'

She shut her eyes, 'You misunderstand.' Her baby doll voice took on an air of mystery, 'It's powerful. I'm still an apprentice.' Hang on, did she mean *Witchcraft?* Vicky's eyes popped open again before I uttered the word. 'I can't speak about it freely,' she said.

That was fine; my mind was still worrying away at the problem of Angela's bike. But after a silence Vicky's resolve weakened.

'The rules that govern all life are available to be harnessed, you see?'

I nodded and she went into an involved monologue about the intricacies of the white arts while I turned over my dilemma, wondering if I'd be able to put off seeing Angela until tomorrow. First thing in the morning I could take the bike to Newbury, get it fixed, and present it to her good as new with an apology for the trouble. There were bookshops in town, I might try and pick out something she'd like, the life of a saint perhaps. The more I thought about it, the more possible it seemed. I had money in my NatWest account.

Sam and Jean returned with the whisky and Dettol. Vicky talked on about her secret coven and I was having vague

171

thoughts about dinner when a familiar figure approached from the road, crossing the clearing towards us. Angela. I got up – better to go towards her with the bike than wait until everyone was settled and we had an audience, I'd already tasted group humiliation during the journalist's visit and didn't fancy another helping.

It was dark away from the fire, and bitterly cold as I dragged the bike.

'Where've you been?' Angela's pale eyes flashed behind her glasses. 'You were supposed to be back ages ago.'

'Sorry, I had a bit of an accident. But I'm fine,' I said, although she hadn't asked.

'What happened?' Her attention moved to the bent bike. Rori wasn't there to help explain.

'I can fix it. I'll take it into Newbury.'

Angela regarded me. Our breath came out in white plumes. 'You can't get it fixed just like that. It needs to be sent away. I bought it in Germany.'

I had a glimpse of her in another life, wearing a knapsack and searching Alpine towns for a collapsible bike. 'Could you let me try?'

'No. Please don't.' Her voice was chillier than the air. If only I'd made Rori leave the pub earlier we wouldn't have been late and Angela might have been more forgiving. 'Can I have the key for the lock?'

'The key. Oh yes.' Oh no. I felt the pockets of my jeans, front and back. It must have fallen out when I fell in the ditch. I checked my donkey jacket, reddening in the dark. 'I think I must have…' I patted myself down again. 'It probably fell in the bush…'

'Of course,' said Angela.

'Maybe I could…'

She looked at me disbelievingly, 'What, pick it out?'

'I suppose not but, but I could get you a new one.' They'd definitely have bike locks in town.

'No,' she said, taking the bike from me, 'I think you've done enough.'

It was only when she'd steered it squeaking towards the fireside that I remembered the candy-striped paper bag, and inside it, the new biro.

19

Curl up and Dye

At home, Maggie was always messing about with her hair. She'd had it mulberry, ash blonde, raven wing and copper. She'd had highlights, lowlights and a pixie crop. She'd had three different types of perm, one of which I'd been persuaded to do for her – which meant a fraught August afternoon in her bedroom with three dozen vicious plastic curlers, the instruction leaflet in eight different languages unfolded on the bed, and a bottle of ammonia solution that made our eyes water. The perm dropped after two weeks, but Maggie wasn't fazed. Every month she bought a magazine called 'Your Hair' filled with dozens of photographs of models, some made-up like extras from a David Bowie video, eyes crazed with space-age make-up. Maggie could study the magazine for hours the way old men could study racing form. But she didn't always back a winner. There was the asymmetric fringe, for example. 'Get them to do it with the lights on next time,' said her mum. Paula didn't go a bundle on what she called 'Tarting yourself about'.

Post-Tony I couldn't be bothered with my hair, and at the camp it was enough effort just to get it washed, so most of the time it stayed under my hat, curled up like a failing creature. But during a brief spell of December sunshine, it had emerged into the light.

Barbel sat knitting something intricate using multi-coloured wool when she paused to consider me, a finger of yarn poised beside her needle. 'Tessa, in your hair you need some fun.'

I put a hand to my head.

'What about beads?' she suggested.

Barbel had learned to braid hair during her travels and could make expertly beaded plaits. She'd already transformed three other women, including Di, who was now walking around with a head full of grey corn rows, like a lady from Barbados.

'We could give you a barnet like mine?' Sam suggested.

'I don't... I'm not...'

She laughed. 'All right Tess, I'm only yanking your chain.'

'But she could have blonde like you?' said Barbel, laying down her knitting. 'I think you make a special blonde, really.' Her voice was going more up and down, a sure sign of excitement.

'You know what they say,' said Sam, 'blondes have more fun.' Sam's idea of fun involved hurling herself at the police.

I wasn't sure. 'You mean bleach it?'

'Like Blondie,' said Barbel, getting off her hay bale to crouch in front of me, like an artist envisaging her new creation. 'It will be brilliant. With your skin so fair.'

'I've got a new box of bleach,' Sam offered.

'But you'll need it for your Mohican,' I said.

'No, I'm thinking of shaving it off, I've had it like this since the squat, and that was two years ago,' she said, brushing a palm along her stripe of hair. 'Tell you what, let's do it together, you dye yours and I'll shave mine.'

I'd never had the courage to do anything drastic to my hair, but then again, I'd never had the courage to live in a community of women protesting against nuclear weapons. Next to Barbel and Sam I felt ordinary; this would be a way to align myself.

'It change your inside when you change your outside,' said Barbel.

I pictured myself with a shock of ice-blonde hair like a militant Blondie. Maybe I could get hold of a black eyeliner too.

For the sake of privacy, we'd decamped to the patch of ground outside Sam's bender. I didn't want loopy Vicky turning up and going on about animal testing. She'd spent a lot of time picketing pharmaceutical companies and got a violent glint in her eye when she talked about scientists and what they did with their pipettes. Wearing rubber gloves, Barbel painted my head with a white cream, which smelled even stronger than perming solution. In forty minutes I'd be Blondie. But the solution had only been on for ten and a terrible burning sensation was already creeping into my scalp.

I wriggled on the garden chair.

'It's got to hurt a little, like this you know it's working my lovely.' Barbel had picked up *my lovely* from a Bristol woman and it was a favourite endearment.

'No pain, no gain,' said Sam. 'Always gets you a bit. Chemicals.'

With a pair of questionable scissors, Barbel had snipped off Sam's mohican and was now engaged in shaving her head with a disposable razor so that, shorn raggedly, she resembled an Irish girl I'd seen in the newspaper, her head shaved in punishment for fraternizing with a British soldier. I fidgeted for another two minutes while the burning intensified. Generally, I was quite good with pain and not a complainer, but this was something new, dozens of molten needles were piercing my scalp. After another minute the sensation was too excruciating to bear. 'Please,' I said, standing up. 'It hurts, it really hurts.'

Barbel frowned, the Bic razor still in her hand. 'Truly? It's hurting so bad?'

'Yes. Please,' I was lurching around, 'get it off!'

'I haven't filled the water basin yet,' said Sam.

The acid pain flowered into one all-encompassing bloom of agony, and I couldn't wait for them to help me, I galloped frantically across the mud with my head on fire. 'Help!' I shouted, slipping, falling onto the knee which was already scabbed from the bike ride, getting up again and running towards the main fire. 'Help!'

Nobody was there, only two startled visitors clutching an M&S bag.

'Are the bailiffs coming?' asked one as I charged past them towards the kitchen, scrambling for the water canister, bending over, trying to heave its mighty weight above my head. It was too awkward.

'Help!' I called, struggling.

'Give it here,' said a familiar voice. I stood bent over, the weight of the canister lifted as a hand guided me to a patch of clear ground and then suddenly, blessedly, the ice-cold water crashed onto my head. I squealed with pained relief.

'Stay still,' the voice instructed. The water kept sloshing. When there was no more I touched my scalp gingerly through wet hair, afraid it would come away, and straightened up. There, regarding me with undisguised disapproval, stood Angela, the empty canister at her feet.

'Thank you,' I said with a shiver. The shoulders of my jumper were splattered wet. She eyed me sternly and walked away without comment, leaving me stupid and sodden, fingering my tender scalp. I was still standing like that when, out of breath, Barbel arrived clutching half a bottle of R Whites lemonade which she was presumably intending to pour over my head.

'Poor lovely,' she said, her eyes large with concern.

I could still feel the after-burn of the acid charring my skin. I reached out for the bottle and took a vivifying swig. I had new sympathy for victims of the bomb.

★

Three hours later my head was still throbbing. As it dried, my hair had turned an unusual shade of greenish orange, the scalp tightening into a bumpy planet of blisters. Jean said I needed calamine lotion, but nobody had any.

A mass of dark blue sky was overlaid with shreds of papery cloud, a collage which drifted and changed, breaking apart to let through pale gold from the vanishing sun. I'd never known how purely enormous the outdoors felt at night. I'd seen photographs of the napalm in Vietnam, the sky shivered and turned dusty yellow, but the sky recovered. It was hard to think what would happen to the sky if a nuclear missile blasted through it. This is something I might have felt moved to talk about if it weren't for the fact I was sitting at the fire beside Angela. For the last few minutes, since Di had left us to witness by the A339 with her placard, I'd been hoping someone else would turn up to diffuse the atmosphere, but no one had. Di always went at commuter time to remind the world we were here. Now and then there'd be toots of support from passing motorists, but these were countered by abuse. One regular rolled down the window of his BMW and shouted 'Go home dykes!' or 'Get a job!' or 'Communists!' depending on his mood.

Angela was absorbing a paperback of indiscernible subject matter. The last time I'd asked what she was reading she'd told me it was an account of the Mau Mau uprising. I'd nodded and added Mau Mau to the list in my exercise book.

Another painful minute passed. Since the incident with the bike and the morning's capers with the bleach, I'd noticed Angela resume the coolness she'd displayed towards me when I'd first arrived.

'I might go and write a letter,' I said, preparing to make a break for freedom. She marked her page with an Embrace the Base flyer and closed the book.

'Have you got a minute?' Obviously I had a minute, I had thousands of them queuing up like empty buses. 'I wanted to talk to you.'

Talk to me? Angela never wanted to talk to me. What she wanted to do was not talk to me, and she succeeded in this daily.

She removed her glasses and rubbed the lenses with the cuffs of her flannel shirt. 'I wanted to ask you...' she replaced them, 'what you're doing here?'

I didn't understand. 'Cruise missiles,' I said, 'the same as you.'

But she didn't seem to have heard and continued in the same deliberate tone, 'Because this isn't somewhere to come when you've got nowhere else.'

What did that mean? Weren't we all equal? No hierarchy? I remembered what one woman had told me at the fireside, how she loved the camp for its egalitarian spirit, the freedom, the sharing, the trust.

'Women have made sacrifices to be here,' said Angela.

'I know that.'

'Do you?'

'Yes.' I had a twinge. Had she somehow got hold of my exercise book, leafed through and seen a few of the early entries about Tony? But in truth I couldn't imagine Angela doing something like that, and anyway the entries about him had dwindled. He'd be in London now, living his new life. Privately I'd imagined a few scenarios in which we'd bump into each other at a CND rally – I'd be standing on a platform making a rousing speech beside Rori and he'd come up afterwards. We'd exchange pleasantries. Can I give you a ring? He'd ask, his eyes full of longing. I'd smile and lay a hand on his arm. *I'm sorry Tony, there's too much to do.*

Angela was still staring at me through her round glasses as if I might have something to add, but when nothing came she unstrapped the canvas bag at her feet and removed a newspaper.

'What's that?' I said. But it looked horribly familiar: *The Berkshire Chronicle.*

'Take a look.'

My heart pumped as I paged frowningly through the paper, pretending not to know what I was going to find and still hoping by some miracle it wouldn't be there. But it was. 'TENKO WITH MUD' ran the headline in the centre pages and underneath a photograph of a journalist with the byline April McCarthy. It had been an offhand comment, a joke to lighten the mood when we'd first started talking in Rori's bender, but plastered across the centre pages it didn't seem very funny. In the newsagents I'd only glanced the headline and a quote, but now it was difficult to resist the urge to read on, even with Angela peering at me. I skimmed the print, my eyes falling on my name.

'One such woman is Tessa, who escaped what she called an eye-wateringly boring job and a broken relationship…' Broken relationship? I didn't say that '…to come and live at the camp. When I ask about the conditions she described it as…' and then the Tenko remark, along with a few choice details about lavatory arrangements, the difficulty of getting water, baths and so on. Oh God. The article was mainly taken up with information I'd given her. Barely a sentence from Jean or Rori had made it in.

'She's twisted it. When I said that thing about Tenko, it was a joke. I didn't mean, I wasn't saying…' My scalp prickled.

'What *were* you saying?' asked Angela, who knew I had no defence.

In one of the birch trees a couple of birds began twittering an early evening conversation.

'You won't show it to the others, will you?'

'Why would I?' she replied in her flat voice. 'Hardly a morale booster is it?' She blinked at me. 'So, to repeat the question, why are you here?'

I didn't know what to say. 'Because it's right.'

'Right for you? Or right for everyone else who's dedicated? If we're going to achieve our objectives we need structure. Rori and myself and Jean are working out a strategy. To put it bluntly, your presence is a distraction.'

'Who put you in charge?' My voice sounded strained, but Angela's stayed level.

'No one put me in charge.'

'Every woman has a right to be here.'

180

Angela held my eye.

'This is a serious endeavour. We might use subversion, but we're not here for a laugh.'

'I care about this,' I waved my hand to include the benders, the pram loaded with firewood, the Welsh dresser, the bent kettle.

'If you really want to further our efforts you could do one simple thing.'

'What?'

Angela blinked. 'Go home.'

I opened my mouth to speak again but nothing came out. On the second try I found some words. 'Is this about the bike?'

'No.'

'Because that was an accident.'

She sighed. 'I understand. But it's one of the accidents that wouldn't have happened if you weren't here.' The fire snapped. She didn't like me being close to Rori, that was it. When she spoke again, her tone was weary. 'You're not cut out for this. Look at yourself. You could get involved at grass roots if you wanted. But I'd advise you to know your limits. After the protest on Sunday we've got more work to do. Serious work. You're a hindrance.'

'Hindrance?' Despite my best efforts, the word came out with a wobble.

'Oh don't get emotional,' she said, leaning back.

'Why not? What about those keening women, they're allowed to get emotional.'

'There's a place for them. They're angry. We need them.'

'Who are you to say what we need?'

'I'm trying to put this before you so you can understand the facts.'

'I'm not stupid, you don't need to patronise me.'

Angela met my eyes. 'You can go crying to Rori about it if you like, but I'm not interested in schoolgirl games. I'm here for a reason.'

'So am I.'

She took the paper from my lap and folded it into her bag. 'Doesn't look like it.'

I got up then and walked away from the fire. Choked with frustration, I headed for the trees, glad to be alone in their cover, weaving through them until the pale outline of Rori's bath appeared. I sat down on its curved edge and took deep breaths, the enamel cold under my jeans.

If only I hadn't spouted off to that journalist. But she'd seemed so nice. I needed to calm down. Breathe. But the more I tried the harder it became. The achy lump in my throat wobbled up and down like a ballcock, forcing hot water to prickle at the rims of my eyes until finally it was spilling down my cheeks. Damn. Once it started it would be difficult to stop, I'd have to rub my eyes, which would go red and bleary and everyone would know I'd been crying, and Angela would know too. I struggled for a few minutes until Mum's voice said *Let it all out*.

The woods smelled mulchy and green and only moonlight directed me as I wandered deeper into the trees, hidden and protected in the glimmering dark. Since that first morning, when I'd staggered into them and found Rori lying in her bath, the trees were my safety, they afforded privacy and comfort, a huddle of slender giant women, always there to gather round. Were trees female? The moon was female, I knew that. The sea was female. But trees? Perhaps they were gender neutral. Angela would know. Bloody Angela. She was no angel, in fact the prospect of her arriving on a cloud, probably holding a clipboard, would be enough to finish anyone off in their hour of need. I should tell Rori what she was really like, petty and controlling, but then Rori might say something and Angela would see I'd acted like a schoolgirl by telling tales, and she'd be right.

At the camp everyone talked about peace. Since coming here I'd remembered the song we sang in junior infants with Miss McClusky, all of us joining hands and singing in our lispy voices,

'Let there be peace on earth and let it begin with me.' It was a nice sentiment, but living it wasn't so easy. Peace demanded all your energy. Peace was exhausting. It's true, I'd been an idiot with the bike and the hair and the *Berkshire Chronicle*, but Angela didn't know everything, she didn't know I'd been trying. She didn't know about my exercise book, the sentences I'd lifted whole and recorded in case I needed them, '…no prospect of justified collateral damage… the boundaries of proportionality stretched out of all recognition.' Things she'd said about human rights and The Fawcett Society.

The birch went all the way to the fence. I kept walking and paused as the trees became denser, taking a deep breath, preparing to turn back to the fire. But a sound stopped me. There it was again. Whispering. I took a step forwards. This time a giggle, which seemed familiar. Another step.

The branches formed a stiff web, and I strained to see into the black pool which contained the voices. Two people, one leaning against a tree, the other pressed in close. Kissing. A hand stencilled by moonlight on the bark. I moved towards another tree to see if my suspicions were correct and what I saw made me step back. The two figures entwined against the tree were shadowy but still discernable. I stood without moving, watching as the bodies twisted thigh to thigh. I edged sideways and lost my footing. 'Shh,' said a voice, 'did you hear something?'

'It's nothing, come here.' A deeper voice.

'Wait.' Silence again. I stood rigid, the breath catching in my ribs, hardly able to make sense of what I saw.

'You're spooking yourself,' said the deep voice. 'It's a wood, stuff lives here. Come on, less talking.'

And in a teasing voice which made me think of a movie starlet, 'Whatever you say.'

There was no doubt it was Rori's voice. She lay down out of sight, twining a long leg around her partner, who lay on top of her and released a low anticipatory groan. Then all I could see was black.

20

Embracing the Base

A little girl sat on her mother's shoulders waving a paper dove on a stick and below her a woman played a clarinet while her friend blew a stream of bubbles through a soapy wand, sending them high into the winter afternoon. I'd never seen so many women: women laughing, women singing, women chatting, women standing staring or pinning mementos to the fence. Some of them belonged to tribes, you could tell by their clothes or banners, but others looked like the women you'd see in Stevenage on a Saturday, middle-aged women shopping with their friends and daughters. And this was only the small section of fence we could see from our crest of slope. No one knew how many had come, but rumours passed along the human chain like a current, creating new charges of excitement: *fifteen thousand* said someone, *twenty thousand* said someone else.

Maggie stood beside me eating a Marmite sandwich. I'd already finished mine. The sandwiches had been handed out, much to her delight, by two men carrying cardboard trays around their necks like ice-cream girls. I told her the men had come from the crèche tent where they'd been stationed. Along with making rounds of sandwiches and cups of tea, they were tasked with looking after the kids and assembling wax lanterns.

We had our backs to the fence. The ground was still soft. In between us and the trees was a mud path along which a constant flow of women was passing. 'I thought there'd be more police around,' I said, trying to see if there were any beyond the curve of bodies snaking around the corner of the fence and out of sight. It was difficult to get a clear view. The path was puddled from the sleet which had fallen overnight and during the early morning, but now the misty rain had stopped and the sky had turned its usual mid-winter, mid-afternoon grey.

'You warm enough, Mags?'

'Fine,' she said, popping the last wholemeal crust into her mouth.

She was wearing tight jeans, pixie boots and a long coat with a fur hood left over from her brother's Mod phase.

'So what are we supposed to be doing?' she asked, stamping her feet for warmth and speckling the burgundy suede of her boots with mud.

'This,' I said. 'I think. I'm not sure. There isn't a plan exactly.'

We shuffled up to let someone pin a child's party dress to the wire. It fluttered, yellow as the skirts of a primrose. Everyone had been asked to bring something to attach, and the fence had been transformed into a chaotic exhibition of baby booties, photographs, poems, messages and art work. Without warning, someone nearby dipped her hand into a polythene bag and thrust her arm to scatter the contents over the fence and into the base.

'Seeds?' she said, offering us the bag as if it contained crisps.

'Don't you need to plant them?' asked Maggie.

'Life has a way of seeing to itself,' replied the woman, chucking another handful. Maggie turned her back in a way that wasn't entirely sisterly and raised her eyebrow at me, then she plunged into the bag and flung a handful of seeds high into the air with a whoop. Most of them fell back down at her feet. She did a couple of star jumps for warmth.

'Your jeans are too tight, that's the problem,' I told her. 'Loose clothes trap the warm air.' I'd learned to dress in layers: a coat over a cardi over a jumper over two t-shirts over a vest. Some women didn't bother with coats because they didn't dry out if they got wet. It hadn't taken me long to start wearing the thermals Mum made me pack.

Maggie was only half listening, she nodded in the direction of a figure weaving a woollen spider's web into the fence. 'What's she doing?'

'It's a symbol.' Webs, witches, Greenham was full of symbols. 'The strength of the web, connected threads, like a network of women. They like that stuff here,' I added, to show I hadn't changed. Even if I had, a bit.

Maggie was still trying to keep warm.

'Do you want to wear my hat?' I passed her my beanie and she inspected the inside.

'When did you last wash your hair?' she said, raising her voice over the clarinet player, who was now wandering like a minstrel behind a troop of older ladies carrying banners for the Ecology party.

'Very recently,' I said, but she'd already pulled it on with a grin.

More seeds showered our heads. The clarinet player began 'You Can't Kill the Spirit'. By now the songs had become as familiar as any chart hit I might have hummed in the bath, so I joined in with the seed flinger whose voice rose in a church choir soprano. Maggie liked singing and joined in too.

I asked her again about home, and she gave me another run-down of work, who'd been going out with who, her new shift patterns at the pub. There was only one Stevenage-related subject I was truly curious about, but I didn't have time to steer the conversation because a familiar voice came sailing towards us.

'Skittle!' Rori weaved through the bodies, an older woman at her side. 'Skittle!'

'She's coming this way,' said Maggie in warning.

'That's my friend.'

'Who's Skittle?'

'It's my nickname.'

'Since when?'

Rori launched herself at me, slinging an arm around my neck. We always hugged, even if we'd only been apart for a few hours. We were as close as ever, and though the memory of the woods had been bothering me, pinching like a blister, I knew today definitely wasn't the day for that conversation. I'd have to wait and in the meantime live as Barbel did, happy in the moment.

'This is my friend Maggie, from home,' I said. 'This is Rori.'

'All right,' said Maggie.

'Isn't this fantastic!' said Rori. Her face was shining and I heard her voice new, the way it must have sounded to Maggie, polished like silver. Dressed in an astrakhan coat with a paisley shawl draped over her shoulders, and a camera hanging from a strap around her neck, the other woman seemed oddly familiar. She smiled the same smile as Rori. Of course.

'You must be Rori's mum.'

'Jocasta,' said the woman, offering a leather-gloved hand.

It was like seeing Rori in thirty years' time, the same green eyes, the same wide mouth that curled up at the edges as if she were contemplating something interesting. Jocasta was what my Mum would have called an Oil of Ulay mum.

'Wonderful to meet you, Tessa,' her tone was warm and husky and she stressed her words, so that wonderful became *wuuunderful*. 'Auri's told me all about you.'

Had she? The thought made me stupidly glad and the scene in the woods receded.

'We've been walking around for ages, trying to take it all in,' said Rori. 'Incredible isn't it?' Her eyes flicked between us. 'Oh, you'll never guess who I saw,' she said, addressing us both. We couldn't.

'Vi.' she said. I drew a blank. 'You know, from the public loos.'

'Oh, *Vi*. Really?'

187

'Public loos?' said Maggie.

'It's a long story,' I said.

'All this creativity,' Jocasta remarked deeply, stooping to get a shot of the yellow party dress on the fence.

'You don't have to photograph everything,' said Rori laying a hand on her mother's arm.

'This is documentary evidence, darling.' Jocasta straightened up. 'This is history.'

'Apparently there are twenty-five thousand women,' I said. 'Maybe more.'

'Extraordinary,' said Jocasta. 'It makes me so proud. How could you not be moved by all this, all this life?' Her eyes darted around and settled on Maggie as if she were expecting an answer. Maggie turned, surveying the heads of the women who poured below us into a dip in the path and out of sight. Open displays of emotion made us nervous in Stevenage.

'Let's have one of you girls,' said Jocasta, shuffling us together.

'You two be in it,' said Maggie.

'No, come on,' Jocasta directed the three of us into position. I stood in the middle and we held our smiles for the flash.

'Now one of the Greenham girls,' she called. Rori's grip was tight around my shoulder. This time there was a problem. 'Hang on,' said Jocasta, and slipped off a glove, 'it won't wind on.' Me and Rori clamped together, swaying each other from side to side until the camera flashed.

'Perfect!' Jocasta surveyed the scene around us again. 'I haven't found the right spot for my memento yet.'

'What did you bring?' I asked.

'Ahh,' she said, and removed from her pocket a photograph of three suntanned children, two boys and between them a little girl of about seven, all sitting on a white boat made whiter by the blue sky and surrounding water. 'Who's this?' she asked. The girl in the sunflower-splashed costume held a fishing rod over the side of the boat, her curls tumbling around her head, a gap in her front teeth as she grinned.

'Aren't you sweet,' I said to Rori, holding the photograph to show Maggie.

Rori laughed at herself. 'Where was that one taken?'

'Quinley, that summer in '68.' Quinley was their home in Cornwall.

'What did you two bring?' Jocasta asked.

'Tessa and Barbel made the most amazing peace symbols,' said Rori.

'We pinned them up near Amber,' I said. Barbel and I had fashioned our contributions earlier in the week by reshaping wire coat hangers into peace symbols and decorating them with beads and ribbon. Jocasta turned encouragingly to Maggie.

'I didn't have much time,' she said.

'Oh, I know, take one of these,' said Rori pulling a packet of luggage labels from her pocket along with a felt-tip pen.

'To write a message on,' I explained.

Maggie made the face of a non-smoker presented with cigarettes. 'You're all right.'

'Go on,' said Jocasta. 'That's why we're here.'

'Okay,' said Maggie, stuffing the luggage label into her coat pocket, 'I might need to, you know, give it some thought.' She eyed me sideways but I pretended not to notice.

While we'd been talking there'd been movement. Five women in matching rugby shirts, each with an individual letter stitched on the front, organised themselves to spell out PEACE. Other women were joining hands.

'Quick sweetheart, they're linking up,' said Jocasta, her camera flashing as the late afternoon sky darkened. Jean had suggested we all bring scarves so that if too few women turned up we'd link together by holding onto their ends, but there was no need. There were women everywhere, moving along the cramped line to let others squeeze in. Jocasta held Maggie's hand, Maggie held Rori's, Rori held my mine, and I held the hand of a woman in a red coat. The chain fizzed with excited energy. 'This is it,' said Rori, 'it's happening.' We squeezed hands.

It was all strangely quiet, and then a distant cry went up and rippled along the human chain until it reached us. 'Freedom!'

'Freedom!' we repeated, raising our joined hands in the air, moving the cry along the line of bodies. The shout carried to the women around the corner out of sight, distantly echoing back to us, 'Freedom!' Spontaneous laughter and cheering. My throat tightened. The women who hadn't got a place in the chain assembled in a ragged line, mirroring us. The cry moved over us a second time, we caught it and sent it on – it carried towards us again and with a whoop we raised our hands in a mass expression of exhilaration. We were here. It was happening.

A helicopter's blade thrummed across the darkening sky.

'It's probably the television,' said Rori, looking up.

Maggie broke out of the chain and waved her arms above her head with sudden energy. 'They might see us on telly at The Volunteer, Tess!'

Rori smiled with non-understanding, the way one might at a foreigner.

I had the sensation of seeing myself as if from above, through the eyes of the helicopter: Maggie knew me and Rori knew me, but at that moment, I didn't know myself.

Dusk came swiftly. By four o'clock the fence was one long jumble of women, half-lit figures in hats and scarves, their gloved hands clasping fire torches and candles. Groups were silent or talking or still singing 'You Can't Kill the Spirit' into the oncoming evening. Moths flittered around the bushes at the fence, attracted to the lights that crowded like a mass of votive candles beside photographs and poems and haphazard flowers, a collective shrine for the deaths that hadn't yet happened, but could if nobody took stock. Maggie said she was glad she'd come, which I took as a personal victory, but now the temperature had dropped and we needed a fire. Rori and Jocasta had arranged to stay with family friends in Oxford, so it was only Maggie and me returning to camp.

Amber gate had swollen with all the visitors, and by the time we arrived half a dozen different fires were burning, creating an extra cheer. Around these fires guitars were being strummed and tents erected.

'So this is it then, this is where you live?' Maggie's boots squelched as she made a semi circle, taking in the scene.

'This is it.'

She fell silent, recalculating some list of information in her head. Was it more or less awful than she'd expected?

'Bloody hell.'

More. I dug a shallow pit using the trowel we kept in the kitchen, filling the space with kindling and crowning the arrangement with a Sainsbury's firelighter from the store box the visitors didn't know about. Not that they'd go near our stuff, most visitors behaved around the camp with a good deal of trepidation, though today was different, I could see that from looking around. Embracing the base had united everyone and put us on a high.

'Didn't know you were such a girl scout,' said Maggie, watching me work.

'I've been learning.'

'Suppose you've got to.' She lit up a B&H and offered me one, but I was used to smoking rollies. 'Why aren't there any blokes anyway?'

'They wouldn't do the washing-up,' I said, fanning the baby flames. 'Anyway, the women wanted to live on their own terms, because the camp is about creating a female space, somewhere away from the male gaze where women can be themselves.'

Maggie was eyeing me curiously as she dragged on her cigarette.

I found us a straw bale. There was a basket of treated timber nearby, a gift from some visitors no doubt, so I arranged some on the fire. The cold fingered our necks, but soon the flames were leaping and gasping into life.

'All I need now is a cup of tea,' said Maggie.

'I can put the kettle on.'

'No, I'll have one in a bit otherwise I'll need to visit that ditch again. I don't know how you stand it, Tessa.'

'You get used to it. Life is so sanitised outside, you forget what it's like to live simply.' I was about to venture a speech about the benefits of returning to nature when she interrupted.

'Talking of basic needs, I nearly forgot.' She unzipped her overnight bag and removed a tin. 'Present from my mum,' she said revealing a round cake iced with a CND symbol in white piping.

'Great, we'll have a piece before I put it in the store.'

She frowned. 'What store?'

'It'll have to go in the supply box. That's how it works.'

'Don't be soft. Anyway, you don't even know this lot.'

'But that's not the point.'

'What is the point?'

'This is a community and it works on shared resources and trust. All property is shared. No profit or ownership.'

'It's a *cake*, Tessa, it's a bloody fruit cake. My mum didn't spend all afternoon making a cake for some Doris she doesn't even know.'

The cake sat on Maggie's lap like an undetonated bomb. Her brow had grown a vertical crease. If I said the wrong thing now, if I pushed the principles of communality, the fruitcake could go off in my face.

'The thing is…'

She looked at me determinedly. 'If we don't eat it, I'm dropping it in the fire.'

'Maggie…'

'Watch me.' She stood up with the tin and held it over the flames. I sighed and gave in.

'Thank God for that,' she said, easing the lid free. 'Thought that was going to be another Tara Mason.'

I laughed. When Tara Mason picked on me at primary school, Maggie had promptly waded in and sat on her.

'So when are you coming home?' she asked. I shrugged, cutting two jagged lumps of cake with my penknife. The cake tasted wonderful, soft and rich with brown sugar and rum. 'Not exactly fun times here, is it. Seems like the locals hate you, and that girl Angela sounds like a pain in the arse.'

It had been a relief to talk about the Angela episode. Since our run-in I'd been doing my best to avoid her though it was difficult living cheek by jowl.

'I've got other friends. Proper friends.'

'What, the posh girl with the hair?' said Maggie, picking out a glacé cherry and passing it to me. My mind flashed to the scene in the woods; that was something I hadn't mentioned to Maggie.

'You shouldn't judge someone by the way they speak.'

'Not just the way they speak,' said Maggie, taking a bite of cake. 'You can't stay here, Tessa. Imagine what they'll do to your hair next time.'

We laughed. The fire snapped and we sat watching it, picking at lumps of cake.

'Your job, is it better than The Old Volunteer then?' I asked.

'You know what pubs are like,' she shrugged, checking for more glacé cherries.

'Ever see anyone we know?'

If she understood where I was going she was choosing not to. All right, if she was going to make me say it. 'Does Tony ever come in?'

'Tony Mercer?'

What other Tony was there? She shook her head.

'Aren't you too busy with your sisterhood to be bothered about men?'

'I'm not bothered about men and I'm certainly not bothered about him. It's nice to be living among women where the conversation doesn't revolve around them.'

The cold was at our backs but our knees and faces were warm.

'Hey, what are they up to?' said Maggie and I followed her gaze to the borders of the trees where a group of orange women were moving their arms in a sideways figure of eight. I recognised the blonde fuzz of Deeksha's hair.

'Rajneeshees. They visit sometimes.'

'Looks like fun,' said Maggie. 'Come on.'

I didn't want Deeksha to think we were laughing at them, but Maggie had already got to her feet and was pulling me up. 'This is my night off,' she said, 'if there are no blokes around we can at least have a dance.'

We'd been to all the worst clubs in Stevenage and if we got to dance we considered it a good night out. We picked our way across the mud, trying to walk without bumping into guy ropes. A woman and her friend were juggling. Two others canoodled beside their tent.

'Bloody hell, Tess, there's a lot of lezzers about.'

'Shh.'

Deeksha greeted us, still swaying her arms above her head, her hair wobbling like a cloud of blonde candy floss. Balanced on a folding garden chair, a tape recorder played a dreamy mix of pipes and chime bells.

'This is my friend Maggie,' I said. Deeksha smiled and kept dancing, making a space for us on the bracken-strewn ground. Music filled our heads. We joined in the dance, turning around and around, the camp behind us, the fire where we'd been sitting and where a new group had now gathered, huddling together for warmth. I felt a deep sense of the shared nature of life.

By midnight we'd snaffled down a third of the CND cake – I could tell it was a third because we'd followed the white wings of the piped symbol – and were both feeling the effects of the Bacardi circulating at one of the fires. A gang of women with dreadlocked hair and multiple piercings had taught an enthusiastic Maggie one of their satirical songs.

Down at Greenham on a spree
Working for the KGB
Dirty women squatting in the mud...

At one o'clock we turned in.

I lit the fat candle I kept in a jar. The ground was sodden outside but I'd lain down hay and plastic sheeting the way Rori had instructed, so inside the bender it was relatively dry and warm.

'Where's the baby Jesus?' whispered Maggie, swirling her torch. 'You are properly mad, Tessa.' She flopped down, laughing, and picked up a large stone with a flower painted on it.

'That's from Vicky. She's a sort of witch. It's called a home stone,' I said, wobbly with Bacardi. 'She blessed it.'

'She did what?'

'She has this ritual, we had to sit around it and she called in our foremothers and instructed them to look after me. And then... and then...' I was laughing now, 'I had to put my hands on it and pray to the goddess. She said it'll soak up all the bad energy and protect me during the night.'

'What, this?' said Maggie, lifting the stone from her lap.

'You haven't seen the other side yet.'

Maggie turned the stone over and stared at it. 'What's that?'

The sides of my eyes were wet, the sentence came out in a convulsion.

'It's a peace snail.'

There was the happy face of the painted snail, his shell off balance, smiling his innocent smile. Maggie looked at me in disbelief. 'A peace snail?' she repeated. We collapsed on top of each other, the way we'd done when we were kids, the home stone between us, its painted yellow petals on one side, and on the other the snail with his amiable smile, turning it over and over, not knowing which side was funnier.

21

Stripping the Fence

It was a few days after Embrace the Base when they came to strip the fence. MoD police officers, soldiers and local volunteers moved along it with their Stanley knives and bin bags, cutting down the decorations and mementos. Me, Barbel and Rori were there too, watching.

Barbel ran to one of the volunteers, a middle-aged man in a cap.

'Please don't do this,' she said as he snipped a sparkly dragonfly from the wire. 'Don't you think it's pretty? Somebody made it.'

But the man didn't reply. He was steadily filling his dustbin liner like a farm hand gathering crops.

'Please. This belongs to someone.' Barbel put her hands up to protect a damp babygro which was next in line for the bag. 'They wanted it to be here.'

The babygro dangled its empty legs and the man, unsure of how to proceed, looked at Barbel, half annoyed, half questioning. He saw her long skirt edged with mud, and her cape made from squares of old curtain which she'd artfully stitched together. He saw her blonde hair braided with beads and ribbon, poking every which way from beneath her cloche hat.

'Please,' she said, still clutching the babygro. 'You don't have to be part of this.'

'Do you require assistance?' called an MoD police officer standing a few yards away.

The man's eyes flicked from Barbel to the babygro, and he opened his mouth as if to say yes, but then thought better of it.

'No. All's well,' he replied, switching his attention to a length of orange wool, part of a tapestry which had come loose. Ignoring Barbel, he clipped it free and held it in his hand for a moment like a horse's tail, before dropping it into his rubbish sack. Barbel turned to us in despair.

'Don't worry B,' said Rori, swinging an arm around her shoulders and guiding her away. '*A luta continua.*'

'But these people,' Barbel said, indicating the clusters of volunteers clearing the fence. Her eyes were large. 'Why must they?'

'There's Vicky,' I said, in an attempt at distraction. We looked down the hill towards her. What was she doing?

'Come on,' said Rori, and grabbing our hands she ran us down the slope. At the bottom, Vicky was crouched down, whispering in the direction of a police Alsatian. Though she coaxed him, the dog stayed at his master's heel.

'Oh no,' said Rori, 'she's doing her animal telepathy.'

Apparently Vicky believed the military were poisoning their dogs' minds and it was her duty to save them. Nobody at camp was particularly interested in Vicky's psychic abilities but she guarded them with a special intensity and we were given to understand that in some indefinable way and at some deep level she knew the secrets of the universe. The dog, aware it was being stared at, twitched an ear and barked. Its handler gave Vicky a wary glance and walked the animal away. Vicky sighed and got up from the grass, shaking her head, and Barbel, always the most sympathetic in any situation, gave her a hug. We stood together steering Vicky's conversation away from stories of animal laboratories and back to the demonstration and its success.

The fence still fluttered with life, but piece by piece the mementos were being cut down and soon it would be stripped to bare wire. I thought about the photograph of Rori as a little girl, gap-toothed and grinning in the fishing boat. Jocasta would be distraught to know what was happening.

As we stood talking, the figure of a woman in a Barbour neared us. She was working her way along the fence, determined not to be distracted by our presence, and as she got closer, steadily tearing down a cardboard rainbow, a spray of peacock feathers, a wooden peace symbol, our conversation fell away.

'Let's save some of the photos,' I suggested. Hundreds had been fixed to the wire, many of children – seated before birthday cakes or building snowmen, arms around their mothers or hand-in-hand with siblings. We began detaching any we could find. I didn't know what we were going to do with them, but it seemed wrong they should end up in a dustbin sack.

The woman continued towards us, pausing at intervals with her secateurs. She stopped beside Vicky, cutting through a tricky piece of wire that held a paper dove: the bird had already been assaulted by the wind and its wings drooped. Vicky screwed up her face and whispered 'Hex' into the woman's ear, hissing like a cat.

'They used to burn witches you know,' said the woman, raising her head. I nudged Rori and whispered *It's her*. It was the woman from LAWE, the one we'd spoken to in Newbury.

'Hello again,' said Rori, pleasantly.

The woman glanced at us without acknowledgement.

Rori began humming, softly. I hummed too. Vicky joined in, so did Barbel until we broke into song.

> *Are you on the side who locks the door*
> *Are you on the side who loves the Law*
> *Are you on the side which wants a war*
> *Which side are you on?*

We continued to sing and she ignored us until, hands shaking with rage inside their gardening gloves, she couldn't contain herself any longer.

'I'm on the side of the decent rate-payers of Newbury, that's which side I'm on, and you're a lot of filthy beggars. We can't sell our houses because of you. This,' she said, waving her hand about to include the airbase, 'used to be a beautiful common until you came along and spoiled it. You should be ashamed.' Two blotches of fuchsia had risen on her cheeks. She stalked off trailing her dustbin liner.

The volunteers were obviously giving us a wide berth because no one else was around, it was only me and Rori and the wind sweeping across the common. Barbel's cape flapped as she and Vicky disappeared further down the hill to rescue more photographs.

This was my chance. After turning it over and over I'd decided I had to say something about the woods. Me and Rori were friends, close friends, she could tell me, she could tell me anything. Surely it was just some kind of mistake, perhaps she'd even been pressured into it. I took a deep breath.

'There's something I wanted to talk to you about.'

'Oh yes?'

She was stooping to detach a scarlet ribbon from a sagging balloon. 'This might cheer Barbel up,' she said. 'She could put it in her hair.'

I'd been trying to think of a way to begin. 'Last week... last week.' I stopped.

'Spit it out, darling.'

'Last week, I was in the wood. And I saw you.' The words came in a rush.

'Saw me what?' she said, manipulating the knot.

One of the police dogs barked on the other side of the fence. I took a breath, light with anxiety. Something told me I shouldn't have started this but it was too late to stop. She straightened up, coiling the freed ribbon around her fingers.

'I went for a walk to be by myself, to think and…' My voice trailed off. She was holding my eye.

'And what?'

I looked away, embarrassed.

Rori nodded and gave a sigh. 'Ahh, I see. In flagrante with the Yank.'

'What if you get caught?'

'This isn't school. We're not doing anything illegal.' There was an edge to her voice.

But what about everything the women said at the camp about the patriarchal militarist society.

'Isn't he the enemy?'

'Enemy?' she threw her head back. 'No, he's a young guy from Palookaville who joined the forces so he didn't have to work in a gas station all his life. He doesn't know anything about the world. And he certainly doesn't know anything about politics.'

I nodded, but I didn't understand. She noted my anxiety.

'You look shocked.'

I shrugged.

'It doesn't mean anything. A few bonks in the cover of darkness. This isn't Romeo and Juliet.'

A few. How long had it been going on?

'It's just sex. You don't think men have the exclusive right to no-strings sexual intercourse do you?'

But there were strings, there were strings everywhere, surely she understood that? We were all strung together. I thought of the wool webs that were woven to annoy the authorities and tangle the police.

'Look,' she said, 'if I'm to live here in the open I have needs to take care of, food, warmth, shelter. Human needs. It's just sex, Tessa. Just another basic human need.'

'But he's one of them.' I turned my head to indicate the base.

'So? Who am I betraying, exactly?'

'The women.'

She sighed, as if trying to explain to a slow child.

'A woman doesn't have to be defined by her sexual relationships with a man. Don't you know that yet?'

I was attempting to translate what she was saying, like someone with only the basics of a foreign language.

'There are women here who are political lesbians. Do you know what that means?'

I shook my head.

'They've decided the best way for women to achieve equality is to paint men out of the picture altogether.'

I nodded.

'So their decision to have relationships with women is a political decision.'

'Right.' Weird.

'But if I'm attracted to someone, a man, should I deny myself my own sexual rights? Isn't that an anti-feminist thing to do?'

I thought about it for a second. 'Couldn't you just do it with someone who isn't a soldier?'

'He's in the airforce,' she corrected. 'And I've told you, he isn't the enemy. He's a kid from the sticks who's bored and homesick and happens to have a fantastic body.'

I didn't want to hear about his body.

'We're not in a relationship. I don't have to talk about him. For ninety-nine per cent of the time, he doesn't even exist.'

She made it sound so neat, but however she explained it, my guts told me it wasn't right.

'What if the others found out?'

'They won't find out. How would they find out?' She sounded testy. 'You're not going to tell them are you?' Her voice had taken on a note of challenge, the one she'd used with the journalist.

'No.'

'Because it's none of their business. It's none of *your* business either really, is it? I mean, I don't know why you were creeping around in the woods spying on me.'

Her words stung. 'I wasn't, I heard voices.'

201

'And you wanted to get the full picture?'

'No.'

'That's very much how it sounds.' Her face had gone cold.

'No.'

She turned back to the fence and fiddled with a length of fuse wire which secured someone's offering: cut-out newspaper photos of Ronald Regan and Margaret Thatcher with the words 'War Criminals' felt-tipped across their foreheads. The pictures were tucked into a plastic punch pocket to keep them dry.

'Don't tell the others, will you?' she said. 'It's not important. It doesn't change who I am, it doesn't change how I feel about anything.'

'But it's not right.'

She turned to me with a glint of fury in her green eyes. 'Who are you to tell me what's right?'

I took a step back, unsteady on my feet. 'Sorry. I just don't want you to get into trouble.'

'Tessa, I need you to be my friend and forget about this.' Her voice softened. 'Pretend you haven't seen anything. You're not going to get all funny about this are you, Skittle?'

'Of course not.'

'Good.' She came towards me and wrapped her arms around me. 'Then let's forget all about it.' We hugged and for that moment the soldier disappeared. But afterwards, as we drew apart, I could still hear the song going around in my head, *Which side are you on?*

22

Under the Weather

We held hands together, we ate together, we froze together, we got sick together. Or rather, we should have got sick together, all things being equal. But all things weren't equal. What began in the morning with a runny nose followed quickly with chills and by early evening I'd retreated to my sleeping bag. I lay there trapped in the bag, trapped in my body, unable to find a comfortable position for my aching limbs and wishing more than anything that I was at home with Mum downstairs heating soup. This wasn't the place for sick people. Sick people needed to be where clean pillows and Lucozade weren't the subject of fantasy. Every drop of moisture in me was sweating from my skin and into my clothes. My cable knit jumper grew heavier and heavier. There was no mental rest either; whenever I closed my eyes I saw Rori and the soldier, his long fingers knotting her curls. The image kept rising up until burying it was impossible, like trying to push a balloon down into water.

A fox screeched somewhere in the birches. I reached up for my torch, found a near empty bottle of water and using its last dribble swallowed the emergency paracetamols I'd stashed in my jeans. They didn't go down in one sluice, crumbly fragments lodged half dissolving in my throat and released a sour, chemical taste. I left the torch on for comfort and tried to sleep, remembering Angela's matter of fact assessment, 'You're not cut out for this.'

I was in enemy waters, making a new effort to save Rori from the soldier when a voice floated towards me. 'Coming…' I croaked, trying to rid myself of the jellyfish tangled around my arm. I opened my eyes and there was Rori.

'Not well.' The words sounded strange, like someone speaking through a towel.

She felt my forehead with the back of her blissfully cool hand. 'You're burning up.'

'Got to stop,' I said. 'Got to, Rori. Promise?'

The bender pulsed like the enormous jellyfish in my dream.

'Stop what?' It was Jean's voice. A silver-haired angel.

'She's delirious,' said Rori, her outline receding now. Come back. Sorry. Don't go.

'Not right,' I told the Barbour angel before everything went black.

Something wet on my forehead. I rubbed it, touching the stuff there. Wet. Pulpy. Were my brains coming out? Oh God, they were, my brains were coming out! Darkness. A caped figure crouched down putting her fingers in my brains. I cried out.

'Shhhh.'

'Stop it!'

The form in the cape started talking gibberish.

'Please don't…' I said, petrified.

'It's an elixir, it will draw out your poisons.'

'Vicky?' I whispered.

A kerfuffle and someone else crawling inside. 'She doesn't need your witchy shit.' Sam's voice. A disagreement. Blackout. The soldier tangling with Rori's hair.

When I next opened my eyes a sallow light had blanched the walls of the bender. Morning? Afternoon? Rori, beside me.

'You've been out of it, Tessa. You've been babbling.'

'Have I? About what?'

'Me,' she said, brushing a curl from her eyes.

'You?'

She lowered her voice. 'And him.'

I blinked, trying to make a path through the porridge in my head. 'It was the fever.'

'I know. I know that.' She sat me forward, offering a beaker of water to my mouth and I sipped. 'But try to forget about it, okay? It's not important, it doesn't mean anything. Nothing for you to waste time on, all right?'

How could I control what my subconscious wanted to waste time on? 'I'm sorry.'

She smoothed a strand of hair from my forehead and her tone softened. 'Anyway, I'm not going to see him anymore, I've made up my mind, so there's nothing to worry about.' I smiled up at her. 'When I was sick, Jocasta used to read me poetry.'

My head felt tender as a balloon. Rori traced her forefinger over my temple.

> *Four grey walls, and four grey towers*
> *Overlook a space of flowers,*
> *And the silent isle imbowers*
> *The Lady of Shalott.*

I shut my eyes, and as Rori's voice threaded mellifluously through the shadow and half shadow of the looking-glass city, I saw her with her hair spread out in wet fronds floating down to Camelot.

The next day, Sam brought me a Pot Noodle, Di brought me menthol vapour rub and Barbel bought me a posy of wild grasses and sang a Dutch song about a field mouse who finds a nutshell. Rori sat with me and left only when I'd fallen asleep. In another twenty-four hours I was well enough to sit at the fire again, wrapped in a blanket, wearing a thermal hat which one of the women used for mountaineering. Angela glanced at me vaguely when I appeared and said nothing. We ate courgette pasta for dinner, which was at least sloppy enough to swallow. But the yearning for a soft, clean bed hadn't abated.

My head felt gluey. When I closed my eyes and touched my eyeballs they felt bruised beneath the lids. While I'd been sick there hadn't been any encouraging news. A group of women from Sapphire gate had tried to get into the sentry box at the main entrance and failed. Two of them had been arrested. The weather remained bleak, grey-dark as a prison blanket and no one was having much in the way of conversation.

While Angela and I kept our dislike of each other private, tensions between Sam and Vicky had risen in full view of everyone and there'd obviously been an escalation in hostilities since the elixir incident in my bender. Trouble started again when Vicky transferred a kettle of freshly boiled water into Alan, her hot-water bottle, a bedraggled thing with a fur cover made to resemble a bear. She was nearly finished pouring when Sam came slapping through the mud.

'What are you playing at?'

Vicky ignored her.

'Did you put that kettle on?' said Sam.

Vicky finished pouring the last drop of hot water into Alan's belly.

Sam answered her own question. 'No, I did. So we could have tea.'

Vicky pulled Alan closer. 'I was cold.'

'You were *cold*? We're all cold. Tessa's been at death's door. Do you know how long it takes to boil that kettle?'

'Have some of this then,' said Vicky in her little girl voice, offering to transfer bear water into Sam's enamel mug.

'Not from that thing.'

'He's not a *thing*. And he's clean.'

Barbel intervened, 'You know, we can't do this fighting with ourselves or we might as well go with them in there, hey?' She pointed towards the base. But Sam wasn't in the mood to keep the peace, and neither was Vicky.

'You're always sneering,' said Vicky. 'I can see you.'

'With your third eye?'

Vicky turned to us. 'You hear her, you all hear her don't you? Why do you have to mock?'

Sam ran a palm over her shaved head, 'I don't have to, it's hard not to.'

Angela's eyes had left her book. Barbel, unable to contain her compassion for the women standing on either side of her, began singing *You can't kill the spirit* in her Dutch/English accent.

But Sam and Vicky had killed each other's spirit long ago.

'Every night you go on and on about all your witchy shit – karma and potions and energies and we've got to sit here and listen to it. Well it's getting right on my tits.' She flapped her mug in frustration. 'I'm here to protest about nuclear weapons, not to listen to that crap. And now I can't even make a cup of tea.'

'Why don't I put on the kettle for us all?' Barbel suggested.

Sam wasn't diverted. 'You shouldn't have to. And we're nearly out of water.' She turned to Vicky. 'Not that you ever fetch it. Tessa's always at the standpipe. I stock wood. Jean cooks. Barbel plays the guitar and makes stuff. Angela organises everything... what do you *do*?' I noticed Sam hadn't mentioned Rori in the roundup, because truth be told, Rori wasn't that fond of housework, or campwork as we called it. Somehow that didn't matter because we all liked having her near, raising our spirits and dispensing hugs.

'And when someone does put the kettle on, you pour it into that...'

Vicky wasn't having any more. She stepped forward and fixed Sam with a stare.

'You are carrying around a lot of dark shadows.'

She extended her arms pointily in the manner of Kate Bush. Sam shook her head.

'Here we go.'

Vicky took another step towards her. 'I'm helping you.'

'If you want to help me you could piss off back to your witchy friends and leave us alone.'

We were all staring at Vicky, bound up in the drama. She swept her arms in a circle and whispered in Sam's direction.

'Don't start with your weird curses.' But Vicky had her eyes shut and was going into full *Wuthering Heights* mode. She spun and twisted, murmuring an incantation.

Three minutes later she exhaled a long breath. 'I've sent the healing of the sisters on you,' she said, recovering from her efforts like a medium after an encounter.

'That's nice,' said Sam. 'Do you think you could ask the sisters if they wouldn't mind sorting me out a cup of tea?'

Vicky's black eyes flashed in the firelight. 'You ought to thank me,' she said, and vanished into the woods. In the morning a note fluttered from a tree saying Vicky had returned to Ruby gate where the energy was healthier. She wasn't the only one who needed a break. I made a pros and cons list in my exercise book.

Here	Home
Rori	No Angela
Learning	Bacon and eggs
Making a difference	Maggie
	Hot bath
	Warm bed
	~~Telly~~
	Telly

23

Bacon and Eggs

Mum moved about behind the frosted panel of the kitchen door and I watched her for a moment, happily contained inside her life, before turning the handle and interrupting it. She gave a start.

'Tessa! What are you... God save us.'

Radio 2 was on and she was wearing her Eiffel Tower apron. Rows of jars jostled for space on the windowsill and on every other available surface. She was pickling again. She took a step towards me and then an immediate step back. 'What's happened to your hair?'

'Dyed it.'

'What with?'

I touched my hand to my head, remembering I was back where personal appearance mattered.

'You're filthy,' she said, taking a sniff at the air, which to me smelt of pickled vegetables and the tang of lemon cleaning spray.

'Nice to see you too.'

'Oh Tessie,' she wrapped her arms around me. 'Of course I'm pleased to see you.' Her body felt warm and familiar and comforting. When we'd finished the hug she held me at arm's length.

'Are you staying? Have you had enough?'

'It's only a visit. A few days.'

I didn't know how long the visit would be, I just wanted time away from the camp, a night in a soft bed, or maybe three or four nights. I didn't want to admit that I'd been lured home by the thought of television and central heating, that I was too weak to hack it. I unlaced my boots and set them outside on the back step.

'Thought you'd agreed to stop,' I said taking off my donkey jacket. The jars were everywhere, all with the labels removed, their shapes identifiable from having once contained mayonnaise or marmalade: she must have been hoarding her empties for weeks.

'Ah well, here's the thing,' she said brightly. 'It's for Paula next door, she's having a bring and buy.'

'Do you think she needs this many?' If there was one thing Mum loved it was pickling. She did everything: onions, squash, marrow, cauliflower, beetroot, until one day Dad said he liked a gherkin as much as the next man, but there was a limit.

'You should be pleased, Paula's doing it for your camp, because she couldn't get to the holding hands event.'

Pickling with impunity. 'But all this veg must have cost a fortune.'

Mum laughed, which wasn't like her at all – money was no laughing matter in our house. She often shopped at the end of the day when the pricing gun was out, and she knew the best cuts of cheap meat and what to do with them: belly of pork cooked slowly, beef skirt, pork hock. It came as a surprise when none of my school friends had eaten corned beef fritters or mince slices.

'Never mind that, what about this hair?'

'I'm allergic to bleach.'

I moved a bag of beets so there was room to sit down at the table, which was only big enough to fit in the kitchen if you didn't extend the leaves.

'What are these?' she said, sifting my hair and touching the scabbed-over blisters. 'It must have hurt, love.'

'Looks worse than it is.' For a while my scalp had been like bubble wrap. 'Can I have a cup of tea?'

'She could have burned all your skin off. You don't drink tea.'

'I do now,' I said, waving her away from my head. The kitchen felt glamorous as a film set. The radio, the rollerblind with its tulip print, the shining chrome of the oven and the lino floor so clean you could eat your dinner off it.

'Where's Dad?'

Mum raised her eyebrows in a *Where do you think* expression.

'Who are they playing?'

'Luton Town.'

I opened a jar of baby onions and munched a couple while Mum filled the kettle.

'You should have rung. I could have got something nice in. What do you eat up there?'

I explained our vegetarian diet of ratatouille, soup and pasta.

'Proves you can eat vegetables when there's no choice,' said Mum. It was true, I'd definitely come round to them, and even tried a few I'd never tasted before. Aubergine was quite nice, but Swiss Chard didn't live up to its intriguing name.

A stream of pure water shot into the kettle, a real kettle that plugged into the wall and only took a few minutes to boil – a white plastic kettle, so white it was almost funny. Mum leaned against the washing machine, arms folded. I crunched another baby onion.

'What?'

She was smiling. 'What have you got on yourself there?'

'It's a bodywarmer.' I'd found it in the donation box. It had possibly once been worn by an Inuit woman. Or man. I took the bodywarmer off because it was unbearably hot in the kitchen and the central heating was making the hair on my neck prickle.

'How many sugars?'

'None please.'

'None?' She assessed me without the extra clothing. 'Have you lost weight?'

I decided not to mention my flu diet. 'Might have. A little.'

In no time she was shaking the frying pan while the kitchen filled with the heavenly waft of bacon. She cracked an egg into the pan and listened as I gave her an edited version of daily life; a version that didn't include blockades, witchcraft or stand-offs at swimming pools. I thought it best to keep quiet about Angela too or she'd only tell me to come home where I had a warm bed and friends like Maggie to rely on.

I began relaying some things I'd learned at the camp. 'Did you know we're renting a Trident submarine from the Americans? It's a ballistic missile called the D5.'

Mum said, 'Is that right?' But her attention was on rescuing a knife which had slid to the back of the cutlery drawer.

'It can send eight nuclear warheads halfway across the world.'

'Ah!' Mum found the knife. 'We look out for you on the news,' she said, setting the plate down. 'Dad thought he saw you at the hand-holding event but it was difficult to tell.'

'It's in this place in Faslane,' I said, ploughing on. 'That's Scotland.'

'But the camera moved too quickly so he couldn't be sure.'

I gave up with the Trident conversation. At least she'd seen Embrace the Base.

'Didn't you think it was amazing?' I asked. The egg yolk glistened and ran deep yellow when I pierced it. Mum agreed that it was.

'Me and Dad are proud of you for standing up for your beliefs, but you don't have to stay there. You've shown your support, haven't you? And they've got all those volunteers trooping in and out. So we were thinking you might want to come home for Christmas and make a new start next year.'

1983. The year the missiles were to arrive. I listened to Mum as I arranged my last perfect forkful: a triangle of bacon fat toast,

212

a slither of white and a smear of yolk with just a lick of tomato sauce.

After the luxury of a bubble bath I dozed off on the bed wrapped in a dressing gown that smelled of washing powder, and when I woke up it took a couple of seconds to remember where I was. The poster of the ballerina reminded me. She'd been there ever since I was eleven and waking from a long fantasy of a grown-up life lived in pointe shoes. I knew ballerinas didn't have the sort of breasts I was destined to develop.

All the clothes I'd managed to live without were waiting in the wardrobe to be re-discovered. I put on a pair of jeans, which needed a belt to keep them secure at the waist, and a red V necked jumper. I'd almost forgotten it was possible to feel warm and fed and clean all at the same time.

The house felt different, the way it does when you come back from holiday. There was a new rug in the lounge with a pink and green floral design and tassels at both ends. Mum's china ladies, holding baskets or petting miniature spaniels, were gathered where they'd always been in a cabinet beside the television, only there seemed to be more of them.

'Shall we go over then?' asked Mum, untying her apron. I'd said I'd go and find Dad in The Volunteer, where he always went after a match.

'You're coming too?' She hardly ever visited the pub.

'Special occasion.'

The three of us sat in the saloon bar, where the drinks were more expensive but you got to drink them in nicer surroundings. Roy, the pub dog, an old lurcher, stretched out his straggly grey body beside the fire. They already had their decorations up and I recognised the collapsible Chinese lanterns from years gone by. I'd tried engaging Mum and Dad in a conversation about disarmament but it hadn't really worked and eventually I'd given in to the pleasurable cosiness of the pub. It felt good to be sitting beside a fire that wasn't trying to smoke you to death, a supply of neatly chopped logs piled high in a dry basket.

'Thought you'd be drinking pints by now,' said Dad, nodding at my brandy and soda. Dad's epitome of unladylike behaviour was a woman holding a pint glass.

'She's got a friend called Rori. Short for Aurora,' said Mum, who liked the idea of me mixing with the upper classes, even if we were doing it on a patch of mud.

Dad raised his eyebrows; he wasn't interested in his betters the way Mum was. 'So when are you back for Christmas? We thought we'd push the boat out this year.'

We'd been talking about it at camp, and if everyone deserted at Christmas, what sort of message did that send out? We needed to stand strong. Even so, I'd never missed Christmas with Mum and Dad, or Christmas Eve with Maggie.

The fire charred up a log until it cracked a fiery vein with a pop and broke in two. We sipped our drinks.

'Is that a new jumper?'

'Your mum bought it,' Dad said, looking doubtfully at his chest. Mum smiled at the pastel pink and yellow diamonds approvingly. It was the sort of jumper worn by men in golf clubs. 'She's smartening me up.' He leaned forwards to Roy and patted his head, 'We're old fellers, aren't we, can't teach us new tricks.' Roy raised his eyebrows, but seeing there were no pork scratchings on offer, closed them again and gave a deep dog sigh. We laughed.

'You could start having a think about new jobs in January,' said Mum. 'Worked hard for those certificates didn't you, don't want to throw them away.' She meant my typing tests.

'Maybe.' I couldn't imagine going back to an office to work as a secretary.

'Me and your dad might even be able to buy you a little car so you can get about. How does that sound?'

Was this an act of final desperation? They couldn't afford to buy cars.

'You can't do that.' I imagined them lying together in bed plotting the best way to get me back home, and felt suddenly guilty.

Mum was smiling. 'We want to.'

Dad nodded. 'Call it a Christmas present. You could choose it yourself.'

'You mean my own car?'

Dad nodded again.

'Seriously?'

Mum laughed. 'How would that be?'

That would be fantastic. I could go wherever I wanted, drive to the Common. Drive home. My mind began turning over.

'Anyway, we've got some news,' said Mum, setting down her Pernod and black. 'We tried to tell you on the phone, but you were in such a rush.'

'The pips were going.'

From the other half of the pub, a cheer went up. A hatched door separated the public bar from the saloon, and if you were positioned in the right spot you could see a slice of the action. I caught sight of a darts player, and the profile of a girl leaning over the bar.

'Back in a minute,' I said, getting up. The girl was laughing, chatting to the barman in a way I knew well as she pushed a row of bangles further up her forearm, accepting her change. I entered the noise of the public bar, breathing in the cigarette fug, ready to surprise the girl who was now carrying a pint and a half, a packet of crisps dangling from her teeth for comic effect. Typical Maggie.

The introduction to Sweet Dreams came on the jukebox, the synthesised pulsing before Annie Lennox's half male/half female vocal kicked in. Maggie walked steadily to a corner table and set the drinks down, dropping the crisps like a cat presenting an offering, and with her mouth free she bent to kiss the bloke sitting there. His back was to me. The room throbbed with The Eurythmics and the cheers of the darts match and everyone knowing it was Saturday and supping up the joy of it with their beer. I was in place to surprise her. She edged around the table to sit down and as she moved she caught sight of me: the expression that washed over her face was horror. The bloke turned in his seat to see what was wrong. He was wearing the denim jacket with the collar up, and there was gel in his hair. He used to laugh about men who wore gel.

Annie Lennox wailed and the room began to tilt. My legs thought they were back at Greenham, stuck in a muddy track. Maggie opened and closed her mouth, then looked to her side as if she might be about to find me a seat so I could join them.

I made a U-turn, not heading back into the saloon, but out into the freeze of the car park where I leaned over, gripping my knees as if I'd just completed a marathon. A minute later, Maggie arrived.

'I thought, I thought you were at that camp.'

Up close, the tarmac glittered. She put her hand on my shoulder, but I shrugged it off. Somewhere unseen a motorbike engine revved and choked. I sat down on a damp picnic bench and pushed my thumbnail along a ridged line of wood. Someone had folded a crisp packet into a tight triangle and stuffed it into one of the slats. I pressed my thumb down and jammed it further in, like a coin stuck in a telephone box. Maggie didn't sit down, she shifted her weight, one hand clasped to the white flesh of her upper arm, a cigarette dying in her fingers.

'I didn't know you were… me and Tony, it's nothing.'

I focused on the stuck crisp packet and couldn't look at her. The bike engine revved again. I'd only had one boyfriend I'd cared about and she had to take him. She had to have the attention.

'Tessa, we were just messing about…'

I got up and went inside.

Dad was on the verge of dozing off, his face ruddy with the fire. 'Hmm… whaa?' he said, springing awake when Mum poked him. I'd blurted it all out.

'With *Tony*?' said Mum, 'What, *your* Tony.'

But he wasn't my Tony. He never had been.

'You stay here, I'll see you at home,' I said.

They both got up.

'No, we're ready for the off,' said Dad, barely conscious, sacrificing the remainder of his bitter, and despite my protestations, Mum was putting on her new coat. When we got outside she squeezed my shoulder and said I was worth ten of Maggie, but kindness only made it worse.

This was usually Mum's territory and I felt sorry for Dad, shuffling around in the car park, abruptly pulled onto an island of female distress.

'What was your news?' I asked, suddenly remembering. Annie Lennox's voice was still going around in my head, the smog of cigarette smoke and Maggie swaying across the pub, that packet of crisps dangling from her mouth.

Mum questioned Dad with a glance. He shrugged. 'It's spoiled now,' she said.

'What is?' I felt queasy.

'Me and Dad had a bit of luck on the pools.'

'Did you?' Perhaps I hadn't got off the bed yet. Perhaps this was a dream. 'What sort of luck?'

Mum paused for a second before saying it. 'Forty-five thousand pounds.'

24

Telly

Three hours later I was lying on Mum and Dad's bed while Mum got ready for the social club Christmas dance.

'I don't have to go,' she said. She was standing beside her underwear drawer in her bra and slip, searching out a good pair of tights.

'Don't be silly, you've got tickets.'

She ran her hand through the leg of another pair, splaying her fingers to check for ladders.

'You could have a whole drawer of new tights now, Mum.'

She laughed to herself. 'Old habits, Tess.'

It was unreal to think of them having money, to think that Mum would be able to go into a shop and buy anything she liked, rather than returning home to describe it in detail before adding it to the store of treasures she carried around in her head: Axminster carpets, microwave ovens, garden tables with holes where the parasols fitted.

'Why don't you come with us?' She'd started putting her face on at the dresser, closing her eyes so the foundation went over the lids and gave her eyeshadow something to stick to. I didn't make any comment, the last thing I felt like doing was sitting in a room with a glass of Babycham watching middle-aged couples do the quickstep. Mum opened her eyes and caught mine in the mirror. 'Don't waste any more time worrying about Maggie Evans, will you? I'm surprised at Tony.' I didn't want to go over it all again, we'd already spent the last hour talking and there wasn't any more I could say or any more of Mum's kind words I could absorb. I'd replayed Maggie's visit to Embrace the Base and couldn't put the pieces together. Had I upset her?

'Why don't you come along, get out of yourself for a bit. Bernie's daughter will be there, you know Karen don't you?'

Mum assumed that if I'd played in a sandpit with someone aged three-and-a-half, we'd established a lifelong rapport.

She moved on to eyeshadow, dabbing and blending a lilac tide along the crease of her lid with a miniature sponge applicator.

'What would you be doing there on a Saturday night?'

'Where?' I knew where, and she didn't dignify it with a response. 'We go to the pub sometimes. Other women visit, the weekenders. We sing. We chat. There are four women who have a folk band, one of them plays those Irish drums.'

'Bodhran.'

'That's it, they play for us, we sit around, have discussions.'

'Sounds like the social club.'

'It's nothing like the social club.'

'We have discussions,' said Mum, tweezing a stray eyebrow hair.

'About what?'

'All sorts. You and your pals haven't invented the art of conversation, Tessa.'

She lowered her tweezers and faced me with her one purple eyelid. Her lips had been blotted away by the foundation. 'You can talk to me if there's anything wrong. I don't mean tonight, with Maggie, but generally. If there's something on your mind.'

'Like what?'

'I don't know, that's what I'm saying.' She studied my face as if she wanted me to confess something.

'I'm fine.'

'You're not, love. Why else would you go and live like that?'

'We've been through this.'

'Outside in all weathers.'

'Mum.'

I ground my head into the candlewick bedspread. 'You know why I'm there.'

'Tessa, it's not right for a woman to live like that. It's unnatural.'

'Unnatural? It's the most natural thing in the world. Living next to nature, in a community, helping each other. Not like living in a little box not knowing who your neighbours are.'

'I know who my neighbours are.'

'I didn't mean you.'

'I've known my neighbours for years.' She turned back to the mirror and pinched the applicator between her thumb and forefinger. 'All those women together, getting themselves in trouble with the police.'

'They're making a stand, like the suffragettes.'

'Let them make it then; you don't have to get muddled up with them.'

'What would happen if no one bothered to protest? If we let governments do whatever they liked?'

'Life would carry on I should think.'

'It would be like *1984*.' She'd got on with shading lilac powder onto her other eyelid. 'That's not the sort of world I want to live in.'

She blinked at herself, making sure she matched. 'Well you don't have to because it's all made up, isn't it.'

She was assessing her lipsticks, lined up soldier fashion in the quilted box Dad had given her as a birthday present. I watched as she applied one then creased a tissue and bit down. 'When I was your age we were out on a Saturday night in our starched dresses having fun. Being young.' She applied a top coat over the blotted coat for good measure. 'There we were, in our gloves and heels, waiting to be asked to dance on a Saturday night.'

Her shoulders slackened with the memory and she was staring past herself in the mirror, as if she'd gone back there to 1956. She shook her head. 'The thought of those girls living in the mud, got up in men's trousers. They think they've worked it all out, those feminists, but what they need is a nice home and a steady man. Some of them have probably been dumped by their fellas, turned them bitter I expect.'

I cringed. Mum caught my eye in the mirror and carried on quickly. 'Sorry love, I didn't mean you. But when you're young, you should be enjoying life. Why don't you come home?'

'How can I with cruise missiles on their way?'

'Oh it's big talk, love. You don't think they're really going to use them do you? Kids with toy guns making a match for each other, that's all it is.'

'They're not toys, Mum. That's the point. One nuclear war head could kill—'

'I know, I know—'

'But it's not right. And it's a waste of tax payers' money.'

'You don't pay tax anymore.'

She wasn't listening. I tried to remember some of Angela's phrases, the ones I'd written in my notebook. I told Mum the government was using the politics of fear, I told her it was because the world followed patriarchal systems and these included the male fetishising of weaponry.

Mum sighed. 'What on earth have they been telling you in that place.' She turned back to the mirror and blinked down deliberately onto her mascara wand before squirting a dab of Charlie on her wrists and behind her earlobes. Then she glanced at her watch and went onto the landing, 'Brian, have you had a shave yet?'

'Up in a minute,' came his voice. He was watching *3-2-1*. If you listened carefully enough you could hear Ted Rogers recite a brain-boggling clue.

'Every time,' she said to her jewellery box. 'Hoops or pearls?' She held up one of each.

'Hoops.'

She fiddled unsuccessfully until I got up and threaded the stem through. There were a couple of fine grey wisps in her hair, but mostly it was brown, the same as mine. Or the same as mine before the bleach.

'What do you think of this then?' She took a red dress from the wardrobe and held it against herself, swirling the material. 'Real silk.'

'It's lovely.' The dress shimmered around her body as she slipped into it. I did the zip and she slid her feet into a new pair of matching heels. Then she sat down on the bed beside me.

'Now, this is for all of us, this money, so we were thinking, me and Dad, when you get yourself a new job we can help you with a little flat, how would that be? Help you put down a deposit?'

She looked so hopeful when she said it. 'I'm pleased for you Mum, I really am, you and Dad deserve it, but it's your money.'

'Don't let that business with Maggie get you down.'

'I'm not.'

She paused to read my face. 'Once we find you some new togs and sort that hair out, the boys'll come running.'

'The boys of Stevenage.'

'What's wrong with Stevenage?'

'Nothing. Nothing.'

Could I be bought off? Work and shopping, was that what life boiled down to? And what would it mean anyway, a life in Stevenage, back in a pencil skirt moving paper around.

'Give us a twirl then,' Dad had creaked up the stairs and was standing in the doorway.

'You need a shave, Brian.'

'Go on.' He knew Mum couldn't resist. She got up and did a twirl so the red dress floated out like the skirts of a poppy.

'A million dollars,' he said. Mum giggled and told him not to be daft.

When they'd gone the house shut down into a small painful box. I walked around it, as if I could outwalk my thoughts, but there was nowhere to go. The neat kitchen with the jars of pickles labelled in Mum's handwriting; the washing-up cloth folded and draped over the taps, the plastic bowl tilted on one side to drain; the bathroom, where I pulled at my hair, snipping a few strands with the nail scissors, not caring how awful it looked, or even that Tony had seen it like that. I walked my thoughts around the house, and eventually sat down with them.

It was the same old telly. I had to wiggle the ariel at the back to get a proper picture on the BBC but there was nothing on anyway, so I turned to ITV where the end of *3-2-1* was playing out. A young couple had won a holiday to a luxury resort and as the man swooped the woman in a circle, she flung her arms about his neck, her long permed hair bouncing up and down. I pictured Tony and Maggie lying side by side on white sun loungers drinking Tequila Sunrises, saw her stretching out to stroke his chest. It was mad really, imagining them together. He was supposed to be living in London by now, leading marches, not sitting in The Volunteer with Maggie talking about – what? What did they talk about?

Perhaps alcohol was the answer, a way to hold back the slow spread of sorrow that was creeping like ivy over my heart. I poured a tumbler of Mum's sherry and flipped through a copy of her *Woman's Own* while the alcohol burned a warm pathway through my chest. Then I poured another. A tear dripped off my nose and wrinkled a recipe for Boeuf Bourguignon. The credits were rolling, the TV audience on a free night out clapped and cheered as if applauding my work. I switched the set off and the house shrank back to silence. Outside I rolled a cigarette, then came in and brushed my teeth and sprayed myself with deodorant all over and felt ridiculous for calling myself an activist when I was too frightened to smoke a cigarette in my parents' back garden.

I thought about Tony. Could he really have once said he loved me? I was so sure I'd loved him, but standing in The Volunteer seeing him anew, the shine had come off him like a cheap Christmas decoration. He looked like any other lad on any other high street. No, what had stung was the shock of seeing him with Maggie.

At ten o'clock I took out the copy of *An Introduction to Feminist Thought* that Rori had passed on to me. After half a chapter I remembered how it felt trying to revise the Corn Laws for O-level history. I closed the book and lay on the settee, unable to make sense of anything: Maggie and Tony; Rori and the soldier; the difference between being respectable and being bored. Mum didn't call herself a feminist did she, but she didn't get pushed around either, so you didn't have to be a feminist, or call yourself one, to stand up for yourself. But then, why wouldn't you want to call yourself a feminist? What was wrong with wanting everyone to be treated equally? And Sam was right, things weren't equal, hadn't women only just been allowed equal pay? And we'd only had the vote for fifty years. Among these thoughts stirred a new one: Mum and Dad have money, there is money where there was none. That was the real liberation for Mum, it meant she wouldn't have to keep cleaning other women's homes. But what if money was all linked in, and what if Mum wasn't a feminist only because she couldn't afford to sit around thinking about feminism the way Rori's mum could?

Outside the window nothing was doing. Everyone had their curtains drawn and their tellies on watching people they didn't know win things. If the four-minute warning went now, this would be my last experience of life on earth, watching strangers get over excited about a free food mixer. This wasn't living. Not like being surrounded by trees and conversation, being free to listen and think. Jean wasn't stuck at home watching telly, she never had been, she was too interested in what was happening in the real world, and so were Sam and Barbel and Di. Even Deeksha, with her orange clothes, was living wakefully. I missed them, and most of all I missed Rori. I wanted nothing more than to be sitting arm-in-arm with her at the fireside. If I shut my eyes I could see her twist the silver peace earrings as she talked. Her laugh. Her long fingers with the almond-shaped nails rolling a cigarette.

Tomorrow promised only the giant waiting room of Sunday with no distractions other than the colour supplements. I made a cup of instant coffee to clear my head and returned to the book. When Mum and Dad came home from the club well after midnight, Mum giggling as she filled the kettle, I was still upstairs reading.

25

Three Little Maids

'Shouldn't complain, I know,' said Rori, reaching out to investigate a soft thistle, 'but the camp doesn't feel like ours anymore. Does that sound silly?'

I agreed, my arm linked through hers. Since Embrace the Base, numbers at Main gate had increased and with the smaller camps catching the overspill, Amber gate had also swollen: benders sprang up overnight like mushrooms and it was difficult to keep track of the new faces at the fireside. Rori plucked the thistle and used it to prickle my ear.

'Hey, that's not on,' I said, wrestling her off.

Not on. Where had that come from? Like *glorious* and *absolutely*, that was a definite Rori-ism. Since my return from Stevenage, we'd spent every moment of every day together, and in the evenings we curled up, sheltering from the bitter cold, our conversations stretching long into the night. She told me about the depressions that sometimes came over her, like blankets she couldn't kick free of. She talked about her family and asked if I minded not having brothers and sisters, and I explained how there'd been a complication after I was born which meant Mum couldn't have more children. According to Dad, she'd stayed in bed for three days after the doctor told her. Lying beside Rori with the jam jar candle between us, I tried to imagine what it would be like bringing her home to meet my parents, how she would look in our front room, willowy and radiant, Mum fussing around, Dad offering up his chair. I remembered the way Mum had said 'Tessa's friend Aurora,' sampling the name like an exotic fruit.

We paused at a clearing in the fence and peered through to see the GAMA compound – the Ground Attack Missile Area – where the cruise were going to be stationed in a few months' time. The silos were half constructed, six enormous bunker garages, but their completion had taken on greater urgency. Gravel trucks were constantly going in and out. We couldn't blockade every time they entered, but we went regularly to the gate in protest.

We walked on in silence for a while and then, needing something to lighten our mood, went back to discussing the party for Barbel's birthday. It was to be a big, morale-boosting event.

'I scribbled this last night,' said Rori, pulling a scrap of paper from her pocket. I read the pencilled lyrics. 'It's for you, me and Angela.'

'Angela?'

Rori frowned. 'Are you two all right? I don't see you talking.'

The cold war was still on. When Angela had spotted me at the fireside after the weekend at home she'd given me a look which clearly said *Not you again*.

'We're fine.' I pictured her face, so small and pale and closed; it made me think of a shop in sunlight with the blinds pulled down.

We continued our loop through the birches, heading back to camp the long way round, through a cathedral of tall trees overlapping above like fan vaulting, stopping to remark on whatever interested us, hawthorn berries, or the rich clumps of fungi which flowered on a dead tree and helped – so I'd learned

– to break down the wood. The shadows amongst the trees deepened and spread, and through their branches the sky turned smoky dark.

Angela and I were never going to be friends, but if we had to rehearse with each other we'd need to make at least an occasional effort, so I decided to approach her after dinner as she scraped veggie curry into the pig bin. A lima bean shone in the moonlight and a spicy waft rose up in the night air. It hadn't been a good meal; Barbel had added too much turmeric to the pot again.

'So you're going to do it?' she said, still scraping. We'd been talking for a minute or two, but she seemed unable to look at me, as if the sight of my face were of too much annoyance.

'Course. But we need to rehearse.' A slop of sauce splashed into the bucket. I'd never found out if the pig bin was actually for pigs, but if it was, their stomachs must be getting extremely dicky by now.

She cleared another bowl. 'I suppose.'

Was that hesitation? I'd never heard Angela dither over anything. She continued to examine the sludge in the bucket before finally meeting my eyes. 'Performance isn't exactly my strength.'

'But you organise everyone at the blockades. And you do speaks.'

'That's different,' she said, 'that's disseminating necessary information, not singing.' She continued to fill the washing-up basin with kettle water, adding detergent from the slimy bottle which had long ago lost its stopper.

'You'll be with us.'

'Yes but…' She trailed off, unable or unwilling to explain the but.

I shrugged. 'It's up to you.' We could ask Sam or even Jean.

She frowned, like a child presented with a challenge she didn't want but was determined to meet, and I tried to soften my voice. 'Honestly, I don't think there's anything to worry about.'

I took a plate from her, stacking it on the wire drainer. Unlike the lima bean, the plate didn't glisten – plates never got properly clean, only clean-er. Angela held my eyes as if wondering whether to believe me, then cast her gaze back to the scrap bucket. I took another plate.

'It's all right, I can manage,' she said briskly. So I left her to it.

We tied balloons to the trees and looped streamers in the branches, and because the day was fine and freezing, the paper chains stayed intact. The weather had become so cold that every in-breath hurt. We'd prepared food and mixed a mighty jug of punch, sloshing in some of the donated booze, fruit juice and handfuls of jaggedly sliced oranges – most of the knives were blunt. Jean chopped up more oranges and added cloves to three boxes of Sainsbury's Cote de Vin, turning it into something like mulled wine, and I wrapped family-size bars of Fruit and Nut inside newspaper for Pass the Parcel, and found a suitable bucket for bobbing apples. Jean had driven to Newbury for party poppers, hats and birthday cake, but luckily we already had enough festive food to feed a female army. After Embrace the Base, donations had poured in, and gifts arrived from all over the country, not to mention Europe, with at least two famous actresses and one rock star signing substantial cheques.

At three o'clock the party officially kicked off and Helene, a French friend of Barbel's who worked as a street performer, dipped her juggling clubs into the fire and began tossing them in a flaming arc. She could apparently swallow knives too, but nobody wanted to risk her with the wobbly breadknife. The women were in party mood, talking, passing around cake in their gloved hands, and the cider had been circulating for a good forty minutes. Significant inroads had also been made in the punch. A woman from Ruby gate turned her battery-powered record player up high.

Rori, Angela and me watched from behind the clump of trees which doubled as the green room, keeping an eye on the performance area, a clearing swept free of rubbish and lit with jam jar candles, our improvised footlights. I'd managed to fashion us costumes from the donations box which might suggest kimonos if you imagined hard enough. We'd whitened our faces with foundation borrowed from a Goth friend of Sam's, applied berries of red lipstick and made our eyes Japanese with black liner. Angela was so pale already her face had practically disappeared.

'Don't forget the shuffling,' said Rori as we huddled.

'And giggle,' I said. 'We've got to giggle.'

'Exactly,' she said, practising a shy laugh behind her hand. 'Are you all right, Angel?'

Angela leaned against the tree as if to support herself. She nodded. Earlier I'd seen her gulping a mug of Merrydown, which wasn't like her at all. 'Ready?' I whispered. With our umbrellas standing in for parasols, we shuffled on as best we could given the bumpy ground.

Rita, our accompanist, gave the nod and began playing the strains of Gilbert and Sullivan on her fiddle.

On cue, I revolved in a slow circle, head cocked. Rori turned after me. Angela half turned. We sang the first verse together:

> Three little maids from Greenham are we
> Come to say no to the NATO army
> Most of the locals say we're barmy
> Three little Greenham maids.

Rori and I poked our heads coyly from our umbrellas as we'd practised and shuffled around each other in a figure of eight. Angela was next to sing a line by herself and Rita played her cue. Nothing happened. Rita played again. But Angela wasn't moving or singing, she was standing immobile and staring at the audience. Rita looked to us for direction. A woman in the front whispered to her neighbour setting off an uncomfortable ripple. Angela knew the words – during rehearsal she'd only needed to glance at them before she had them perfectly. Rori and I exchanged a look. Suddenly understanding that something was required Angela opened her mouth and her voice came out, thin and tremulous, barely a whisper.

One little maid in the cells is flung.

She was supposed to crouch down protecting herself with her umbrella, but me and Rori picked up our lines anyway. 'Two little maids in attendance come,' we sang, shuffling towards Angela, who stood like a block of granite. 'Three little maids is the total sum, three little Greenham maids.'

On instinct we continued, taking her lines between us as Rita bowed with extra vigour.

Most of the papers find us scary
All very loud and quite contrary
Not quite a ladies' seminary
Three little Greenham maids.

The song continued. Angela managed somehow to assume the final position, the three of us peeking out from our umbrellas, kneeling at different levels.

The crowd clapped and whistled as we shuffled off, and backstage by the tree, Rori reached her arm around Angela in a hug.

'Sorry,' said Angela, her voice still faint. She dragged the back of her hand over her mouth smearing the lipstick berries, then said she needed to get changed and disappeared while Rori and I filled paper cups with punch and seated ourselves in the audience.

'What happened?' I whispered.

Rori shrugged. 'Mysterious.'

When Angela reappeared, clean of make-up and zipped securely into her parka, she didn't sit down with us but began busying about, sorting mince pies onto paper plates and tidying a stack of half-empty boxes which had nowhere to go.

'Dear Angel,' said Rori. 'I don't know if she's a party kind of girl. Some people detest them. My aunt Clara hasn't celebrated a birthday for twenty-five years, but then there's Jocasta, she'd have a party every night of the week if she could.' She pinched a glazed date between her thumb and forefinger before biting it in half. 'If she were well enough to be at parties every night, which, quite frankly, is highly doubtful. My father had to bring her home in an ambulance one evening when she went berserk in one of their friends' gardens and fell off a trampoline.' She continued chewing. 'Skittle, these are luscious, like toffee.'

I tried to imagine Mum going berserk on a trampoline but it just wasn't possible.

Angela still hadn't come to sit down. Now she was standing by herself, breaking up boxes. 'Yum,' said Rori, packing another date into her mouth. There was no love lost between us, but Angela was obviously unhappy, and what was the point? It was only a song. I went over. The cardboard juddered in her hands.

'You're missing the other acts,' I said to the back of her head. She didn't reply. Her shoulders tensed, she picked at a peel of tape and tore it violently along a seam of cardboard. 'Look, it doesn't matter.'

'What doesn't?' She stopped tearing.

'You know, the song.' Now she grabbed at another strip of tape. 'It was only a bit of fun…'

'I don't want to discuss it,' she said, throwing another flattened box on the pile.

'Sam's on next.' Sam had been working on a comedy routine which wasn't for the easily offended.

But Angela wouldn't turn around. 'Could you go away?' she said, and carried on ripping.

By the time it was Sam's turn to come off, the women were stamping their boots and banging pots. There were demands for more, but like a seasoned professional, Sam had already cracked open a beer and was basking in the afterglow, surrounded by groupies. Before we had time to let the cheering die down completely and put the music back on (the woman with the record player only had three records, Leo Sayer, Songs from The Musicals, and Hits of 1980), a woman spoke up.

'I have a poem.'

According to our running order, we'd have a short break then Deeksha was going to sing – before she'd joined The Orange People, she'd been a successful session musician. We hadn't opened the entertainment to everyone, but when the woman unfolded herself from her crate, there was nothing we could do to stop her. Besides, this was a place of equality where everyone had the right to be heard – even if her name wasn't on the bill.

The woman must have been over six feet, with large hands and a head of soft hair, the sort of hair you associated with a baby animal. She stood before us in the height-reducing stance of the very tall, her weight shifted to one hip. It occurred to me that she was about the right height for the American serviceman. The audience hushed. The woman scanned her piece of paper then dropped her arm to her side and began to recite from memory in a voice much louder than anyone expected: *You, with your weapon shaped like the penis.*

Rori looked at me with raised eyebrows.

The woman rocked as she spoke, inching towards us as we stared back, caught in her headlights. All laughter ceased. The metaphors were bold and disturbing. Menstrual blood. Vultures. Somewhere after the fifth verse, Rori took out her tobacco tin and began rolling a cigarette, whispering something about sincere feeling resulting in appalling poetry. I remembered my Tony poems and stayed quiet. She offered me her cigarette.

'Where are your gloves?' I whispered, inhaling.

'Lost them,' she replied, considering her red hands and nestling them into the pockets of my jacket for warmth.

We were arriving at the poem's excruciating climax, a scene of apocalypse, the earth powdered with white dust. After the final line, the tall woman continued to rock on her toes, looking to the horizon as if she could see the poem becoming smoke. The audience clapped and whoever was in charge of the record player acted swiftly because Leo Sayer came on immediately singing, 'You make me feel like dancing.'

The party resumed its rhythm.

'Having fun?' asked Jean, sitting on the seat which Barbel had recently vacated. She and Di were dancing together, the beads at the end of Di's cornrow plaits skipping as she moved.

'Yes thanks.' And I was, we all were, except perhaps for Angela, who stayed on the periphery – what she needed was a book, but even Angela knew that reading wasn't acceptable party behaviour. It was the strangest but definitely one of the best parties I'd ever been to: here I was outside in the freezing cold, numbed through but among friends who cared for each other and trusted one another, not at home in Stevenage watching telly, not reading a paperback in my bedroom, or in the pub with Maggie listening to her latest list of conquests. Maggie. I nudged away the painful memory of her dangling that packet of crisps in her teeth.

After some party chatter, Jean lowered her voice and asked Rori if she'd told me about the Christmas Eve plans.

'I wanted to pick the right moment,' said Rori.

'What plans?' I asked.

'I think now's as good a time as any,' said Jean. Sam and her groupies had joined the dancing and were jumping about with abandon.

'Some of us are planning to break into the base,' said Jean.

'To get to the missile silos,' added Rori. I pictured a wall of soldiers barely restraining their slathering Alsatians. 'There's a double layer of fencing, but we've found a weak section.'

Jean checked me for a response. 'But we wouldn't expect anyone to be involved who wasn't aware of the consequences.'

'Consequences?' I shifted on the crate.

Barbel twirled holding a length of material, winding and unwinding it around herself and Di as they danced.

'We don't know what the MoD situation is. They could charge us with offences relating to the Official Secrets Act,' said Jean.

'We'd be arrested?'

Jean nodded. I thought about prison. Suffragettes being force-fed. Rori put her arm around me, 'Oh Skittle, we'll all be together.'

I looked at Rori, her green eyes, like a cat's glinting in the darkness. This was it, I'd made a commitment, this is what I was here for and this was my chance to be courageous. This time I'd be properly involved, not like during the blockade when I'd ended up on the sidelines.

'What's the plan?' I asked.

Rori grinned and squeezed me to her.

The party went on for most of the night; we stripped the willow, bobbed for apples, played anarchic musical statues, but by midnight things were winding down. Rori and I had been talking about the action as we huddled around a satellite fire we'd made for ourselves, warmed with cider and a quantity of DIY punch. She snuggled into me, resting her head on my breast. A bird clattered in the braches and was still. I was thinking about the action.

'This will be the most serious thing I've ever done. This is something necessary, isn't it, something that really matters?'

She took my gloved hand and held it to her cheek. 'Lovely Tessa,' she smiled, 'best beloved.' I pulled one of her ringlet curls; it sprang back in a quick coil.

A twig snapped in the fire.

She smiled again, cradled her bare hands around my face and kissed me, very gently, and then with greater pressure, on the mouth.

Part Three

*Gonna Lay Down
my Burden*

26

Meetings

'Unfortunately,' Ron Hitchcock rolls his pen between thumb and forefinger, 'there's nothing I can do, Mrs Perry.'

Ron is representing the council's Your Community division, but despite the fact we've met twice before, he refuses to call me by my Christian name. Deciding to hold the meeting here in our cramped office was a mistake, especially on such a hot afternoon, and while we've been talking two dark patches have blossomed in the armpits of his blue shirt. Turning on the fan will create a paperwork tornado. If only he'd at least loosen his tie.

'Even if we had the resources to re-fund this project, I'm afraid you're not grant ready,' he says, moving his gaze to Frieda.

My heart sinks. Grant ready, like market facing and measurable outcomes, is part of the synthetic pseudo business language which gets trotted out at these meetings.

I refill his water glass. 'But we're running smoothly,' says Frieda, edging our year-end accounts over the desk. 'And we've had so much good feedback,' I add, gesturing to the corkboard. He's barely noticed the display we've created around the office walls. The thank-you notes, the photos of happy pensioners and school children.

'I can see you've done good things.' He sighs and sits back with an expression of weary patience. 'Nevertheless there was some reservation expressed about your pedagogic practice.'

Pedagogic practice? I think for a moment and recall Oak Lane, the Head of Year stalking towards me at the end of a workshop, *I thought you were going to discuss recycling*, she snapped.

'Do you mean Oak Lane Academy?' I ask. Ron makes no comment. 'The thing is, with older students, bright students, conversations tend to open out.' She'd reprimanded one of the kids for asking what she called an inappropriate question, and I'd let him ask it anyway.

Ron glances at his notepad. 'As well as nuclear energy, it seems you were facilitating a debate about direct action...'

'No, I wouldn't say facilitating.' The power of official language. 'There was a discussion, one of the students mentioned the coal-fired power station in Kingsnorth.'

'And there was also reference to...' He glances at his notepad, the squiggles unreadable from upside down, '...nuclear missiles.'

I scroll back in my memory. Occasionally someone asks how I got involved with campaigning.

'It's not your responsibility to lecture students about the whys and wherefores of nuclear disarmament, Mrs Perry.' A strand of hair is curled damply on his forehead and I feel a huge temptation to reach across the table and give that pink head a good hard slap. Not to hurt him, just to wake him up.

'We carried out nearly seventy workshops last year, some were more spirited than others, but there shouldn't be a remit against debate? Not in a school.' His expression tells me that whatever suspicions he had are now confirmed. I press on, 'We certainly wouldn't want to prejudice students in one direction or the other... our purpose is to...' I reach for a word, '...empower them.'

Empower. I realise the word has come to mean nothing, it's another entry on the list of jargon, the word Pippa used as she stood in the kitchen after our argument, her reason for taking part in the beauty pageant.

Ron touches a thumb to his brow. 'These are funds from central government. We're compelled to make efficiency savings. You understand.'

A sheen of perspiration glitters his forehead. I look to Frieda.

'We've been working very hard to develop our connections with the local community,' she says, reminding him of the community gardening scheme we've piloted. After drama school she appeared in a high-profile advert for washing-up liquid, and now she gives Ron the full beam of her Sunshine Rinse smile. I run my eyes down the pro-active verbs pencilled along the margin of my notebook: foster, harness, maximise, engage, enthuse, ready to seize on anything which might be of help.

Ron is not impervious to Frieda's smile, and his gaze lingers on her curiously, like a man in a boring shop who's found something of interest.

'You've evidently put in a lot of energy,' he says. 'And that's commendable.' He stops browsing and returns his eyes to me, where they settle with businesslike regard. 'But as you know, these are challenging times. Our resources are diminished and the green market is extremely competitive.' Green market? We're not looking to produce the next generation of happy shoppers. I say nothing. He clicks his ballpoint and tucks it into the breast pocket of his shirt. 'I'm sorry Mrs Perry, but there are other organisations tendering for similar education work.'

Frieda is making one last attempt to talk him around, but no amount of Sunshine Rinse is going to save us now. The meeting is over. That's it. Without our schools and community contract we've lost sixty percent of our funding; we've no reserves to speak of and we can't compete with charities who have actual advertising budgets. But this isn't Ron's problem and already he's buckling his briefcase.

'Oh, Mrs Perry,' he says when we've shaken hands at the door. My heart skips: a sudden idea – he's remembered a source of revenue reserved for small environmental charities in Cambridgeshire. I give him my full attention. He smiles, a genuine smile, slightly shy. 'I wanted to ask… it was you on that make-over programme, wasn't it?' The dream dissolves. 'Only my wife's a big fan. She was wondering, what's Jude like in real life?'

Frieda leaves the door to the street open so a breeze can blow through, and now that its clatter won't disturb our conversation, I switch the fan up high.

'Do you think they'd give me a part in *Me and My Girl*?' I ask.

She smiles, and I do too, because it's better than succumbing to a long despairing wail.

'We could always get the collecting tins out,' she suggests.

We attempt a few more ideas for funding, but our hearts aren't in it. Soon Frieda will be gone, tap dancing her way around the regional theatres of Britain and I'll be sitting here scratching my head alone because there's no money to replace her. We finish off the day's work and I complete the workshop plan for the rest of the week.

At five-thirty Frieda reaches for her shoulder bag.

'Don't worry, you'll come up with something,' she says, gliding a comb through the fine wings of her blonde hair. 'You always do.'

'Do I?'

'Absolutely. You're the most resourceful person I know,' she says, applying tinted lip gloss. Resourcefulness was a habit we developed at the common – rain-capes made from dustbin liners, earth ovens dug under the firepit, the mug tree made from a real tree. But I don't have any good ideas for magicking up cash.

Frieda smacks her lips together. 'That should do it.'

She's seeing a film, and as she tells me about it the thought arrives that I would happily swap lives with her, pop the lip gloss

242

into my bag and whiz off into the evening sunshine. She snaps the compact shut. 'How about you, any plans?'

'Just a quiet night.'

My mind travels the route home, enters our house and there we are, the Perry family, Dom upstairs strumming his bass guitar while me and Pete occupy separate ends of the living room, trying to make it to bed time without inflicting or experiencing fresh pain. Our communication has gone down to the bare minimum, and though we're still sleeping in the same bed to keep up appearances – Dom's brown eyes monitor us over the dinner table – we're only clinging on. Our marriage is crumbling. All day I carry traces of it underneath my fingernails like soil from the garden.

Five minutes later Frieda's gone, leaving a cloud of scent behind her. I sit for a while, watching the multicoloured pipes of the screensaver making and remaking themselves, thoughts whirring with the fan. Something she said gives me an idea.

The collection tins are in the bottom drawer of the filing cabinet, and with my heart beating, I dig one out, drop it into my backpack and lock the office door behind me.

★

The wheels of my bike slice through shapes of bright light and shadow, following the commuter traffic out of Cambridge, past the cream stone of college buildings as they gradually give way to featureless road, a petrol station, a row of shops and then the junction I'm seeking. Two more turns and I've found the cul-de-sac, a slope of compact houses; first homes for new families or last homes for the retired. A little boy in a Thomas the Tank Engine t-shirt runs through a sprinkler and his mother smiles as I pass with my collecting tin.

Number 78 is a well-kept semi-detached with a neat front garden and two terracotta pots of marigolds balanced on the white exterior windowsills. I fumble the gate latch. Lavender bunches haphazardly along the path and three foxgloves bend towards the front door, which is half panelled with smoky glass. On the letterbox a discreet handwritten sign reads No Junk Mail Please. The sun has dipped behind the house and my arms feel weak, as if they're carrying something much heavier than a plastic box with Easy Green stickered across the front.

The doorbell's three harmonic notes are loud, they send a chime of alarm through my arm and into my chest and all at once I have an urge to flee. In a bid for distraction I begin to count the petals of a marigold. Fifteen, twenty-five, thirty-two, and no one comes. Better not to know, to turn back and get on the bike in the low evening sunshine and cycle away. But then a blurred shape appears behind the glass like the shadow of a fish underwater and the shadow swells until the door swings open.

She wipes her hands on the tea towel slung over her shoulder and wary regard softens as she sees the tin, the tin which explains my presence on her doorstep. I press it forward. 'I'm collecting for a charity. We're called Easy Green.' If it is her, has Pete told her any of this? Along with a denim skirt, she's wearing a washed-out pink vest, and without a bra her breasts make the shape of two shallow bells. She's what, five years younger than me? This knowledge pulses through my head followed by *Perhaps it isn't her at all, perhaps it's her mother.*

If she knows who I am there's no indication because she's looking at me with something that borders on sympathy, encouraging me to speak, the way people encourage the shy or the afflicted, trying to draw them out. She nods. 'Oh yes?' An Irish accent. She's Irish. Why is this surprising? I begin to recite some information about the charity, an automatic spiel. Her skin is Celtic, naturally fair, but she's trained it to withstand the sun and a spray of freckles decorate her shoulders. There are whispers of grey coming through her dark brown hair. Her face, although pleasant, is unremarkable, nothing like the face I've imagined with its soft pout and coltish eyelashes.

'So you visit local schools? I've taught at quite a few in this area.' She says this brightly because it links us; it gives us something in common. That immediate intimacy so often found in female conversation with its undertone of *Like me, I'm no threat.*

Then it is her. It is almost funny, so far removed is she from the woman who's been sashaying through my head. Her eyes are a greenish grey. Her mouth... what is this mouth like, the mouth that's been pressed to my husband's, the mouth that's tasted his skin? It is a mouth. It is an ordinary mouth, the lips a little thin.

My thoughts are escaping in all directions, I'd gathered them tightly but now they're a clutch of balloons rising and separating, and she gives me that sympathetic smile again.

'Hang on a tick. I'll get my purse.' She dips back into the house. Her feet are bare and the toenails painted with a polish the colour of aubergines. She returns and drops a pound coin into the box. The money makes a hollow rattle. 'Are the neighbours not feeling generous today?'

'I've only just started.'

'Oh right.' She nods, puzzled by my method of beginning a collection in the middle of the street.

'It's a nice road. Have you lived here long?' I ask wondering if she has cooked for Pete, that tea towel slung over the shoulder.

'Um... about four years now.'

'And you like it?'

'Sure.' She is holding the purse. 'It's very friendly. You'll find that as you go around.' She checks behind her, as if her name has been called. Where is the kitchen? I would like to go inside and lift the lids of her pans, investigate her fridge to discover her tastes, make my way through the rest of the house to pick up the photographs in their frames, read the spines of her books, sort through her wardrobe, her bedside table, examine the contents of her bathroom cabinet. And I want to tell her I have a right. I need to know. And she needs to know too, about the insomnia, the effort it takes to drag through each day, to get out of bed and into the shower and into the office and the panicky feeling which never quite disappears, which follows you everywhere, as if you're about to speak to a thousand people.

She's taken half a step back.

'Where do you teach?'

'I'm private tutoring just now,' she says. 'Exam season. All those anxious parents.'

Does she have children of her own? She shifts her weight from one hip to the other and now her face is guarded – she wants to go, to step back into that calm life she has for herself behind the front door, where other men's wives do not turn up unexpectedly, she wants to slip back there free as a fish. She has a hand on the door, swinging it ever so gently when a black cat appears and winds around her legs. 'Oh,' she half laughs, the sudden flash of velvet against bare skin.

'He probably wants feeding,' she says, stooping to run a hand along the animal's body. 'Eat eat eat, that's all you do,' she says fondly. This is my cue to go.

My heart speeds. I part my lips. All I have to do is open my mouth and out it will come, the inconvenient truth, those words which will alter the course of her evening and the course of mine, and whatever is cooking inside that mysterious kitchen will burn. *I'm Pete's wife.* The roses on the wallpaper at daybreak. Our shoes still muddled in a heap by the wardrobe, just as they were a month ago when I didn't know she existed, when her naked body wasn't settled between us. She straightens up and we make eye contact. Her face is expectant. And I want to ask her *Do you know what this is like? Do you know what you've done?*

I begin, 'Do you…?'

She leans forwards, the better to express her empathy.

'Do you want us to put you on our mailing list?'

She holds her hand up in refusal. 'No. If you don't mind. I can hardly keep up with the mail I receive.' She smiles for the last time, wishes me a good evening and closes the door.

27

Silent Night

At half-past four in the morning, I stood arm-in-arm with Rori. We were waiting our turn to climb a collapsible aluminium ladder and go into the base. Three days had passed since she'd kissed me and in that time neither of us had spoken about it, nor had we kissed each other again, but I'd replayed the kiss a hundred times in my head, trying to remember what had been in her eyes when it happened. I wanted to talk to her, to know what it meant, although I thought I knew already. And anyway, talking about it in those terms might cheapen it, whatever it was. What was it? Had I fallen in love with her? Even whispering the idea made me uncomfortable, and yet what else could this be?

I thought about her all the time, I thought about her and I thought about the destruction of the world, and in my mind the two had become connected, because if there was no world there would be no Rori. In a dream, I'd knelt beside her dead body – which was perfectly intact after a nuclear blast, white and limpid like the Lady of Shalott's – and woken with a start to find her lying safe beside me. Stretching out a hand I'd touched her cheek in the half light while she slept. If I felt this way, then surely she felt the same? She had been the one to lean forward, to cradle my face and press her mouth against mine. And if she hadn't kissed me again perhaps it was because she was waiting for me to kiss her? I would. I wanted to. First we just needed to scale the nine-foot-high fence.

There were at least forty of us taking part in the action, though we couldn't see the other women clearly and only caught snatches of excited whispers and nervous movements in the birch scrub. I could hear Rori's breathing. All day I'd been questioning my courage, but she'd calmed me, and now we were here, poised in the darkness, a gauzy darkness relieved by torches beamed towards the ladders.

'Your wings are crooked,' I said, adjusting them.

She checked behind her. 'Thanks, Skittle.'

I rearranged the tinsel fixed around my beanie. It was Christmas Eve and we'd decided to make the action celebratory. Someone had sourced various bits of festive costume along with a bag of angel wings. In addition, we were all wearing tabards decorated with luminous peace signs to identify us as demonstrators – rather than terrorists – in case things got hairy. Things *getting hairy* was Jean's euphemism for *In case we get shot at*. Getting shot was the main thing I was trying not to think about.

The woman setting up the ladder was called Jenny and she worked in the outside world as a paramedic. She was a safe pair of hands, at least. At the top she unfurled a roll of carpet rescued from Newbury dump which she laid protectively over the double coil of barbed wire, and there she balanced like a circus artist perched on a high wire, her sparkly deely boppers catching the moonlight as another ladder was offered up. This second ladder she lowered to the other side of the fence so we could manage the descent. A few seconds later came a thud and crackle as she landed.

'The ground's not too bad,' she said, her face to the wire. 'You've got to be quick.'

We'd decided to keep a chain going – each woman who went over stayed to help the woman following after. Two other ladders

248

went up along the fence. I stood behind Rori in the bracken waiting my turn, a fine spray of rain coming down on our faces out of the black night, like mist from a sprinkler.

Sam appeared beside us and performed a clunky pirouette, she'd dressed as a Christmas fairy for the occasion, a pink ballet tutu pulled over her army trousers.

'How are you going to get over in that?' I said.

'I'm not taking it off. I got it specially,' she said, giving a curtsy. We began giggling. After a whispered discussion we agreed Sam should remove the skirt, throw it over the fence and put it on when she reached the other side. A woman with a misshapen silhouette ascended the ladder.

'What's she got on her arms?' I said.

'Cut-up tyres,' replied Rori.

'Why?'

'In case of police dogs,' said Sam through the shadows. 'We'll be all right. I've got a few aniseed balls in my pocket, Alsatians hate them.'

'We won't have time to feed them sweets,' I said. 'Hey, we should have got tyre shoes. Boing. We could have bounced straight over.'

It wasn't funny, but the tension had made us dizzy with anxiety, and I was still snorting alongside Rori when I heard another whispered voice.

'What's wrong with her?' I straightened up to see Angela, unadorned except for her tabard, staring at me.

'Nothing,' I replied, straight-faced.

She gave me a sharp look and pushed her specs up her nose. 'Once we're over we need to stay low and wait until we're together, then we can run forwards,' she said. 'Does everyone have the number of the solicitor?'

Everyone had. I'd written the digits in blue biro on the backs of both hands.

'This is it,' said Rori, drawing us into a triangular hug. I had my arm around Angela's bony shoulder, the feel of her, so light, almost snappable. She and I drew away from each other as quickly we could.

The queue was moving. It reminded me of the first time I'd waited on the ladder at Stevenage swimming pool to jump off the high board, trapped at the top, no way of going down again, heavy splashes as the invisible bodies fell forwards. I followed Rori as she climbed. Despite the beams from the torchlight, it was nearly impossible to discern shapes with any clarity. At the top I cocked my leg over the carpet, clinging and wobbling, no idea where to put my feet.

'Swing your left foot,' Rori whispered from below. I felt my way with the toe of my boot, found the rung, descended halfway and waited to guide the next woman down. Through the shadows a hat appeared and then Angela's white face. She got to the top easily enough and then manoeuvred her leg and halted with a muffled Ouch.

'What is it?'

She was lying on her stomach, one leg behind her on the ladder, the other caught in a prickle of barbed wire.

'If you stay still, I can…' I climbed back up and put my hand on her leg.

The wire had twisted in the material of her trousers and she was stuck. We were supposed to help each other. 'Let me,' I whispered, and tried to lift her leg, but she forced free and with a rip, her trouser tore. She wriggled to reposition herself for the descent. I gave up and went to crouch in the bracken with the others, our tinsel and deely boppers springing from the undergrowth.

More flightless angels thudded to the ground, bouncing to their feet and hugging. They obviously hadn't heard Angela's advice to keep low in the bracken, or were too excited to remember.

'Is this everyone from Amber?' said Jean from somewhere close by.

'Not quite,' I said. The small round figure of Di emerged over the fence. 'Tessa!'

The voice came from behind and I jumped as Sam rustled out of the darkness in her tutu. 'I can't get the thing done up at the back.' Hysterical all over again, we took turns fiddling with the zip and hooks.

One minute I was grappling to get Sam's tutu back on, and the next everyone was running. I didn't hear a command, we simply went with the flow of movement, my hand in Rori's, her hand in Angela's, running out of the trees, tack-tacking across soft ground, and then over the runway towards the ghostly outline of the silos. Up ahead, the first women had reached them and were scaling their sides. Mounds of concrete, they were only half-built, with steel rods sticking out of them like spoons from giant upturned Christmas puddings. We followed the women and then we were clambering onto the silos too. My boots were still gluey with mud and I leaned forward for balance, scrambling to get up, Rori just behind me, up and up until we must have been nearly forty feet high. And then we were standing on the surface, rubbled like a moon crater, the black airfield spread out below.

Rori reached to hug me, her paper wings beating as we jumped up and down. Everyone was embracing, elated. More women were making the ascent. We offered our help. Hands gripping hands. More hugs. A high-pitched ululation, that red-Indian noise I'd heard on my first night and now understood to be defiance. The nearly full moon drifted from behind a cloud. We were standing on top of the place where the missiles would be stored; a drawbridge door was in construction on one side of the silo for the purpose of letting them in. In the freezing air we waited for everyone to gather.

Someone stepped forwards and asked to sing. Di.

She began in a good steady voice, the only sound but for the crackling of plastic sheets harnessed to the silo. We instinctively held hands while the words rang out, *All is calm, all is bright.* Stars picked at the black sky. The woman beside me cried softly. The magnitude of where we were and what we were doing swelled between us and when Di finished singing it was a moment before anyone spoke. Then a few women cheered and clapped, their gloves deadening the applause. Barbel thrust her arms out. 'We're here!' she called 'Peace! Happy Christmas!' We were laughing. 'Happy Christmas!' we shouted.

After that a woman from the folk group started thrumming a bodhran and Barbel, who was now well practised, played her recorder while Jenny picked up a flute, and we sang songs from the camp. We'd instinctively formed a rough circle. Rori's face shone beside mine. Jean raised her arms and we raised ours with her, processing clockwise, our black silhouettes against the deep blue sky like a chain of cut-out paper dolls. Christmas Day. The circle gathered pace. We added a hop and a skip. The stars whirled above us.

I lost track of how long we were dancing, ten minutes, fifteen. Underneath our feet the space designed to house the weapons, and above us a sky that went on and on. For a while I felt separated from my body; part of the other women and part of the sky.

And then came the sound of a siren.

There wasn't a plan for what happened next.

'Americans,' said Sam from her place in the circle. 'Must be.'

'Don't stop!' said Barbel. I tightened my hold on Rori's hand. Adrenalin coursing through my heart. Distant barking echoed now as we continued to rotate, raising our voices.

'Skittle,' Rori turned to me, breaking from my clasp. 'I'm going to look over,' she said, moving towards the silo's edge. 'Hang on!' The gap closed and I went to follow her but another voice said, 'Are they coming? The police?' It was the woman on my other side, I could see she was younger than me, perhaps only seventeen. 'It's all right,' I said, clutching her to calm us both. We continued to rotate.

The whoop of more sirens soon followed. And voices from the circle,

'Are they MoD?'

'Can't tell, keep dancing!'

'We did it!'

'We've done it!'

And yet more sirens. Jenny stopped playing her flute and the circle broke. Barbel played on. Women were hugging or calling out, or dancing in pairs and threes. Where was Rori? I shouted her name. The sky had grown a shade lighter, but it was still too dark to see clearly. 'The Americans can't touch us,' said someone I'd only spoken to a few times. She had a blunt fringe and her expression was calm. 'They have to wait for the police.'

Was that right? Suddenly I didn't know what I should be doing. Some of the women were sitting down in protest. Where was Rori? I wound through the women, crossing uneven ground to the other side of the silo, and there was the outline of a body climbing over the edge. I knew from her curls and the line of her shoulders that it was Rori. I shouted. She turned briefly, her face half shadow, but she didn't pause, she kept moving, the paper wings bobbing on her back. 'Wait!' I followed, calling her name, keeping her in sight as I skidded down the steep face of the silo until my boots met with earth. Long-legged, she ran.

Military vehicles gathered on the other side of the silos, their sirens tearing through the early morning, and she didn't slow, she was running towards the inkiest trees clustered at the fence. My heart hurt, but I ran behind her, my breath came short and sharp, but I could nearly touch her. I reached out, grasped one of her angel wings, but she didn't slow. Instead she pulled away and as she tore free I fell. She turned. We were near the bracken. I cried out with the pain coming from inside my boot. I tried to kneel but couldn't get up. She stood three feet away, breathing hard. She looked at me and her expression was of someone at first alarmed and then withdrawn, as if she were witnessing an event many miles distant in which she could play no part.

'Rori, please,' I heard myself say. She took a step back, another, and then she ran, disappearing into the black, and I was alone.

Unable to force myself upright I gave in and lay still, fingers curled around the papery angel wing. Sounds from far off, a dog barking, a loud hailer. My ankle throbbed until pain was all I could feel.

And then someone coming near and a voice I knew. 'What's happened?' Angela was kneeling beside me.

'I'm all right,' I tried to tell her, but the words didn't come out, only a jerky sob.

'Lean on me.'

'It's okay.'

But it wasn't okay, nothing was. I raised myself and leaned on her slight body. Lights flared behind us at the base, a policeman was shouting through a loud hailer but whatever he was saying was drowned by a helicopter circling overhead. We stood isolated. *Breathe, steady breaths*, came Angela's voice. Two police officers were running towards us and then my arm was pulled so vigorously behind my back I thought it might break.

'She's not resisting arrest,' said Angela as they cuffed her.

'Shut your mouth.' The policeman had his face up close to hers. 'They ought to shoot you lot on sight.'

'She's injured,' said Angela.

The policeman marched me forwards. 'Trying to earn your Holloway wings are you?' he said, and I realised I was still grasping the torn paper from Rori's back. I dropped it on the mud. As we neared the vans, we saw other policemen carrying down the women who refused to walk off the silos. Di was hustled along with her hands held behind her. Some of the women continued to sing as they were arrested, snatches of song travelled on the air.

'You lot are taking the piss now,' said one of the policemen when they'd clanked the door of the van shut. There were six of us inside, all cuffed, separated into wire cages. Two of the women were still singing. The van smelt of dogs and diesel.

'Shut your noise, will you?'

The women sang louder. One of the officers began Land of

Hope and Glory, and when that stopped he talked about what he'd do with us if it was up to him.

I'd had nightmares of being in a police van, and now it was actually happening. My face came back at me reflected in black glass.

'Can't you take these cuffs off?' said the woman beside me. 'They're digging in.'

'Should have thought about that before you went on your little spree.'

'Which station are you taking us to?' asked Angela. At a sharp turn in the road we swerved to one side and my weight shifted abruptly, sending a new and violent pain to my ankle.

'We ask the questions, darling.'

After that Angela was quiet. I shut my eyes. Rori had run. She'd abandoned the action. She didn't care what happened to us. And it was plain as the cuffs on my wrist that she didn't care what happened to me.

28

A Two-Seater Sofa

'I don't understand why he…'

'Why Peter,' corrects Valeria, because one of her rules is that we only refer to each other by name. 'Why Peter…' I never call him by his full name, only Mum does that, '…always has a problem with what I'm doing.'

Valeria is haloed by the glow of the Tiffany lamp at her shoulder. Petite and calm, she sits with a notepad on her lap, her black hair wound into a coil and fastened with a silver chopstick. She waits for Pete's response. He shifts on his side of the sofa, a dusky pink sofa which blends warmly into the room's burnt oranges and mustard yellows.

'I don't have a problem, it isn't like that…' His body is angled towards me but he speaks to Valeria. 'The point is, I don't think Tessa enjoys half the things she does.'

Valeria is attentive, she notices folded arms, she's keen on eye contact. Perhaps remembering our session on Better Communication, Pete lifts his eyes to meet mine. 'I'm not going to encourage you to take on every cause you find. It's got ridiculous.'

'So I'm ridiculous?'

The remark is automatic and defensive, and defensiveness is another of the code red words we learned about in Better Communication; but that was some weeks before we found ourselves picking over the problem of infidelity.

'I didn't say you were ridiculous. I said, I'm saying…'

Pete sighs with closed eyes and pinches the bridge of his nose, like someone who's lifted an uncomfortable pair of glasses, but he doesn't wear glasses and I find the gesture annoying. 'What about the Justice and Peace group at the Catholic church?' he says. 'You don't even go to church.'

'It's only a couple of hours a month, they needed someone to help steer it.'

He folds his arms and sighs again, returning his attention to Valeria. Is he really criticising me for attending a Justice and Peace group when he's been messing about with another woman? But we are not meant to be talking about her this week, at least not directly, that was for last week when I learned what Pete was so unwilling to tell me at home: the details. They'd slept together twice apparently – that took place in her neat little terrace. I recalled her running her hand along the black cat, imagined a bedroom with the curtains drawn, marigolds drinking in the sunlight below. Pete narrated in a low voice. Valeria looked between us and I looked at my hands to the scuffed wedding ring. I thought of a boy at primary school who used to pull out matchboxes from his pockets and slide them open to reveal dead insects, nobody wanted to look but we all did. Valeria waited for us to negotiate the silence afterwards. Pete told me he loved me, told Valeria he loved me, told me he loved me again. But that was last week. This evening we're supposed to be using our session to get at the reasons for his infidelity so we can find a way back to wherever it was we were, the place when we were happy. Or at least happier than this.

At our very first session Valeria asked us to say what we loved about each other. I said I loved Pete's good humour, his shaggy hair, his kindness – and other things which were difficult to explain to Valeria, or probably to him, because we don't sit down and tell our spouses why we love them, unless we are drunk perhaps, or they are teetering on death, or we've only just met them and need to quantify it to ourselves. I love, used to love, the way he let Pippa dance on his feet when she was little. I love the way his tongue pokes out of the corner of his mouth when he's slicing an onion into wafers. I love the way he – used to – put up a tent, the easy swing of the mallet as the pegs sunk down, the way he'd smooth the ground sheet and lay my sleeping bag down first, checking it for comfort. I love his fascination for old dead kings and queens, the way he'll bring their first names into conversations as if he knows them personally and understands their dilemmas. All sorts of things I love about him. Loved about him. Love about him. And more painful than the thought of him in bed with another woman is the idea of him sitting face to face with her in the corner of a dimly lit country pub – where was it they went? – holding her hand, explaining the workings of his heart.

A car passes in the road and there's the creak of a floorboard upstairs: Valeria's husband, shut in his study until the less happily married find their way home. I imagine him up there sitting on the bed in his socks, finishing a crossword, sipping a whisky, waiting until the coast is clear. Or does he have the television on a low volume? I've never met him, never even caught sight of a photograph though I've scanned the room. Then again, why would Valeria spread her family mementos about – happy days by the river, intimate holiday dinners – it would be cruel to remind us what we're missing, all of us who arrive to sit stiffly on the two-seater sofa hoping for rescue.

When we first decided to ring the bell to Valeria's house we thought it would be a gentle steer when we needed it, a way to get us back on course. Neither of us knew we could risk making things worse as we stripped back the layers and confronted each other with the sort of hurt which might better be left in a box marked Do Not Open. Pete told Valeria in the second session that he felt we were simply occupying the same space, that we were more like housemates than man and wife. Co-parents. I said we used to have projects we enjoyed together but he'd lost enthusiasm. He said I was never happy unless I had a tub to thump. I said if he looked sideways once in a while he might see there's a world outside the living room. He said if I sat down and relaxed once in a while I'd notice it had other people to solve its problems. So it went on until Valeria held up her hands and called for a halt. By then there were empty boxes everywhere. Although none of them were yet marked Supply Teacher.

Pete is telling us both, me and Valeria, about the other commitments which displease him. He mentions Heston Fields. I say that in principle I think he'd support the campaign to save the field, but he won't because I'm running it. His antagonism feels perverse.

'It's not as if you get paid for any of this extra work,' he says.

'Is that what irks you, that it's voluntary?'

'No, you know it's not, but I don't understand why you go on like this.'

'Go on?'

He sighs and leans back, 'Sorry... you're good at what you do. She's excellent...' he tells Valeria. 'But it's an obsession.'

Valeria asks how Pete's comments make me feel. This is a phrase she's fond of.

The rubber plant splays its shiny leaves. The plants are here to remind us of life. Renewal. Suddenly I feel weary to my bones.

'Sorry,' I say, fighting off a yawn.

'If you're tired why don't you do less?' he says.

'That's not an answer.'

'Why isn't it?'

'Because if everyone sat back nothing would get done, I just want to get things done. I've got a duty.'

'Duty?' He gives a dry laugh. 'You're not the Queen. No one's waiting for you to open a hospital wing.'

'It might be helpful for Tessa to unpack this,' Valeria says. She gives me her steady gaze. '…Duty, that's an interesting word.'

Is it? I don't want to do any unpacking. I want to sleep and not think. The time's nearly up and I want to get out of Valeria's pink womb. She writes on her notepad. There's no point trying to sit here explaining ourselves to each other or ourselves to ourselves. Whatever Pete might have loved about me seems so lost that he hasn't even tried rediscovering it but has made a path through the foxgloves and marigolds to somewhere he can find a warm bed and a warm body.

'Tessa, I know this is hard for you because you've been hurt. And Pete, you know this is hard for Tessa too, don't you?' He nods, dipping his eyes to his knees. 'But we have to face some difficult aspects of ourselves.' Pete is a tree man, that's why I love him. Loved him. Love him. Beardy. Solid. Rooted.

'Shall we leave it for this evening?' I say.

Valeria glances at the clock.

'I can't excuse what I did,' Pete says. 'But I regret it.'

'You are trying to excuse it… you're making it sound as if I'm never at home… as if I drove you to this.' The room is too red and too warm.

'Perhaps what Pete is feeling is that he doesn't have enough of your attention when you are with him,' says Valeria.

The shelves bear a collection of trinkets, not the sort of trinkets Mum favours, porcelain ladies and china spaniels, what she calls her knick-knacks, but postcards, a brass elephant, a carved wooden bowl. Amidst them is a glass paperweight with an indigo swirl at its centre. It always captures my attention, that inky swirl of glass, a miniature tempest forever in the act of storming. Impossible to touch. Impossible to calm.

The session ends. We make another appointment. We say goodbye to Valeria. We walk to the car in silence.

29

In the Cells

Angela sat leaning against the wall with her knees bent up in front of her, maintaining the silence. She'd buried down into her parka, both hands in the pockets, and her eyes were shut. I sat at the other end of the bench staring at the whitewashed brick, unable to reconcile what had passed, everything crashing together: the fear of scaling the fence, the elation of standing on the silos, and Rori, running without looking back.

A shaft of weak morning sunshine entered the cell through the smallest of high windows. My left ankle was puffy. I'd taken my foot out of my boot and there was no way it was going back in again, but at least the physical pain of the ankle was some distraction from the doomy music playing in my head.

There wasn't much to look at, but what there was I recognised from episodes of *Juliet Bravo*: a bench built into the wall, a folded grey blanket, a door hatch into which a policeman could push his face. In one corner of the cell stood a simple toilet without a lid. Neither of us, please God, would have to use it. If I needed to go I'd bang on the door. I glanced at Angela, her brow furrowed in concentration. This wasn't how it was supposed to be. If I'd ever imagined incarceration, and I'd tried not to, there was always a gang of friends present, we were making each other roll-ups and confounding the authorities with our good-natured solidarity. There was almost definitely singing. And in my imagination I was always with Rori.

'What will they do with us?' My voice came loud in the chilly space.

Angela twitched. A chain of beads spilled briefly from her pocket and she tucked them back in without opening her eyes. Rosary beads. That's what she was doing. How had she managed to hide them from the police when they'd confiscated my rolling tobacco and sealed it up in a clear plastic bag?

'They'll leave us until they've decided what to charge us with,' she said, her eyes still shut.

'How long will that be?'

She shrugged.

'Could it be... could it be something to do with the Official Secrets Act?'

Another shrug.

For pity's sake, we were locked up together and she was playing the plaster saint. A minute passed but she said nothing else.

'What are we going to do?' I asked.

'Wait.'

'But... it's Christmas.'

'They won't let us go yet.'

I wasn't sure what our bail conditions would be if bail was to be granted. Mum and Dad could afford to put up the money now, but it would mean telling them what had happened, and I couldn't do that – especially not on Christmas Day. They'd been so happy after their pools win. No, if I was going to make one phone call, I wouldn't ring them, I'd phone the solicitor whose number was still inked in smudgy biro across my hand.

'Have you been arrested before?' I asked. Angela opened her eyes and nodded.

'What happened?'

'The first time they cautioned me. The second time they wanted me to agree to be bound over.' She noted my blank expression. 'It means you have to agree to keep the peace. But I refused so they took me to court.'

'And you got off?'

'No. I got six days.'

I didn't ask what it was like in prison. I could take a guess. Oh God. I tried to think of the suffragettes.

From the corridor came the sound of clanging as a drunk was slammed, slurring and protesting, into a cell: 'Ope the fuckindoor,' he hollered. But the door wasn't opened and the man was left shouting into nothing and to no one. Angela closed her eyes again. Every thought I had joined a stream of desperate others until they were smashing like lemmings over a cliff. The wall wasn't much of a distraction, but it was all I had, and I began counting the whitewashed bricks. I'd got to three hundred and seventeen when a young WPC entered, her blonde hair pinned into a bun, a sprig of tinsel clipped to her lapel.

'You girls fancy a cup of tea?'

'Yes, please. Do you think I could have an aspirin too? It's my ankle.'

She glanced at my fat foot. 'Can't really do that without my colleague, he's in charge of the meds box and he went home an hour ago.'

'Surely you can give her something?' said Angela.

The WPC considered my foot. I'd swung it onto the bench to keep the blood flowing. 'Got yourself in a right pickle, haven't you,' she said, shaking her head like a wise older sister. It was the most sympathetic thing anyone had said since our arrest.

'How long are we going to be held?' I asked.

But the WPC didn't know. She said she was only here to offer us tea and did we want sugar. I asked for two. The door banged shut. Angela retreated into herself.

After she'd gone I couldn't remember where I'd got to with the bricks. What was the point? It was all such a mess – my

263

attempt at activism had come to this: the pain, the cold, Rori, prison. Biting the inside of my cheek wasn't working. I tried chewing on my nails instead, but they tasted bitter from the ink the policeman had used for our fingerprints. Sod it all. I was going to have to cry. As the ache in my throat relaxed into a sob, the relief was instant. Angela opened her eyes in time to track the first tear as it skipped off the end of my chin.

'You shouldn't have come back to the camp,' she said in a weary voice.

'I wanted to,' I replied, juddering. 'Anyway, it's nothing to do with you.'

Anyway came out as A-a-any-way. There'd been a time when the thought of crying in front of Angela would have been the ultimate humiliation, but what did it matter now? Nothing mattered.

'I'm not judging you. But protest is hard. It demands sacrifice. I tried to tell you.'

Not judging? She was always judging, even if she wasn't saying anything, *especially* if she wasn't saying anything.

'You're not perfect.'

She took off her round glasses and rubbed the lens with the hem of her flannel shirt. Without them her face dipped into shallows, like a snowman whose eyes had been stolen. 'I never claimed to be.'

She replaced the glasses and the pale eyes reappeared, the eyes that moved so coolly around recording every detail with the precision of a surveillance camera. And then she closed them again, re-engaging with the beads in her pocket. Well that was typical, shutting out anyone who didn't come up to her standards.

'What about Barbel's birthday?' I said, rubbing a sleeve across my glistening upper lip. I didn't want to mention the song directly, but at least I'd got her attention. Her eyes were open. 'You make mistakes too.' Why couldn't she at least admit she was human?

There was another silence. I didn't think she'd respond but then she said, 'I didn't want to sing.'

'Why did you then? You could have refused.'

Because she couldn't stand the idea of me and Rori doing something together that didn't include her. I told her this.

'No, it wasn't that.'

'What was it then?' The man in the cell down the corridor was making more noise. 'What?'

'I wanted to show him,' she said quickly.

'Show who?'

She looked away. 'My dad.'

'What's it got to do with your dad?'

There was only the reverberation of the man banging out a drunken rhythm on a metallic surface. A policeman arrived and told the man to stop. When Angela spoke again she'd drawn her knees higher to her chin and was talking to her boots rather than me.

'He was always in the centre, whatever the occasion you could hear him above the crowd.'

If I'd ever had any notion of her father, he'd been a version of her, bespectacled, serious, surrounded by leather-bound volumes.

'He always made us get up when there was company, my brothers and sisters…' she paused. 'He used to make us sing, but I couldn't do it. I'd try, but my nerves got me and my voice…' She stopped, seeming to forget I was still there. '*Run off to your books*, he'd say. And they'd laugh. Good old Brendan, the centre of every party.' Her voice had gone to a whisper, her words disappearing into the cell wall along with all the other secrets it must have absorbed. 'But he'd make me get up the next time. And the next. He enjoyed it.' The silence pulsed between us like an extra presence and I tried to imagine Angela as part of a big family, intimately connected to other people, brothers and sisters, and a father dragging her into the centre of a crowded room.

'But surely that was years ago. It doesn't matter what he says.'

'No. It doesn't matter.'

I shifted my sore ankle. I should have stayed silent, let her stay silent. But now he'd been hauled out, this father with his loud voice, he had to be acknowledged.

'What does he think of you being at Greenham?'

She stared at her boots and shrugged. 'He died in May.'

The information settled on me like a fall of snow on bare skin and I remembered what Rori had said about a bereavement.

'I'm sorry.'

The man along the corridor was being moved, raising his voice in a less determined protest, exhausted by his previous efforts.

I shivered.

'Have the blanket,' she said, realigning her body to its former position.

'We could ask for another one,' I said.

She shook her head. The blanket stayed where it was, folded between us. Angela closed her eyes, returning to the images behind them – her father, the Virgin Mary, the arms race. The dull square of light sharpened briefly on the cell floor. I shut my eyes feeling worse than ever and tried to sleep.

30

Down by the Riverside

I'm supposed to meet Angela at a café beside the Royal Festival Hall, but the train is stuck on a tree-lined track outside Cambridge and we haven't moved for nearly half an hour. There's been a mumbled announcement about signal failure, apologies for any inconvenience and we're elbow to elbow because the train is only three carriages long when it should be at least four. It's warm. A woman with a home-counties hairdo fans herself with a magazine and a baby in the next compartment begins to fret. Newspapers creak and whisper as pages turn in the limited space. Why today? You don't want to keep someone waiting when you haven't seen them for nearly thirty years, especially not Angela Mullen. I picture her zipped into her parka, stirring a cappuccino and checking her watch. Of course she won't be wearing the parka anymore, but I'm finding it difficult to update her. And what are we going to talk about anyway?

The bars on my mobile are two miniature flat bricks: they quiver and are still. I can't access my messages to see if there's anything from Pippa. Since our argument I've managed one short phone conversation with her, but now she's in London visiting a friend so we've arranged to meet up later for dinner. Somehow we need to smooth things over. I gaze into a nest of brambles and remember primary school afternoons, the simple mother-daughter transactions, the presentation of a painting done in chalky poster paints, mixing a mug of hot chocolate while she talked about her friends. Somewhere around the age of fourteen she started to wander away from me and she's never come back.

A heavy man in the seat opposite is wheezing softly. He opens his briefcase and removes an inhaler, shakes it, tilts his head back and sucks in. When he exhales an after-cloud of Ventolin hovers around his mouth and nose, giving him the look of a dragon trailing smoke. He catches my eye and smiles self-consciously; I smile back and look away, reminded by Mum's voice that staring is rude.

The train eases forwards. We snap out of our stupors, glancing past each other into the trees on either side of the window which begin to inch past, trunk by trunk, before another judder brings us to a stop. The air fills with more low-level sighing.

The trees are so close I can see the twiggy branches growing from their trunks and the blades of light behind, and while I study the dark and light shapes, my thoughts creep into a familiar thicket where bodies are twisted together. I wonder what the supply teacher looks like naked.

The café is vibrant with white-aproned waiting staff, and the coffee machine gushes as they circle the tables. I texted Angela to explain the delay, and she's bound to have gone by now, but I scan the room anyway, feeling oddly exposed, my eyes passing over two elderly ladies, a blonde woman who looks French and who is holding two fingers in the air to signal the waiter, a stylish couple who might be Italian tourists, and a man in a pink shirt eating poached eggs. There's also a group of women about my age, a couple flushed with love and staring into each other's eyes, and two mothers attempting to chat while their toddlers run free. Fatigued from a dash across Hungerford Bridge, I take a seat at an outside table. It's a Tuesday, but the South Bank is alive and it's good to sit in the dappled light watching the flow of life passing by in all its variety. My phone says three missed calls, and I'm just about to ring Angela's number when there's a tap on my shoulder.

'Tessa.'

I turn around and it takes me a moment to answer. 'Angela?'

'I was waving at you,' says the petite woman in the cream suit.

'I… I thought you were French,' I reply, still confused.

'French?' She laughs.

French? 'Sorry. Only… I wouldn't have recognised you.' I tell my face to look normal.

'Evidently,' she says. 'I've a meeting around the corner, that's why I'm suited and booted.'

Her hair is still blonde, but brighter, cut into feathery layers, and the round glasses have been replaced by chic designer frames. Her skin is lightly tanned and the sprinkle of freckles on her nose give her a girlish look. She smiles and says it's great to see me, swooping forwards to kiss me continentally on both cheeks, and because I'm not quite recovered from the surprise I simply sit there offering my face rather than joining in the greeting. The only thing that remains the same is her stature: she's slim, but in her outfit she appears slender, rather than scrawny, the way I remember her from camp. I explain about the signal problems, feeling strangely incapable after all these years.

'Never mind, you're here now,' she says, taking the seat opposite. 'It's a pity we don't have much time.' Her northern accent is there but it's softer and inflected with something vaguely transatlantic. In my head I continue the struggle to connect her to the image I've been carrying around for nearly three decades.

'I was looking out for a redhead.'

I shrug, uncomfortable at the memory, 'It wasn't really me.' It took sixty-five quid and four hours in a salon to get back to normal, well, better than normal, my new hair is cut into a shiny chestnut crop.

'You look great either way,' she says, and I return the compliment. I would like to sit her down and stare at her for a good five minutes, uninterrupted.

'Thanks so much for coming; I wasn't sure how you'd feel getting an email out of the blue.'

'A little surprised.'

'Only a little?' She raises an eyebrow.

'Quite a lot.'

'There you were on TV, large as life. I couldn't believe it,' she says. I cringe as choice moments from the programme go shuttling through my head. 'I always look out for *Make Me Over* when I'm home.'

'Do you?'

'Oh yes. Was the filming fun?'

I decide not to go into the details. 'It was interesting.'

'Ah, *interesting*.'

I think of myself standing in the orange trousers waving my arms and mention the drastic way they cut the final edit.

'Can't trust the media, we should have learned that years ago,' she says.

I register the smile, natural and relaxed, a comfortable smile. She leans over the table conspiratorially and a small gold cross glints at her neck.

'Tell me, what's Jude like in real life?'

'A tad bonkers to tell the truth.'

'I knew it,' she sits back with a laugh, and I join in. I am having a laugh with Angela Mullen. It's too strange. As she speaks I can't help trying to find the old Angela in her face. Yes, her eyes are the same pale blue, quick and intelligent, yet she is altogether changed. Not simply the hair and the clothes but her manner. The word that comes to mind is light. She is *lighter*.

A waitress appears and I order a tuna salad and an orange juice. Angela asks for another coffee because she's already eaten.

We smile and I'm not sure who should say something first, but she speaks, an attempt to calculate how long it's been since we last saw one other. I remember clearly, the conversation, the cold bright sky, my thoughts afterwards, but I feign puzzlement until we agree on an approximate date. I ask if she comes this way much for work.

'Now and then. Blackfriars. The Lancing and Turner building.'

'Oh, you're in insurance?' I need to know about this new Angela, the person who has out-manoeuvred her younger self.

'No, advertising. They're clients, I have to update them on a project.'

Advertising. Really? I feel like running onto the pavement and shouting to release some of the accumulating incredulity. 'Sounds exciting.'

'Can be, when we're working on a good account. This one's fairly dry. Still, have to keep the wolf from the door somehow.'

Judging by Angela's appearance this particular door must be in a smart neighbourhood. 'I always imagined you'd become an academic,' I say. A woman surrounded by books, a woman whose purpose is to correct and instruct.

'I was for a short while. Too many hours for too little pay. And academics are a cynical bunch.'

She considers me and something of her serious young self shows through. 'I was intrigued by the work you're doing.'

'They didn't show much of it on the programme.'

'No. But I looked you up afterwards. Easy Green, isn't it?'

'That's right.' It's slightly unnerving, the idea of being looked up by Angela. 'To be honest I'm not sure how long we'll be able to keep afloat. Funding cuts.' I explain something of our recent problems.

'Have you ever tried corporate sponsorship? Business likes to raise its green profile these days. Sorry, awful expression.'

'I've had a go, though we're so small, there's not much in it for them. But I've a meeting later with a potential donor at a trust, so fingers crossed.' We talk about work and I tell her I've been in various not-for-profit organisations all my life – fundraising, communications – and when she asks more about it, I catch myself trying to make my employment history sound more dynamic than it's actually been, because communications largely relates to the churning out of various charity newsletters and reports. Eventually I manage to turn the conversation to her career. She tells me she was teaching at a college in the States when she started doing a little freelance copywriting for a friend's agency and found she enjoyed it.

'How long were you in America?'

'Fifteen years.'

Of course, she left Greenham to go to Seneca, the peace camp in New York State.

'America was a revelation after England; the climate, the people, the Can Do. Funny, after all that Anti-American propaganda we spouted to find that it was so many things Britain wasn't. It felt like reaching the light – especially after a British winter. And a Greenham winter at that.'

We reminisce with grim relish.

'Strange days,' she says to herself, twiddling a sugar sachet.

I'm not sure how to interpret this; didn't we have a cause worth fighting for? And wasn't she on the front line? She catches my expression. 'What I mean is they were strange days for me, personally. Looking back I can see I wasn't at peace with myself about quite a few things.' Her eyes settle on a pigeon as it pecks for crumbs and I nod, hoping she'll explain, not wanting to probe. The waitress arrives with our order. Angela sips her coffee and I spear a chunk of griddled tuna steak.

'And of course I was terribly religious in those days,' she says.

'Were you?' I reply, remembering only too well.

'Oh yes. I wanted to be Joan of Arc. I'd be in my little tent saying one novena after another for the deliverance of the world. Life was all about the struggle.'

272

Protest means sacrifice, her words come back to me across the years.

'I thought you had it all worked out.'

'Did you?' She seems genuinely surprised.

'You always knew what was what. I remember arriving that first night and you were sitting at the fire with your parka on reading the paper...'

She groans. 'God, that coat...'

'And I was this girl who'd just got off the bus from Stevenage, and hardly knew which way was up.'

She laughs and sets down her cup. 'When I look back it makes me think of that Bob Dylan lyric, *I was so much older then.*' She looks into her coffee, 'I felt quite shabby afterwards about the way I went on.'

'Did you?' My fork wavers and her eyes lift from the cup to meet mine. By the way she's regarding me it's clear what she means is, *The way I went on at you.* Whatever I was expecting from a meeting with Angela, it certainly wasn't a confession.

'I was so uncompromising. Clinging to my rosary beads, clinging to a cause, but the fact was, at that time I was mired in these terrible feelings of grief, and other complicated emotions I couldn't sort out.' She doesn't explain what these emotions relate to, but she says something of the grief. 'It was a bad year, 1982. Me and my dad, we'd always had a difficult relationship, if you can call it a relationship, and I feared him, but even so I wanted him to be proud. Or if not that, I wanted him to understand me a little. But then suddenly he was dead, heart attack, and no chance to put things right, none of those father-daughter conversations I'd longed for, so I threw myself into saving the world.' The phrase strikes me and I file it away. 'Not that I wasn't sincere, I was probably too sincere and I believed in disarmament passionately, but there were other complicating factors.'

Her face is briefly shadowed like the young Angela's, and I feel compelled to lighten it.

'Well, let's be honest, you had your work cut out with me. I was all over the place. Do you remember rescuing me when Barbel tried to bleach my hair?'

She laughs. 'You did attract a certain amount of calamity. Even so, talk about uptight, I was the living definition.'

What happened, I want to ask her, what happened to the girl in the parka and the little round glasses? Maybe it's related to the gold cross at her throat, maybe the patron saint of tortured young women came down and performed a miracle over her. As if anticipating these questions she says, 'If I hadn't got myself a decent psychotherapist in the States I probably wouldn't be here. I think that saved me, I honestly do.'

The sun makes a stripe on the table. I think of Valeria and her tranquilly decorated sitting room, and take a bite of fish, trying to reorganise my head. This is Angela; this is not Angela.

'Better than Greenham stew?' she asks.

'Much.' The salad has a lemon dressing and its tang complements the smoky tuna and croutons. We recall some of the meals from the camp and Angela recounts an incident I didn't know about when Vicky the animal rights fanatic caught Jean sitting in the camp van with a Chinese takeaway and went berserk. We discuss Jean fondly.

'You know who else I used to like?' says Angela. 'That lady who hardly spoke. What was her name, the Welsh woman?'

'Di.' I picture her at the roadside with her placard or quietly trailing a rubbish sack.

Angela smiles. 'That's it. She had the right idea; just got on with it.' She takes another sip from her coffee.

Has this become marginalia to her? It would surprise her to know how deeply those weeks have imbedded themselves in my life, and yet the experience affected her too, she's said as much – only not in the way I'd assumed, and that knowledge makes me suddenly unsteady, wrong-footed. She tells me that Barbel went on to become a filmmaker, they exchanged Christmas cards for a while before losing touch. I think of Rori but don't mention her, and neither does Angela. I want to ask Angela what it was like living in America and I want to know who she is now, because this whole encounter has been different, very different from the way I imagined it. But she has an eye on her watch and says she ought to get moving, that she's sorry we don't have more time. 'What are you up to now?' she asks. I'm about to mention the Stop the Cuts rally in Trafalgar Square but this news might interest a very different Angela, so I tell her I'll prepare my notes for meeting the Adams Foundation. She fastens the buckle on her leather shoulder bag which bears the monogram of an Italian design house. For a split second I'm calculating what it might cost.

'Will you let me think about Easy Green?' she says. 'There may be something I could suggest.'

'Yes of course, that's kind.'

What hasn't changed is her ability to take charge convincingly: I can imagine her directing teams of people with absolute assurance, covering each agenda point with swift clarity.

'It's been great to see you, Tessa,' she says warmly, and I lean forwards to kiss her cheek. It's as if we're lost best friends, not two women who begrudgingly shared a muddy tract of land. In my head I remove her from the frame in which she's been stuck all these years, holding a copy of John Stuart Mill's collected essays at the fireside, frowning at me when she thinks I'm not looking. We promise to email and she disappears into the sunshine, a gleam of light coming off the Thames behind her.

After she's gone, I take a walk along the riverside and stop at a bench beside a carousel which is playing a Simon & Garfunkel melody with the jaunty grind of an old-fashioned organ. Its painted horses are rider-less except for a girl and her boyfriend, his arms wrapped around her waist as the horses rise and dip. A white passenger boat glides underneath Hungerford bridge, and as it emerges Angela's phrase *Saving the world* re-enters my head. The girl I knew with the closed, intense face has gone. But that Angela has been travelling with me all my life and now that she's transformed into an advertising director who wears immaculately tailored suits and shakes her head despairingly at her former self, I can't help feeling unsettled, and something more than that. Although difficult to admit, the word that comes to mind is cheated.

As I'm turning this over, my mobile rings and Pippa's name flashes up. We chat for a few minutes; I try to describe my encounter with Angela, and Pippa's listening but I sense she's waiting to break in. She does at the next pause.

'Grace has got tickets for this gallery thing tonight, it's completely last minute but she's asked if I want to be her plus one. It starts at six.'

The carousel is no longer rotating and another melody plays as it awaits new passengers.

'Shall we meet earlier then?'

She's tentative. 'Thing is, we're in Portobello, so by the time I get to you it'll probably be time to go back again, because we have to get changed and everything.' She hesitates and it's difficult to know if this is the truth or if she doesn't want to see me. 'But I mean, I don't have to go, you know, it would be nice to meet up…'

Come and see me, I want to say. *I miss you.* 'Never mind, you go and enjoy it, love.'

'What will you do?'

'Oh, I'll be all right, I'm sitting in the sunshine. And there's a rally I was going to drop by at.'

'Oh yeah,' she says, and her voice takes on a strain of fatigue. 'What is it this time?'

31

Fires

After Reading police station they moved us back to Newbury and I was put in a cell with Barbel, Sam and two members of Sapphire gate: Nel, a yawning woman in her twenties who kept saying how much she wanted a spliff, and Bernice, a red-haired American with a gutsy laugh who reminded me of a grown-up orphan Annie. There we stayed, eating shepherds pie from plastic bowls and rearranging our limbs periodically in the cold space. Our hearing took place the day after Boxing Day in a panelled room where we were asked to confirm our names, charged with breaching the peace, and instructed to return in a fortnight for trial. Then they released us into the fresh December morning.

On the steps of the magistrates' court our supporters had gathered. A woman I didn't know thrust a limp handful of snowdrops at me, their stems wrapped in damp newspaper, while another woman with a port-wine birthmark kissed my cheek and called me sister. I kept hold of Barbel's hand as the world rushed at us: the biting wind, the white roofless sky, and the swell of women singing songs from the camp and chanting *We Don't Want Cruise!* their fists punching the air. I stood in the middle of them like a fake celebrity, shaken to the root by the police cells, the clanging doors, the keys. I looked about.

'Where's Rori?' I said, raising my voice above the crowd, searching the faces. We blinked at a photographer's flash and his colleague asked me how I felt. I tried to make sense of the scene. She wasn't there. During the slow hours of confinement, I'd replayed the memory of her running away, and finally concluded that it must have been a moment of panic, that she'd have regretted it and would come to make her peace.

One of the supporters pushed towards us, rosy-cheeked and smiling in a purple suede coat. 'We came in the van,' she said. She meant the camp van, which had been entrusted to another woman from Amber gate.

'You're not insured to drive it,' said Jean, taking the keys from her.

'It's all right, we've got lots of cars,' she answered, as if Jean had made an entirely different remark, 'everyone will get a lift.'

The last time we'd seen it, the van had been white – or whiteish – but as we followed the girl in the suede coat, we saw an enormous daisy blooming in green emulsion from the bonnet.

'We did it this morning,' said the girl. 'It wasn't just me,' she added modestly, 'some of the others helped.'

Walking behind Jean, we circled the van. A spider's web had been painted on the side door beside yet more flowers, and the back doors were newly branded with a red CND emblem. Every member of LAWE would know where to target their rotten eggs.

Jean sighed. 'Let's get back,' she said, hooking a strand of silver hair behind her ear and settling into the driver's seat. I climbed in gingerly behind Barbel, my ankle still tender, and our new supporters rearranged a collapsible ladder to make room. They wanted to know what it had been like on the silos, how the police had treated us, if we knew that we could justify our action by using the 1969 Genocide Act, which incorporated aspects of the Geneva Convention. On and on they went while Jean drove us out of the town centre, its Christmas decorations and strings of colourless bulbs drab in the daylight. I rested my head against Barbel's shoulder, and as she fielded questions I let my mind work against the questions of the last forty-eight hours. Why hadn't Rori come? Perhaps she'd felt too ashamed? That was probably it, she'd be back at camp, waiting for us. The girl in the suede coat hypothesised about political policy using whatever she'd picked up from her International Relations course at UCL, and suddenly I felt older than her mother.

A fire made the only point of brightness in the dull afternoon as we followed the track towards the congregated women, the ground churned to slurry by the work of so many extra boots. Our settlement had grown. A number of Ruby and Sapphire gaters had joined Amber gate. I recognised Bernice, my red-haired cell mate, and a hoard of new visitors had arrived too. A sheet of blue plastic served as weather protection, decorated with snakes of bedraggled tinsel, and under it a dozen women sheltered from the drizzle which flecked the air like iron filings. A donated armchair had been dragged to the fireside, one armrest gashed and spilling yellow sponge, and it stood beside other oddments of furniture, the trestle tables, and an old pushchair with the hood protecting a pile of blankets. Stackable plastic chairs, the sort you'd see in school halls, were scattered higgledy piggledy in the mud and the rubbish heap had grown mountainous, over-spilling with Sainsbury's bags knotted at the handles. Di moved around with a black bin liner doing her best to collect refuse. Another group of women sheltered from the wind under golfing umbrellas.

Stripped of its chocolate Santas, the Christmas tree stood where we'd left it, listing more noticeably to one side, a toy elephant, once fluffy but now soggy, attached to its uppermost branch. Inside a shopping trolley, pots were piled high, a frying pan driven into their midst, flaking with skins of fried egg, and an empty gas canister lay on its side in the mud beside a camping stove on which a pot of soup bubbled. I'd been looking forward to the gypsy homeliness of the camp with its rich smell of wood smoke and earth, the silver birch crackling with birds – but now my heart dipped.

One of the visitors got up and offered me her crate, its ridges filled with milky mud, and I sat down without argument. The fire blazed high as a bonfire. Where was Rori? Was she collecting wood or making a rare trip to the standpipe? We needed to talk in private. During the van journey I'd been rehearsing our meeting in my head. It was going to be difficult, but I knew I had to forgive her because she was bound to be feeling terrible too, as terrible as I'd felt in the police cells without her.

Angela sat at the other side of the fire with a paperback as if she'd never been away. We exchanged nods.

'Hey, baby, we're famous!' said Bernice, thrusting a paper my way. PEACE WOMEN DANCE ON SILOS.

Another Sapphire gater who'd also been arrested gave a whoop. I recognised her from that first blockade – thin-faced with a shaven head and a rat's tail, dressed in canvas overalls, she had an animal name, what was it? I raked through until I found it. Cat.

Talk turned to solicitors and court appearances and the recounting of prison anecdotes as the Sapphire gate women constructed spliffs. Cat made the point that we'd invalidated the fence.

'They can see we're serious. What's that fence worth? Nothing. A gang of women like us can climb straight over it.'

Sam got up to tend the soup. 'If we had bolt cutters we could go in and out without ladders.'

She was right. The fence was only an idea, I saw that now. It had been erected in our imaginations as much as anything, and it was up to us to un-imagine it: we'd cleared the fence with ladders, why not cut a hole in it and make a door? The discussion flowed, I listened, fading in and out, my head filled with Rori. She'd been gone too long to be at the standpipe.

Could she have been in town and somehow got left behind by the van.

'Have you seen Rori about?' I asked Sam. She shrugged.

'Rori?' said a woman from our gate. 'She went to London to see her family.'

I let the information sink in. London? She'd returned home as if nothing had happened? No, it couldn't be true.

Jean had already excused herself and retreated to her tepee. Perhaps if I could sleep too it would calm the sudden dread feeling in my heart.

Inside my bender, buried down under a quilt, a figure lay sleeping. I whispered Rori's name in the gloom, softly at first, then more urgently. The figure twitched and moved her head above the bag. A tuft of black hair stuck out. In normal circumstances, waking a sleeping woman would be against all camp etiquette, but these weren't normal circumstances and after a shake on the shoulder the girl came to, rubbing her eyes and introduced herself as a friend of Ava's.

'Who's Ava?'

'Oh,' she blinked with surprise as much as fatigue, as if I couldn't possibly not know. 'She's head of the Women's Society at UCL. She's *amazing*.'

'Is she the one who painted the van?'

'That's right.' She grinned, on the verge of starting up more Ava conversation.

'I need to sleep,' I said with a sigh.

'Oh, sorry. Course.' The girl shuffled out and I took her place. 'We had a late one last night,' she said, crawling to the exit with a yawn. 'Isn't it *amazing* here. Were you on the silos?'

'Yes,' I said, and shut my eyes before she could ask anything else.

Even with the help of the extra quilt and a nearly dry pillow, sleep wouldn't come. All I could see behind my eyelids was Rori's face. How could she have done it, abandoned us, not just me but all of us, gone running and kept running until she was home? If I didn't mean anything to her then didn't the camp mean something? After an hour I went back to the fire and sat in silence, my mood darkening with the sky.

And then, on the edge of dusk, she appeared, an outline at first, moving with that familiar swaying stride. Tired to my bones and trapped in a dialogue of righteous anger, I watched until she became distinct, dressed in a new sheepskin coat and wearing a red hat topped with a white pom-pom. It struck a wrong note, that hat, it spoke of a frivolity we'd left behind three days and a lifetime ago. In addition to her rucksack she carried two turquoise carrier bags with wine-coloured string handles. I sat with my sore ankle, nursing a mug of bitter tea. She'd seen me, I knew she'd seen me well before Barbel said, 'Look, Tessa is here too.' Noticing I wasn't moving towards her, Rori came over and bestowed a flittery kiss on my cheek. Her hair smelled newly washed. 'Hello,' she said, before moving away to greet the other women without another word.

'I picked up a few bits,' she said, dipping into the turquoise bags to unpack an assortment of treats: a bottle of liqueur, a box of chocolate biscuits, a giant wedge of stilton. Barbel clapped her hands. 'Oh and some of these,' she pulled out two boxes of Christmas crackers. 'From my mother. Just for fun.' The women who didn't know her watched her with the sort of admiration I'd seen many times before as she swooped down among us like a fabulous Christmas angel. At the other side of the fire, the Sapphire gaters began a song.

This was supposed to make it all right was it, this show of generosity? The song grew louder. Angela had closed her book and was talking to Rori, but I couldn't hear the conversation. She didn't even glance in my direction. Christmas crackers gave way all around with the snap of gunpowder strips and laughter, gifts and jokes spilling from their broken centres. Barbel delighted in her glittery hair clip, fixing it immediately to one of her plaits, and the woman beside her tried to start a game with a miniature deck of cards while Sam clipped on a plastic moustache and read out jokes in a music hall style, hitting an imaginary snare drum at every punchline.

My attention returned to Rori, who was now distributing gifts. Angela unwrapped a new book. Sam accepted a hat with furry earflaps to protect her shaven head from the cold. 'It's Russian, it's called a Ushanka!' called Rori. Barbel unfolded a case for her recorder. Di shyly unravelled a new Thermos flask because her old one had been cracked by a stone from a passing motorist as she'd sat witnessing at the roadside.

Rori removed the last gift, the largest of all. If she thought she was going to buy me off like this, she was wrong, very wrong. I sat quietly, one eye on the fire.

The women had stopped singing. Sam was ladling soup.

Rori held the present to her body. 'Has anyone seen Jean?'

But Jean was still asleep in her bender, and the gift went back in the bag.

And that was it. I remembered lying in the mud, looking up to her for help while sirens whirled around the black airbase.

'Thirty-two of us got nicked,' Sam was saying, as she filled a bowl for Rori. 'We should rename you Lady Luck.'

With shaky hands I took a last sip of tea.

'Chaos wasn't it,' said Rori, accepting the bowl. 'I hardly knew what was happening.'

She dipped a finger in the soup and tasted it.

'You knew enough to run,' I said.

She looked directly at me then, the silly red hat protecting her curls. But I wasn't going to be silenced. She was a fake, a beautiful fake: this was a game to her. Wasting hours in a freezing cell thinking about her, not knowing what to tell Mum and Dad, willing to make a sacrifice for the sake of peace, for the sake of her. The memory swam back, standing dumbstruck in the smoky pub, Maggie with her mouth on Tony's – the way I'd left without saying a thing. But this was different.

'It's a blur,' she said, checking Sam who was adding more liquid to the soup. Rori didn't care about the camp, she didn't care about us. She probably didn't even care about the weapons.

'You probably had to get back to your boyfriend,' I said.

She didn't answer, but met my eyes and gave the slightest shake of her head: a warning. But she had no right to silence. Not now.

'Boyfriend?' said Sam, slowing her ladle. 'Have you got a boyfriend, Aurora?'

Rori said nothing but her eyes returned to me and she stood very still.

'Why don't you tell them about him?' I said.

Alert to the strains of discord, Barbel put her arms out towards me. 'Come, my lovely. Have some soup. Split peas. You haven't eaten.'

I shook my head. I felt a tightening at my core. My attention fell back to Rori.

'Not as if there's anything to be ashamed of?' I said.

The rest of the women seemed to recede until there was only the two of us and the fire jumping between us.

'No,' she said. But it wasn't an answer, it was an instruction.

I held her gaze.

'Tessa…'

The black sky. The fire. The kiss. Prison. 'She's been sleeping with a serviceman.'

'What?' Sam frowned, then laughed. 'Don't be soft.'

The women around us stirred like sheep unsettled.

'It's got nothing to do with you,' Rori hissed to me, her eyes flaring.

'An American,' I said.

'A Yank!' repeated a voice. 'She's had sex with one of them?'

'It's a wind-up, right?' said Sam.

'But it isn't true, Rori,' said Barbel, her face serious. 'Really, you have not been with one of them?'

'It's not like that,' she said.

Someone gasped. Sam stared at Rori with open disgust. Exclamations from other women, and No! from one of the Sapphire gaters.

'What's it like then?' asked Sam, the new hat making her into someone else, a Russian stranger fierce with anger.

Rori raised her voice. 'This is personal, it has nothing to do with...'

Cat came forwards. 'The personal *is* political!' she cried, 'what's more political than your body?'

Other voices. Four, five, six voices. The women around us came back into focus. They were all joining in.

'These women have been locked up, and you've been fraternising.' It was Debbie, the woman I'd sat next to in my first blockade, wearing the same hat with the CND badge. When she said *these women*, she gestured to me.

'Shame!' came a cry usually directed at the police. 'Shame! Shame!'

Angela stood up. 'Let's be calm. Please, be calm.'

But no one wanted to be calm, they wanted to rage. I raised my arm uselessly, a conductor ignored by his orchestra, unable to control the discord.

Rori stood at the edge of the group, fearful.

'Please, listen, it doesn't mean anything,' she said.

'Doesn't it?' said Cat. As she neared her, Rori dropped the bowl and pea soup splattered the ground.

'No, no. Nothing.'

Di sat down on a milk crate, a black bin liner in her hand, folding herself to stillness.

Sam was furious. 'It doesn't mean anything? Of course it does, it means everything. *Everything*. And what does this camp mean, us getting slammed up, is that a nice little upper-class game too?'

'Don't bring class into it,' said Rori.

'Why not?'

The visitors looked on nervously under their golfing umbrellas. I couldn't make it stop.

'This is my home,' said Rori. Her face cracked with tears, but no one gave her comfort. She was standing at the edge of the fire now, alone. I'd seen her cry before, but then she'd let me put my arms around her.

'Run back to Daddy,' said Cat.

Where was Jean? We needed Jean.

'Shame! Shame!' chorused more Sapphire gate women.

'Stop it!' I said, but not loudly enough and no one was listening.

Rori turned and walked quickly away from the fire towards the road. I went after her, calling her name, increasing my pace, my ankle throbbing. 'Wait!' I called. 'Where are you going?'

'Away!'

'Where?'

She faced me. 'Away. What does it matter?' Her voice caught in a sob. 'Want to send me some hate mail?'

'I'm sorry.'

'No you're not,' she gasped between breaths. 'You enjoyed it. I bet you've been waiting for just the right opportunity haven't you?'

How could she not understand? 'You left me. You ran.'

'I can't look after you all the time.'

'But you left me,' my voice was loud and out of control. 'We were locked up. You didn't even wait at the camp.'

'I went to see my mother, she's a mess at Christmas.'

From where we stood we could hear both traffic sounds and the voices of the loudest women at the fire.

'You shouldn't have joined the action, if you were worried about being caught.'

'How dare you tell me what I should do!' She was shouting. 'Why should I be a good little martyr?' She threw her hands in the air, her voice choking, 'Everything is royally fucked up because of you. Have you, in your little suburban head, any idea what you've done?' It hurt to look at her.

It was wrong, all wrong, it shouldn't be like this. 'But you left me.'

'You! This isn't about you.'

'But…' The tears were rushing down my face. 'I thought…'

'No you didn't, there was no thought. Why do you want to hurt me? What have I done to you?'

'I wasn't, I didn't…' My hands fell to my sides. How could I explain to her what I couldn't explain to myself, that I loved her. We were breathing hard. 'Why did you kiss me?' I'd said it. Finally.

She shook her head. 'Kiss you? Because I felt like it. It was spontaneous. It didn't *mean* anything.'

No it didn't mean anything. What could it possibly have meant?

She looked back at the scrappy benders, our patch of muddy ground. 'This place is all I've got. I made this my life. Now I've got nothing.'

'I'm sorry.' She walked on and I followed. 'Please stay.'

She whipped around. 'You're even more naïve than I thought.' Her voice was full of disgust.

'Let me talk to them.'

'You've done enough.'

We were nearly at the road. She picked up speed and I went after her, but she turned aggressively, telling me to leave her alone. I wanted to press a finger to the beauty spot near her lip. I wanted to pull her to me and beg for forgiveness, and then she'd be able to feel my heart struggling against her and know it was breaking and she was breaking it.

She put her hand in the pocket of her new coat. 'You might as well have this,' she said, her face empty. 'Happy Christmas.' She turned and walked into the dark.

I fumbled the box open. Inside, on a bed of dark blue velvet, lay her peace symbol earrings, their silver sheen catching the moonlight.

★

I felt as dead as winter. But I couldn't leave. As part of our bail conditions we had to report to Newbury Police Station every day. I was with Jean during one of these visits when the desk sergeant asked if we'd seen a newspaper. We were at the front of the line and the rest of the women formed a shambling queue behind us. Registering our blank response, and pleased with himself, he reached under the counter for a tabloid, flicking through until he found the right place. He folded the page back and laid it before us.

'There you go.'

LADY MUCK SLEEPING WITH THE ENEMY.

I scanned the four short paragraphs below the savage capitals. They told the story of Posh Peace Girl's Bonk with US Airman. They'd got hold of a photograph of Rori in an evening gown. Also illustrating the report was a snapshot of three hardcore members of Sapphire gate during a blockade, a photo of Rori's family home, and a snatched photo of Jocasta with her head down wearing a scarf and fitting her key into her front door. I felt giddy, a wave of nausea rising through me.

In among all those new faces at the fire it would have been easy to plant a journalist. I thought of Rori hearing of the report, and Jocasta seeing the news, their name dragged through the mud. What would her father think? It was all my fault.

Jean sighed and pushed the paper back over the desk. 'This is of no interest to me,' she said. 'Is there anything else or can we go?'

He raised his eyebrows, 'All publicity is good publicity, isn't that what they say?'

The rest of the women were waiting to file into the station, all the women who'd interrupted their lives to witness for peace. I lowered my head as I passed them.

32

Miss Student Body

'Are you sure about this wig?' I ask Maggie. We're making our way from the bar, which is the main point of illumination and dazzles bluely like a swimming pool at night. Everywhere else is inky dark.

'Blonde suits you,' she replies over her shoulder, half speaking, half shouting because a heavy baseline has begun to reverberate from an early '80s hip-hop track, so loudly I can feel it in my heart. It's years since I've been inside a nightclub and this cavernous maze, which has the surround sound of a multiplex cinema, is a far cry from the glitterball hang-outs of my Stevenage youth, their tricolour disco lights and boxy amps.

Tuesday night is '80s night at the Punch Bowl in Ipswich and everyone is encouraged to dress the part. Tonight is also the regional semi-final of Miss Student Body, which is why we're here, me in my stone-washed denim and Maggie doing a fair impression of Carol Decker. Maggie insisted on the outfits; she said they'd help us blend in.

'Where shall we sit?' I defer to Maggie because she was always the one to decide: back in our teens it was all about being noticed but tonight it's more about camouflage.

'No one will spot us here,' she says, stepping gingerly up two shallow stairs, 'I can hardly see my own knees.'

By no one she means Pippa. When I mentioned the competition to Maggie she threw back her head and laughed, *Wouldn't you love to be a fly on the wall?* And that one casual remark has somehow resulted in us driving across the east of England dressed like extras from a Bananarama video. Our plan is to slip into the club, watch the competition and then slip away. But the operation is more than idle curiosity on my part: it's being done in an effort to understand my daughter, to shed the blinkers of what she calls my lefty prejudices. Despite its name, I want to believe that Miss Student Body is for confident and even, yes, empowered young women.

Our circular table overlooks the low runway around which a young crowd is assembling. A veil of dry ice begins to roll over the platform like lakeside mist.

'What *are* Rockshots anyway?' I ask, eying up the screens emblazoned with electric pink branding. The contestants must be waiting behind them.

'Flavoured tequila shots. Yuk.' Maggie pulls a face. 'One of their reps came into the pub. Taste like melted ice-pops laced with booze. How's the G&T?'

'All right. It's taking the edge off.' For the last twenty minutes I've been swinging between nervous excitement and all-out anxiety. 'Think I'll ditch these,' I say, unrolling my legwarmers.

'They go with the outfit,' she says, laying a restraining hand on my arm.

'I've had my share of looking daft recently,' I say, then immediately regret alluding to the make-over show because we've agreed to put it behind us.

'Honestly Tessa, I thought I was helping out, thought it might even bring you and Pete closer together...' She knows about Pete and the supply teacher, but I don't want to go over it all tonight. 'Still, it's not as if I'm a relationship guru, is it?' She shrugs and takes a sip from her blue-tinted glass. 'Actually I'm having a break from the internet stuff.'

'Are you?'

She nods. 'It's wearing me out.'

'You'll meet someone, you're bound to,' I say pointlessly because what do I know, and what if she does and he turns out like her ex-husband Rick who got himself a gambling habit and worked his way through their joint account? And who says she'd be happier if she met someone anyway? How many relationships start off the same way, two people sharing a lovely bubble which carries them high over the dreary factories of daily life until they're dropped onto a stretch of waste ground, blinking, wondering what happened.

'What's on your mind?' asks Maggie, and I check myself.

'Nothing.' I raise my glass, 'Here's to a good night out.' We clink and chat about nothing much until a brassy fanfare sounds and a voice announces: 'Ladies and Gentlemen, welcome to Miss Student Body.' Squeals from the crowd. My stomach turns over. 'Please welcome your host for the evening…' I've a feeling the host in question is behind the screen giving his own introduction '…Gary Bunch.' Maggie squeezes my arm and Gary springs on stage looking suitably pumped up, his hair a study of highlighted spikes. He addresses us with holiday camp bravura before introducing the four judges who each take their seats at the foot of the runway. One of them is the owner of the nightclub, a porky chap in a cummerbund who looks all set for a dinner dance.

'Are you ready Ipswich?' cries Gary after some more spiel. Ipswich confirms that it is and Gary's voice hits a high. 'Right then, let's meet the girls!' He waves an arm to herd them in and the sound system erupts with a diva belting out a song the crowd knows – something about letting me show you what I've got – and a dozen young women stride onto the runway dressed in party outfits. They've obviously been instructed to dance because there's plenty of jigging and twirling. One girl mimes the stirring of a giant bowl of invisible cake mixture.

'There she is!' says Maggie. I catch sight of Pippa, her hair falling in loose curls around her shoulders. 'She looks fantastic.'

And she does. Moving fluidly in a short tulip-shaped skirt with a long-sleeved red top, she spots a friend in the crowd and waves.

'Let's hear it for our Miss Student Body finalists!' calls Gary, still whooping up the audience. When the contestants have done a circuit of the runway they form a line, ready for Gary to approach with his microphone. They are all lovely and all wearing numbered wristbands. 'And what's your name?' he asks a tall girl in a sequined mini dress, turning to the crowd as if to speak on their behalf. He could very well have a day job demonstrating food mixers in shopping centres.

The tall girl, Eve, tells Gary she's studying medicine. Cue a toe-curling remark about doctors and nurses. Eve laughs along because seven years at medical school must be expensive. He moves down the line, giving out vital statistics and engaging in the same embarrassing banter. Is this irony? It's hard to tell. And is he meant to be sending himself up too? I remember Dom in our living room, crossing one giant Goth boot over the other and shaking his head.

'And next we have...' My heart is bolting as the mic is presented to Pippa. She leans towards it and gives her name.

'P-p-p-p-Pippa,' says Gary with a stagger. 'And what are you studying over there in Kent...' He glances at his clipboard but thankfully doesn't have any double entendres for European Studies and Economics. Seeing her up there I feel the same anxiety as when she played the Fairy Godmother in an infant school production of Cinderella.

'So you're here to win?' asks Gary.

'I'm here to have a good time,' she replies, less comfortable now, one hand locked to her hip.

Is she having a good time? I take another sip of gin and tonic and try to relax, but the next thing to come out of Gary's mouth puts paid to that.

'I heard a whisper that someone in your family wasn't a big fan of this competition.'

Pippa seems surprised by the question and hesitates. 'My mum wasn't too keen.'

'And why's that?' asks Gary cocking his head in mock innocence.

Pippa stands too close to the mic and it pops. Gary pulls it back. 'Um, she's a bit old school.'

'What?' I say aloud.

'Is that right?' says Gary, who then asks her something about burning her bra, which elicits cheers from a group of lads in the front. Pippa bites her lip then remembers to smile. It's like watching a car crash. The only problem is that my daughter is one of the victims and there's no way I can pull her from the wreckage.

'Is this as bad as I think it is?' I ask when the girls have finally been interviewed and the break arrives.

Maggie grimaces. 'It's pretty bad,' she says like a doctor confirming test results. 'I'll get you another drink.' She's gone for ages and I sit in the deafening gloom, wondering whether to leave. Duran Duran pumps through the speakers. A girl with a charity bucket is circulating, and when Maggie sets down the drinks there's hardly time to discuss what we've seen before Gary is back to introduce the talent round. The crowd has swollen. The anticipation is palpable, reminding me of the one and only time I went to a greyhound race, that moment before the traps sprang open.

By the time Pippa is introduced we've had one too many contestants singing warbly American ballads and the audience are restless. My fingers play fretfully with my nylon hair. Please don't sing, I whisper, trying to remember if I've heard her sing anything since she used to entertain us with The Dingle Dangle Scarecrow. When her name is called she walks on wearing the party outfit and high heels, a basket over her arm. Some sections of the audience are talking amongst themselves. At the centre of the stage she stops, puts the basket down and signals for music. But the music isn't the intro to a ballad, it's a burst of Scott Joplin, and from the basket Pippa removes three beanbags which she throws and catches in a simple loop. After a few seconds she halts, silences the music, gives the crowd a knowing look and replaces the beanbags. The incidental chatter dies down. This time she removes from the basket a banana, a tangerine and an apple, holding up each piece of fruit deliberately. She cues the music again, flings the fruit up and begins to juggle. A few cheers. I'd forgotten all about her childhood talent. When she was little she'd to come to rallies with me, there were always kids for her to play with, and by the time she was thirteen she could juggle five beanbags and do tricks. At a change in the music she dips into the basket and removes another banana which she presents with a theatrical bow.

Standing square, holding the four pieces of fruit, she throws the apple up and follows it with the orange, but she's off balance and catches them prematurely, rocking on the high heels. *Come on Pip*. This time, she kicks the heels off and stands barefoot, looking at the top centre of the imaginary arc to keep focus. One banana goes up, the tangerine, another banana then the apple until she's throwing and catching in a fluid loop. She walks in a circle, faces the audience and reverses the direction of the loop to the sound of applause. As the piano music reaches a last chorus she changes the pattern by crossing the bananas so they're arcing high over the other fruit. The urge to call out like a stage-school mum is nearly overwhelming. Me and Maggie are already clapping hard even before the music stops.

'She's got to win with that,' cries Maggie.

'I know!' I yell back, high with pride and excitement.

Gary returns and asks where she learned to juggle. Smiling naturally now, she invites him to have a go. The audience urges him on until he's forced to try. When he does the beanbags fall to the floor with a thump, thump, thump. Pippa takes the mic and gives instructions but Gary's not getting it. After the second attempt he takes the mic back, thanks her again and directs her to the wings. Still feeling the glow of maternal pride I watch the last acts pass before us – a girl limbo dancing under a length of bamboo and another playing a bass recorder. Pippa could definitely walk away with this. Definitely. Suddenly I'm glad we came, glad to be wrong, glad I'll be able to tell Pippa this. And then Gary introduces the final section of the competition and my heart drops like a beanbag.

'*Swimwear?*' I say to Maggie. 'He's not serious?'

But he is. On they come a few minutes later in a flourish of flesh and assemble side by side to a roar of alcohol-fuelled cheering.

Eve the medical student is first up and she sashays forth in her black bikini and sarong, which she whips away at the end of the runway, pivoting to appreciative whistles. Gary rubs his eyes in mock amazement. 'What about that ladies and gentlemen.' Eve takes her spot beside him.

Maggie calls Gary something in Anglo Saxon.

My eyes dart back to Pippa who's now wearing an orange one-piece and a pair of heeled sandals. *Run away!* I want to shout. Miss East Anglia is followed by Miss Cambridge who appears in a high-cut yellow costume. And then Gary raises the mic to his lips and calls for my daughter.

The diva music ramps up as she walks the runway wearing an uncertain smile and not much else. At Gary's side she casts her eyes to the crowd, some of whom are yelling out.

'Looking lovely. How about a twirl for our judges?' Gary's in charge again and he's enjoying it.

Poor Pippa. She smiles and agrees she's having fun, though her body language says otherwise – she's standing stiffly, four strangers giving her marks out of ten. Oh God. Gary consults his clipboard, ready to ask one of his inane questions – if you had to choose, which of the seven dwarfs would you date? – but just as he's starting to speak there's a commotion. Two figures spring on stage. One has a megaphone. She shouts something indistinct which becomes clearer: *Grades for brains not for bodies!* The contestants group together like gazelles.

'What's happening?' says Maggie. I'm on my feet. Gary doesn't know what to do, and nor does Pippa. The megaphone wielder clutches something, and with a rapid movement she hurls it at Gary, but he dives out of the way and as he does, a cloudburst of blue powder hits Pippa on the side of the head.

Pippa! I'm shouting her name, pushing through the crowd to reach the stage. The bouncers get hold of the two protesters but half a dozen others rush up. They have more bags of powder. 'Stop!' I shout, and then there's strong light and I'm on the platform with my daughter, who is frightened and half dressed, blue powder spread like a swathe of bruising over her face and shoulders. 'Leave her alone!' I shout, trying to snatch another of the bags. Pippa is frozen with shock. The crowd are in uproar. Gary's professionalism has slipped and he's swearing.

'Mum…?' There's horror in Pippa's voice. A bouncer grabs me from behind.

'I'm her mother!' I shout, trying to wrestle him off. With my arm still locked in his he asks Pippa if it's true, his face an angry orange suntan. She backs away but says it is and he lets me go.

Two fat-necked bouncers are shoving the protesting girls off stage but yet more dive out of the crowd to replace them, skipping around and unfurling a banner which reads 'Miss-ogony' in luminous letters. The DJ cranks up the music. A girl in a princess costume and heavy boots is running after Gary, attempting to bomb him and despite everything, it's gratifying when she lands a bag of purple flour on his head.

Pippa disappears behind the screens with the other panicked contestants and I follow into the backstage chaos where girls are shrieking and a woman in a Rockshots t-shirt is trying to calm them down. There's a lack of light and the floor is strewn with clothing. Pippa blinks at me from her half-blue face. 'What are you doing here?' She says it as if I'm the one who's thrown the powder. 'And what are you wearing?'

Raising a hand to my head I remember the blonde wig and pull it off.

'It was for '80s night.'

She stares disbelievingly. The dye is smudged against her shoulders and arms and as she wipes her cheek a streak of colour transfers to the back of her hand. A new thought occurs to her. 'Did you organise this?'

'What?'

She gestures, 'Whatever that was… that protest.'

'No, oh Pip. No. We came to… to support you…'

'Who's we?' Now she really looks appalled. 'Is Dad here?'

'No. No. Me and Maggie.'

'*Maggie?* You came for a laugh?'

'No!'

'What then?' She kicks off the high-heeled sandals and puts a leg into her jeans.

Another girl in a swimming costume is close behind her, squealing to a friend about this being a complete bloody joke and what she's going to do when she finds out who those mingin' feminists are. Pippa grabs a sweatshirt from the floor and pulls it over her head, marking the neck with dye. I want to help but she's scrambling about, unzipping her bag, digging for tissues to wipe her face.

'The juggling was brilliant, Pip, I haven't seen you juggle for years.' She's worsening the powdery smear as she wipes. 'Where are the loos, let's get you cleaned up.'

She turns away. 'I can do it.'

'Oh, love.'

'You were right, OK. Is that what you want?' Her voice is controlled desperation. 'This was a mistake.'

'No, no. I don't care about being right…'

But she's not listening. A t-shirt flies sideways as she roots in the clutter. I want to tell her I don't care about proving points. I want to comfort her. But she has her back to me.

'Do you want me to go?' I ask. She doesn't reply. Still holding the scratchy wig like the pelt of some ruined creature, I re-enter the pandemonium.

33

Butterflies

News of Rori's affair with the American circled the camp, repeated in whispers. Some of the Sapphire gate women who'd come to stay at Amber showed me a new respect, because the way they saw it I'd been willing to sacrifice my closest friendship for the sake of my principles. But I didn't want their admiration. If they could have seen my heart turned out like a pocket with all its contents spilled onto the mud, they would have known the truth.

Conversation centred around the forthcoming trial and how we'd deal with it. The women who'd never been arrested sat at the feet of those who had, listening as they recounted stories of court appearances. A woman called Liz said she never stood up when the clerk asked everyone to rise, and they'd stopped threatening her with contempt because it was more trouble for them in the end. She told us the legal process was designed to be official and intimidating but we shouldn't be afraid. She said the term for someone who defends herself in court is Litigant in Person and we didn't have to use solicitors. The tall poet from Barbel's birthday party said she'd be happy to write a poem for anyone who wanted to use it to represent herself, and we thanked her but no one took her up on the offer.

All the time, as the conversation rumbled on around the fire, another stream of talk was going on in my head in a quieter voice; I was telling Rori I missed her, I was telling her I was sorry and I'd make everything all right, if only she'd come back. Over and over again I saw her walking away into the dark.

Mum still didn't know about the trial. When I'd phoned to tell them I wouldn't be home for New Year she'd started agitating, 'When are you going to stop all this nonsense?' she said, before Dad cut in on the new extension. We still had to report to the police station every day, so I couldn't have gone home even if I'd wanted to. I said why didn't they treat themselves to a nice holiday, and Mum's voice came back on the line saying how could they go and relax in the sun while I was still living at that place. I said I'd be down soon and everything was all right, and asked about the new carpets to try and keep things light, but when Mum said goodbye there was a catch in her voice and I knew she was only a second away from sobs. Poor Mum. She'd be in a terrible mess if I went to prison, even worse than the one I'd be in. I didn't think, even in my most heroic imaginings, that I'd be able to cope with being locked up. If there was an opportunity to escape Holloway, I resolved to take it. I'd agree to be bound over.

New Year's Eve stayed dry but a bitter wind came blasting through the camp, threatening the fire. We sat tight, arm-in-arm, drinking donated sherry from plastic cups, and when Barbel played 'Down by the Riverside' on her guitar, we swayed side to side as she sang in her Dutch accent, 'I'm gonna lay down my burden down by the riverside, ain't gonna study war no more', rousing us for the chorus. After that Jean sang the words of 'Old Lang Syne' in Scots, 'An thers a han, my trustee feer! An gees a han o thyn! And we'll tak a richt gude-willie-waucht, fir ald lang syn.' I thought about Rori and couldn't swallow down the pain in my throat. It was too dark for anyone to notice, and our eyes were always streaming anyway because of the wind and the smoking fire – only Angela took note. Her eyes danced over my wet face and I turned away.

'To peace, my lovelies!' sang out Barbel as we hugged and toasted each other. 1983: the year I would turn twenty, the year the missiles were due to arrive. Everyone said we could stop them coming – public opinion was on our side and hadn't the Tories got a big-gun advertising agency to help them win the propaganda war? They were afraid. There was an election coming up.

The weather turned colder and frost hardened the mud into swirls like Christmas cake icing. The ground stayed white all day until it disappeared into the four o'clock dusk. We built the fire up as high as we could, glad of the wood deliveries which came more frequently since news of the Christmas action had broken. Two days before the trial, I was sitting around one of these high fires with Barbel. Mid-afternoon was the worst time of day, the dead hours between two and six before everyone regrouped and dinner was prepared, a bottle opened and the conversation and singing began. I'd been trying to read but couldn't concentrate. Barbel had been re-knitting an old scarf but had given up because even inside her gloves, her fingers were too cold to be nimble. My mind drifted to a time only two weeks before when she and I were sitting around the fire laughing with Rori.

I'd decided to tell Barbel about my decision to be bound over. When all was said and done, I knew Angela was probably right, if I couldn't spend a couple of nights in a police cell without falling to pieces, then the prospect of being locked up properly and receiving a criminal record would definitely be too much. I was about to start this conversation when Jean arrived to ask if I wanted to work on the tapestry for a while. A visit to Jean's tepee was always a good thing; it felt special, like being invited into the staffroom, a chance to sit on one of her cushions and talk about the world. I followed her across the stone-hard ground.

During our conversations in the tepee, I'd learned that Jean was born in India and lived there for twelve years before her parents sent her to boarding school in Sussex where her childhood abruptly ended. Before that she'd enjoyed a barefoot, game-playing life climbing trees and splashing in rivers. Her parents had worked with a group who supported the Indian freedom movement. When we'd all gone to see Gandhi together at the cinema in Reading, Jean had wept.

'Are the butterflies finished now?' I asked.

Jean passed me the elephant cushion and I sat down. But she hadn't opened the sewing basket yet to unravel the embroidery which she'd been finishing for a local campaign group to auction. I'd helped sew the stems of the poppies, and Jean had carefully worked her needle to make leaves and butterflies. There were only a few finishing touches left around the border.

'Tessa.' She reached across, laying a hand over mine. Her gloves were navy with elastic around the wrists and leather padding on the insides for extra grip. My gloves were rainbow striped and I wore my fingerless mittens over the top. 'I'm afraid something terrible has happened,' she said. The elastic on her right glove was pulled tighter than that of her left. 'Tessa.' She was waiting for me to look at her, and when I did, her face sprang into focus, concerned, serious, the expression of a surgeon breaking bad news. Except that this wasn't a hospital, no one was having an operation, I was here in her tepee. A shadow went through me.

'Rori has died,' Jean said, fixing her eyes to mine. 'I'm sorry.'

I'd misheard. No. She'd only been gone five days.

Her blue glove on my striped glove. 'How? How can she..?'

'She drowned, Tessa. I don't know the exact details. I read it in the *Times*, only a snippet, but I wanted to tell you before you found out.' Her voice was coming from a long way off.

'You must have made a mistake. It must have been someone else...'

But her voice remained calm, as if she wasn't aware of the storm crashing and destroying everything in range, turning everything to sticks.

It had happened in Cornwall, said Jean. With nothing to grip hold of I felt myself swirling and choking too, Rori rising and submerging, and then the image of her face as I'd seen it last, empty, one curl falling over her eye. I saw her walking alone into the water. *It's harder to drown than you'd think.* My teeth began chattering, and then my legs and arms were jittering and shaking, as if I'd been pulled up spasming from a freezing sea.

'It's the shock,' said Jean. Her arm went around me, solid and real. She held a flask to my lips, its fumes rising. 'Brandy,' she said. Me and Rori, drinking brandy side by side, the pub alive around us. 'Come on dear,' came Jean's voice. I opened my mouth to speak but the words didn't come out and instead I swallowed them with the brandy. *It's my fault.*

34

Bourbons

'You know what you can have in your coffee now?' I raise my eyebrows in expectation, waiting for Mum to tell me, and she does with obvious pleasure. 'Amaretto syrup.'

We're discussing café society. 'Remember when having coffee in town meant a cup of filter in British Home Stores?' This is something I've noted before but that's not important, the important thing is that Mum gets to chat happily on for a while, the burgeoning coffee shop scene of Stevenage having become something of a pet subject in recent years.

'That one near the bus station is good, but they leave the gateaux in the fridge too long. Who wants chilly cake?' she says, twisting one of the pearl buttons on her dressing gown. 'Mind you, the tables are always spotless.'

It's ten o'clock and we're settled on the sofa before bed. I've a morning workshop at a local comprehensive so I'm staying the night rather than catching the train all the way back to Heston. Home looks the same as it always does, cared for, polished, orderly. The conservatory they had built after their pools win is lovingly attended to, its orchids and glossy-leaved rubber plants, the liberty-print armchair where Mum sits in the afternoon with her crossword.

On the television a Mediterranean chef assembles an elaborate dessert, but neither of us is paying much attention and my gaze wanders towards the figurines.

'Is she new?'

'Couldn't resist,' says Mum, reaching for another Bourbon.

The ballerina stands in an arabesque beside her sisters: the milkmaid shouldering two heavy pails; the three shepherdesses with their crooks; the rosy-cheeked farm girl; the fine lady in her fancy hat and empire line frock coat; the Dutch girl in shiny clogs. All of them have been helping to keep Mum company since Dad died three years ago.

'Are you going to tell me what's up then?' says Mum, and when I turn from the china she's studying me. I'd tried to keep up a convincing stream of conversation over dinner and washing-up, offering snippets of news about this and that, local happenings, neighbours. I also recounted the fundraising picnic in Heston Field: she particularly liked the description of Dom offering close-up magic tricks for a 50p donation. Thankfully, the day was a huge success – sunshine, steel band, cake stalls, bouncy castle for the kids – and with some last-minute effort we managed an impressive turn out. The local paper chipped up and took photos. Pete was in one of the pictures wearing a Save Heston Fields t-shirt underneath a striped apron. He'd been due to take his lower-sixth on a field trip to York that weekend, but mindful of our sessions with Valeria he'd arranged for a colleague to cover and offered to man the barbecue instead. The supply teacher has changed things.

Mum still has her attention on me. She seems alarmingly old tonight, the fine lines of her face easily traceable without foundation or rouge. Naturally I haven't mentioned the Pete situation. She loves Pete, has done from the first day he entered our living room, filling the space, his head inches from the

305

ceiling. 'Isn't he tall, Tessa?' she'd said afterwards. Gregory Peck, John Wayne, Jimmy Stuart, she'd always liked tall men. She and Dad stood shoulder-to-shoulder, and though he was solid, with a broad builder's back, she liked the notion of being swept upwards. And she liked Pete's family too, *professional people* she called them, a GP and a music teacher, a cousin somewhere who worked in the Foreign Office, all part of that upwards sweep.

She's still waiting for an explanation. 'You're all out of sorts,' she says matter-of-factly. Impossible to imagine her on a two-seater sofa giving up her most intimate feelings. *Me and your Dad just got on with it*, she once said.

'I'm fine.'

'You're not fine, I'm your mother and I know.'

I flop my head back and laugh, exasperated. 'Mum, I'm forty-eight.'

'What's that got to do with it?'

I never tell her anything that'll worry her, but I'll have to offer something, not the supply teacher, not the discontent that's been churning like a waterwheel since meeting Angela, not the scene in the Ipswich nightclub with Pippa smothered by blue powder, but something. I say we're having a few problems with the charity. She listens and asks questions until she's satisfied.

'Just your job is it? No more run-ins with Maggie?'

She knows about the make-over show-down, but I assure her we've patched it up, and she sips her tea. 'Well, I'm glad you're pals again,' and her voice becomes factual. 'She can be a bit silly.'

'But you love Maggie.' Mum's known her so long she's almost like another daughter. She likes her verve and her lipstick and her high heels, her breezy manner and her gutsy laugh.

'Yes. But she's a bit silly,' Mum repeats. 'Always has been. Remember all those get-ups she used to have on herself? And the hair!'

We recall a few of her more memorable experiments: the Medusa-style perm; the blonde asymmetric fringe; the bridesmaid's dress cut down and dyed crimson.

'I used to think you'd have preferred her for a daughter,' I say, half to myself, regretting the hurt which passes over Mum's face. 'Only, you know, I wasn't much good at fashion, was I?' A memory of the day I left for Greenham: Mum and Dad in the kitchen, me with my Doctor Martens and rucksack, Mum turning to Dad as if he might be able to do something.

'Come on Tessa, as if that matters.'

'Sorry,' I say, knowing she would have loved us to go through the Littlewoods catalogue together all the same.

'Anyway, they didn't do a bad job on you, those TV people. I thought you came out a treat.' She takes me in. 'Even so, I prefer your natural hair colour.'

She tells me again how she watched the programme with her friend Shirley. Recently she's begun to repeat herself. In my own cowardly way I find it easier to ignore the signs of her ageing rather than to see them close up, that way she can stay here forever in this house wearing her frilled dressing gowns and eating biscuits.

'Shirley said they could teach her daughter-in-law a thing or two – have you ever met Dawn? She's one of those poor things with the thighs.' She draws her hands apart illustratively. 'Wears these terrible tight jeans, like sausage skin.' While Mum is sidetracked by Shirley's daughter-in-law, I begin to imagine Angela at home watching the programme. I decorate her house with original art works and Eames chairs, then wonder if there should be a few children's toys or teenager's clothes scattered around. Perhaps it's a modern and functional place, the home of someone who devotes her life to work. Is there a portrait of the Madonna in a discreet alcove? I remember her at the Southbank, the small gold cross at her neck falling forwards as she laughed, a wave of sunlight brightening her blonde hair. Is she a contented Catholic now? Perhaps she's made enough sacrifices to earn that privilege.

'A woman I used to know from Greenham Common got in touch recently.'

'Did she? One of your chums?'

'Not especially. She saw the show, we met up.'

'That's nice. Did she fancy a make-over too?'

'Not exactly,' I recall Angela's Italian shoulder bag. 'She works in advertising these days.'

'Is that right?' Mum nods approvingly. 'You could have had a job like that if you'd wanted. Be better than trekking all over the countryside for no money wouldn't it?' She smiles to let me know she's joking, but only half joking. I don't comment because for the first time I've started to think the same thing, especially after our funding review collapsed.

It's been another long day; part of it spent giving a school's workshop in Peterborough. When I split the class into groups and gave out questions for discussion, a girl with brutally scraped back hair and a lot of eye make-up regarded me with dismissal and said that as long as the lights came on when she clicked the switch she didn't give a shit where the power came from. Her friend laughed. The teacher was chatting to her colleague at the back of the room, and too tired for a confrontation, I carried on. Everyone has bad days of course. But then, why not have a bad day and get paid for it?

Angela's company website, MPP (Mullen, Powell and Porter), a sleek affair of sliding graphics, has her photographed in black and white, back lit and self-assured: Angela Mullen, Creative Director and Partner. I pondered that photo for much longer than necessary, and her passage through life; the years in America, her career in academia, then the transfer into a new world of immaculate cream suits. Meanwhile I've been trying to push boulders up mountainsides for about 53 pence a week. That photo of Angela gave me a stricken feeling I couldn't quite explain. Over the years when I thought of the common, she was one of the people I held clearest, her round glasses, that pale face peering out of the parka into a book or away into an imagined future. Her phrase about protest requiring sacrifice stuck with me, but was that advice delivered by a different person? Has she had her therapy and reinvented her life as if none of it mattered? I can't tell and it's not the sort of question that can be easily asked, but it lodges in my chest.

'How long did she stay there then, your friend?' Mum never says Greenham, she says *there*, or *your camp*, and on occasion *that place*.

'Angela? She left before I did.' That reminds me, I didn't ask about Seneca, the peace camp in New York State where she was bound.

'Smart girl.'

It bothers me that Mum's so intransigent after all this time. She catches my sigh.

'Well,' she says, 'bunking down in the mud for heaven's sake. I never understood it. You were a girl, weren't you, young for your age I suppose, but as to those middle-aged women. Married women, some of them.' She shakes her head.

'Plenty of married women came, and plenty of men supported them. Those women were there because they had convictions, Mum.'

'Maybe so, but they didn't have to give their convictions to you.' She shakes her head, as if at some private memory. 'Convictions don't always do people good.'

'What do you mean?'

'You weren't the same after you came back from that common. It was like you'd shrunk and grown all at the same time.' Her voice is serious. 'They did something to you. They changed you. You came back different.'

I wonder who Mum's *they* are, and even as I wonder I know she's right, I did come back different. It's just that she's attributed the change to an army of radicalised women.

'No one was brainwashing me, Mum. You could have come if you'd wanted. Seen it for yourself.' It strikes me that a visit from Mum would have been the last thing I'd have wanted back then.

'I nearly did,' says Mum, 'when you didn't come home for Christmas. Your dad stopped me, said we should leave you be.'

'Did he?'

She seems vexed at the memory. 'You weren't the sort to be living under a canvas sheet. You thought you were, but you weren't.'

She sighs thinking about it, that shadowy period of time, just them in the house, scanning the papers, waiting for me to ring from the Newbury phone box when I couldn't always get there. She would have been worrying about the worst, whatever her version of the worst was. Motherhood in the eighties: a world without texts.

'So Dad was all right with me staying?'

She purses her lips. 'We didn't see eye-to-eye about it.'

'Really?' Hard to imagine Dad being insistent, he was so mild, and in truth it was usually Mum who had the last word.

'In fact,' a fond note enters her voice, 'he became your number one defender, got into a row with Bob Potts about it all.'

'What, Dad and Bob Potts?' My mind skids about at the idea of Dad arguing with anyone, least of all Bob, long-time manager of the Old Volunteer, loud and ruddy, pink ham fists clenched around the ale pumps.

'Some of them in there were having a few cracks about the women and your dad got his hackles up. He'd done his stuff by then, his research, he knew all the arguments. He kept a scrapbook.' Mum waves to indicate the side cabinet. 'Probably in one of those drawers.'

'Honestly?' The idea of Dad cutting out clippings with the kitchen scissors is incredible.

'Oh yes. He really blew his top with them, came back here steaming. Didn't go in there for a month.'

Tomorrow I'll hunt out the scrapbook and see what Dad was collecting, but not tonight; tonight I don't want to think any more about that Greenham Christmas and everything that followed. My gaze wanders back to the ballerina's porcelain slipper.

'So will you be seeing your advertising friend again?'

'We're keeping in touch.'

Whoever Angela is these days, she's been true to her word when it comes to Easy Green, and since our meeting at the riverside she's invited me to Feel Good, one of the new and fashionable summer festivals her company helps promote. She's offered me a stand in the charity tent. When I mentioned this to Pete he suggested coming along too. I've wanted us to get back into camping for years, but not like this, as a last resort, the two of us zipped together in a last ditch attempt at intimacy. But Valeria tapped her pen against her notebook and said we should see the festival as an opportunity. So now it's arranged.

'Is it just work that's bothering you?' says Mum, still uncomfortably attentive to my mood.

'I'm fine... I just... I think I'm a bit over tired that's all.'

'You go at things too hard, Tess,' she says, 'why don't you at least drive down when you visit instead of mucking about on those trains?'

That's another conversation, but it's too late at night to discuss carbon emissions. Not that I want to. The energy efficiency leaflets for pensioners. The polystyrene cut-outs for primary school children. Suddenly it all feels so pointless. I think of that girl today with the hard face.

Mum sets down her cup. 'How's everything with Pippa?'

With that 'everything' I take a guess that Pippa's rung. If Pippa can talk to Mum, why can't she talk to me? Probably because I've made it that way. Too judgemental. Too quick to fill her with my own ideas.

'Did she tell you about the competition?'

Mum nods. 'Sounds like quite a night.'

She anticipates my question before I find a way to say it.

'Pippa only confides in me because I'm her old granny, it doesn't matter what I think.' Mum doesn't keep giving her opinions all the time, that's probably the truth of it. 'She wants you to be proud of her, Tessa.'

'I am proud of her.'

Mum doesn't comment further, and settles back on the sofa. 'It'll pass. Quite honestly I never knew what was going on in your head when you were Pippa's age, couldn't work you out. And you and Pippa aren't so different, same stubborn streak.'

It's painful, the knowledge that I've got things wrong with Pippa somewhere along the way, and failed at so many other things I wanted to get right.

'You look dead beat, love.' Mum shuffles over and puts her arm around me, frail now, so that when I lean into her I can feel her bones under the quilted dressing gown.

'What is it Tessie?'

'Nothing.'

'You can tell me.' At that moment I love her more than anyone in the world. 'Touch of the mid-life crisis is it?'

'I don't know. I've been thinking about the past lately, that show stirred it all up, I expect.' The past with its liquid language, *Time and tide, Water under the bridge,* but this water never truly passes, it washes back and forth bringing its freight of memories, all those faces, and that one face in particular.

After three or four quiet minutes Mum turns off the lamp. 'You'll feel better after a good sleep.'

'I've got a few things to do before tomorrow,' I say, thinking of an unfinished grant proposal.

'Never mind about that,' she says, moving my laptop bag out of reach. 'Come on missy, up those stairs.'

35

The Muncher

I was stirred from sleep by a commotion and sat up, straining to make sense of the jumbled sounds. It was early morning and I hadn't been asleep long – after two weeks in prison I'd found the return to camp disorientating, even though I was glad to be back among friends. Now there was shouting. Machinery. Shapes moving outside the walls of the bender. I pulled on my boots and when I peered outside my worst suspicions were confirmed: bailiffs. One crossed the centre of the camp carrying an armful of tarpaulin from somebody's bender, stomping past the flameless fire pit towards a machine like a dustbin truck – this must be the muncher I'd heard about. A woman dragging the nylon chrysalis of her sleeping bag stumbled in the other direction. Conflicting voices echoed through the clearing, '…orders from the council … my home…' and fragments that were indistinct, phrases that clashed and careered into each other, male and female voices coming underneath or overtop the constant grinding of the truck. '…out the way there… Stop!…' and in an accent which sounded like Barbel's the word *please*. But unlike that first night, when the local youths had arrived in their car, the women weren't able to force the men away; no ululating cries could dispatch them back into their vehicles.

One of the bailiffs, wearing gloves like a bin man, a donkey jacket over his round shoulders, lurched towards Rori's empty bender carrying a large-handled knife, presumably to hack through the strings and branches which held the frame. With a desperate heart I dived into my own bender to gather what I could – jeans, jumpers and the little pile of Rori's belongings I'd saved after she went – stuffing my trainers into my rucksack, snatching my sleeping bag and running with it towards Jean's tepee. The handful of women camping at Amber gate were moving in panic, grabbing to save what they could and I nearly collided with Angela who appeared out of the mist holding the portable typewriter. Sam clutched a stack of paper bundles from the fridge and followed behind. 'The van!' she shouted. 'Get stuff in the van! Who's got the keys?'

'Jean,' I said. My sleeping bag overspilled my arms, slippery and difficult to grasp, so I dropped it and ran to Jean's tepee. One of the bailiffs was already there, turning everything upside down as Jean did her best to reason with him, wearing pyjamas under her coat, her hair in uncharacteristic disarray.

'Council orders,' said the man, who had his arms around a wicker basket, a cigarette on the corner of his lips.

'Keys,' I mouthed to Jean behind his back as he lugged the crate towards the muncher. She took them from her coat pocket and threw, I snatched them out of the air as the bailiff turned, the crate of Jean's belongings clattering with him. Forgetting to go back for my rucksack I ran across the foggy clearing towards the van which was parked under the trees a short distance from the road where Angela and Sam were waiting, and quickly we began piling stuff inside.

'We need to fill it up with everything we can and move it to the public highway, then they can't claim it,' said Angela, dumping the typewriter on the back seat.

I returned for my things, telling the other women to take

whatever they could to the van. Already my bender was in the process of being destroyed: a bailiff pulled at one of the walls and a whole sheet of plastic came away so that for a second I paused to see it lifting through the mist like a weather-beaten sail. He tugged another sheet and the entire frame gave way, but I didn't have time to watch and went running to salvage what was left in the kitchen – saucepans, cutlery. Angela struggled with a roll-up mattress and between us we got it to the van while the benders collapsed one by one around us. The men worked quickly. The same one who'd been carting away Jean's belongings set about pulling down her tepee, the last structure standing. A furious Jean shouted at him but he carried on regardless.

'We're taking stuff to the van,' I said as calmly as my adrenalin-fuelled body would allow. She looked on, clutching an armful of her clothes, a candy-striped blouse draped over her arm, and reached into the tepee, which now flapped open at the seams, to try and retrieve a zip-up holdall.

'Leave that, we've got to clear the lot,' said the man, tearing the canvas free as if he were unwrapping a giant ice-cream cone.

'My clothes. Where's your decency?' said Jean. But the bailiff didn't want to talk about decency; he had a job to do.

I grabbed the bag for her. The man stopped unpeeling the canvas from the tepee frame, and seeing where my hand was going next, he snatched Jean's Indian print elephant cushion and threw it out of reach. I remembered the embroidery, all those hours of labour, and scooted past him to pick up the sewing basket.

'Come here!' he said, discarding the cigarette from his mouth. I had my hands firmly on the basket. 'Give it over. You lot shouldn't be here,' he said striding forwards, but I dummied him, racing as quickly as I could to the van. Angered, he followed, knowing nothing about what was in the box, only that it was important.

'Sam! Sam!' I shouted as she piled two garden chairs onto the back seat. 'Start it!' I clambered in with Jean's sewing box, the bailiff's shouts growing louder, and we slammed the door, panting, as Sam wiggled the unwieldy gearstick, ground the gears and steered onto the road. The bailiff's face receded in the wing mirror to the sound of our cheering. 'They'll want to clear the other gates next,' I said. Most of our camp must have gone into the jaws of the muncher by now.

'You get out and help the others, I'll take the van and warn Ruby gate,' said Sam.

I jumped out and ran back towards the camp in time to see Barbel try to wrestle her guitar free. 'No!' I yelled, going to help. But there was nothing we could do. The man had the guitar by the neck and threw it in an arc towards the muncher. Barbel shrieked. The muncher didn't discriminate; it guzzled anything they fed it. With nothing left to save, we watched as two of the men hauled the Welsh dresser up off its feet and lowered it into the mouth of the machine.

An hour later, there was nothing left, only a handful of women sitting in the mud beside a shallow pit where the fire usually blazed, a few ragged bits of debris strewn around. One long pole staked in the ground was all that remained of Jean's tepee. They'd even torn down the WOMEN AGAINST CRUISE banner.

'Shall we put the kettle on?' I said. Jean gave a smile.

'Have we still got one?' someone asked.

'It's in the van,' replied Sam, who'd returned from warning the others. 'Anyone seen the teabags?'

Di, who'd been sitting silently on the log opened her coat. 'For emergencies,' she said, unfolding a polythene bag with a dozen loose teabags inside. Everyone laughed. Everyone except Angela who sat unmoving at the end of the log, staring a thousand-yard stare.

'Angela,' I said, rousing her out of her trance. 'Help me gather some wood.'

'Come on girl, stir your stumps,' said Sam, giving Angela a friendly shake on the shoulder. 'Can't do anything without a fire.'

Angela got up automatically, without seeming to register who we were, and did as she was told.

36

Feel Good

It's day two of Feel Good and the nine-hundred-acre site is thick with activity. Thousands of people swarm over the grass in search of entertainment or food or something they haven't quite decided on yet. From my station in the charity tent, I catch glimpses of the human traffic: a group of teenage boys dressed in togas, a golden-limbed mum with her golden infant bobbing in a papoose, couples swigging cider from recyclable pint glasses. Pete is out there too somewhere, a programme marked up with his must sees, and apparently Pippa is here with her university friends, but I haven't seen her. Since the Miss Student Body fiasco, mother/daughter relations have reached an all-time low. There haven't been any phone calls, only text messages to Pete. I am very definitely persona non grata. Despite this I continue to scan the crowds for girls with long chestnut hair.

The festival is cleaner and altogether more attractive than any I've known, with theatrically designed canvas spaces set up to host hundreds of events. Whatever you're feeling – poetic, jazzy, funny, thirsty – there's a dedicated space for you to feel it in. The Feeling Thoughtful tent is propped with giant book-cum-armchairs, and audiences gather inside for lectures by popular scientists or TV historians, while those who are Feeling Flirty can visit the red-feathered marquee to watch burlesque performed on love-heart-shaped stages. Smiling twenty-somethings wander around giving out free copies of *The Guardian*, or trial sachets of herbal hand-wash, and little flowered vans patrol the grounds collecting rubbish and attending to the wondrous paraphernalia: talking toadstools which offer directions, networks of stepping stones which light up magically at night. If you don't want to be performed to by the roaming jugglers, singers or stilt walkers, you can always relax in the super-sized trifle, an arrangement of beanbags and squishy cushions. Entire families are welcome to lie back in the custard while couples drowse below them suspended in jelly.

Angela's company, MPP, has been promoting Feel Good since it began, growing it from what she called a boutique cultural event to a place everyone wants to visit – teenagers, hip young families and the youthfully retired. It'll be the perfect platform for Easy Green, she said. So here I am in the Feeling Caring Zone, slotted between Save the Children and Amnesty. Looking around on the first day, I couldn't help suspecting the charities had been handpicked to promote the right image: there's plenty about human rights, environmentalism and overseas development, but not much in support of battered women or nasty degenerative diseases. Still, I'm happy to be among the chosen and grateful to Angela. Each charity takes a turn to run a workshop in the Feeling Factual tent next door and the scattering of people who turned up to mine were among the most relaxed audience I've ever addressed, content to sit back and nod appreciatively before making their way into the sunshine to queue up for enchiladas or just have another nice flop on the grass.

A stream of footage from the sexiest charities is projected on a screen, interspersed with clips of celebrities promoting the causes nearest their hearts, and between unpacking a box of leaflets my gaze falls on a soap actress who's describing a well-building project in Tanzania. Dressed in a simple black t-shirt

318

she offers high cheek-boned sincerity as the camera moves in for a close-up and the charity strap-line glides under her chin. I'm pondering our chances of securing the patronage of a local celebrity for Easy Green – perhaps a Look East presenter – when I catch sight of Pippa on the other side of the tent. Not a look-alike this time, but definitely my daughter. A spark of joy fires in my chest like a wick flaming on a long-dead candle. She's with a boy and they're moving in a circular path around the stands. I have a flashback to our last meeting, me in the stonewashed denim and blonde wig, her smeared with blue powder. Never mind, she's here, she's come to see me. I wave a leaflet in the air and track her arrival through the crowd.

'Hello, Mum.'

It's not an unfriendly hello, but neither is it the voice of loving enthusiasm. I resist the urge to hug her, unsure how it'll be received. She's wearing the sort of outfit that seems to be popular, spotted Wellingtons and a short floaty dress that flares out prettily revealing an expanse of tanned thigh. The festival is bursting with teenage girls working the tantalising gap between welly and skirt. To keep it casual she's slung over an old cardigan, recognisable as one of Pete's, the sleeves rolled up to show off her bangles and wristbands.

'We've got some time to kill, and Mikey wanted to have a look in here so…'

In one breath the flame in my chest is extinguished, but I carry on smiling.

Mikey is tall, good teeth, drainpipe jeans and Ramones t-shirt. Perched on his head is a little straw trilby. He has beautiful features and speaks a hybrid of public school dampened with estuary English.

'You didn't say your mum was an environmentalist.'

Pip's eyebrows lift, as do mine, because the way he says environmentalist is the way someone might say concert pianist.

'Yeah, she's been into the environment and stuff for years, I mean for as long as I can remember.'

319

I'm waiting for the crack about me signing her up to The Woodcraft Folk at birth but it doesn't come. Mikey nods. 'Not like some of this lot, jumping on the bandwagon,' he turns his head to indicate the people outside the open wall of the tent. A new line is forming at the vegetarian risotto shack: options include porcini mushroom, grilled aubergine, and Tuscan bean. Never mind burgers and chips, this festival offers everything from macrobiotic salad to French bistro classics. It's the first time I've seen Bouillabaisse served in a field. While Mikey pours serious scorn on the middle-class masses, Pippa stares with a serious expression too, but hers is serious adoration and is directed at his neoclassical profile. When he's finished despairing, she says, 'Mum was at Greenham Common actually.'

I swallow the overwhelming desire to laugh.

'Right,' says Mikey.

I'm fairly sure he has no idea what Greenham Common is or was, but he pays the information due reverence anyway and in order to spare him the bluffing, I change the subject and ask what they've been to see. But after a brief rundown, he turns the conversation back to Easy Green. Pippa is quick to answer his questions and the guttered candle flares into life again – this might be the first time she's stood beside me with something like pride rather than embarrassment. He soaks up the information from Pippa and says to her, 'So you're into this too?'

'Yes. No! Well…' She regards me fleetingly, a glance that is almost an apology. 'Not like Mum exactly… when she was my age she was a hard-core protestor.' She offers information about Greenham and as she does, Mikey regards me with extra admiration and I realise with new and swift understanding that Pippa is under a misapprehension. The version she has of her teenaged mother is nothing like the truth. Her face has become concentrated. 'She was living outdoors and everything, and from what I've read…' She's read about this? When? 'It was

320

really hard, fetching water from a stand pipe, dealing with the police…' Somehow she imagines me as a former heroine of the frontline. 'There's no way I could have done that.'

'Pippa, Pip…' I place my hand on her arm to stem the flow, 'I had next to no idea what I was doing back then.'

She faces me, puzzled.

'But you were in the camp, weren't you? You left Gran's and went to live with those peace protestors.'

'Yes, but it didn't mean I knew anything. I stumbled to Greenham partly by accident.'

She positions her head at a new angle, as if she's misheard, and I explain something about Stevenage and Tony and wanting to reinvent myself. Mikey glances from mother to daughter and seeing this is family business, moves tactfully along the trestle table to browse a stack of leaflets. As she listens, I sketch a picture of Stevenage in the 1980s. My days of copytyping. The lure of activism.

'But what about *Never let a man be the reason for your decisions*, that's what you used to tell me,' she says. I shrug. 'And you went off and… you mean, a bloke dumped you and you went to live on a common…'

'It wasn't exactly like that.' She's staring at me in disbelief. 'There was a bit more to it…'

'That is desperate,' she repeats. I shrug, contrite. Mikey interrupts politely to remind Pippa that Little Boy Roots is on in the Feeling Wordy tent.

'He's a slam poet,' she informs me before resting her eyes on Mikey once more. I haven't been inside the graffiti-sprayed spoken word den yet, only heard the poets echoing outside and admired their swagger from afar. 'We better make a move,' says Pippa, consulting her festival brochure, then adds, 'but this subject is not closed.' I hold my hands up in surrender, which elicits a grin.

For the next two hours, until it's time to leave the stand and meet Angela for coffee, I am foolishly, deliriously happy.

Suitably casual in flip-flops and jeans, Angela sits opposite me on a picnic bench, dipping her chopsticks into a box of Thai noodles while I sip a black coffee. She's wearing minimal make-up, only a sweep of mascara to emphasise her eyelashes which, as I remember, were so fair they almost disappeared. We've been discussing Easy Green.

'What's your mission statement?' she asks.

'We don't exactly have one.' I tell her some of the things we do, the energy advice service, and the schools workshops, and the gardening project. She interrupts, chopsticks aloft.

'This is the problem, Tessa, you're attempting too much. You're unfocussed. You need to project a single, clear message.' I nod, remembering the young Angela and her bullet points. She takes another mouthful of noodles then adds as an afterthought, 'And you should reconsider the name.'

'Really?'

'*Easy Green*, it sounds like an airline for hippies,' she replies, neatly pinching a cube of tofu. I try not to feel bruised: she's directed lots of charity campaigns, she knows what she's talking about, and I trust her in the way I trusted her at camp, the girl with the clipboard ready to oversee all eventualities. 'You need to concentrate on defining your brand, raising your profile, diversifying your funding streams, all that stuff. We should arrange a strategy meeting.' I'm touched by that use of *we*, grateful she's making it her business to help.

On a nearby stage, a small Andalusian woman is stamping and clicking in an impressive display of flamenco and the audience cheers her on. I take another sip of my rapidly cooling coffee. The morning began with blue skies, warm buttery light filtering across the grass, but since midday the cloud has moved in and the wind has changed direction. A delicious smell of green curry comes wafting over, reminding me of the less appetising aromas of the common and the long hours and days when we had nothing to do but sit and chat or stare into the fire. Or, if you were Angela, work through a pile of books. I picture her deep in her parka, deep in a Russian novel.

'What's amusing you?' she asks.

'Oh, nothing. I was thinking about Greenham, what we would have given for some of this entertainment.'

'There was always the women's puppet theatre.'

'True.' I remember something else, 'What about that girl who visited once with the harp? Dragged it over the mud.' We agree that making our own entertainment was part of the challenge. I nearly mention Barbel's birthday party but edit myself in time, 'My kids can't live without their technology.'

'I know, even here we're offering Wi-Fi pods,' she remarks. 'It's a modern disease, the fear of boredom. There's a name for it.' Two blinks are all it takes for her to find the word. 'Thaasophobia. As opposed to Theophobia.'

'What's that?'

'The fear of God,' she says, tilting the box. 'I might have suffered from that myself once.'

A crocodile of children winds through the crowd, following a woman in orange pantaloons who leads them onwards while clanging a pair of cymbals. Feel Good kids don't have to settle for the usual climbing frames and face-paint; they're invited to learn circus skills or devise their own plays with the assistance of professional acting troupes. I marvel to Angela again about everything on offer.

'People come for the entertainment, but they're really paying for something else,' she says motioning to the glut of recycling bins, and the fresh fruit stand and the Feeling Caring Zone, 'All this helps to create a mood. People like being in a community, and that's the experience they get here, even if it's only for a long weekend.' She's right, the atmosphere is co-operative, relaxed and almost self-consciously friendly. 'And research shows that being green, or rather perceiving oneself to be green, makes us feel good about ourselves. So we push that.'

'Hence the solar-panelled shower blocks?'

'Better to have them than not. I love this festival, but no one's here to solve global warming, they're here to have a good time and they don't want to feel guilty about it.' She says it matter of factly, and looks to the crowds migrating between tents. 'In the end, what everyone wants is some great entertainment, a few drinks, Pad Thai,' she lifts the empty box to indicate herself, '…and a nice fuzzy feeling on the way home in the Prius. Of course the ultimate answer is to consume less, but the world would stop spinning if that actually happened. So it's our job to deliver another message: consume *differently*. Make a *difference*.' A cloud of applause rises and breaks from the flamenco stage. 'People like you are rare, Tessa.'

'People like me?'

'People who aren't just talking the talk.'

She's waiting for me to speak and I do, awkwardly. 'You just have to remind yourself what's important and what isn't.' I don't mention the fact that between conducting home-visits to discuss cavity wall insulation I've been tormented by daydreams set in swanky advertising offices, none of which feature conversations about reflective radiator panels.

'And what isn't?' she asks.

'I don't know… shopping.' This is the first thing to enter my head, and definitely the wrong thing to say given that Angela works in advertising and hers could be the hand that helps to feed us. But she isn't offended.

'The truth is people like stuff. And they like new stuff. Novelty. It makes life more joyous. I have a good lifestyle – could I give it up now and live in a one bedroom house and never buy another designer frock or try a new restaurant? Probably. If I had to. But I don't want to. In the end you make a choice.' I listen to see which way the conversation will go. 'I mean, obviously I *recognise* the argument that we're conditioned to buy more than we could ever possibly need.' I meet her eyes, unnerved by her ability to second-guess my thoughts.

'Sorry, I didn't mean to sound pompous. I think I might be a little jealous of your choices actually. There's nothing glamorous about what I do.'

She smiles; the ground is safe beneath us.

'When I think back, it's hard to believe we lived like that on the common.' Her tone is unsettling. 'It seems unimaginable to me now.'

The young Angela never complained about the weather, she never complained about anything tangible like wet feet or poor food. Her grievances were large and global.

'One of my toenails went black and fell off,' she says in sudden memory and laughs, startled anew. 'Probably from wearing those same wretched boots.'

'Really? I had no idea.' Why would I have had any idea about Angela's toenails? They were as private as her feelings.

'I limped around for about three weeks.'

I picture a ring of booted feet propped on hot stones at the fireside. While we were chatting and joking Angela must have been hidden away in her tent, ministering to her toes. 'Everything's easier when you're young,' I say.

'True,' she says, 'but think of Jean and all those older women who gave up their comforts…'

Jean must have been ten years older than we are now when she arrived at Greenham.

'She was one of a kind,' I agree.

The conversation turns back to Easy Green and Angela swipes her phone to find us a meeting date.

'It's good of you to give up your time like this,' I say. She knows we can't afford to pay, but she shakes her head. 'Pleasure. Anyway, you're helping ease my corporate guilt.' She glances up, 'It's not as if I don't occasionally wonder why I didn't become a human-rights lawyer.'

'Why didn't you?'

'Honestly? I wanted to have more fun.' Angela and fun were not two words I would have equated once upon a time. 'On the flip side, if the business is earning enough we have some flexibility about which clients we take on, so we can work with the people who need us regardless of their budgets.' She catches something in my expression. 'Alex, my partner... Alex says advertisers will tell themselves anything for a good night's sleep.' This is the first time she's mentioned her personal life and my ears prick up.

'What line of work is Alex in?'

'Academia – Development Studies.'

A few light spots of rain darken our picnic bench. I'm poised to ask more about Alex but my breath catches before any words form – a figure weaves through the benches, pulling up the hood of a red sweatshirt. I straighten, alert as a gun dog. It's her, I'm sure it's her. Angela is talking and I tune back in with half an ear. She's saying something about a party '...one of the festival sponsors is putting it on, they're a client. Nice company, they make the cider you've probably seen everyone drinking.' I'm keeping one eye on the red hood. 'It might be useful for you to meet, see if we could get them interested in a relationship...' The figure in red is queuing at a food stall, it's her turn to pay. 'Are you all right, Tessa?'

Angela follows the direction of my gaze.

'Sorry, yes. Think I've seen someone I know.'

Two more drops of rain catch my arm. Faces tilt skyward. 'We'd love to come. Listen, can I text you...'

Umbrellas go up. I'm on my feet. A bare-chested musician stops playing his African drums and runs them to shelter. I follow the red hood across a stretch of open grass towards a network of stalls which drip with beads and scarves and tie-dye skirts. Two women in front are struggling to put up a fuchsia golfing umbrella and when they succeed everything goes pink, but I manage to overtake them and yes, she's still in view, pausing at the walkway which connects two main arenas, taking shelter under a cedar tree. Rain flicks at my eyes and bodies pour past, fresh from the Feeling Funny tent. She takes a bite from the hot dog then checks her phone and returns it to her pocket. What if he's sending her messages? Oh God, what if they planned it together? Perhaps that's what happened, he decided to meet her while I was rattling my charity tin all day.

My body feels light as I approach the tree. The wet wind changes direction carrying a surge of world music over from another field before veering away again. We're close to each other, as close as you have to get to ask a stranger the time and indeed when she faces me she thinks the answer to a question is expected.

'Hello.' I try to keep my voice steady.

She frowns slightly inside the hood, wiping the side of her mouth with a paper napkin. A strand of hair whips across her face and she tucks it back. I thought she might recognise me but actually no, I hadn't thought that far at all, only as far as not letting her slip away, and my heart is pumping as if it's still on the chase.

'Do you recognise me?'

She bites her lip, half apology, and considers for a second. 'I don't think... but you do look familiar. Sorry. Were we at college together?'

'No.' That's all. I want her to guess again. She hesitates, confused.

'Was it a PTA?'

'No.'

Any conviviality is all but gone. 'Then I'm sorry but...' Her face lightens as the answer comes, 'You came round collecting...' She's pleased to have remembered yet this satisfaction is overtaken by further confusion because what I say next throws her off balance. She asks me to repeat it.

'I said I'm Pete's wife.'

The pearly inside of the sausage glistens and falls from the bun.

'Peter Perry.' I say his name.

'Sorry, I don't quite.' More people are channelling over the walkway, a few are running for shelter under the trees. 'But the

327

charity… you said… are you…' her voice falters. 'Are you stalking me?'

'*Stalking* you?'

The rain gathers force. Neither of us moves. It's what Mum would call a clear-up shower, but nothing has been cleared up. Not yet.

'What are you doing here?' Her voice has a note of demand, coloured by fear.

I blink at her, incredulous. 'Isn't that the other way around?'

'Look, I have nothing to say to you,' she declares and still holding the empty bread roll, walks away towards the busy thoroughfare. I hurry after, against the crowd and against the rain, dodging a group of lads, a Superman cape flaring out behind one of them, hurrying to catch up, and when I do I stand square in front of her, because I have to know.

'Are you here because of him?'

She's breathless and when she speaks the Irish accent is more pronounced. 'No… no, I didn't even know he was coming.'

'So what are you doing here?'

'Trying to have a good time. Like everyone else.'

Is that true? I don't know what to believe anymore. Whatever has to be said, has to be said now.

'We've got children!' The words are louder than I expect and two women in flowered rain-capes nudge each other and pause to watch, as if this were a piece of close-up theatre, part of the entertainment. The supply teacher becomes quiet and official.

'I'm not having this conversation,' she says and turns away.

But she's not going to brush me off like an awkward parent, this woman who's been circulating in my thoughts for weeks. 'How convenient for you!' I shout at her back. 'How bloody convenient!'

She stops, hesitates and then retraces the few steps towards me. The crowds are still herding past, rained on, exuberant. When she speaks this time her voice falls away. 'Look, I promise you, it's over.'

328

Her eyes meet mine for the briefest second and I see in them something I recognise, something I've experienced myself, on a different expanse of wet grass many years ago; the dim sorrow of rejection. A little girl wearing a fairy outfit and a cagoule sploshes by hand-in-hand with her mother.

I stand still to watch the pink gauze of her wings bob into the distance. When I look back, the supply teacher has gone.

37

Departures

Two days after the eviction, I lay in Rori's bath imagining my way through one of her books, a collection of Greek myths. Every goddess had her face. When Actaeon lingered in the wood to watch the beautiful Artemis bathe, I saw Rori turn towards him, fierce and lovely, surrounded by nymphs. She cried out with fury and transformed him into a stag.

The afternoon was bright but cold, and the bath's high sides were protection from the wind. It was a relief to slip away to read, especially since there was almost nothing left of Amber gate, only six of us sitting around like refugees in the mud, trying to keep our spirits up. The two other camp members had gone home, leaving me, Jean, Sam, Barbel, Angela and Di. We'd managed to fashion a new shelter for ourselves with donations, one long tent-like structure which accommodated us all, but there was hardly anything left of our original camp. The bailiffs had crammed everything we owned into the mouth of the muncher, but they didn't know about the bath hidden in the trees. We'd survived. The rebuilding hadn't begun in earnest yet, but we had shelter and food. The women were regrouping. *A luta continua.*

Sunlight turned the leaves to yellow medals. If I had no one else to talk to, there were always the trees, and they kept my secrets, however dreadful. If I whispered her name at night, the trees themselves would bring it back, *Rori, Rori, Rori.*

Lying where she'd lain, I thought of her that first morning, crunching on a carrot. She'd once said that boarding school had prepared her for the meals at camp. During my two weeks in Holloway I'd eaten the sloppy macaroni cheese and grey stews without complaint, although I'd had little appetite. An edgy, queasy feeling stayed with me all day and all night. At camp, the missiles hovered on the edges of our imaginations though we'd never seen them up close, only television images or newspaper pictures, but the prison with its metal and echoes and frigid spaces was frighteningly real. For the first time I saw what it meant to be poor and disenfranchised and brought down. I shared a cell with a woman called Ronda who told me she'd been locked up for shoplifting. Her mother was looking after her two kids, and her boyfriend was in Pentonville for doing something she wouldn't talk about.

For the first two nights I didn't sleep at all. On the third night I dreamed of Rori walking into the sea alone on a Cornish beach. She swam up to me and tried to pull me down with her until I woke up gasping and screaming. 'What is it?' said Ronda in the darkness.

'I've killed someone,' I whispered into the pillow. If she heard she pretended not to and hushed me until I was quiet.

During the day we sat in a high-ceilinged room assembling dolls. We had to fit their plastic body parts together: two slim legs, two slim arms, torso with two smooth bumps for breasts, the final plunk of a head with long nylon hair in either blonde or glossy brown. Bernice from Sapphire gate wouldn't do it, said she was having nothing to do with brainwashing little girls, and there was a scene with the wardens. She got transferred to the laundry instead, where she had to load and unload sheets from the dryers and couldn't sit down all day. I stayed silent, plunking the heads onto the dolls and fitting them into their beach wear/party wear: it was strangely trance-inducing work and helped me not to think. They paid us £1.65 a week. I bought tobacco and chocolate and shared them with Ronda.

Ronda couldn't see why the camp women were there when they didn't have to be, but she listened when I tried to explain about the weapons in my own words, without Angela's statistics and vocabulary. I didn't need to try and impress Ronda anyway. 'No peace in this life,' she said. She'd been bringing up her kids since she was sixteen, she'd taken beatings for them, she'd stolen for them and she'd been locked up for them. She knew about causes. She said she was glad if we were doing something that was worth it, and traced her long nails through her plaited hair so they made a scratchy sound. Ronda took pride in her nails, she painted them with care using two coats of acrylic polish and filed them so they formed squares with level tips, not rounded tips the way Mum did hers. She offered to do mine one night after lock up, but I'd bitten them down so far there was nothing left to polish.

When I got out, I circled the base with my eye to the wire, looking for the tall airman, but I never saw him again. Perhaps he'd been posted somewhere else. Perhaps he was dying of a broken heart. More likely he was simply getting on with his invisible life in there, doing whatever it was they did to prepare for the arrival of the missiles. Mum and Dad wrote me a letter on blue Basildon Bond notepaper, which was delivered to Main gate. I'd never had a letter from them before. They wrote on one side of the paper each, Mum's handwriting round and neat, like the writing on the labels she attached to pickle jars, Dad's sloping and narrow. He passed on football results and made a couple of jokes. Mum said she wanted me to come home. But I couldn't go back to Stevenage. That girl had gone.

Thoughts of my parents and prison and Rori went through my head as I lay in the bath that February afternoon reading passages from the book, turning them over as the trees moved overhead. I didn't notice Angela until she was standing nearly beside me. She raised a hand and we exchanged hellos.

'If you're looking for firewood, they had a delivery at Ruby gate, they said we could go and pick some up. There isn't much left here.' A lot of the visitors had taken dead wood and even a few branches, there was no brushwood left at all.

'No. I wasn't looking for wood, I was looking for you. I wanted to say goodbye.' She looked even thinner than usual.

'You're not leaving?'

Of all the women I knew at camp, I imagined Angela as the very last person to go.

'I've been discussing it with Barbel, and I'm going with her to the States.' She regarded me through her glasses.

'What for?'

'They're creating a peace camp like this one.'

'Seneca?'

She nodded.

'What about us?' I said, because I couldn't help it.

'I think I've done all I can do here. Anyway,' she smiled, a brief, tired smile, 'you know what you're doing.'

'But you can't go...' She stood at the foot of the bath, a shaft of pale light falling onto her hair. 'I know we've had our differences but the camp needs you.'

She pulled at a stray branch which wasn't yet ready to bud for spring. A truck passed distantly, the sound of it scoring through our exchange. 'I can do good work at Seneca, pass on what we've learned here.' There was no point trying to persuade her if her mind was made up. 'My stuff's packed.'

'Don't imagine that took long.' We exchanged a smile. Should I hug her?

'So.' She maintained her customary intense expression, but it didn't unnerve me anymore. 'I'll be off.'

'Right.'

I stayed where I was, in the bath. 'Good luck.'

'Thanks.' She blinked at me from behind the glasses. Then she made her way back through the trees. I watched the outline of her parka as she moved like a quick woodland creature, half in camouflage, until she disappeared.

38

An Orange Tent

We are here to raise a glass of complimentary cider to mark the festival's end. It's nine o'clock and the party is in full flow. It is a corporate event and yet somehow the tent has been transformed into a fairy grotto: the walls are draped with sheer orange cloth and strings of amber lights seed the decorations so that everything has taken on a soft sparkle.

Pete is holding a chargrilled prawn by its tail. I haven't told him about my encounter with the supply teacher and don't intend to.

'You look lovely,' he says.

'Me or the prawn?'

'Both.'

My sundress is green cotton with a white daisy print and it flares out in a 1950s' swirl. I bought it on impulse from one of the stalls – it's secondhand, but in the language of Jude I prefer to think of it as vintage.

'I can't remember the last time we were at a party,' he says casting around. There are still a variety of hats on display but fewer wellies.

'Bill and Trudy's Christmas drinks, we always do that.'

'Not last year. You were in Faslane. Don't you remember trying to get back, the snow?'

He's right. There was a demonstration at the Trident base. Fifteen hours on a National Express are hard to forget. But aware this conversation could taint the mood, I turn his attention to the dancers who've begun lindy-hopping beside the swing band, and together we watch as the guy rolls the girl over his back and cradles her in a catch.

We haven't spoken of it but we know this evening is important. It's our last before the return to Heston. At first I thought Pete would do anything to make things right, but then I started to feel less certain, noticing a new resignation in him, as if accepting the roles we'd been assigned for the rest of our lives: I am the time-pressed wife; he is the undervalued husband. After the awful weeks spent half talking, the hourly counselling sessions – that box of tissues planted between us – it's quite possible we could give up, decide to share our parental responsibilities and nothing else. But three nights in a tent have forced us back to each other and this morning, in the half-light, we let ourselves roll together, his mouth on my neck, then my breast, an old-new tenderness.

A waiter offers us canapés.

Pete tells me that Dom's band have changed their name again. This is a good conversation topic, it connects us: we are Dom's mum and dad waiting to stand at the back of his first gig, arms around each others' waists.

'What is it now?'

'Death Squad Training Camp'

'Bit dark?'

We recount their other incarnations. Francis Bacon and the Biros was our particular favourite, but this didn't stick. There was an unsortable argument in which everyone wanted to be Francis Bacon and no one wanted to be a biro.

The party continues to fill up and judging by some of the fabulous ensembles, a man in a gold shirt and a couple wearing matching velvet suits, some of the guests are performers. While Pete finds another drink, I go on a recce to find Angela and spot her in a circle of people. She's wearing a Feel Good t-shirt and a pair of wide linen trousers similar to the ones Jude wore for the make-over show. She waves me over. This time I'm ready for the continental kiss.

'Fab dress,' says a woman in a cowgirl hat who's introduced as Meredith Porter, one of the partners at MMP. 'So how do you two know each other?' Meredith looks first at Angela, then at me, diamante studs glinting in her hatband.

Angela and I exchange a glance, wondering who's going to say it.

'We were at Greenham Common together,' she says after a pause. 'Back in the day.'

Meredith is delighted to have this information. 'Angie, I didn't know you were at Greenham, you kept that quiet!'

'Did I?' It's the first time I've seen her look uncomfortable since our re-acquaintance.

'Was it all lentil stew and singing? God, did you actually *live* there Angie, in the mud? How amazing!' Her face glows.

Angela seems vaguely unsettled, but Meredith carries on, demanding full details. Other people get pulled into the conversation, including the girl beside me who works at the agency; her cheekbones are dusted with glitter and she's wearing the sort of outfit Pip would definitely approve of. Together Angela and I explain a little of what it was like to construct a bender, or de-ice a frozen standpipe or fan a dying fire back to life with a Tupperware lid. The conversation wanders amiably and returns to the festival and life in the outdoors.

'I have to say, the pop-up yurt was a godsend,' declares Meredith, 'I've slept so much better than last year and the kids love it.'

Pop-up yurt? I wonder if she's joking but no one else seems surprised.

'We've completely cracked it this time,' she continues. 'What you need is a double thickness king-sized blow-up mattress and you're away. Earplugs too, naturally. Absolutely can't stand overhearing other people's bathroom conversations first thing in the morning. Ugh.' She shudders. 'Jules brought this amazing tea-light chandelier, adorable, and I pinned up a Bedouin throw to make it more homely. The only thing I'm *desperate* for is a hot bath.'

A man in a flowered shirt who may or may not be called Giles says, 'What about a bathhouse, wouldn't that be a festival first?' And while the conversation courses on, an image floats towards me of that long-ago woodland bath, its exposed pipes and lime scaled interior, a lacy canopy of spring leaves.

Angela turns away from a discussion about a Mexican installation artist to speak to me. 'Did you manage to find your friend earlier?'

'Friend?'

'Whoever it was you rushed after.'

'Oh, no,' I recall the meeting in the rain, the supply teacher peering from her red hood. 'Wasn't who I thought it was.' I can still see her in my mind's eye and that expression, an appeal to be set free. Well, we're free of each other now.

Angela nods, distracted by someone over my shoulder.

'That's our client,' she says. 'I'll introduce you later. And I must meet your husband.' She excuses herself and I search the crowd for Pete.

When I find him he's at the bar chatting to a striking woman with a head of auburn curls. The woman has placed her fingers to her neck, amused by something he's saying, and for a second the muscles in my stomach tighten.

'There you are,' he says resting a hand on my arm. 'I've just been hearing about your friend Angela's adventures in... where did you say the place was?'

'Austin,' replies the woman in an American accent. 'That must have been, what, twenty-five years ago. More. 1983 I think.' She's directing the information towards me, filling me in. 'Angie was backpacking in the States and I was travelling after college,

338

we got talking on a Greyhound bus and six weeks later we were working on a ranch. Though she couldn't actually ride a horse back then.'

'I didn't know that.'

'No?' says the woman taking a sip from her wine. Her gaze is cool, self-assured.

'We've been out of touch for a long time.' I try to picture Angela whirling a lasso.

She smiles, waiting for more information. Pete steps in, 'Sorry, this is my wife, Tessa. She and Angela were at Greenham Common together.' And before I can ask her name, the woman widens her eyes. 'So *you're* Tessa. Of course,' she says, and she smiles her American smile with new warmth. Pete turns to pick up one of the miniature kebabs being offered around on orange trays.

'So was Angela travelling after Seneca?' I ask.

'After where?'

'Seneca. The peace camp in New York State. She was going there after Greenham.'

'Oh that's right. Yeah, I forgot about that,' she says, also reaching towards the kebabs, 'she stayed a few days if I remember.'

Only a few days? That can't be right. Angela had gone there to become the British arm of Greenham in the USA, that was the plan; that was why she and Barbel left. But I don't have time to ask because one of her friends appears apologetically beside us.

'Sorry Alex, can I borrow you, slight drama with the cake.'

Before I can say anything else, the American woman excuses herself, leaving me to stare after her.

'Have you had one of these?' Pete asks.

'Alex? Is that woman called Alex?'

He nods, sliding a curl of green pepper from the skewer.

'Do you know what she does?'

'Why?' he asks, licking his thumb. I repeat the question. 'Works at the LSE, I can't remember what she teaches. Development something... what is it?'

I'm reassembling the pieces of Angela's life to make them fit. 'I didn't know she was gay.'

'Who?'

'Angela.'

'Is she?' he says, 'No big deal is it?'

'Of course not. But, Angela?' I think back to what she said that first time we had lunch at the South Bank, not just about her father's death, but the other things she was struggling with, and it makes perfect sense.

As I'm sorting out my thoughts Meredith reappears in her cowgirl hat along with her glittery-cheekboned young colleague, who seems to have something important to say to me.

Angela was so contained, so bound up in that parka, and then she unzipped herself and walked free.

'...so I can't work it out, I keep thinking we've met before, I'm sure we have.' But I don't need to announce my TV identity because she suddenly snatches at the air as if snatching a gold coin. '*Make Me Over!*'

'That's it!' says Meredith and before I know it, I'm being quizzed all over again, only this time it's not about midnight raids over the perimeter fence, but that burning question: what's Jude like in real life? Pete shifts from foot to foot, as if the ground had started to warm up beneath him. He can only relax when the subject moves on.

'Funny, all the years I've known Angie I never knew she was at Greenham,' says Meredith. 'That explains her fondness for ethical accounts, I expect.'

The glittery-cheekboned girl asks what I do these days and I mention Easy Green.

'That sounds brilliant, it must be really...'

Rewarding? I nearly suggest before she supplies the word herself and repeats it with emphasis,

Meredith steps nearer and declares in a stage whisper, 'It's not as if we don't have a social conscience in our industry... half the junior staff are scurrying around volunteering with the Samaritans.'

340

'Yes, but it must be fantastic to go to a party and actually be proud of what you do,' Lara insists, and five minutes later, I'm telling her about the schools workshops and somehow we're discussing nuclear fuel.

'But we're all going nuclear aren't we,' says Meredith, readjusting her hat. 'I thought the Greens were behind it these days?'

'Some. But it's not necessarily the best solution…' I'm about to dip into the familiar waters of uranium mining when Pete excuses himself. I feel a tug of annoyance at his not very subtle disappearance – visiting the loos is more appealing than listening to his wife yak on about renewable energy. Everything had been going so well this evening. All the signs were there for another frolic in the tent later. But I suppose one romp in a tent does not a marriage mend.

Just then an amplified American voice comes over a microphone on the far side of the tent. 'Ladies and Gentlemen…' The DJ softens the music. 'We have a birthday girl among us!' calls Alex. 'Where's Angie?' The tent ripples with movement as she's sought out.

'I didn't know it was Angela's birthday,' I say, accompanying her through the tent.

'Tomorrow,' she says. 'The big five O. Wears it well, doesn't she?'

A crowd has formed around a colossal pyramid of profiteroles, and Angela is there too, flushed, one hand to her cheek as Alex starts everyone on 'Happy Birthday' in her good loud voice. When we come to 'Happy Birthday dear…' I'm singing 'Angela' when everyone else is singing 'Angie'. After the applause, Alex puts an arm around her in a sideways hug and there are cries of *speech*.

'Can't see you!' comes a voice from the back. Angela is presented with a chair and made to climb onto it.

'You haven't come to listen to me, so I'll keep it short.'

'Like you!' calls Giles of the flowered shirt. More laughter.

She thanks her creative team, the cider company, the performers, and says how proud she is to be involved with the festival. 'And thanks to Alex for this fantastic cake, which I have no idea how to cut.' She smiles down, then raises her glass. 'And here's to feeling good.' A cheer goes up. I'm pleased to be one of Angela's chosen; despite the fact I don't know who she is anymore. 'To Angie!' someone calls, and we repeat the toast, raising our glasses high. There's still no sign of Pete, so I find Angela and wish her a happy birthday.

'You're not fifty yet are you?' she asks, and I tell her I'm a little way off.

'That's right, it's me and Rori who were close in age,' says Angela, taking a sip of her champagne. 'I think I was a year older.'

'Who's Rori?' asks Meredith eying her shining pile of pudding.

'Aurora Fletcher,' says Angela. 'A girl we knew at Greenham, looked a bit like the young Diana Mitford but with a tumble of curls. I think we were all half in love with her.' She takes another sip of champagne, eyes on the bubbles as they break in a fine column, and then her expression lightens. 'She had quite a spirit. I remember once the two of us were giving a talk in Oxford...'

'A speak?' I say.

'That's it. A speak! God, I haven't thought of that for years. And after it was over she had a wild burst of energy and tried to make me stay up all night drinking; we'd met these students in a bar and she persuaded them to steal a punt and take it down the Cherwell. The college porter came out and read the riot act.' She smiles at the memory. 'I suppose if she didn't have that reckless streak she might still be with us.'

'What happened?' asks Meredith.

'Isn't she the girl who drowned?' says Alex. Suddenly I don't want to be caught in the heaving swell of the orange tent, trapped in this conversation, but there's no way to escape.

'It was very sad, but evidently they'd done it before...' says Angela, glancing at me as if to cue me in. But I'm not following what she's saying. She turns back to Meredith. 'She was cliff diving with her friends, I think they call it tombstoning now. It was something they did every New Year when they stayed at her family home.'

'God, how awful,' Meredith remarks. 'How old was she?'

I'm watching Angela's lips moving but it's difficult to connect this with what she's saying. I'm remembering the afternoon that Jean told me; the heat of the brandy, the dreams of Rori wading into the freezing sea, stretching up her arms to be saved. My mind is struggling to untangle the conversation, groping for clarity like someone swimming through seaweed, and when I speak the conversation has drifted to another subject, away from the dead girl who no one could save. I address myself to Angela while the others are in discussion.

'But I thought...' My throat is tight, and I force the words out, 'I thought Rori drowned herself.'

She looks at me with a creased brow. '*Drowned* herself? Whatever made you think that? No, it was her and her friends. They had some insane ritual where they'd go down to the sea and jump in at dawn. Her mother told me. I got in touch with her after Greenham.' I think of Jocasta, pinning her photograph to the fence. 'With everything that had happened, the family wanted to keep the press out of it as much as possible.'

Angela's words come filtering down to me as if from a great height and it's a moment before I can articulate anything. I lower my voice until it's barely audible and when I speak, it's almost to myself.

'I always thought it was my fault. I was the one who drove her away.'

I stand there trying to make sense of it. 'It was because of me that she went to Cornwall. After we had that...' I leave the sentence unfinished.

'That scene over the serviceman?'

343

I nod, still ashamed to remember it.

Angela shakes her head. 'She would have gone to Cornwall anyway, she went every year. Besides, she wasn't going to stay at Greenham much longer, I could see she was getting restless, the thing with the American was just a distraction. Oh, hang on, Tessa.' She looks at me with concern. 'You didn't really think…'

But I did. I did really think, I did.

39

Peace

It's an August afternoon and we've spent a couple of hours wandering over a stretch of heathland, passing grasses and gorse and purple-flowering heather, stopping to read the information boards with their illustrations of nesting birds, Dartford Warblers, Woodlarks and Nightjars. When Maggie offered to take me for a day out, a pre-birthday treat, she said it was my choice, we could go anywhere, a health spa or the races or Kew Gardens. She didn't expect me to say Greenham Common. The runway has been uprooted, cycle tracks and conservation ponds landscaped into the flat space, and the whole area is contained by a simple waist-high fence strung together between wooden posts.

We've nearly finished our picnic and I'm remembering what it was like setting off to Newbury on that first October day.

'You told me I should have gone to Butlins.'

'Did I?' She laughs and shakes her head. 'I don't remember that. All I know is you were doing that secretarial job and then things didn't work out with…'

The sentence hovers before us, a dragonfly in the warm air.

'Didn't work out with who?'

Two boys are running a kite, and I remember Jean telling me about the high winds that bowl over the unprotected expanse, strong ground winds that could have been disastrous if they were carrying pollutants. Maggie rolls a cherry stalk between her thumb and forefinger.

'We never did talk about it, not really,' I remark, as lightly as possible.

After Holloway and then the eviction, I spent a few more weeks at the camp before going home, on Jean's advice, to re-sit my A-levels. Like the good head teacher she was, she encouraged me to think of my future, put my head down and work. There was no question of returning to an office, and I couldn't have sat transcribing the little tapes for Mr Hirschman because all that seemed like a lifetime ago. Mum and Dad didn't mind what I did, Mum wouldn't have minded if I'd set up my own clown school as long as I was out of *That Place*. Maggie and I patched things up without reference to Tony, and then I headed off to university in Leeds and threw myself into my politics degree, signing up to every society and action group going.

Maggie gives in with a sigh. 'Go on then, what do you want to know?'

'Tony Mercer,' I say, brushing my fingers against a knapweed flower, 'why did you go out with him?'

'It was years ago, I can hardly even remember.'

This isn't the truth, and she knows I know.

'All right. All right.' She thinks. 'That time I came to visit, when everyone was holding hands...'

'Embracing the Base.'

'That's it. I drove home in Mum's car. It took hours getting out of there behind the coaches, and when I put the key in the front door there was no one in. Mum and Dad were at work and the house felt, well, I felt, sort of... empty.'

I let the image of that sink in a moment. Young Maggie sitting on her bed, forlorn. Maggie didn't do forlorn.

'I don't know what it was Tessa, honestly. I was bored. He was bored. I didn't even fancy him, but I felt left behind. You were off with your friends, saving the world, probably never coming back...'

'But didn't you always say he had a wonky eye.'

'Did I?' She laughs.

I say his name out loud, 'Tony Mercer, I wonder what he's doing these days.'

'He married a pharmacist and went to live in Leicester.'

I turn to her. 'Did he? A pharmacist? You never said.'

She shrugs and offers me a last dip into the bag of cherries. 'God, Tess, have you been carrying that around all these years?'

She asks how things are with Pete. I tell her they're improving slowly and think about our final visit to Valeria's Georgian house, that warm orange space where she assembles the chips and fragments of other peoples' relationships like mosaic pieces. We'd sat watching a shadow tick along the wall, lightening and darkening a shelf of books, and I'd glanced over at Pete, stiffly nodding at Valeria's suggestions. And when she'd talked about making time to share experiences together, breakfast in bed for example, we caught each other's eye, giving and receiving the same thought, *How did we get here?* In that exchange were the years of all our other exchanges, and I felt a gap was closing. Afterwards we went to a cafe in the square and drank coffee in the sunshine and watched other couples passing through Cambridge and didn't speak much. On the way home, when we stepped off the train, he took my hand.

The sun brings a spray of daisies into focus and I lick the sharp cherry juice from my fingers and tell Maggie about our new plans for Easy Green and the meetings Angela is helping organise.

'Bit of luck bumping into her again,' she says before raising an eyebrow and adding, 'maybe I did you a favour with that programme after all...'

We look at each other and laugh.

I close my eyes, feeling the sun on my neck spreading like a silk scarf, thinking of all those protesting women, wondering where they might be now and what they might be doing; the thousands who stood in the freezing mud holding hands around the base, the hundreds more who camped overnight or sat for months with their backs to the fence. The curious. The committed. The accidental.

After another few minutes the sun is lower and Maggie stretches. 'I was thinking we might get a glass of wine in one of those Newbury pubs. That's if they let in the likes of you.'

She reaches for my hand to pull me up. But there's somewhere else I'd like to have a look at before we go.

The old GAMA compound is the only area that's still sealed off from the public. We can't see much through two layers of fencing, but Maggie and I have our faces to the wire and are trying to distinguish the faint shapes of the missile silos. Still camouflaged with grass, they suggest burial mounds, tombs from a lost civilisation. A notice reads:

SCHEDULED ANCIENT MONUMENT
THIS ENTIRE SITE (INCLUDING FENCES) IS PROTECTED UNDER THE SCHEDULED ANCIENT MONUMENT ACT. DAMAGE TO IT WILL INCUR UNLIMITED FINES AND IMPRISONMENT VIA THE CROWN COURT.

What are they monuments to: The Cold War? Peace? Perhaps they've been left as monuments to our worst uncertainties, all those possibilities we have to find ways of living with.

'We made it to a Heritage site after all,' says Maggie as we stare in. 'What did they do with the missiles in the end?'

'Destroyed them. The Russians did a spot check to make sure the silos were empty, I remember reading that.'

The path is overgrown with clusters of fern and birch scrub.

I tell Maggie about driving through Reading in the van with Rori and Jean, and buying ladders to get over the fence, how we hid them in the woods until the dead of night. She likes the idea of Sam in her tutu vaulting over the fence.

The roll-top bath is long gone, of course, but on one of the silver birch I trace the strings from a bender embedded in the growing bark. There must be artifacts buried in the mud, left for archaeologists to dig up: an empty reel of yarn, a rusted fork, the detachable mouthpiece from a recorder.

'So how about that drink?' says Maggie.

'With you in a minute,' I say, and return to the fence, feeling for the photograph in my shoulder bag. I take one last look at it, at the creased faces of two young women with their arms slung around each other, laughing into the unexpected flash of a camera. A dove on a stick blurs in the background. I twist the fusewire so the photograph is secure, attach it to the fence, and leave it there to flutter in the late afternoon light.

Acknowledgements

Research for this novel was significantly aided by access to The Greenham Common Collection at The Women's Library, and The Imperial War Museum's Greenham sound archive. I would like particularly to acknowledge *Greenham Common: Women at the Wire* (Harford & Hopkins, eds); *Walking to Greenham* by Ann Pettitt (Honno); *Common Ground* by David Fairhall; *Thank you Greenham* by Kate Evans, and Beeban Kidron's documentary film, *Carry Greenham Home*. Thank you to everyone who was generous with their time along the way, particularly Dr Sasha Rosenheil for answering my questions, and Ann Pettitt for reading the manuscript.

Various liberties have been taken in the name of fiction. Although a scene is set at the first 'Embrace the Base' protest, the scene where the women climb the silos is not a representation of the actual New Year's Day protest. Amber gate and the other gates mentioned are invented, as are all their members.

Thank you to Sarah Ridgard, Natasha Soobramanien, Helen Smith, Sandra Deeble, Roger Mills and his class at the Mary Ward Centre. For financial assistance, thank you to The Arts Council. For encouragement at just the right time, thank you to Isobel Maddison, Rowan Pelling and the Lucy Cavendish Fiction Prize.

Special thanks to my agent Zoe Waldie, and to my editor Penny Taylor and the team at Seren. Most of all, for limitless patience and good humour, thank you to Stephen Keyworth.

SEREN

Well chosen words

Seren is an independent publisher with a wide-ranging list which includes poetry, fiction, biography, art, translation, criticism and history. Many of our books and authors have been on longlists and shortlists for – or won – major literary prizes, among them the Costa Award, the Man Booker, the Desmond Elliott Prize, The Writers' Guild Award, Forward Prize, and TS Eliot Prize.

At the heart of our list is a good story told well or an idea or history presented interestingly or provocatively. We're international in authorship and readership though our roots are here in Wales (Seren means Star in Welsh), where we prove that writers from a small country with an intricate culture have a worldwide relevance.

Our aim is to publish work of the highest literary and artistic merit that also succeeds commercially in a competitive, fast changing environment. You can help us achieve this goal by reading more of our books – available from all good bookshops and increasingly as e-books. You can also buy them at 20% discount from our website, and get monthly updates about forthcoming titles, readings, launches and other news about Seren and the authors we publish.

www.serenbooks.com